THE MAGISTRATE

Kingfisher Sparrow Books
by M.E.J.Powell

DASHI TRILOGY
Dashi
The Magistrate

THE
MAGISTRATE

M.E.J. Powell

KINGFISHER SPARROW

Cataloging-in Publication Data
Powell, M.E.J., 1966 –
The Magistrate.
1. Powell, M.E.J. (Mark Evan James), Characters–Dashi.
2. Powell, M.E.J. (Mark Evan James), Philosophy and ethics.
3. Philosophy in literature.
4. Philosophy.   I. Title.

ISBN 978-1-7750848-4-6

(v1.1.3

Great thanks to
Denise, Judith, Ruth, Shannon
and of course Sue

AUTHOR'S FOREWARD

Beginning the second book of the Dashi trilogy right after the first was overly optimistic. It takes time for water to refill a well.

Also I knew the book was a challenge to myself – to work out my own political views. My sympathies, all on the side of the underdog, were too easy to be real. I do not accept being without some compassion for even the worst people. Any philosophy of mine needs to pass through the needle's-eye of empathy or I consider it unlivable.

I began the work in September, 2017. By January I realised that my practice was not strong enough. I didn't know what I was saying – not in my daily life, in my body. I was over my head, drowning. I therefore stopped writing and focused on diving deeper. I tore into meditation and my philosophy with ferocity.

Where in the first book mistrust as grief was salved by the firebreath. Now it was the wall of habitual thought that needed release. So I broke every stone I could find to break, and vowed to continue until there were no stones unbroken.

By mid March I had managed to make myself so sick I thought I was going to die. I am not given to the use of this phrase. Little did I know that if you release your minds' contents that quickly you get something like a vacuum. Consciousness, without form in which to flow, is like not being able to breathe in. A grey blankness that only slowly begins to reform itself. For several days after a particularly enlightening revelation I drank nothing but ginger tea to keep my stomach from emptying itself. Therein I salvaged a theme of poison.

By summer, three of my teeth had broken and I'd acquired fourteen(!) cavities. My hygienist wept for me because she thought I must have a violent terminal cancer, like that of a friend of hers who'd passed. "I'm ok, I've just pulverised my minds into smithereens." But it was those empathetic tears, cried for me, someone she didn't really know, that moved me – one unselfish ripple in a sea of takers that nudged my boat towards shore.

When you go digging into negative capabilities – that is, when you leave the maps behind on the ground and wander with only an inner song as compass, you disappear into your own trust. Out there I embraced absolution. And I gave it up to heal. Returning to it as my only tool with new found respect.

In truth – I am unmade and remade. Healed bones set into funny and unfamiliar shapes. As yet I've not completely given up the culturally exhorted habituation to comprehension. Though with time another way opens. I touch those burning gates of heavenly energy now with cautious care. If I have time – it will take the time it takes.

I try to not over excite myself, nor return to the ashes of my former being. It is not insistent. It sings to me to be at peace.

But do not let me make you think the experiences were terrible. I have floated in an endless expanse where there are no concepts, no self, no thought, and yet it was fathomless; a darkness, yet there was golden light; there was no one but the most penetrating vanishing all-encompassing indifferent loving kindness. I glowed for weeks on end. Stone cold sober.

Many would stop there. The womb of consciousness. Surely *that* nothing was foundational enough. But although I can explain how to get there (just follow your complete ignorance into the void) I knew not everyone could follow. It wasn't enough. There was more to be done.

Remember, I am also trying (for some mind's reason) to condense tangles of mystical insight into a cogent engaging story. (I am aggrieved that so much of comprehension's transformations are internal without adequate language to parse its syntax – would that I could give you my thoughts directly.) Hence art.

In looking through my notes at the time I find an occasional verse:

An unknown becomes
itself known –
! imperfect ! individ-
dual: a beautiful
tyger awakes.

In pursuit I am unrelenting. Or I was. A greater part of what I learned about myself was that the willful behaviour that had brought me this far was, of course, itself now sticky. And this was the why of my making myself sick. Forgiveness was granted then for the worst offender: myself.

By April I had returned to the bumpy writing road. April of the next year. Sporadic writing from the time in-between filled hundreds of pages of disorganised notes. By May I had collated some of them. There was productivity self-recrimination. My publisher pushed for September. I felt annoyed but ultimately grateful, at least after she stopped telling everyone that I'd blown my due date. It was fine that I took my time. I was doing more than writing a book, I was writing myself so that I could write the book with authenticity.

"Don't eat sugar," said Gandhi.

If I was to also write the book after this one, then I had better get the whole story straight. By which I do not mean the narrative of the novels. As a practicing imperfectionist, I have no idea what I am writing about – that is for the other minds to work on – I just show up and take dictation.

Of course, I still went another distance beyond (just to see) to find the mirror beneath the void, of which one can say not much, except that I agree, although I do not know why, and it makes me chuckle – my reflection in the river of the great consciousness. How could it be otherwise?

This is the stone I cannot break. I stand upon it as the foundation. Finally my ship comes to rest upon the mountain. But that's not where my life is. It's just a book I can close.

climbing the mountain
reaching the top
still on the ground

Thus in the year 2020 I cross the first draft finish line on the last day of February. It is not an explanation of my journey, nor a way to replicate it, but its expression, as best as I am able. I'll put some small explanation in the back I think, but not clutter up the story with maps. That would make it a map and not a story, and it apparently wants to be a story. I'm sure it will sound like dream language. Perhaps it reaches towards myth – that which points outside itself – which needs to be experienced not explained…

Well, I guess you'll just have to read it.

I thank your curiosity,
M.E.J.Powell
Victoria, Canada.

First draft – 12:09 Feb 29 2020
Second draft –2:51:51 Oct 27 2020
Final draft – 2:21:02 December 21 2020

THE MAGISTRATE

I

Dashi and the Mistress

By the evening the master had left the palace and returned to his cloud-hidden mountain. By night, the near full moon cast its eternal light into the walled garden, on tree and arbour, and on the magistrate, Dashi. He wandered its hedged paths seeking sanity. He found scented flowers. Because of the light of the moon, of what colour flower, he could not say, but he gathered them.

Presently he realised he was not alone, "Who's there?" asked Dashi.

"I am here," said the mistress, coming out of the shadow of a tree. To her heart she held a bouquet of flowers.

"Ah," said Dashi, "I was gathering them too."

"They are yours to gather, magistrate," she replied, "I am stealing from you."

Dashi laughed. "Please call me Dashi, mistress. And you may pick every flower in this garden." But pointing to a small but handsome tree with long leaves and tiny white blossoms near the fountain, "Except those," he joked.

"Ahh... Then those will be the ones I will want the most," she said, "My Lord."

Dashi smiled. "I expected you to go with the master."

"No, I prefer the comforts of the city," she replied.

"Ah," said Dashi nodding.

"May I be so bold as to ask a favour of the new magistrate?" she asked.

"Only if you call me Dashi," he said. "What do you need?"

She said, "I would like to return to my old quarters at the palace, if I may. My present dwelling is, as you know, somewhat draughty."

"Of course," said Dashi, "Nothing would please me better than your rightful return."

"I thank you My Lord... Dashi," said the mistress.

"Here," Dashi said, "take these too." And he handed her the ones he had picked. "I am looking for the right mind to be in, not flowers."

"What's wrong with flowers?" said the mistress peering over the almost two dozen she held in her arms.

"Nothing," said Dashi, "It just wasn't what I wanted."

"What was it that you wanted?" she said.

"I don't know," confessed Dashi.

"Then how do you know it wasn't flowers?"

II
The Caterpillar

Out in the courtyard the braziers burned, one aside, to keep the magistrate warm, if not to add to his imposing figure, black draped and seated on an ornately carved heavy red chair, on a platform raised over all. Dashi looked into the fire. The grey smoke ascended into a sky of the same colour.

The man the mistress had brought from the provincial capitol had remained for a few days, before conveying the former magistrate and her torturer partner to the governor for trial. He stood to one side at the bottom of the steps, dressed all in nearly black, blue silk. His pudgy fingers grasped each other behind his back as the prisoners, chained together were let in. Dashi turned his attention just in time to see the sensual red lips of the blue man part, revealing a smile of tiny yellowing teeth.

To the other side of the blue man stood, at the bottom of the steps, the executioner, a bloody chop block before him and a basket full of human heads. The blood was pig's blood, and heads had been removed from those who had been killed in the previous fighting, many, the sons of those now standing in chains. Nevertheless the blue man from the court had asked for permission to lead the interrogation of the conspiring elites with this display.

The first prisoner was dragged forward, pushed roughly down onto the block. The executioner raised his axe.

"Does the prisoner," began the blue man, "swear complete and undying allegiance to His Imperial Majesty and August Sovereign, the Divine Emperor, ruler of all under heaven?"

The man croaked a strangely high and strangled affirmation.

"Your excellence?" the blue man said turning to Dashi.

Dashi stared down at the quivering man. He wore beautiful clothing. If it had not been for Dashi's charcoal robes and wide brimmed hat, this frightened man would have considered Dashi beneath him. Would have sneered.

"Next," said Dashi.

The blue man surprised that no word of pardon had come, as they had discussed, but did as bid and brought the next prisoner forward. A middle aged woman, again in fine and expensive clothing was dropped to her knees and her head was pushed down on the bloody chop. She peered into the basket below and wept.

Again the blue man queried the wealthy woman as to her political loyalty, to which Dashi, the magistrate, was supposed to say, "Pardoned."

This self-styled aristocracy had not just capitulated to the murder plots of magistrates, the poor, Dashi's own brother, his master, himself and a host of others – but had conspired. All the while taking for themselves the spoils. All the while the croplands surrounding were so badly mismanaged, that the city lay in near constant famine. But they, who were the wealthy, ate. But they, who were important to the functioning of trade, still ran things. Because it was not from them the city collected land taxes to send on to the capitol, but from the farmer's fields. Thieves in silk robes. Stealing to survive was one thing and stealing to engorge another.

Dashi was supposed to pardon them, but he stared into the fire, breathing out slowly from between his barely parted lips. Only pausing to say, "Next." If the blue man was annoyed he showed no sign of it, but continued bringing them forward, one by one to be frightened half to death and receive no pardon. Dashi looked up. One of the prisoners was staring at him – their gazes met.

Dashi stood, "How dare you!" he yelled. "Face down on the ground!" And the guards pushed their faces into the stone pavers. Dashi wrapped his wind flurrying robes around him and marched down the steps. Some of them still held themselves off the ground by their arms, Dashi looked to the captain of the guard to come forward, and mimed, stamping with his foot for the captain to instruct the guards to put their boots upon their backs to force them down all the way, so they felt the weight of being crushed into the dust.

The magistrate stood silent. The pennants behind the dais snapped in the wind, but no other sound dared intrude.

"Do any of you *not* swear allegiance to the emperor?" said Dashi. There was no answer. He nodded.

"I want to talk to you…" said the magistrate, his mouth straight and thin as an arrow, "about luck." Dashi abruptly grabbed the basket and furiously hurled its contents – which bounced madly, as if merrily, open mouthed and dead eyed, towards the enchained. A few slowly rolling that last distance to the prostrate – who turned their heads, who retracted at the touch of death, who winced inwardly in pain.

"These young men were not lucky," said Dashi. "These young men, because of a conspiracy made… with her!"

Dashi paced slowly in front of them. He held out his hand. "Captain give me your sword." The captain straightened and then dutifully removed the sword from its scabbard and offered its hilt. Dashi took it.

"Put out your hands," said Dashi to the prisoners. When they were slow, he shouted, "Put out your hands!" and those who still refused the guards pulled their hands out in front of them.

"These young men... were *your* hands and feet," said Dashi, and he walked along them, gently dragging the tip of the sword in between their outstretched arms. "It was you who benefitted most, put them in harm's way. And one can only conclude you did not care what happened to your hands," he said, and he began to walk behind them now drawing the flat of the blade over their extended ankles, "or your feet."

"It is very unlucky to not care, don't you think? A strange affliction. But I think I know why," he said, coming round to the front again, "You do not understand luck.

"Right now, you are thinking that you are unlucky. But that isn't true." Dashi motioned with the sword at the scattered heads. "*They* are the unlucky - My brother, was unlucky - I and my master, would have been unlucky." And Dashi kicked a head towards the prisoners.

"You see, if one has seven golden cups, and you lose six, then *you* - would consider that unlucky. But this is not right... this is not right. Because you still have a golden cup!" the magistrate shouted, "And that is very very lucky indeed. Perhaps you can regain your fortune.

"It is when you have nothing. When there is no cup of life. That," Dashi said," is bad luck."

"That is what bad luck means," he repeated, "All the rest - while you live and breathe, is good luck. This is what I am telling you. That today... you are very lucky to live." Dashi breathed out heavily, and gave the sword back to the captain with a nod.

"From today you will have reformed your unlucky ways," he said, "returning what was taken in humble offering, so that you might continue your very great luck.

"And what is more lucky, is that you are going to favour me with your reformed luck, joining me each and every day, at sunrise, for meditation, such as my master has taught me.

"We begin tomorrow," said Dashi, who promptly left, his flowing black robes billowing out in the wind like a dark sail cast on a dark sea.

He came into his chambers like a storm. Throwing off his robes in a heap. The magistrate Dashi went abruptly to the window and stared. He saw the trailing streamers in the distant clouds, it was raining further up the valley.

"Did it not go well?" asked the mistress. Dashi was strangely used to her suddenly being there, or suddenly not there.

"No," said Dashi, "They are all guilty as hell." He watched the clouds on the mountains. "And I do not trust them. But all I could do was to fill their selfish hearts with fear," he said. "And worse – one of my minds, enjoyed it."

"Brilliant," said the blue man, striding into the room with Dashi and the mistress. "Beyond my expectations," he gushed. "Ferocious. Terrifying. Unpredictable. Even I was afraid. But..." His eyes moistened, and his voice tightened with emotion. "To make them come to you every day... like dogs, checking in with their master. It's beyond... Simply amazing. A master stroke."

Dashi didn't know exactly how he felt about this praise, but it wasn't favourable. He hadn't planned any of it, it'd just come out of him.

"They will come every day?" asked the mistress of Dashi.

"Yes," said Dashi nodding, now considering his necessary role in his command. "They will come to meditate with me."

"Ah," she said.

Dashi swallowed. "I will teach them the fire meditation the master taught me."

She nodded and said nothing else. Dashi waited in the silence. "If you have any insight you wish to share, your assistance in this matter would be appreciated."

"I will consider," said the mistress, and that was all.

"What matters is that they come to heel," said the blue man.

"What matters," said Dashi, "is that they change their minds. The old way is done. I cannot have them thinking it will continue. Nor can they wish for its return. I drove a spear into its heart. Now I must give them the new way... but I don't know what that is yet."

"Absolutely, Your Lordship," said the beaming blue man, pressing the tips of his pudgy fingers together. "We have the utmost faith in your abilities. The governor will be well pleased with my report," he said.

"That means you will have free reign," the mistress said, translating its meaning from court speech.

"I will return to the capitol tomorrow morning with your sister and her pet. We dine this evening to toast your rise to power." The blue man clapped his hands and bowing retreated from the room.

Dashi watched him go. "Power... yes. But there are many things to do," he sighed, "and dinner is far away."

"My Lord," said a voice beside Dashi, who swung around abruptly to face it. Seemingly too abruptly, as the boy dressed all in black cringed, but only inwardly – as if to receive a blow without protest or any signal its violence was unwarranted.

"Yes?" said Dashi.

"My Lord, we are assembled. Ready for your approval," said the boy.

"Who is?" said Dashi.

Dashi re-donned his robes and hiked to the main hall, where only yesterday there had lain bodies that he and the master had stepped over, and pools of spilled blood ran down the steps in steams from near the great chair at their summit. Today, no sign any stain had ever touched their surfaces. Nothing had sunk in, nor made any lasting mark upon the room. It felt to Dashi as though an army had come in the night, magically replacing the entire room with a pristine duplicate. Spiriting away its unsightly disturbance.

The hall he tread led directly to the throne. At his appearance, as one, the hundreds assembled, filling every space of the hall and even outside the double doors, went down on their knees in supplication. Dashi looked out over the tops of heads, their black hats, those with robes near the front, all aligned in perfect rows and columns. He, the magistrate, sat. Robed, as they were robed. He placed his hands on the arms of the great carved red chair. A bell sounded.

One robed bureaucrat at the front rose. "We pledge our allegiance and fealty to His Majesty the emperor, and his governor and his magistrate. My Lord, we are your servants." And they all bowed just a little lower to the floor. "We humbly await your inspection, My Lord."

Dashi breathed. It calmed him, it centred him. Just then a flapping of wings came in at the door. A hawk. To the consternation of the assembled, it flew about the room, confused to find itself in this space, and promptly flew back out again. The previously prostrate remained conspicuously silent.

The room was as before, but not.

The magistrate looked out over the mass of black clothed backs, feeling their communal desire to melt into the stone floor, so abjectly did they cower. Something in the unexpected visitation spoke of a presage of which Dashi didn't know, but moved him nevertheless.

"Tomorrow," spoke Dashi, his pace measured, "the previous... the false magistrate and her co-conspirator, will be transferred to the provincial capitol where they will face trial." He thought a moment, the different paths he might take, weighing each mind that spoke a suggestion to him.

"I suspect they will die for their crimes. But today, I offer you mercy." His voice reverberated off the stone. "Any who are complicit in these crimes. Any whose benefit was due to the previous regime. Retire - quietly," he said. "I offer, you disappear. Leave the city and seek your life elsewhere, without the stigma of a long prison sentence."

Dashi, the magistrate, said, "There will be no pursuit. Do not ever return. There is nothing here for you anymore except your judgement." He stood. "Tomorrow, I will receive you again - those that remain. At that time I will make my inspection." And Dashi left the hall.

The room as before, but not.

"But the schedule, My Lord," said the black robed bureaucrat standing in a cluster of several others, each burdened with scrolls and book and pieces of paper.

"I need a moment," said the magistrate.

"You have many items. The itinerary is rather tight," said the bureaucrat.

"A private moment," Dashi hinted.

"Of course, My Lord."

To the magistrate's quarters they all moved as one, flocking at his very heel, pressed in behind him like a murder of crows.

Dashi felt as though his back had just become infested with ticks and the birds had come to feed.

"Wait outside!" commanded the magistrate.

"Of course, My Lord," they intoned.

As soon as Dashi closed the door behind him he grimaced. He began to grieve. What have I done? And all that grieving came through his breath. Imagining the fire, as the master had taught him and pushing the grief into the flames. The death, the change, the absence of his master, again, after only just reuniting. He was so beside himself he could have sworn he heard a stifled sob from inside the room.

"My Lord?" - came a knocking.

"Wait!" yelled Dashi more forcefully than he meant to - and he inwardly cringed.

"My Lord- Yes, My Lord," echoed the genuflection.

Dashi grabbed up a stool and pushed one leg through both the rings of the two brass pulls of the double doors. He looked around.

He told himself that last night he must have come through that door to this chamber. Perhaps it had been the shock. But the lavish carved ebony bed, the red silk covers, the tassels, the table, the settee, the bottles of wine, and cabinets and cupboards and wall hangings with birds and flowers and mountains, and armies, and so on... He was sure he'd never stepped foot in here before in his life.

He was also sure he didn't want to be here now. This was too much for him. A smaller more modest bedroom would suffice. But outside there were black clad scroll and book and paper carrying schedule keepers - with items. And an itinerary! Which he was meant to proceed through as due course. This was duty. And Dashi remembered what the master had said about shoulds - so like a good student he looked for an escape route. The window!

Dashi opening the shuttered window in the far corner looked down. A small tile roof ran along just underneath the window and then a straight drop to cliff tops above the river, overshadowed by his master's mountain. If the fall didn't kill him directly there was always bouncing and drowning.

The bureaucrats began once again to knock heavily on the door. Dashi threw his hat on the floor and then took one look along the wall to see there were more windows - one of which was open. He'd been in tighter places as a kid with his brother. So the magistrate of the city, in his ceremonial robes of office, snuck out onto the small roof. Dashi edged his way along. He was trying not to look down. Then his foot got stuck in something. He had to look down.

At dizzying height he saw the toe of his boot caught up in the robe's hem. He lifted his foot but the cloth just followed. He tried to put his foot out to rip the fabric, but it stretched. He would have to draw the cloth up in one hand, but that meant he'd have to let go of the mortar joints his fingertips were grasping to keep him from toppling over backwards. Dashi leaned back on one leg and held on with the same hand, reaching down with the other to pull his robes off his boot. He drew the cloth up to his mouth and bit it to hold it in place, gagging himself. He wondered whether or not he would release it if he fell, and what last single important word he'd say.

Then inch by inch he continued along, until he found his way to an open window.

Peering in, it seemed to be some kind of office, with a large table in the middle of the room, and maps on the walls. No one was there. Dashi pulled himself in at the window. His foot slipping as he did, but he was already in. A clatter on the cliff rocks below made him look – a dislodged tile, smashed. He let the robes fall from his mouth.

There were two exit doors. He went to the first door. Carefully opening it, he peered in. The door led into the magistrate's bed chambers – from where he'd just come. This was the magistrate's study.

Dashi looked at the window, "Well, that'll save time," he thought. He went to the second door, and peered out likewise, into the hallway. Still knocking on the door, they even cawed like crows, and presently one of the black robes came running, he brought guards who began banging instead of knocking. As if louder would be more effective. Perhaps they thought he hadn't heard.

Sneaking back into his chambers he retrieved his hat and then, in all the noise, when they were looking away, the new magistrate crept down the corridor, away from the guards, his entourage and their scrolls and books and itinerary, to explore the palace on his own.

"O Master," Dashi said, when he was sure no one would hear him,"I did not understand what I wished for." But the empty hallway could not answer.

The corridors were a matter of confusion for Dashi. It had been some time and he was pretty sure the crows would have given up. At least he was far enough away he could no longer hear the banging. They may have called for more guard to smash down his door. Dashi grimaced, he thought he'd better go back.

The way from the hall of judgement he probably could have navigated, had he been at the hall of judgement, which he wasn't. Instead intending to return he found himself somewhere else entirely.

He wandered purposefully, pretending to be striding confidently, should some black clad minion appear, but none did. Two corridors diverged at an intersection and he, not knowing which was correct, or what correct might mean, chose the one that seemed barely brighter. As he marched forward into what was definitely a different way than he had come, he faintly heard singing.

Drawn to it, Dashi made his way through doorways and halls. Here there were women servants who bowed to him, and were unable to see his return bow due to their eyes being cast down. Dashi found the deference markedly disturbing, its formality mechanical. Yesterday they would have laughed at him. Today in robes... was only the magistrate here now?

Where was Dashi? he thought, as the location of the woman singing became clear, coming from a corridor through a grand open archway ahead. And finally to an open door. Dashi entered. The tall room, painted all the way to the ceiling with fanciful, coloured birds, trembling trees and flowers, held low wooden couches, gilded and carved, with embroidered pillows: azure and crimson and imperial yellow; a carpet of tranquil oceanic blue, woven with flying dragons; and in addition a coterie of women in robes of every colour. A radiance of colour. The singing abruptly stopped and there was more bowing.

"Please," said Dashi, bidding them to stop that, "I was drawn to the sound of the music."

"We hope we didn't disturb you, My Lord," said the girl who'd been the singer and who, youngest of the others was wearing the shorter style which allowed one to see her feet, which were bare. He must have been looking because the girl blanched visibly, and curiously, thought Dashi. She moved like a cat to put a low table in between them. It was only then he realised who she was.

"You're the master's granddaughter," said Dashi with a smile. "I didn't recognise you. Are you living here as well – with your grandmother?"

"Yes, My Lord" she nearly stammered. This annoyed Dashi. Before it was depressing his mood, but now it was annoying.

"I command you... to stop treating me differently!" he said.

She looked him in the eye. "Would you have commanded me before, My Lord?" Dashi knew they both knew the answer was, no. "Then I will treat you as before, when you do," she said.

He said, "Would you at least sing, then?"

She tilted her head. "Are you commanding me, My Lord?"

"I don't – but I'm afraid my attire does," he said looking down at his official robes. "You will have to decide for yourself," he said, finding a place to seat himself among the cushions and ladies.

So sweetly she sang.

Dashi decided he ought to make his own itinerary or he'd forever be at the mercy of other people's lists. By simply choosing a direction the magistrate was able to find himself outside, and again following the sounds, subsequently found the captain of the guards watching his men sparring in the yard.

"You train them hard," said the magistrate.

"My Lord," said the captain," That's because they became soft under the previous administration."

Dashi watched as sword met sword, spear duelled spear, or one met the other. He said, "They appear capable."

"They're fat and lazy, My Lord," he said, "But not for long."

"Captain," said the magistrate, "I need a few men to accompany me to deal with the situation with the hovels outside the city walls."

"How many do you wish, My Lord?" said the captain snapping to attention.

"A dozen should do," said Dashi, "Send them to the northern city gate to await me."

"I will send them to await you at the earth gate, My Lord," he said.

Dashi nodded. "Also we should clear the forests of the bandits. I can show you where."

"I understand," said the captain, nodding, re-evaluating the new magistrate.

"Can you make use of more men?" asked Dashi.

The captain frowned, "More men, My Lord? I think we'll be able to deal-"

"I will offer amnesty to all the bandits if they join my guard. They are used to fighting for my brother; now they will fight for me. Can you train them?" said Dashi.

"Indeed," said the captain, re-re-evaluating the young magistrate.

"Good. If you follow the ditch, just off the road, running between the fields where the sorghum is planted on either side, it will lead to the edge of a forest area. We walked in the water; that was why you couldn't find our foot prints. The ditch flows from a stream. Continue following the stream and you will pass through forest and eventually come to a rocky gully. Head along that and you will come to the camp which lies above the fallen tree. However I suggest you stop just when you come in sight of the tree and deliver your message from there. Just to be safe. Go to the kitchen, ask for some apples to leave as a promise of good will."

"Yes, My Lord," replied the captain.

Dashi nodded and turned to go.

"My Lord," said the captain.

"Yes?" said Dashi turning back.

The captain hesitated, weighing his words. "It is a very good plan, My Lord," he said simply.

"Let's hope so," said Dashi.

Dashi considered the problems in front of him. He wasn't thinking about them so much as looking within for answers. This day, today, he felt it crucial to set the tone. To show everyone how he was going to change things. There was no point in telling them. Let them know him by his actions.

Only now, ascending the steps two at a time nearly tripping on his robes, they would just know him as the clumsy clod. He angrily pulled off the robes to carry under his arm, cutting through his palace to get to the front gate.

He would rally the people, as best he could, to work together. He articulated this to himself, but realised he'd already decided it - this morning, dealing with those who only thought of themselves: the traitors - plus a sea of ministers of this and that who no doubt aided and abetted.

But to be fair, he thought, this really applied to everyone. Even himself. He too had selfish desires.

"What," thought Dashi, striding down the hallway, "do I want out of this? What are my minds aiming towards, even if I do not realise their quarry."

"Magistrate, Dashi," said the mistress, dressed in a flowing pale green robe, as Dashi rushed past by her doorway.

He halted. "Mistress," Dashi said, bowing.

"I am surprised to see you here. I was of the understanding that you had barricaded yourself in your room."

"Oh," said Dashi, "There was a misunderstanding. I'm sure it will get sorted out."

"If I may ask, where is My Lord off to in such a hurry?" she asked.

"No, hurry," said Dashi, "save for the hours of light left. I am determined."

"What are you determining then?" she asked.

Dashi laughed, "Yes, exactly." He said, "I am determining how others will consider my character by my actions."

The mistress said simply, "You have no idea what you are doing?"

Taken aback Dashi paused. "No," he replied, "I'm being swept along by a river."

She nodded deeply, "This is why you'll be a great leader."

Dashi looked into the eyes which looked into his. She seemed taller. "Would you like to join me?" he found himself asking.

"I'd be honoured. To where do we go?" she said taking his arm with her long fingered hands.

Until she asked he hadn't exactly known, but now he did, "We go to my people," said Dashi.

"I walk more slowly now," said the mistress. "It will give us time."

"You think I will be a good leader, then?" said Dashi, offering his arm.

She said nothing.

"I'm not fishing for compliments. I'm diving for answers, and wonder if I am in the right waters," he said. "I've never been magistrate. I was never even a leader."

"You have always been a leader," she said. "You just never had anywhere to lead people."

Dashi smiled. "Mistress, I'm so glad you're here. I understand why the master left; I have to do this on my own. But you make me feel less adrift, knowing I can trust your counsel," he said. "If you would give it."

The mistress said without hesitation, "If you can keep it," and squeezed his arm.

They left the palace, and descended towards the inner gate, where Dashi and the master had slipped in only yesterday. How strange these walls that once held him away, now held him to their breast. Sun broke through the clouds. He noticed it had recently rained – the hot earthy stone scent now rising with the steam in the morning air.

Here he was. Dashi, the magistrate, living in this palace. Ruler of the city. The mistress on one arm and his robes waded up under the other. Dashi walked in silence. Silence, however, was not what could be heard. Outside the palace wall a din of voices shouted.

Annoyed by the commotion disturbing his reverie, Dashi said, "Well, open the gates," to the guards standing, looking at each other, wondering what was going on outside the wall.

They pulled back the heavy doors and revealed the tumult. In the outer courtyard where Dashi had once protested the previous magistrate, people were pushing each other and shoving each other. Yelling at the top of their voices. Pointing accusing fingers in each other's faces. All looking thoroughly miserable and self righteous. My people, thought Dashi.

"Excuse me mistress," said Dashi, dropping her arm, and handing his robes to one of the guards. The two guards from the inside drew behind to block the gate, as the two stationed outside the gate unsheathed their swords and fell behind the magistrate as he waded into the crowd.

"Silence!" shouted Dashi.

A few people at the back kept fighting and Dashi motioned with his eyes for one of the guards to bring silence to those as well, which he did by knocking them both on the head with the pommel of his sword. Dashi frowned at this but he'd already put his hands on his thighs and was looking from one side of the mob to the other. The sun was peeking out now and stood behind him. The brim of his hat hid his eyes. He hoped he looked magisterial. He further thought that he had better.

"Why are you shouting outside my gate?" he said.

There was silence.

The magistrate, Dashi, said, "Well?"

"We come because he took our- It was ours, you're the

one that took- My husband has run off with that- Lies! Look how she-" and they all started in at once until angry shouting had again resumed.

"Silence! Silence!" shouted Dashi. "Control yourselves," he said when they had come to a stop. "You there," he said, picking a woman who's dress spoke of modest but comfortable means, "Why are you here?"

Now on her own without the crowd to bolster her, she said, head sunk into her shoulders, "I want a judgment."

"About?" said Dashi.

"I had some washing, My Lord, and it was- I had it hung, and one of my," - she blushed - "garments disappeared." She squared her shoulders. "My best one too. Stolen!" she exclaimed, shooting the woman beside her a dirty look.

"I didn't take it. I already told-"

Dashi immediately raised his hand for silence. "Say nothing. I take it you all need me to adjudicate your cases? Raise your hand if this is so." Dashi faced a sea of raised arms. "I have other business today-"

"We've been waiting months!" shouted out one of the people. The guards turned. And while eyeing the guards' pommels there was a soft, polite, murmur of agreement.

"The old magistrate hasn't even left yet," Dashi said, holding his palms open in an appeal for reason. "Tomorrow is a holiday. Be glad," he said. "Tomorrow we will begin," and he said with emphasis, "Together. To mend what has been broken. But..." he said, "I cannot do it all in a day. I'm sure I've been left a backlog that will take time. You have been patient. Be patient a little longer."

The crowd seem mollified by that.

Dashi turned away. "Mistress," he said and she again took his arm, and they began their journey through the streets to the north gate. Two of the guards fell in behind.

It seemed like a different city now, thought Dashi.

"You have acquired a tail," said the mistress, smiling.

"I think it's their duty," Dashi said of the guard.

"Look further back," said the mistress. And indeed when Dashi looked there were a number of people following them. Dashi wondered what they wanted.

Intuitively the mistress answered, "They are curious as to what we are going to do."

The magistrate and the mistress strolled arm in arm. Children ran ahead and soon the shopkeepers were standing at the door and people leaned out of their windows to see the new magistrate out walking in full daylight.

"There once was a tiger. A huge tiger, the like of which no one had ever seen. And so it came to be known that the ruler of the province would pay handsomely for its pelt to adorn his throne room floor.

"Hunters tried to trap him. They used nets. But he was so ferocious that no sooner would he be caught than he would rip the ropes to shreds. They made cages. But he shattered them into twigs. They dug a great pit. But such was his size that in a singe leap he was out. No rope could hold him, no cage keep him, no pit was so deep he couldn't climb. In this way many hunters lost their lives, until no one would dare try.

"One day a mysterious woman appeared in the village. She said she could catch the tiger. The villagers laughed. This angered her. 'You will see,' she said 'I understand the mind of the tiger.' So she walked away from the village, the sound of their laughter still echoing, and out into the jungle.

"She found a clearing. She took a rope and lay it in a large circle around the area, and in its centre she placed a handkerchief of her own. Then she sat, just at edge, inside the circle. She hadn't waited long when the tiger appeared, ready for battle. It roared, and began to sniff at this new trap. The woman made as if she was trapped inside the ring and could not move.

"The tiger ignored her. Boldly it leapt right into the ring. But nothing happened. With its great paw it battered at the rope, and still there was no trap. It sniffed at the handkerchief which smelled of the woman, who pretended to try to get away. The tiger walked about the trap, and then perplexed, it sat down in the centre, right on the handkerchief.

"The woman knew then she could move a little closer. Little by little she inched closer until she was almost beside it. When the tiger left, she followed. Whenever the tiger would come to a place she thought it might rest she would move as close as she could and then place the handkerchief down and wait.

"Soon the tiger got used to sitting on the handkerchief. But by now she could get so close she could pet it. The woman scratched the tiger behind its ears, always being sure to defer to its moods. After many many days in the jungle she simply picked up the handkerchief and walked into the village, and the tiger followed.

"When the villagers saw the tiger walking behind her they were frightened by the woman's magic, and called her evil. But she just laughed, explaining, 'Only a tiger can catch a tiger.' "

"I don't understand," said Dashi. "She's really a tiger?"

"No, of course not," she said.

"Do you mean then the tiger trapped itself by choosing her and therefore was no longer free?"

"Choice is the question. Danger comes in many disguises," she said.

Dashi said, "What danger?"

The mistress said, softly, and charmingly, as though saying something about the weather, "They are surprised you are so bold to walk out in the open."

The thought had never even occurred to Dashi. His eyes widened. This was dangerous.

She smiled and waved at the shopkeepers. "You went into the palace unarmed to oust my sister, and now you appear bold as a tiger. This is a good impression."

"I had no idea I was doing that," said Dashi.

"Exactly," said the mistress. "If you were doing it for show, that'd be obvious – and they'd know you were weak. But clearly don't give it a moment's thought – so you are strong."

Dashi smiled at some children hanging out a window and waving back at them said, "You mean I'm a fool."

"Yes."

As the two neared the earth gate, a dozen of his guard awaited, "Open the gate," said Dashi, and the larger outer gates to the city were opened. Dashi glanced up at the mountain wishing himself luck.

Nearby now, the tattered hovels, shacks, lean-tos, huts and cooking squats, scattered across the bare, rutted, dirt field outside the walls, awoke to calls of alarm as the guards drew near. Peopled sparsely, as the majority were now out in the fields, the youngest of children and the eldest of elderly protecting them, oozed out of the encampment to meet this new threat.

Dashi put up his hand for the guard to stop.

"It appears muddy here," said the mistress with distaste.

Dashi looked at her, and the mud, "I'll bring them to you."

And again, he realised, here he was, striding off, by himself, into the camp with mud up to his ankles. A couple guards broke off from the main and circled at a respectful distance, keeping Dashi in view. He wondered what it meant about him that he was so careless, impulsive, unmindful.

"Un-mindful," he realised, laughing at his predicament, a little. "Oh master. Where are you? Everything I learned from you is gone and I'm right back where I started," he thought. And while he knew, or a mind inside said, that wasn't really true – at the moment, as the day churned around, surging past him, sweeping him along in its river, it certainly felt that way.

"It's all right," he said to reassure the worried faces that met him at the camp, "The old magistrate is gone."

"Who's the new magistrate?" a scrawny, elderly man asked.

Dashi looked down, now remembering how he'd thrown off his new office's robes in a fit. "I am," said Dashi.

"You, Dashi?" The man smiled a semi-toothless grin.

"It is funny," said Dashi, smiling, "but Yes, I'm the new magistrate. See the hat."

"Where'd you get that hat?"

"It's the magistrate's hat," explained Dashi.

The old man's eyes opened wide, "You'd better give it back. That's why the guard has come. Give it back!"

"No, I'm the magistrate. It's my hat." But no sooner had Dashi said this then the old man whisked the hat off his head and gamboled with surprising quickness, towards the guards waving it in the air. "Here it is! The hat. I took it. I don't know why. Please, take it back," he pleaded, looking directly at the mistress, "I'm very sorry I took it. And I accept whatever punishment is necessary for hat stealers."

The guards stood immobile, not sure what to do. Dashi came up behind the old man and snatched his hat back. "It's my hat."

"Don't listen to him," said the old man. "He's just trying to take the blame. I did it." And he snatched it right back. "Dashi's always been a bit weak in the head. Him and his crazy brother. After their father died and their mother ran off..."

The guards stood immobile, though if you watched them closely they jiggled very slightly.

"Stop. Stop," said Dashi, and asking for intervention said, "Mistress?"

The mistress gently took Dashi's hat and put it back where it belonged, on the head of the new magistrate. "He is the magistrate. Dashi is magistrate. Hard as that may be for you to believe."

The old man stood flabbergasted. "One of us?" he said.

It nearly brought tears to Dashi's eyes. "It's true. And I appreciate your heroism."

"Oh," said the man. "That was so they didn't kill everybody - it wasn't for you."

That makes sense, thought Dashi. "Still, it was brave," he said.

The old man thought a moment. He shrugged. "Some things you have to do."

Dashi nodded. "Bring me into the camp - to show I mean no harm."

The old man thought about that. "All right." And he turned and walked towards the shacks.

Dashi accepted the invitation, of sorts, and followed.

The children came out to see him. "Dashi, Dashi, Dashi, Dashi, Dashi," they said, as he walked among his people, the news being spread by the old man. This had been home at one time, different parts of it, at different times, living here, living there. Now, that he saw it again he truly saw it – it was an affront.

They all gathered around him.

He stopped. "Look. Everyone. You know me. I can make things better now. For all of us." And Dashi knew whatever else happened that when he said 'us,' he meant these people.

"Return to your houses beside the fields. You don't have to stay here anymore. The farms are to be yours once again." The old folk looked at each other and Dashi knew what thoughts went between them. Regaining status was fine, but they sold the stolen food to those inside the wall from here. In the fields they would again be without money. If he continued, as previous magistrates, taking nearly all the crop to send for the imperial taxes what would they have?

"And in its place we will build a market so that we can bring your crops to sell." Their expressions looked dubious, then brighter, and continued alternating as they weighed this idea.

A face in the crowd caught Dashi's attention. "Nano!" called Dashi.

At hearing her name Nano's curiosity turned to fear and she quickly began trundling away. "Stop, Nano!" called Dashi. But she kept going. At this point a guard appeared from the other direction and stood in her way, turning her about to face Dashi who was coming to meet her.

Seeing him, she gasped and threw herself on the ground at his feet. "My Lord, master, Dashi, forgive me. Please,

I'm just a foolish old woman. I didn't realise what I was saying, I was so hungry."

Dashi lifted her off the ground to standing. She wore so many rags she looked large but she weighed no more than air. "Then let's make sure you are never hungry again," he said. "Come, I want you to meet someone." And he led her back to meet the mistress.

The mistress had folded her arms so that her hands had disappeared up her sleeves.

Dashi said, "Mistress this is Nano. She was one of the nans who raised me and my brother." He was pleased to make their introduction but he could see the embarrassment of Nano, covered in filth as she was, the mistress, beautiful in silks, and both of them near the same age.

"Hello," said the mistress.

"My Lady," said Nano. She looked at the ground. And then she said in her gruff voice, "Are you looking after this one now?"

The mistress smiled. A big smile like Dashi had never seen her smile. "Yes," she said.

"All right then," said Nano.

"Mistress, I have an idea," said Dashi, "I find many people have lost their manners during... the previous reign. Do you believe this is true?"

The mistress said, "It is always true."

"Very well," said Dashi looking at Nano, "I think if I were to ask all the nans to discourage rudeness that this might improve the character of the people. What do you think?" said Dashi.

The mistress considered. "Improving the character of the people is dangerous. The mind that discerns better can very easily tell itself to discern that which it doesn't like as the enemy of the better. Often with a disavowed advantage going to the giver of the advice. If you must do something, encourage instead. Better yet still, teach them the secret of your great success."

"What *is* my secret?" half whispered Dashi. The mistress just looked at him. Then her and Nano's eyes met. "Oh, you mean the master's meditation..."

The mistress waited.

"I'm already going to be teaching it to the merchant families. I can't teach it to everyone," explained Dashi.

The mistress smiled. "Of course," she said – and sighed.

"Your own people," said Nano.

Dashi summoned an aggressive and concise argument from within, looked at the two older women and changed his mind. "There are two of you; I am surrounded," he said. "Fine I will teach the nans – then they can teach everyone else. Is that acceptable?"

"As your first negotiation, I concede: it is acceptable," said the mistress.

As the mistress and Dashi returned to the palace, the mistress slowed her pace. When Dashi showed concern she brushed it off as being tired, which Dashi understood, he was tired as well. He looked up at the dark clouds rolling in off the mountain. There had been quite the conversation about farming the land, Dashi's purpose to his visit, when Nano waved everyone over:

"Why are the crops failing?" he had asked.

"They make us plant them in the same place every year."

"Who does?"

"The officials."

"Who are they?"

Shrugs, "They're your officials."

"Why... Never mind. Go back to farming properly. I'll deal with whoever it is who tells you otherwise. Do you need help with your old homes?"

They thought about it, and looked at each other. "No."

"Do you need help with making a market here?" he said, indicating his dozen guards at the ready.

"No."

Dashi blinked. He paused. He felt the way they were feeling. "You do not trust whoever I might send?"

And they all looked at their feet. Until Nano, "Damn right, we don't. No offence to you Dashi- uh, My Lord."

That said, the dam burst. "They're always getting in our way... All the rules... Always yelling orders..." said the assembled outside the shanty.

"All right," said Dashi holding his hands up. He could see that this would be a gesture he would find himself using a great deal in this new position.

The elderly man who'd taken Dashi's hat said, "They don't know soil from dirt." And he nodded once, and spat on the ground, indicating that this was the holy truth. And everyone else also nodded at this sagacious articulation.

The magistrate, Dashi said, "I'll take care of this."

And many smiles blossomed around him.

Dashi was hungry. In his palace he sat at the head of a long table. Servants came and went, bringing the feast before them. Dashi had never dreamed of this much food. The blue man, the mistress, her granddaughter waited, seated beside him.

The blue man was saying, "...exactly what we needed, a people's magistrate. Brave. Fearless. I hear rumours already that our new magistrate battled with the jailor in a duel," he laughed, waving his hand around like a sword. But Dashi was not listening. He was aware of the young boy who was standing beside and slightly behind his chair. As did boys who stood behind the others, he noted, the blue man and the two women.

Dashi waved him closer. "Hello. Why are you standing there?" he asked under his breath.

"My Lord?" said the boy not sure of what was being asked and not wanting to answer incorrectly.

"What is your job?" asked the magistrate out of the corner of his mouth, still half listening to the blue man go on, just in case he said something useful. "...a perfect day," he was saying.

"I'm your taste tester My Lord."

"Taste taster?" said Dashi repeating his words.

"Yes, My Lord," said the boy, "I test the food in case it's been tampered with."

"Tampered?"

"My Lord..." the boy, now being very uncomfortable with the conversation. Haltingly he stated it, "Poisoned."

"Ah," said Dashi and looking about the table with a different mind. They were sitting down to feast while those who attended them most intimately, eating from their plate were potentially attending their own funeral.

"What if," said Dashi, "they use a slow poison? Despite your eating it, I would still die, as of course would you."

This line of questioning was frightening for the boy who swallowed hard. "Yes, My Lord," was all he said. All he could think of to say.

"You were the tester for the previous magistrate?" asked

Dashi, going on despite the boy's discomfort.

"No," he said, "This is my first day."

"Mine too," said Dashi trying to lighten things – intolerable things – somewhat for the boy and somewhat for his own thoughts which darkened.

They were interrupted by the arrival of a roast pig, and voices of appreciation. Carried aloft by two men with great fanfare and laid before the guests, glaring through its glistening glaze. Dashi was now even hungrier, and maybe because of that his gut led his thoughts more than they would have otherwise.

"Ah," he said, to the two who had brought the pig to the table, "and which of you is the chef?"

The two looked at each other. They bowed. "Neither of us is the chef, My Lord."

"No chef?" said Dashi, "For this? A great meal that we are about to have? That we are about to celebrate? Get the chef at once. Bring him here. None of us will eat a thing until he is before us to receive our appreciation."

The two who had borne the plate retreated in an undignified scramble.

Dashi tapped the table. "So," he said, making magistrate conversation, "are the former magistrate and jailer made ready?"

"They are My Lord," said the blue man.

"I will instruct my guard to keep people from pelting them with stones," said Dashi, with a smile on his face but not in his heart.

The blue man nodded. "It is well that they arrive in good condition." He curled his lower lip just ever so into his mouth.

Dashi looked towards the door. He tapped on the table. He glanced at the feast and his stomach growled.

The scent of food. Was there anything more beautiful he thought. He took his eyes from the feast. "I am glad you have joined us," said Dashi to the mistress's granddaughter. "As I was glad to hear you sing." He turned his head to the mistress. "She sings beautifully."

"Musical talent is part of the family," said the mistress.

"That's right," said Dashi, who could now hear, as they all could, raised voices far away but coming closer. "Your sister was very musical. I recall the master saying this to me." And Dashi turned his head to the door, and awaited the noisy arrival.

The two men, plus a couple of guards dragged the struggling chef into the room. At the sight of Dashi he went pale and then clawed at his captors, trying to break free. Dashi swallowed hard, and indicated a place for them to seat the chef at the table. And together with much effort they forced him to sit, and then withdrew. At once he again tried to escape. But they again firmly pushed him back into his place.

Dashi inhaled, and blew angry hot breath into the his belly's fire. "No need to be so humble. Look at all this beautiful food," he said exaggerating, opening his arms wide. The blue man was watching the chef intently and was now leaning back from the table. "Come," said the magistrate, Dashi, "I insist you have the first mouthful of everything."

The chef just sat there quaking with cold sweat.

Dashi sighed, "What do you feel is your best dish?" Dashi picked up his own plate, and began to serve for him, spooning it with delicacies. The chef said nothing. "How long have you been chef?" Nothing. "Do you like the work?" Dashi asked him. The chef sat as if made of stone.

"Offer him some pig," said Dashi to the boy behind him, who moved to beside the chef and cut a delicate strip of pork for him to eat. The chef turned his head as the boy set it before him. And then the chef grabbed the knife. And the boy.

He held the knife to the boy's throat just as the captain came bursting into the room with more guards. The chef turned his head at their entrance, and a strike from the mistress's granddaughter on his elbow allowed the boy to break free. Whereupon the chef jumped up knife in hand, slicing through the air at the attendees, like as at hornets, or ghosts, as the captain, advancing with the other guards, drew their swords.

Trapped, the chef lunged at the table and Dashi pulled the granddaughter away thinking her the next target, but the chef fell upon the roasted pig, hacking it with the blade and biting it directly. Chewing, ripping, smearing, crying, he lay half on the table, and rolled over masticating, head tilted backwards staring right at Dashi – chewing and gnashing, his mouth open in defiance.

This stupid cow of a man didn't plan this, thought Dashi. "Who do you work for?" he said, and the man spat half-chewed pig clumps at Dashi's face and all over the other dishes.

"Oh!" said the mistress with indigence. Who up until now had been silent. Who up until now had been the model of dignity. Who looked with anger at Dashi as if to say, "Enough!"

Indeed. "Get this pig off the table!" said Dashi, "Get both of these pigs off the table." And they hoisted the chef's bulk up, who now standing, glared at Dashi. And then he looked in pain. The guards tried to hold on to him as he began to twist and convulse. All the while he grinned and grimaced. Mouth foaming, as his face became redder and redder. And then he began gasping, choking, becoming heavier in the guards' arms, until his head hung limp and the half chewed roast pig splattered down his front and onto the floor.

Everyone gaped in silence. The only sound, the rain outside the window.

Dashi looked to the blue man. "A perfect day," he said.

In the dark, as it rained and rained, the ditch, at the edge of the people's newly ploughed field, eroded - disclosing a small skull, quickly filled with pelting water.

Dashi rode a horse to the cheers of the people lining the street to the south gate. They threw flowers. He stopped just inside the wall, awaited there by the mistress sitting in her palanquin, and her guard, with shiny helms, pikes, and rifles, all bedecked with festive ribbon.

The cavalcade of marchers, censer swingers, musicians playing a jaunty tune while the drummer beat out the march rhythm, each in actuality trained fighters in disguise - shook the ground in military step, followed gracefully by the blue man riding resplendent in his carriage. The magistrate and mistress showed their respect as he departed. Earlier the blue man had disgorged presents from the governor: well wishings for the new magistrate. Fancy things: cloth, carvings of elegant artistry which the mistress admired, and guns. Things to steal, thought the magistrate. Dashi was hoping for a place on the mountain.

Following the blue man's carriage were more guards, and horses pulling wagons, and more guard again. Dashi knew that the boxes on the wagons were now returning full of the swords and rifles previously carried in the floor of the carriage. He watched it go by, his former professional interest piqued.

Last was an old cart with bad rough wheels and a tiger cage. The cart sides and deck were covered in slop and filth thrown by the people: mud, dead rats, horse manure, anything the people could find to throw. But no stones. The captain had gone in front forbidding it as people on either side were just as likely to hit each other. The stones ungathered at their feet. A little mud or rat never hurt anybody.

The two in the cage, dressed only in ripped old sack, cowered with their backs to the onslaught. It was only because of his point of view, Dashi mounted beside her palanquin, that he saw - as the cart bounced through the wall's gate, the previous magistrate turned and looked right at her sister - who waved.

The black dressed men, a dozen, two dozen, they flocked and rose in noisy clouds, bringing in bundles of yellow papered books with printed red tissue at the front, and scrolls of paper, all wrapped with string.

"Here are all the regulations and laws over which you are to adjudicate," said the court clerk. "There may be some you are not familiar with. So I have had them collected for your convenience." He said this impeccably without a trace of sneer. "May I offer my congratulation on your appointment My Lord. I look forward to working under your guidance."

Dashi looked at the piles of paper that surrounded the table in his study, and upon every flat surface, astonished at the consequence the words: "Come in," had manifested. Dashi looked up at the court clerk, also dressed in black, very much like the others, but with an air of, what Dashi took to be, bureaucratic confidentiality.

Dashi was tired and merely gazed at this man before him. He looked him up and down. In truth his thought drifted to thinking about a dark mountain pass, though never taking his eyes off the clerk. He said, "These should be taken to the mistress. Ask her where she would like them."

The clerk bowed, backed away and left. Presently the black cloaks scooped up the books, and scrolls just as quickly as they were laid down and in moments Dashi was sitting alone again, his table bare.

"What do they say?" said Dashi.

The mistress, dressed in green, receiving yet another scroll from her granddaughter, also in green, said, "They say what you are allowed to do, or must do, or under almost no condition should do."

"So many though," commented Dashi.

"Yes," she said, "This is the lives' work of an army of mediocre minds adding stipulation upon decree upon requirement. Always adding, rarely subtracting, never concerning themselves with cause."

"And I am to follow all this?" asked Dashi, alarmed.

The mistress smiled. That is, her mouth widened and Dashi took that as a smile. "No, no. You are magistrate.

May I add, of somewhere unimportant where the people are, frankly... expendable, as far as the emperor is concerned. No, all you have to do is maintain the laws that would offend the emperor should you veer from their edicts. Anything else is at your whim."

"Life and death?" said Dashi.

"For those who live here, life is half of all they have to cling to - the other half being resentment. Even the wealthiest have only faded glories," and she tilted her head slightly. "I will have the appropriate scrolls put in your chambers."

"I can't read," said Dashi. The granddaughter, although looking away, busying herself with the scrolls and appearing not to be listening, straightened up, her hands still.

"Oh yes, of course, My Lord. Your master mentioned you had some lack of facility in this. No matter, come back tomorrow and we will read them together," she said. Again she smiled. "I will advise the clerk that all documents are to come here."

Dashi thanked her, and the granddaughter went back to looking through the scrolls, although more slowly than she had.

Dashi's backside hurt. Outside, all day the sun had shone, the skies glorious blue, bold with sunlit clouds. But Dashi sat in the chair dealing with an endless backlog of cases. Day after day. Dashi could barely remember one case from the next for all the backstabbing, squabbling and tears. When the great doors opened for the next petitioners, the scent of the spring wafted in on beams of sun, before the doors were closed up and the next trial began under torchlight, flickering.

He also realised he was very hungry. He'd risen late and had run, yanking on his flailing cloak while doing so, in order to be on time. An action he realised later, by way of raised eyebrows, was not becoming for a magistrate. Next time he would walk and they could wait. With only a plain bun, and the bitter green cake the mistress insisted he eat for his health, his stomach grumbled.

Worst of all they brought papers. Documents, and contracts and legal precedents, and notices from the higher courts and it was all incomprehensible, even if he could read it, Dashi felt mortified, adjourning those cases saying because of their complex nature they'd take more time and that he explicitly wanted to clear out the bulk of the backlog and not let getting caught up in the technicalities of this type of caseload that would slow up the process of dispensing simpler judgements. Meaning he planned to ask the mistress. Just leave the documents to be considered, thank you, next.

When the court officers next opened the doors, Dashi could see by the colour of the light that the sun was starting to set. He'd been here all day. The sound of hooves announced the next case, as the officers brought through a horse.

Dashi laughed, "Leave the doors open," he instructed the court guards, regaining his composure, "for ventilation."

The sun was so beautiful. And coming in low its yellow light made the hall seem warm and festive. The officers led the horse right to the bottom of the steps of his magistrate's chair.

"And what is your case?" Dashi asked the horse.

"I am being denied a stall by the innkeeper," said a high

voice.

Dashi looked around for the one who had said this, and his eyes fell on a small man in black. One that Dashi had taken to be one of the court officers. They all looked the same, all dressed the same.

"What is your position?" said Dashi.

"I am the assistant keeper of the records," he said, and offered papers.

Dashi waved them away. "Which records?" asked the magistrate.

The man raised his eyebrow. "The records of the city? I am the third assistant to the city chronicler," said the man, sounding unsure.

Dashi asked, "Where is the inn keeper?"

Annoyed, the bureaucrat said, "He's not here."

"That's why I asked," said Dashi watching the horse in his courtroom relieve itself onto his floor. "Are you staying at the inn?" asked Dashi, with a tight smile.

"No."

"Ah... Then why should the innkeeper rent you a stall?"

"I wasn't renting it."

"What do you mean?" said Dashi.

"It was my stall. I used it. I'd been using it for years and now he bars me from entrance," said the man, his voice rising in pitch.

Dashi said, "You mean for free?"

"Of course," said the man. "I'm the assistant to the chronicler."

"Third assistant," corrected Dashi. "Why... let me think how to put this... To what benefit is it to the innkeeper to house your horse?"

"Because everyone who does business in the city is listed by the chronicler," he said.

"And–" said Dashi.

"*And–*" repeated the assistant, "it's important for his business that people know which establishment is the best to stay in."

"Ah," said Dashi, "I'm beginning to see the picture. You mean for a favourable word from you, the innkeeper should give you a stall in return."

"Exactly," he said in self-evident tone.

"How long have you been keeping your horse there?" asked Dashi getting all the evidence he needed.

"Fifteen years," said the black dressed bureaucrat.

"Did he ever try to do this before?" asked Dashi.

"Only in the beginning," he said, a grin coming to his face.

"But the last magistrate found in your favour," grumbled Dashi, along with his stomach.

"Of course."

" 'Of course,' " repeated Dashi. "And what you want is for me to force him to take this animal into his care?"

"Yes," said the small man.

Dashi looked at the dung on the floor. "And this is why *you*... have brought *a horse*... into *my* courtroom?"

"Yes," hissed the exasperated bureaucrat, putting his hands on his hips.

"Very well. Guard, take this horse to the inn in question and place it in the stall–"

"Good," said the third assistant chronicler.

"– and then tell the inn keeper it's now his horse, in lieu of payment for fifteen years board," ordered Dashi, who stared down the shocked little man in black. "And as for you–" said the magistrate, "it's 'Yes, My Lord.' "

"You magistrates don't understand a woman's point of view," she declared, peering at him over her glasses.

"Actually the last magistrate was a woman," said Dashi, "The one that shut down your shoe store."

She gazed slack faced at Dashi, as though struck dumb. Dashi creased his brow. Then - as if suddenly awakened - a wind up toy sprung back to life, "Anyway, my mother did it, and my grandmother, and her grandmother," she said, "and so did I, and my daughter." And she put out her feet from under her dress to show. They were very very tiny. Dashi had never seen any feet so small among the women farmers, or the women who sometimes came to the thieves' camp. They looked like doll's feet.

All he could think to say was, "You have extraordinarily small feet."

"Just so!" she said, "Then there's no reason for the ban."

Dashi nodded.

"Let me open my shop again," she said.

The magistrate said, "I don't see why people who wish to buy-"

"Excuse me, My Lord," interrupted the court clerk who seemed genuinely upset by this exchange, "Forgive my impertinence but the emperor has explicitly forbid it. It is considered cruel and unnatural."

"Ah," said Dashi, "Is this true?" he said to the woman, who had turned her head down and to one side. Was it in shame? - or an immobility caused by being lost to curiosity - perhaps for an insect on the floor - one visible only to her. "Did you know the emperor has forbid this? But you come before this magistrate, asking me to rule against it, to allow you to sell your tiny shoes, knowing full well this would be against the emperor's laws?"

"His laws, My Lord," she said, "But they're my feet."

"Mistress, I am well pleased with your handling of the army of black crows who dog my heels," said Dashi, "But if you would, teach me the art of politics," he said. He was back in the women's area sitting on the silk couch, looking at painted birds chase each other in the ceiling.

The mistress eyed him, "You might as well ask me about the art of mugging," she replied, "It is a craft. For me I will reserve *art* for skills yet greater."

"Actually," said Dashi, "It takes a bit of finessing to- I'm just saying."

"Craft," said the mistress, "As I said."

"Not art."

"Exactly," she replied.

"Mistress, will you then teach me the craft of politics?" asked Dashi.

"You've seen it. Mud and filth. Power-lust and debasement. Rise and fall. What more do you need to know?" she said.

"You have said that I ought to avoid improving the character of the people, that instead they can be encouraged. The nans will do that for some. What about the others?" asked Dashi.

The mistress was silent. She said at last, "The reason improving the people's character is not to be done is - it's dangerous. It's dangerous because by doing so you encourage people to say - this is good and that is not. This is also why you do not just tell them to improve themselves. Stuckness is stuckness because it lacks the very tools, and often motivation, to stop spinning about.

"Although the nans may encourage by rudely calling people rude, this will not help. It is the merchants being taught this by you that will be the real source of the encouragement. They will prosper, and that is what interests most people."

"You mean they will do it because they want what the rich have? But not for their own sake?" asked Dashi.

"Yes," she said, "For the image, they like of themselves, as rich and powerful. The nans however, show the breathing is no rarified technique. Their invectives will be viewed as zeal for the practice. As there is no reason for the people to latch on to it as anything other than a means, they will not get caught up in trying to determine its potential good and bad ends."

"Is that important?" asked Dashi.

"It means you, Dashi, may know this, you may even be able to teach it effectively, but it is not from you, just through you. This means they will ignore that you have brought it. In doing it, they will take it for their own without attachment. Thus it makes an effective medicine with only the problem of self congratulatory puffery," she said, "but that's a constant."

"But don't we want them to understand why they should want to trust?" he said.

"Should?"

He rephrased it in his head, "Is the understanding of the way in which one's minds work not important?"

"It's very important," she said, "Too important to be tossed in the street like straw. You wish to understand. That is you. And it is a long journey.

"Other people want to get on with living. They have no interest in thinking. That is who they are."

Dashi said, "But if they wanted to know–"

"If they want to know, then by all means teach. However, keep it close to you, and whatever you do, do not try to improve them against their will. Do not try to trap them. They will resent it. Even if they just imagine you are trying to do so, they will resist."

"So then what is the craft of politics?" he asked.

"The craft," said the mistress, "is the ability to manipulate the people into wanting what you want them to want."

"Isn't there a positive side to it?" asked Dashi.

"That is not politics," she said.

"The master said that the people need to run their own affairs without interference from magistrates," said the magistrate.

"I'm sure he said that if people were unstuck, and allowed to mature naturally, without being manipulated by those with bad intent, there would be no need for them being manipulated by those with a so called good intent," she said, "The difficulty is like that of health. A healthy body may come to injury but it repairs itself. Once it is compromised too far by external interference then it requires medicine, an external interference, to restore it to self-repair. That is, if you know what medicine to employ. If you can rightly assess the dosage. And the frequency."

"And if you are not sure?" asked Dashi.

"Then you are just as likely, actually more so, to kill the patient rather than heal," she replied.

"But if the person is already sick–" said Dashi.

"Better sick than starving, you mean," she said. "That depends on how sick you get. If one catches politics one can end up dead rather suddenly. If you do not know, and basically no one does – the best path is to do no harm. Leave the people alone and concentrate on removing the conditions that led to the sickness, or in this case stuckness. The better course is to keep people healthy."

"Isn't that interfering?" countered Dashi.

"Certainly. Healers interfere on behalf of their patient. But the patient comes to the doctor. I don't go out distributing medicine to people in the street. First they must want it. They must be sick of being sick.

"And second it must be rare, or kept seeming that way. Otherwise the people will disregard it as common. Much disease can be treated by drinking water. But it falls from the sky and the people have not learned to appreciate it. They are stuck. Their minds are conditioned to desire scarce things: gold and trinkets."

"Like the gifts from the blue man?" said Dashi.

"Ah," she said, "You'll not catch me so easily, My Lord. It is not the material out of which it is made. It was what I mean by art. The carvings themselves could have been made from compressed cow dung and been perhaps even more beautiful."

Dashi said, "Do no harm, I understand, but what of the people who are already sick? Already stuck. Some of them are so stuck I cannot understand how they think. Further, some of them are dangers to themselves, to others. They are contagious. What then? As magistrate I can't just sit by and let them harm others. Isn't that what the master tried? Isn't that why an iron fisted magistrate was sent afterword?"

"Already that hat is so heavy," said the mistress. "If the people by their sickness harm others, if by their sickness they are contagious, it is still the patient, in the case of politics, the people who must request the intervention. Else it is your will in this, and if in this, why not in that, and if in that, why not completely. Do you understand?"

"Yes, mistress," said Dashi.

"It is the same as I said for improving character. Whatever is good and bad for you, when mixed with power, it becomes enforced medicine – for their own good. If they come to you, then do your best – which will require maturity of mind to increase your discernment.

"But sometimes you will treat the wrong disease. And they will die. Or you will fail to do enough of what's right and they will die," she said, "Greater discernment is the best means."

"I understand. What is then the best practice to attain maturity of mind?" asked Dashi.

"Ah. That's for your master to teach, Dashi. I'm only here to instruct the magistrate... My Lord," she said, "However, I do not think it oversteps my authority to say each mind needs to attain its wholenesses and that forcing is counter productive to that."

"Forcing myself," said Dashi.

"It always begins inside. How can one seek a good for others that is also good for oneself – without really knowing what is good for oneself? The good is not an object to be found out in the world but a condition of being whole. The greatest of wisdoms can be spread upon the earth at the feet of the stuck, but they will not see."

Dashi nodded. "Thank you mistress. Your counsel is wise. I will try to wait for the people to ask me to help them so they do not resist," said Dashi.

"You will wait a long time," said the mistress. "People are stubborn as mules. That's why the ancient rulers created the craft of politics."

"Master," said one of the merchants coming to the magistrate who was preparing to sit for meditation. The others were seating themselves in rows in the courtyard in sight of the gates far behind, and along the long outer wall to their left - facing at some distance a blank corner wall. This had no significance in and of itself, it was merely the place closest to the gates that was warmest and most out of the wind as dawn crept over the walls.

"The master lives on the mountain. I am just a student of the way, like you," Dashi said adjusting his sleeves, noticing the elder women sitting among the merchants. On that first day the nans shuffled in and sat behind them, and the merchants had looked a little affronted. Then gradually they formed a column beside them. Now they mixed with conviviality. Dashi internally nodded, which appeared as a subtle external nod that the student interpreted as an invitation to go on.

"My Lord, I feel angry and I have tried to burn it away but it returns," he said.

Dashi paid attention. "At what?" he asked.

"When my wife, or someone in my house does something wrong, if they drop something or are careless, I become disdainful and contemptful of them. I lash out. It's as if I felt they were doing it on purpose. I know they are not, but I am angry as if they were," he said.

Dashi thought a moment. "Perhaps you are not burning the wood but the flame," he said, and then wondered where that thought had come from. He continued, "You yell at them when they do something wrong?"

"Yes."

"What do you do when you do something wrong? If you make a mistake?"

"Oh, I hate making mistakes," he said, "It makes me

so..." freezing mid-thought.

"Angry?" Dashi asked.

"Very angry," he said.

Dashi nodded thoughtfully, "When you were a boy what happened when you made a mistake?" Dashi could see the quiver that went through the merchant. "Mistakes were not to be made?"

"No," confessed the merchant.

Dashi said, "Burn that."

When Dashi went walking out in the city, his city, as he passed doors and shops the people gave him wary smiles at first, but slowly they softened and began to feel that this time might be different. They honestly liked the new young magistrate, despite the fact that he was nothing but a country clod, and they suspected he'd been elected because no one else was foolish enough to take the position. They hoped he'd survive long enough to make things better.

Outside her window a bird called in the night. The mistress, not feeling well, dined in her quarters with her granddaughter and the magistrate, lanterns lit.

The dining plates returned to the kitchen. A discussion of bureaucratic misdeeds ensued. The mistress offered to direct appropriate investigations. Then, drawing table pulled out, brushes were brought forth, while court documents, having been explained, sat upon another table.

"Mistress, how should one free the people?" said Dashi

standing across the table from her, but out of the way of the lantern so as not to cast shadows on the paper.

She looked up, lifting her inked brush off the image of a lone tree. "Why would you want to do that?"

"The master said it is necessary to free the peoples' minds," he said.

"Ah. That is different. You must distinguish those," she replied and continued her painting.

Dashi waited. She held her sleeve just so, and the brush just so, and took up the ink just so, and quickly, efficiently, drew strokes across the paper. When she raised her hand and stood back, her granddaughter would remove the painting and replace it with a fresh piece of paper.

During the interval Dashi took advantage. "Do you wish me to expand on that?"

"Do you need to speak to think?"

"I might," he said.

"Go ahead then," she said and put brush to paper moving quick with purpose.

"The people's minds should be freed," he said.

"Should?" she replied.

"As a best course of action," he responded.

"Best?" she rejoined, her head down working.

Dashi sighed, "Being free."

"Free is what the thief tells you it will cost," she said, "What kind of free?"

"Unstuck free," said Dashi finally.

"Who is to be unstuck?" she asked.

"The people," said Dashi.

"All at once?" she queried.

"No, separately," Dashi said.

"All right. Therefore..." said the mistress lifting her brush.

He said, "Therefore to free the minds of the people is about each individual, whereas freeing the people is about the crowds."

The granddaughter took the finished piece away, and interjected, "Drive them from the city?" Earning her a look from her grandmother as she replaced the paper.

"And-" continued the mistress, dipping her brush.

'And-' thought Dashi, watching the marks appear before him, upside-down, "- Ah! That the political solution is top down, rather than bottom up, because it does not address each individual it is inferior," he said.

The mistress painted a river, or what Dashi tilting his head to see, thought looked like a river. "And-" she said, turning and blotting the brush, leaving dark tracks that were stones along the river.

Dashi considered. This was obviously subtle. A painter was speaking. Counter intuitive perhaps. He crossed his arms and emptied his mind. Letting his eyes unfocus. Dropping his questioning. There he stood, for a time, until something made him look up. A giggle. The granddaughter had her arms crossed, shoulders back, and so too the mistress. They were amused. Dashi put his arms down.

"Why did you just put your arms down?" asked the mistress.

"You suggested I was too stiff," said Dashi.

The granddaughter clicked her tongue, "Tsk, tsk, tsk," shaking her head slowly.

"We didn't say anything," said the mistress.

Dashi replied, "You didn't have to."

They nodded.

"Too determined," said the mistress.

"What do you mean? asked Dashi.

"I mean your right hand doesn't know what your left is doing." The mistress gestured her hand and the grand-daughter immediately placed a fresh piece of paper before her. Without a thought she painted.

"Ask me what I am painting," she said.

"What are you painting?"

"I don't know," she said and the marks appeared here and there, in the blanks. Unconnected, unintended. She picked another brush and began in red. Placing drops among the long twists of grey. Dashi wondered if these were fish, or more ominously blood dropped in the river.

For the first time Dashi interrupted her flow, "How do you know what to paint then?"

The mistress made a large complicated stroke at bottom and then she handed the finished painting to Dashi with the same speed as she had made it.

A fox sitting under a cherry tree.

"An inner desire, that the people like you, is dangerous in your position. Never," she said, "promise the people what no one can give them. Do not even think it – or you may show it, or worse say it. And you'll regret it."

Many of them jostled into the courtroom. Many had tried to clear their boots of mud, but some had not and the result was that they all tracked it around. The court clerk looked disgusted and caught the eye of every other court official he could to express his disdain.

"Order!" said the magistrate from his chair, "Or something that approximates it." They all settled down. Most of them, anyway. Some continued to talk until the bailiff rapped his staff upon the floor. Then there was silence –

and just a few whispers.

"All right, I have been thinking about how best to do this. Because many who previously owned the land are dead and have left no descendants. Because some land is better than others, because some need to support more people I have decided that whatever I do, I won't be able to make all of you happy. So consider that what I am going to do will make all of you unhappy to some degree, but also better off in general." Dashi paused here while they whispered until the bailiff rapped his staff again.

"I considered giving all of it, to all of you to have in common. But I realised if there were arguments, then those arguments would likely break along family lines into feuds. Therefore the total land and its quality has been looked at and will be divided among the twelve families. The parcels will be divided along the existing ditches and paths. That way all arguing will be with those who are like you," he said and stopped at the murmuring, which seemed to contain a lot of questioning sounds.

"That is, each family will receive, by draw, one parcel which is adjusted to be of equal quality and size," the magistrate clarified. "No family may have two farms. I have chatted with the nans about who's related to whom, to make sure the numbers of each family are relatively equal, and because most of you are already intermarried, you can work out who goes where."

A man stepping forward said, "Dashi?" a strangled sound came from the direction of the court clerk's throat, followed by a floor rap. Chastised, he corrected his address, "My Lord... If you give us back the land, can't the next magistrate, if you'll excuse my saying, just take it back again?"

"I'm not promising anything for the future," said Dashi,

"Who comes after me will do what they do. But I have an idea.

"We want each farm to be productive. If unsuccessful, each family will not be able to pay the emperor's land-fees and forfeit the land. And of course starve. It is in your best interest to do better for everyone.

"I am also assigning a liaison to each parcel who will report back about how the farms are doing. If the liaison interferes and should the farm produce less than the other comparable farms, they will be sentenced to work the farm, under the farmer, for a period not less than ten years.

"Any magistrate coming after me, therefore, already has complete control if they wish through the liaisons already established and the liaisons have every reason to not get involved except to help you, and if they overstep their bounds and ruin your crop then they, not you, are to blame and dig ditches for a decade.

"If all that seems fair enough, you will find in front of you a bowl with twelve stones. Each has a number and represents a parcel of land. You will draw straws to establish the order of the draw. Once you have it, that is your land. Should you have a preference, you can barter one for another. Agreed?" said the magistrate. And they chatted a moment and then nodded their heads.

"Read the list of family names," said Dashi, watching as the lots proceed. He felt pleased with himself, thinking of this. Working things out wasn't as hard as it seemed.

Dashi had finished the court and was marching along to see the mistress. "My Lord," said the court clerk, walking stiff legged to catch up with the magistrate.

"Clerk," said the magistrate.

"My Lord," he said somewhat winded. "The land. You do understand," he said.

"I understand," said Dashi. "It is being returned to its rightful owners. Also, those who actually know what to do with it, so that we can all eat, and I can pay the taxes."

"Yes, true, true, My Lord. Well said. But a merchant is of a lesser rank than a land owner," the clerk alluded.

"And?" said Dashi wondering where he was going with this.

"And many, say I, most of the exiled society..."

"Society?" queried Dashi.

"Nobility," answered the clerk.

"Courtiers," countered Dashi.

"Yes, as you say, they, most of them, had their lands taken away from them when they were sent here, and it is only natural for them to desire to have lands that they may continue in the manner to which they are accustomed," and he spread his hands upward as if that truth explained itself, while bending his head to his left shoulder and stretching his face into an unpracticed grin. And there he froze, batting flirtatious eyes like an badly aged painted lady.

At first Dashi didn't know what to do, so he did nothing. Waiting to see if the court clerk would continue. But he just smiled.

And as the magistrate did nothing – so too the clerk continued to stand there. Only his eyes began to shift and he began slowly nodding his head as if to lead the magistrate along into agreement.

Finally Dashi was aware of his own tiredness, and the creeping fingers of hunger, "Clerk," said the magistrate,

72

"When the emperor chose to strip these persons of their lands, I am sure, it was not his intention that they should just go get more elsewhere. And certainly not that they steal them from his own tax base, by making them less than productive. If however you wish me to solicit a definitive answer, I can have a letter to the capitol drawn up to clarify this. I will consider its wording so that the *full* situation is *fully* comprehended by the receiver."

The clerk fully put down his open hands, and the partial smile. "I don't think the emperor need be bothered."

"Me neither then – that saves time," said Dashi in a helpful tone. And the clerk bowed and backed away down the corridor in the opposite direction from Dashi's dinner.

Dashi liked the new head chef – the positive comparison was easy. He often took his meals down in the kitchen with the staff, or when that wasn't convenient, especially for the mistress, the chef joined them at the magistrate's table. Food tasters were now banned from the palace. His former taster had been given the position of runner for the new magistrate, and couriered the court documents needing to be considered. When not employed with that, he brought food from the kitchen and ate with them when there.

Despite the opulent ingredients that were housed in the kitchen, both Dashi and the mistress preferred simple fare. The mistress had selected the new chef, pleading her delicate stomach. Rice and a single flavourful dish of meat and vegetables, in a simple sauce, was common. A persimmon, held in underground storage, was served after dinner.

What Dashi enjoyed most were bowls of rich brown broth overflowing with dumplings. He'd insisted they find someone who could do that. He preferred to eat these in the kitchen rather than in front of the mistress, who ate so elegantly that one couldn't fully enjoy the exquisite gastronomic experience of dumpling slurping.

It was a pleasure to laugh with the kitchen staff, who seemed like a family. One kitchen maid was all gossip about the previous magistrate and told tales of the last chef and his mad outbursts – which they attributed to drink, as he would occasionally disappear into the meat locker for long times coming out crazed, with bloody smock and half-dripping wet. It was at these times they were most afraid of him, and they were glad he was dead.

Dashi raised his glass. "May his soul find freedom in death that in life he could not."

The staff smiled peculiarly at each other and drank.

At evening's end, the kitchen crew prepared for tomorrow, hanging pots, replacing dirty cloths with clean ones, putting up wood for tomorrow's fire. "So what do you do when you aren't being my runner," asked Dashi of the boy across the table, as he poured him some more wine.

"My Lord, I sleep," he said.

"I'm keeping you up," apologised Dashi.

"No, My Lord, I enjoy sitting at the table."

Dashi nodded. And then he began to tear up. "It is nice, isn't it? So simple. Just to be warm. Full bellies. Kind faces," said Dashi sighing.

"I know what you mean, My Lord," said the runner.

"All right," said Dashi, "Get to bed," he said.

"Tomorrow I sit again in the red chair. And you will run the halls to the mistress."

"Thank you, My Lord," said the boy untangling his legs from the table bench. He bowed and departed. Eventually so did the rest of the kitchen staff, one by one. Drinking wine, Dashi sat alone. The deaf girl who kept the embers burning in the night came in, but refused an offered drink. So Dashi finished the bottle, and took another to his room.

"The procedure is to change the ownership of the parcel, but the records of who owns the parcels appear to have been lost," said the mistress.

"Lost?" said Dashi.

"Misplaced more likely," she replied.

"I see," he said, "And without the records..."

"Without them there can be no transfer of the lands. Besides your proposal was to reallocate the lands. To draw boundaries anew, was it not?"

"Yes," said Dashi, "I felt that would be most fair and also productive."

"Well you can't just do that either," she replied.

Dashi considered this. "If there are no records of ownership to transfer, then there are no records of any boundaries for those lands. It suggests these lands are therefore common lands of the empire. Which means that as the acting magistrate I can assign these lands in order to further the common good of the empire. In this case, by increasing the lands productivity, thereby creating more grain to be given in taxation, and thus strengthening the imperial treasury. Is that not so?"

"I am persuaded that it is," she replied, "But what of the original ownership deeds? What if they should suddenly appear again?"

Dashi put his hand to his heart, "I have it on the best authority from my service that no such documents now exist. Any documents subsequently found are therefore forgeries created by swindlers trying to steal the land from the emperor," said Dashi, "I should think there would be some harsh penalty for such a crime. Please have the bureaucrats look *that* up – assuming the books of statutes haven't all been lost."

"You are wasted here," said the mistress.

The magistrate went to the fields. He took a horse from the stables, as it dawned upon him that presently they were his horses.

It was good to feel the wind and watch the trees and grasses sway. He passed through the farmyards where the abandoned houses were being painted and patched, reclaimed and remade.

Though his bed chambers were warm, and the court room decidedly not, he knew from experience these dwellings hadn't been even as good as that – when he'd lived in them. When the farmers had been cleared from the land and encamped in what was now the market outside the north city gate. When the previous administration wanted the people close by so they could control them, or just to keep them from being happy, or to...

"Why drive the people from the fields?" Dashi thought, wondering. It didn't make any sense – like most rules, he concluded.

But the lush green and a playful breeze removed all thought of politics from Dashi's minds. Today he'd passed through the market, and the people waved at him, and he waved back. New vegetables were appearing at the stalls, along with buyers: cooks and their assistants, the servants of the rich and the townspeople themselves. Noticing the ground was still muddy in places, he wondered why the farmers weren't included into the storefronts that sprawled in the town.

Looking back at the rescued homes with chickens and children and curling chimney smoke spiralling away on the breeze, Dashi felt real hope. Something he'd not felt for the people, he thought... perhaps ever.

It was funny to Dashi that drafty leaky country dwellings, a quarter of the size of his bedroom and from which he'd dreamed of escape when it was there he lived, had their own appeal. 'When the roof falls in you just move to a house that still has some,' - one of his brother's expressions.

As he rode though the upper valley he spoke to the farmers, "Bad crops," they said and shook their heads. They always said that in case a capricious god might be listening, but Dashi knew what that meant.

Dashi stopped to talk to whom he recognised as the daughter of the woman who made sleeping mats from reeds. She was cutting down weeds with a homemade angled blade with a handle and piling animal straw mulch and river mud on top, "The crops are growing," she said - echoing the statements of several others.

The magistrate nodded. "Ploughing soon?" he asked

"No," she said, as had the others, "No ploughing this year."

"Ah," said the magistrate, as he had with the others, but

this time he didn't ask why because none of the others knew why.

She stood and leaned on her tool, "Dashi," she said, beginning a question, "I mean, magistrate..." And then she looked at her shovel. "My Lord..."

When she didn't continue he prompted, "Yes?" Dashi said finally.

"Do you have a woman?"

"No," said Dashi, a smile... and then quickly not. Because a laugh rose up to the absurd question – when mere weeks ago there'd have been no such question. And then, he felt instead the sadness for her wish to escape a life of subsisting toil. He, the magistrate, said to her, "I promise everything will become better."

The magistrate stood smiling in the square outside the walls of his palace just about where he himself had once stood protesting. Some men with buckets stood by. On the wall someone had painted 'I promise everything will become better.' The mistress, who had just read it to him, stood beside him on his arm, made 'tsk' noises.

"You don't approve?" said Dashi.

"Can you make *everything* better?" she asked.

"Well... not everything," he said. "But I am pleased at their optimism."

The mistress tucked her hands into her sleeves, "My advice is scrub it off the wall before too many see it and become *pleased* you'll solve all their problems for them. Consider how *optimistic* they will become when you can't," and added, "It's cold. I wish to be taken back inside."

Secretly he was pleased, but Dashi led her back, nodding his assent to the crew who began to remove the words written upon the stone.

The warm air was still. Still warm, Dashi tilted his head back, his eyes heavy and his body drooping down. More laws, more paper.

"We have our first report," said the mistress.

"From who?" said Dashi, rousing himself to continue lining the brushes up on the table, in a row, equidistant and so their ends matched.

"The nans from outside the city and wealthy who sit with you - every morning," she said.

"Them," said Dashi, "What did they report on?"

"On the state of the people, their mood," she replied.

"I don't recall asking them to do that," he said.

"I did," she replied, "If you are to win, and politics is about winning, then you must know which way the people are leaning."

"We could just check to see which way the wind was blowing," joked Dashi. It fell flat.

"The report says, in summary, the people have had their trust sucked dry by a series of parasitical magistrates," said the mistress.

"Oh," he said.

"It says they keenly desire someone capable, and fair," she said.

"I believe in fair," said Dashi, "Did the master ever talk to you about the ship wreck and the cake?"

"Cake? No we never discussed cake," said the mistress.

"It was about fairness," commented Dashi, moving the smallest brush a little further in.

"Would My Lord like to hear my opinion?' she queried.

"That would be fine, please do," said Dashi.

"As an herbalist, if I were to come to be given a city to care for, to improve the health of the people, I would follow protocol. First, I'd assess the levels and kinds of health and disease. Second, assess the multiplicity of sickness causing conditions. Third, remove the worst and easiest of the unhealthful conditions. Fourth, promote many different healthy exemplars. Fifth, introduce multiple strategies for health self-improvement. Then sixth, you reassess, at every level, and repeat the process.

"If done properly, the people will gradually get better but not really know how it was done – meaning, as it will be considered a good thing, they will decide that they did it themselves. Which is already partially true. Therefore they will do more of it, and it will become more true, until that is just the way it is," she said, and brandished the report.

"As magistrate it is exactly the same, only you are dealing with the stuck minds of the people. One, what kinds of stuck people are there? Two, what things are keeping them stuck? Removing the worst and the easiest, third. You want to get it done. If something will require ongoing effort then beware. Do not get bogged down in implementation. You also do not want a protracted war. Choose something that won't be missed. It may be that through subsequent integrations this problem will solve itself.

"Fourth, introduce multiple exemplars of integration to which people can aspire. If there are many, each will find their own inspiration. This leads to, five, multiple strategies for self-integration. For maturity, wisdom, beauty, wholeness..."

"As many as there are minds, I take it," said Dashi.

"Exactly so," she said.

"It would be advantageous therefore to know how many there were and of their nature," said Dashi perking up.

"O, I agree," said the mistress, "If the leader is mature, they certainly would need to know," she nodded, "But that is why *you* have advisors, My Lord."

The magistrate called to him his runner. "Tell the treasurer," Dashi had checked if he had one, and what his duties were, "to decrease the taxes by a tenth – but do not tell the people. Tell him the increased crop yield will make up the difference." The runner sprinted away.

The people seemed stuck on worrying about their next meal. That could easily be attributed to the shortage of food. Dashi knew if they were to learn to divide the cake well, whatever way that was, they first had to have enough cake not to want just to steal it. The crops were still in the ground, not much he could do about that, but he could increase the amount of money they had by not taking as much.

Dashi had decided however, that if he told the people he was dropping their taxes they'd be happy momentarily, but then he'd have focused them on how still high they were. Better just a lightening of their burden without them noticing. Better that things were getting better, but not in so many words.

It was the same with the more punitive laws from the previous magistrate. Dashi simply repealed them. Whether they knew it or not, the people were in this at least, more free.

Once again therefore he went to the stables and chose

the tawny stallion he liked. But this time he'd had ribbons tied to its tail. And that exuberance, which was really all he felt he had, would express that things were to be better. Or at least that is what he thought about it afterwards. So the magistrate rode out of the gate like a storybook prince, and went galloping into the countryside, with many pausing to watch him.

The crops were looking lushly magnificent. Out on his inspection he'd been amazed by their vigour and health. He chatted among the farmers as he'd always done. Only now they didn't say, "Too many questions Dashi, we've work to do." Instead they answered politely. And truthfully, from what he could tell.

They no longer tilled the soil, they explained, instead they covered the ground with leaves and straw. When he asked why, they said – the rice fields – they flooded them. When pressed further, they explained the water suppressed the weeds – why not do the same with mulch to smother? Dashi remembered this as the technique the master also used for his own garden. But why the change? At this, they shrugged.

Whatever the approach, it was working. This at least would be a success that he, as magistrate, could, while not take credit for, bask in its glow. Considering this he also realised if the crops had been a disaster, he could have found an excuse probably involving the previous magistrate. Insinuation being the art of politics.

Again Dashi sat in the chair, in his full robes, looking down from on high upon the prisoners. The two men he knew. Unnecessarily announced by the black robed court officers: this was their fourth appearance. Separately: drunk and disorderly, with a deep ingenuity for starting brawls. When their twin paths met, it was hatred at first sight. And they'd been destroying property in their devotion to destroying each other, since. Bonded in chains, they stood before the magistrate, with bruises and black eyes and dried blood.

"Why?" said the exasperated magistrate.

He breathed in and looked off exasperated, exhaling. To be judge: to deal with people's inability to judge for themselves. "Tell me why I should let you go free? – even whipped!? – even fined!? What difference would it make?" Dashi rapped his fingers on the arm of the chair. His stomach grumbled. "When we all know, you'll be right back here."

He was trying not to be resentful of this. To see them as flawed creatures as he himself was flawed. And the flaw presently was he was annoyed to have them clanking and cluttering up his hall with their chains.

The two looked down the whole time. They gave no defence. They did not engage.

Said Dashi aside to his runner, standing to his right, "They seem so docile presently."

"Like naughty children," said the former taster boy.

"Ah... and am I then parent of these devil twins?" asked Dashi.

"They are old enough to be my parents many times over. They ought to be parents for themselves," said the boy.

"And yet they are not. This is just as I was saying at dinner. I care, yes. But how must a society shoulder *this?* When it is wanton... dangerous... disrespectful... and repeatedly so?" he asked his young friend.

"Perhaps it is only in their own company, that judgements, of whatever mind, can be understood," said the runner bringing to bear what Dashi had been relaying to him of the master's teaching.

"You mean understood by the people who are like them?"

"If there are any," said the boy.

Having lived as a thief among thieves Dashi understood who was like them. Him, for one. Though not as violent, he understood being mad at the world. Resentful of one's poor lot in life. Well, he couldn't complain now.

Still this kind of headlong destructiveness needed to be met, as his brother had done, with a hard wall for hard heads. Considering, Dashi marvelled at how his brother had always made the punishment seem like their own fault.

Dashi nodded. "All right," said Dashi aloud, and turning to face the prisoners he addressed them with his magisterial voice, "I can find no better punishment for the two of you – than each other. You are each other's twin.

"As you seem to like being put in chains, my judgement is for ones to be specifically fashioned for you. You shall be bound together as a three legged man. Your hands will be bound close to your chests, allowing you to eat and dress and so on, but stopping you from hitting one another. Arrangements will be made to alter your clothes so that you can take them on and off.

"I hope for your sakes, after you've enjoyed some time trying to sleep, eat, dress and void your bowels, which I have no doubt you will make as unpleasant an experience for each other as possible, you will appreciate this pointless feud as a mirror of your own poor attitudes and consider the idea of a truce."

"Never," grumbled one of the two.

"What?" said Dashi, leaning forward at this challenge to his authority.

"I'd never be truced to this bag o' shit!" he shouted out, as if to make the whole world hear this oath. "No matter..." he growled with an absurd grimace at the other man – who spat in his face.

Howling anger, the roaring two tussled fiercely in the midst of the courtroom, knocking over the bailiff who tried to stop them, overturning a table covered with court papers, crushing and ripping the papers under their dirty boots.

"Order! Order!" yelled Dashi over all the other yells for order, as the court officers and guards struggled to bring the battling toughs under control.

Dashi sighed and glanced sideways at his companion. "Like an old married couple," Dashi observed, in a voice he recognised as his brother's sneer. The boy smiled and stifled a laugh. But Dashi was past humour. How dare they turn his court into a mockery.

When the pandemonium twins were finally wrestled into submission Dashi glared down at the two – forgetting to be sympathetic. He rose like a great black crow from his chair, and pointed his finger at the prisoners "By the power invested in me... I hereby declare you man and wife. Let no one break this bond of holy matrimony."

The courtroom was shocked silent. And then it chuckled. And then it began to laugh out loud.

The magistrate continued over the din of laughter, "If you return again to this court, you will be banished from this city, to return on pain of death. Take them away. And see to it that they start their life together properly blessed," he said gesturing – scattering the gobsmacked prisoners with thrown imaginary flower petals.

"Court is adjourned," said the magistrate as he and his assistant withdrew to get something to eat.

Soon they fell into boyish mirth and amicable chitchat.

"All I said was that we should... If we try to get the people to help us find the trouble makers in their midst then... then they can be dealt with," said Dashi. "The captain thought it was worth trying. Everyone we've asked has agreed, but then we've had not one culprit exposed."

"Lucky for you," said the mistress.

"How is this lucky?" asked Dashi.

"Because it means they retreat from politics," she said. "Because they cannot tell between ruthlessness power for gain, and necessary strength – therefore they come to resent all intrusions."

"You think I need to be more sensitive to their feelings?" he said.

"To your power, My Lord. The emperor sits at the centre of the web of society. So too, in a lesser way, the magistrates."

"You mean I'm a spider," said Dashi.

"No, spiders make webs. What gets caught up in them are those who seek power for their own sake. The office of magistrate, executed correctly, is a glorified catcher of mad dogs – removing the violent from society so that it may continue," she said, "For all the emperor's power, despite physical luxuries, his armies mostly fend off invasion – an ongoing concern and no less a disquieting and troubling occupation than yours."

Dashi said, "One can also use an army to attack."

"A tyrant will attack. This is the summation of being

stuck in identity, power and survival. For an emperor to seek status – what need is there for grandiosity except feelings of inferiority? It means he is weak.

The weak man serves only himself, or in the case of my sister, herself. These tyrannical values are normalised. They appear in the laws and customs. They are reflected in the buildings and banners. One is then surrounded by aggrandisement. When the people only respect spectacle, the kingdom is already lost.

The people will naturally come to reflect the weakness. They will steal and hoard. They will bear false witness, thinking their status can protect them from accusations of not being loyal enough. Fine things will be coveted to enhance one's prestige and to be used as bribes. Unwanted attention will be diverted from one oneself by driving down another's reputation. It will not be long until it is the emperor who is in danger," she explained, "People who are used to being preyed upon like nothing better than some vulnerability they can attack," she said. "When the people become lawless by imitation, eventually the tyrant finds no army is large enough to stop their lies from burrowing into everything – and thus come themselves to a sticky end."

"What about your sister? She was magistrate for years," said Dashi.

"And it was the captain that reported you and the master had been killed, rather than face the consequence of failure," she said, "Whole empires have fallen because impossible orders were issued that, on pain of punishment, no one dared fail. So therefore everyone lies. All the way up the chain of command, a conspiracy of silent deceit.

"Self-fawning weaklings through presumption of the glory of their word – that it shall be so – show not true power, but conceit. Laws are not edicts by the gods. True power requires no show. Not for others, not for pride. It is cautious as if walking on ice."

"The fox and its tail, I remember the story. I must take care with my power," said Dashi extending his chin nobly.

"At least a tyrant pretends to true power," she said, "Yes, you could be the hero – make a government which addresses the people's needs," said the mistress, "Have medicines and abundant food and army presence so people feel secure. Have flags and songs and such so they can feel they're part of something valued. Make systems of trade, and money, and rules with judges. Make universities where the useful truths will be studied. And top it off with some religion so they can have a unified cosmos. Each separate layer would work.

"But what if you've created incompatible rules? What if your reason is not omnisciently perfect?

"We could ask the people," said Dashi.

"How much more quickly will the people lose respect if a ruler goes about asking them to help him? Or when he opens his decisions to debate? He has the power. Does he know how to deal with the unruly or not?" she said.

"True power must be seen as considered and reasoned," said Dashi.

"True power has nothing to do with politics," she responded with force. "Nor reason."

Dashi shifted his weight, considering. "It would help them also, to be part of the decisions," he countered.

"For half of the people in this city nothing matters save appearances, power and survival," she said.

"You keep repeating those three ideas," Dashi observed, "What are they?"

"Ask your master. I only agreed to teach you about politics," she replied.

Dashi winced. "Terrible tactics for survival. It doesn't make it right," said the magistrate.

"No, but it does explain why people don't want to inform on each other," she said.

Dashi said, "I thought you just said they did."

"Oh, they will, but it's a dangerous move. I'm sure if you keep asking, someone will offer you a sacrifice," she said, "but it will be to their personal advantage. They'll just make the system complicit in taking down an enemy, that's all. Do you really want to tempt them with this power? You are lucky they do not snatch it, and praise you falsely.

"And to that end, when into this stuck mess arrives a kind hearted person with hopes and dreams of a better society, an individual who would attempt to free the masses - giving power out like pastries," she said, "You'd just be making tiny tyrants."

"I'm a dreamer," he said.

"O yes, very much so," she said with a tiny smirk playing on her lips. "But that isn't the problem. The problem is that you are impatient for improvements. You've been head dog catcher mere months. You think you can bend the people to your will so easily? The tyrant has come to live inside them - even when the outer one is driven away."

"Ah, but once they realise... they have swallowed the tyrant - then this can be healed," said Dashi.

She said, "But you'll not be able to discuss this with them - for they do not trust, no matter your trustworthiness."

"Ah," said Dashi, "Trust. I see."

"And telling them the problem is inside them will seem like pointing fingers," she said. "There is nothing to be gained and everything to be lost in pushing forward, My

Lord." The mistress bent forward, "No matter how superior your purpose.

"They may even assume your good intentions are some trick, and fear reprisal when you change your mind. Having been under the heel, they will not tell you the truth. But worse, if they come to suspect you are weak, they will mock you behind your back, and lie outright to your face."

"How it is that I have lived near this town all my life, seen what I have seen, but still am surprised by people's maliciousness?" said Dashi.

She said, "You keep hoping."

"It's probably not very smart," said Dashi.

"Wanting the best, for everyone, is... sweet," she said.

"Naive, you mean," said Dashi, and folded his arms across his chest.

"I mean what I say, My Lord. If you want my words, then hear me. If you don't want them, send me away," the mistress said.

Dashi uncrossed his arms. "I apologise," said Dashi.

"My Lord, don't apologise. It makes you look weak. I told you," she said. "A northern town is no place for weak men."

"I'm... listening," he said.

"Good," she said. "Understand this then. Lots of people have lots of ideas of what constitutes the good. Will you merely be another salesman yelling from your stall in the bazaar? Again, what if they don't want to? What if they choose another truth?"

Dashi remained silent.

"The difficulty you are having is twofold," she said, "One is that the meaning of their life is their mature experience of themselves. If they are not there, then everything you busy them with is only a distraction from their maturation. Anything you could offer is arbitrary and will not suit anyone. Any attempt to bribe the people will distract them from the simple existence of their nature. Tyrants force, and the people burrow in. Do gooders also force them and the people will get stuck in manners, conduct, and protocol. Thus the good will become an evil."

"So then I will encourage them to mature," said Dashi.

The mistress said, "The other is because you yourself do not possess your own matured consciousness. Whatever mistaken form of government you conceive has already in it the seeds of its inescapable downfall. With no awareness of the true nature of themselves within, even a good promoted as being natural, would be itself not based in the natural way, because even those conceiving it are not themselves being natural. The best they could do is mimicking what was explained to them."

"Oh," said Dashi.

"Maturation is natural. Don't add to their lives, remove obstacles. Teach people how to feel relief. Don't belabour that it's good for them. That's just giving them the temptation to give themselves airs. Or for you to pat yourself on the back for being beneficent.

"If it makes their lives better, they will understand this. If you are reduced to arguing for it, then you are forcing and they will become cunning in making your good a bad. And even should they submit, the seeds of begrudging compliance will be mixed in with this good. Only through the direct experience of the awake individual, or their works, can the picture become clear. Only when there are enough free people will you have a free society. Then everything will just happen of its own accord and it will seem as if you have done nothing. It will be - just how it turned out. Then no one will bring cases to judge because they'll work it out for themselves, and you can go fishing."

"Oh," said Dashi again.

"The craft of governing is to know what the people need, and to offer it," she said.

"What do they need?" asked Dashi.

"Once there was a man who wanted to be a success, but who could not dream," she said, "He had tried many many occupations, but none of them brought him the success he desired. He therefore wanted a dream to tell him at what he would be successful. Because his minds were filled with worries, all night long, he hardly rested, and never dreamt. He thought, how can I have a better life if I can't imagine one?

"Every night he went to bed hoping. Every morning, he arose to go about his tasks still with no dream in his heart. And every day he looked worse and worse until people began to comment that he should get more sleep.

"One day the old midwife appeared on his doorstep. She insisted that he couldn't sleep because he was secretly afraid he wouldn't hear his dream when it came. The cure, she said, was to take a rooster into his house to be sure he didn't oversleep.

"Not knowing what else to do, the man took the rooster into the house. But the rooster clucked all night long, keeping him awake.

"So the old midwife said, so you can sleep, you will now need a cat to keep the rooster afraid to cluck. So the man got a cat – but it just mewed at the fearful rooster that clucked all night long.

"So the old midwife said, so you can sleep, you will now need a dog to corner the cat. So the man got a dog – but it just barked at the cornered cat which mewed at the fearful rooster that clucked all night long.

"So the old midwife said, so you can sleep, you will now need a cow to bully the dog. So the man got a cow – but it just mooed at the bullied dog which barked at the cat which mewed at the fearful rooster that clucked all night long.

"So the old midwife said, so you can sleep, you will now need a horse to menace the cow. So the man got a horse – but it just neighed at the menaced cow which mooed at the bullied dog which barked at the cornered cat which mewed at the fearful rooster that clucked all night long.

"Finally the man couldn't take it any longer, and he banished all the animals. A peace fell upon him, and that night he slept like a baby. The next morning he arose with a dream in his heart. And he never worried about being successful again."

"Ah – worry gives you insomnia. That's one I can understand," said Dashi.

"Actually, it's about how single-mindedness disrupts natural flow – even if one's obsession is to correct the flow. Thus," said the mistress, "Perfect government is a contradiction of terms. Governments are created by the learned, not the wise. More so because they do not know the difference between the two and think their learning the pinnacle of human achievement. They have no sense about being. They do not understand ignorance. They cannot perfect imperfection. They have faith in their learning but no faith in faith as its basis. In short, they are stuck being young adults who think they already know everything," she said. "No matter how you define it, there is no way to create a painting by explanation."

"Right," said Dashi, nodding, though not really knowing what she meant. "But when I sit with the others in the courtyard and explain how to burn away stuckness, am I not doing exactly this?" he asked.

She said, "Offering the people the firebreath, to reclaim minds they've rejected – this is not organisation as you know it. Nothing is done, so nothing is left undone."

"Just to fill out my education," said Dashi, "If I were going to do it wrong, if I didn't care to make people well again – then what would be the way to govern?"

"Simple," she said, "You would choose what you originally suggested - keep people isolated by making them suspect everyone is a potential informant, but with the addition of lies, fear, manipulation and unrelenting brutality."

Dashi was breathing. Before the sun or anyone else arrived Dashi had a few moments to himself. To clear his minds. To burn. To burn deeper. He inhaled and breathed down on his anger. But the anger remained.

He was concerned he was becoming changed as magistrate: churlish and resentful. He felt he owed those before him unbiased emotion. As unbiased as he could be. It occurred to him that in the past he'd often not expressed his anger. Worse than pushing it away, he'd made it invisible. Like it wasn't there.

Only it was there. Even what he thought of as his better judgements were no doubt tainted with it. In between one thought and another, a little space, a line, a demarkation, a crack in between, where the thought he'd made invisible, hid.

His thumping heart told him he'd found what he pretended was not there. No doubt it appeared in the corners of his sincere smile and every effort of his hands, if one had eyes to see. Invisible then only to him. What before was a private sham was now a public display.

What was he so angry about? He'd come to peace with the past. Or so he thought. Perhaps it was the opulence. The inequity weighed on him. The seeping into his soul of attitudes substantiated by the walls around him. Their values becoming his. But then he felt the same way about the gnawing of destitution. It was why he sought the master of the mountain.

"Master," Dashi said to the air, "If living for free in palaces *and* abandoned shacks, both cost too much - what is it to be free?"

The morning courtyard sit was becoming lighter as spring advanced into summer; the empty courtyard awaited the coming students and offered no illumination.

"Mistress," said Dashi, "this office I hold..." He paused in thought, "I find myself beginning to feel the power of it is mine - that it's in me and not in the hat and robes. I burn it in practice but if I don't remind myself, I slip into forgetting that when I leave, I will just be Dashi."

"Well that you worry," she said. "Some people do have power - to strategise, to lead, to fight, to heal, to persuade. They are authorities on what they can do or know. Bureaucrats however have merely positions of authority. A completely different thing.

"But those bureaucrats become used to the life of power. They think it is their due. They become arrogant. If you want to see what a person is like - promote them."

"Yes, I can see this," said Dashi, thinking of the inn

keeper's horse, "the question is how can *I* remember?"

The mistress nodded, "Once there was a farm yard with five brother pigs who grew up together, rooting the ground, clearing away the brush.

"One day the farmer made a pen. One of the brothers was chosen to be prize pig, and live in the pen and receive the best of food, as much as he could eat, indeed enough food for all of them, and all without working in the fields.

"The other pigs said, 'Brother pig, we rejoice in your good fortune.'

"But the prize pig said, 'You are just envious of all that I have. This is not luck! I have come here on my own skill and therefore with you I will share nothing.' The other pigs protested their good will, but to no avail – and to them – the prize pig turned his tail.

"With only the prize pig to eat all that food, day after day, very quickly, he, the prize pig, grew bigger and fatter, and wider and heavier.

"Then one day the axeman came and the prize pig cried out, 'Help me my brothers!' "

Dashi sat in the morning, upon a low dais. The sound of the rain striking the large canvas awning, strung taut pole to pole, caused his mind to wander to places which he then burned – a slow, and methodical wildfire, scorching the landscape of rejected thought.

If he waited for the people to speak, why not induce them to speech? Why not ask of them what they would have for rule? He burned it.

The master's granddaughter's bare feet.

Should... Would it not be right... Surely it must be right

that they choose their own judge? Perhaps even... emperor?

Again - the granddaughter's bare feet quickly disappeared behind the table.

Dashi, annoyed, went to burn it, but couldn't bring himself to want to burn her feet. So he found where the memory had landed inside him, and burned that until it was nothing but a cinder.

Following its own natural course the falling water pooled at his feet.

A dozen people looked at the new message scribbled on the outer palace wall. The magistrate exiting his palace, passing behind them, looked at the people. The people looked at him and waved. He waved back. That was enough, and they nodded knowingly amongst themselves - and they grinned.

Meanwhile the magistrate flowed onward into the familiar labyrinth of streets in search of dumplings.

"Your fairness will be lost on them, My Lord," said the court clerk, after a gruelling court session.

"It is not lost on me," said Dashi turning back to see the clerk catch up with him in the hallway.

"Of course," said the clerk, "You are a man of virtue. What I mean is that there are methods of order and stability. In order to have security one must have a system of merit, and system of punishments for transgressing the system. The people care nothing for stability, until it is lost, of course. They concern themselves only with their immediate gratification."

The tired magistrate said, "Their gratification is their common humanity. What they desire is a soft bed, something to eat, and someone to love and protect them. It's as those things are frustrated that they become cunning and greedy. Or perhaps their delinquency is a replacement for something else. As to stability, it is their individual stability that is collectedly the stability of society - despite the system.

"I am now going to gratify my desire for dinner, if you wish to join me."

Outside it poured rain - again - still. This made the petitioners look more bedraggled than usual. But Dashi was warm and his lunch sat very pleasantly in his stomach. The cases were slowing to a trickle. He would be all right he decided.

The clerk announced the two women who came before the magistrate, Dashi. "What is your petition?" he said from his chair atop the stairs. They stood silent. One woman carried a swaddled baby on her back. "You," he said.

"My, My Lord, I gave this woman my baby to care for her, but now the old magistrate is gone I wanted my baby back," she said.

"Is the baby in question not the one on your back?" asked Dashi, clarifying.

"No, that's her," said the woman with the baby.

Dashi nodded with a slight tilt to his head. "Then why are you here?" he said bemused, and wearing his patient face.

"You have your baby-" began the other woman.

"Order," said Dashi, to the second woman.

The first began again, "I can't give her two copper, and she says she needs it back. I give her the one I didn't spend - it's all I had in the world - and I only gave my baby so she could have a better life, but now you're here, your highness, we'll have food enough - I thought - I want my baby back!"

"You just came and took it!" accused the second.

Then both, "Now we're out in the fields again... ...Gave her to me freely, to place her in a good home... ...so I can care for her myself... ...I care for her just fine, just like I care for all of them... ...but she doesn't behave right! Just look at her! ...feed them, I clean them-"

"You said you were going to put them with good parents." interrupted Dashi.

"They don't grow on trees, your honour. But there *she* was," she spat, "You gave her up and I paid. I was the one caring, with all the others in that dark room- Sleeping rooms are always dark!" she interjected, rebutting an aspect of the dispute withheld.

"Stop!" said Dashi, his hands raised in that gesture. The woman with the baby had unslung its carrier and came forward showing the baby to Dashi. The court rose as Dashi arose from his chair, his robe reflowing around his legs he descended the steps. Dashi looked at the baby in the carrier.

"See?" pleaded the woman, "Her eyes aren't focused, she won't look at you, she said, her face he could now see, was long with worry, "She should look at you."

Dashi pushed back the patterned red cloth around the child's face, to see. It looked like a baby.

"When I was a boy, the nans sometimes sang to me, and

stroked my hair," said Dashi. "Do you sing to your baby?" he asked.

"Every day," she replied.

"Sing more," suggested Dashi, "I think you're doing all the right things. Just keep doing them. She's been through a difficult experience for a baby." And now the woman started to cry tears of guilt.

"She'll be well. And maybe one day, if she's very unlucky, maybe she'll become magistrate," he joked. The crying woman gave a wan smile.

"So," said Dashi, turning to the other woman, who had her lips held tight in anger, only worsening her case. "You said you would care for the child..."

"And I did! I do everything. I even pay–"

Dashi held up his hand. "And as you've said, this you did. However, you also said you would place the child with parents." He turned his attention back to the child. Some mind said something he couldn't hear. "This you did not do."

She protested, "But payment was–"

"...yes, two copper, yes," mumbled Dashi, looking at the baby girl, dismissing that bothersome feeling. He turned to the woman with the child, and speaking in a lower voice, Dashi said, "And as it happens, you now wouldn't have wanted that."

"No, My Lord," she said.

Dashi stepped back up the stairs, speaking, "Therefore," said the magistrate, "Half of the contract is fulfilled and half not." Dashi sat down in his chair and ordered his robes. "I therefore award one copper back to the mother for services not rendered. Which she says she has already spent."

"You should be happy it's alive," sneered the woman.

"Are you happy your baby's alive?" asked Dashi of the mother who was humming to her child.

"Yes, My Lord," she said looking at her daughter.

"She is," said Dashi to the woman. He tilted his head and smiled, opening his hands, "Case closed."

Dashi sat in his own chambers. He breathed and he counted: one, two, three... he counted up to three hundred and seven before he stopped. He couldn't tell.

He went to find the mistress. When he entered her quarters through the open door she was not in, but her granddaughter was. She was tying ribbons onto lanterns.

"Hello," said Dashi, who scooped up a handful of ribbons so that she didn't have to return to table where they were laid out.

"My Lord," said the granddaughter, smiling, picking a ribbon out of his hands, and tying it in a neat bow.

"May I ask a question?" said Dashi.

"Of course, My Lord," she said smiling, tying yet another ribbon.

"Do you know how many minds there are?" he said.

"In your case, My Lord, only one. Excuse me," she said without a smile, and left Dashi standing bewildered, holding ribbons.

Dashi wandered about the palace's many corridors that turned and twisted. What is going on in all these rooms, he wondered. Sometimes he would quietly open a door and look in. Often he would find a group of scribes at tables, writing. Oil lamps provided light. The reddish walls about them were entirely shelved, for books, and with many small drawers, each with a label and carved brass pull. Save for the one he thought said 'Health,' he didn't know what was in the rest. What were they writing? Did they write all day? Why so many?

When the master had made the labels for the herb packages, he wrote words onto the wrapping paper such as: snow lotus, or monkey's blood. Dashi would remember that pattern. When they were in the street, or a shop he would point and ask and the master would tell him and Dashi would remember the words. But there were so many, and snow lotus and monkey blood, came up in conversation rarely.

Today Dashi opened a door and found instead of a room, another corridor that snaked into the palace, ending at another fancier door. Dashi entered. The room was dark with only the light from a high window, but Dashi could see it too was filled with books. Not as the previous ones had been, just around the perimeter, but row upon row of shelves of books and papers, with tables piled high, "How much of the palace is just for storing writing?" he said aloud.

An answer returned, "Seventy three rooms, eighteen thousand, three hundred and nine official volumes not counting books of taxes and records, which comprise at least that volume again. Do you need me to find the count on those volumes?" said the old voice.

"No," said Dashi, "I was... I just spoke aloud." Dashi looked around for the source of the voice and located it on the opposite side of one of the tables.

The only part that could be seen: the shine from the top of their bald head, tilted downward, "Oh, said the voice,

"That's too bad."

Dashi said into the darkness, "Why would you want to count the volumes?"

"Something to do," said the man. "No one comes into the library much any more." And Dashi could hear him rustling around and then a match was lit, and that light put to an oil lamp, which then moved towards him.

"Did they used to?" asked Dashi rounding the table to find a small, old bent-over man dressed in standard black, though around his waist he wore a red sash.

"My yes, they were always looking up a point of law. Some edict. Some tradition," he said, "The last magistrate didn't need tradition."

"I understand," said Dashi, looking at his lined face approach.

"Do you?" he said, "It's a fine thing, very rare these days. Now how can I help you?"

Dashi was close enough to the man now to see the man's milky white eyes. "You're blind," he said.

"Of course, I'm the librarian," said the stooped blind man.

"How can a blind man be keeper of books?" said Dashi, "How can you find anything?"

"I know where they all are," he said, reaching out with his hand to the shelf beside him and running his hands along the spines. "This is a book of laws pertaining to travel. This is a book for the correct drawing of stars and their patterns. This is a book that explains eggs."

"Eggs?" said Dashi.

"Yes."

"What is to be explained about eggs?" he asked.

"I don't know, I've never read it, but that is what it contains," said the man.

Dashi could understand skipping over that particularly unscintillating volume, "You have an impressive knowledge, though. It must have been a great sadness to have lost the ability to read," he said, considering this the mirror of his just learning.

"No. I've been blind since examinations. I told you I'm the librarian," he said.

"You've never read any of them then?" said Dashi, shocked.

"You can't just let anyone go reading the emperor's books," he said.

"And you know this just by feel?" said Dashi.

"Yes," he said, "I've memorised all the volumes and what is in them. That is the training for librarian."

"What if someone moved them around?" Dashi asked.

"They do that sometimes. But I'd just put them back," he said. "Now, again, is there something you require?"

"No," said Dashi, puzzled by this office, "I only remember a few words, so I can't read."

"I have a new book on how people remember things, but it was taken out recently," said the librarian.

"Wouldn't matter as I can't read it," explained Dashi.

"Ah, yes," said the man and was silent a moment. "So why are you here then?"

"Good question. I was just walking about the palace, trying to learn what's where," said Dashi.

"Why?"

"Because I live here, and I should know where everything is," said Dashi.

"Why should you know?" said the old man scolding, "If someone wants to send you somewhere, young man, then they will direct you. Who are you to be poking about the magistrate's halls?"

"Indeed," said Dashi laughing.

"You think it's funny do you?" the librarian was serious now, "You just wait until the guards catch you and haul you in front of the new magistrate."

Dashi was about to say. "I..."

"I hear he likes to give unusual punishments," said the bureaucrat in black coming further forward into the light, "Not so murderous as the last, but with a cruel streak this one. An illiterate country clod! Thinks it's funny to tie men together. To marry them! And then what everyone knew would happen, because they couldn't get away: one killed the other."

Dashi inhaled involuntarily.

"Yes... exactly," said the librarian to this rare listener, "Then the one flees, before he gets caught, still chained with his enemy flopping behind him.

"So time goes by. Next seen, he's burst out of wherever he's been hiding, dragging the rotting corpse of his enemy, still chained to him, mad as the moon, with this maggoty mass oozing out behind him, and he goes to the butchers and steals a cleaver. Even though I'm blind I can imagine the look of horror upon the people's faces. And the smell must have been terrible.

"And what was he supposed to do? He must have thought if he waited long enough the other will rot and fall off. So he hacks the other up to get free. But they said his leg was already infected. And then he ran away still in chains. Quite mad."

"Did he escape the city?" asked Dashi glad the blind man could not see his ashen face.

"Not without the guards gutting him. Use your head, boy," said the librarian. "But you listen to me about that magistrate. He's..."

"I was kidding, saying I just wandered here," Dashi said then.

"What?!" the old man interrupted, "Wasting my time?"

"Actually I was sent by the magistrate, for a map of the palace," said Dashi

The old man moved away far quicker than Dashi would have guessed him capable of. He shuffled across the room to a desk and felt through some scrolls. "I heard he'd taken on a runner," he said smiling and held our a rolled map to Dashi to receive. Then his face squeezed this way and that with concern, "Those are just the rumours I hear. I don't know anything. I'm always in here," he said and waved his hands around at the library. Then, "Please don't tell the magistrate what I said," he pleaded.

"Don't worry," said Dashi, "If that is what happened, undoubtably the magistrate has already been made aware. I will say nothing."

"Thank you, good boy, thank you. Come back any time you want, I'll make tea. You can borrow anything you like."

"I still can't read," said Dashi.

"Boy," he winked, "- there are books with pictures," and he nodded up and down with a broad reptilian smile.

Dashi and the boy came to the mistress's quarters to ask her to dine with them and found no one present, but the granddaughter had resumed her tying of ribbons after he'd left. The room was quite festive. And there upon the table, also tied with a ribbon was a book. Dashi wondered if this was the book on remembering things that the librarian said had been removed.

Dashi wondered what the ribbons were for. He stood for a time wondering if someone might come. They didn't. Then he wondered if chef had anymore of the duck he'd prepared yesterday. So the two of them left for the kitchens.

Thus the room stood empty for a time, and the book remained upon the table.

"Congratulations very much on your birthday," said the granddaughter.

"Is this my birthday?" said Dashi.

"It is spring," said the mistress, "That's what your Nan said. Close enough."

Dashi said, "Ah."

"We have a gift," interjected the granddaughter, which caused one of the mistress's eyebrows to rise.

"Indeed," said the mistress, "We do." She backed out of the way revealing the book sitting where Dashi had seen it, bow and all.

Dashi removed the ribbon and began turning the pages. The first page was the fox sitting under the tree. And every page thereafter was also a painting by the mistress. They began simply and then grew more complex: there were trees, people, animals, and above most of them were black squiggles that Dashi knew meant whatever that thing was. Pages and pages of paintings, with those in the back becoming more text-heavy and less illustrated.

"I thank you most heartily for the beautiful book," he said. "Now I understand what you were painting. I will cherish your fine artistry, and place it in a place of greatest honour."

"The book is only the half of it," said the mistress, "In addition," the mistress said clearing her throat slightly, "my granddaughter will tutor you in reading it." The mistress gazed sideways at her surprised granddaughter.

"Of course," said the granddaughter, bowing, her smile much like her grandmother's, thought Dashi.

Dashi felt a surge of gratitude. "I humbly give thanks to the friendship you've offered," he said returning the bow, "I only hope there will come a time when I may have the good fortune to return the kindness you have shown."

As he was looking downward, Dashi only saw the feet of the granddaughter suddenly run away. He immediately looked up and turned, to catch her in flight, but she'd already silently disappeared out the door.

"Was it something I said?" said Dashi.

"Yes," said the mistress.

Sitting. Dashi adjusted his robes against the light rain.

Sitting. Now that Dashi had uncovered his lost anger he felt better generally. However, the integration of the anger was proving, not so much difficult, as slow. It seemed while some irritations could be burned off, others had to take their own course.

Sitting. He wished he could move them along, and sitting was filled with his minds looking for ways to integrate faster. He hoped there might be some new exciting revelation. But it was just trust again.

He breathed in, and he breathed out.

He thought to himself. "How does one trust?"

By trusting, he was answered.

"What image is that most like?"

It is most like standing still – but knowing that the ground around you is falling. The world is large and it appears immovable, but nevertheless you are in motion. You are falling.

"I think I prefer just trusting," he thought to himself.

And some mind said, *What you mean by trust – that's just suspension of disbelief. Trust is being with what's changing. This is why integrating feels both like standing – and falling. Moving, but going nowhere.*

"Hm," grunted Dashi out loud, and a few students opened one eye to peek. Dashi sat for a time eyes closed. When he opened both eyes he spoke about trust.

Sometimes when they sat, Dashi would notice the sounds from the square beyond the wall. Sometimes he was listening to himself and didn't hear it. Sometimes he thought to ignore it. Sometimes he thought better of that thought and listened. Many feet passing. The guards would say "Hey!" Many feet would move on.

In being aware of these passings – ignored and listened to, Dashi had become aware that the foot traffic and the noises of the guards had increased over the last while. On this particular windy day the guards were shouting and grunting, making the magistrate curious as to what must be going on in the square to cause all the fuss.

"Continue," he said to the group and placed his hat upon his head. He stood, and briskly walking to the gate, said "Open," to the inner guards. All the meditators turned around to see what was happening, except for those who thought they shouldn't notice – and those attending to inner being.

The gates swung open. Outside in the square was a smattering of people seated on the ground, and the guards were trying to get them to move along.

The magistrate stomped up behind the guards who turned, hearing him coming. "We are meditating. Stop pestering these people and be quiet," he said and stomped back in through the gates which closed behind him.

He returned to his place. He removed his hat. He sat and said, "I continue," closing his eyes, placing his hands comfortably on his knees and breathing out a slow breath of fire.

"Mistress," said Dashi, as they walked in the garden, "Do you know how I can best improve my awareness of my minds?"

"Yes, My Lord," she said and bent a cherry tree limb to smell the blossoms.

Dashi sighed, and thought about his master. "Would you tell me?"

"Yes, My Lord, I would," she said and faced him, patient as a mountain.

"Mistress," said Dashi, "Please tell me how I can improve awareness of my minds."

"Burn them," she said.

Dashi replied, "I have been practicing that every day. What comes before my mind, I purify. When that recedes, I burn the next thing. I burn the darkness, and I burn the light. I burn each feeling and thought to release what is stuck, but I feel I am not getting anywhere. And yes," said Dashi, "I have burned the expectation that I should get somewhere, or there is even somewhere to get."

"Excellent. Maintain your practice," she said.

"Is there more that I can do?" said Dashi.

The mistress held out her arm for Dashi to take, they walked to the pond where the fish approached the water's edge at their footfalls. "How many fish are there?" she asked.

Dashi looked into the depths of the waters. The fish swam about. "It is hard to say, they move back and forth so they are difficult to count. Some more readily come to the surface and the depths may hide yet others."

"Magistrate, do you know how many minds there are?" she asked.

Dashi replied, "The master wouldn't tell me."

She regarded him, and then nodded. Looking into the pond, she said, "Perhaps you are counting the same fish over and over, or different ones as the same one." She walked on. Dashi followed.

"Well, perhaps... if I understood how many minds there were, I wouldn't be," he huffed.

She nodded. "Perhaps," she said, pulling another flower down to steal its scent, "My Lord, a mind is like an image. A map, your master would say.

"When freeing oneself, one first sees all the memories. Then one sees they are but illustrations of memories. One then sees the brushmarks, then the type of ink, and finally one sees the paper: its tooth and texture and colour. How much it influences the created image. And then one sees one's own hand. What am I talking about?" she asked him.

"Point of view," said Dashi.

"Self nature," she said, and walked slowly to a bench. "Sit with me, My Lord."

Dashi sat beside her.

"There are things which I will leave to your master to instruct. However, this much I feel I can reveal. The frustration you are experiencing is because although you have removed the insides, there remain the shells of habitual thought.

"You are coming to the end of the first meditation. Your master will teach you the next meditation when he feels you're ready for it."

"Another meditation," repeated Dashi.

"Yes," she said.

"How many meditations are there?" he asked.

"One," she said.

"But I thought you just said..."

"It is the same meditation, but deeper," she replied.

Dashi sighed, "All right," he said, "How many deeper versions are there?"

"Three," she said.

"What's the third?" he asked.

"You don't even know what the second is," she said.

"All right, what's the second?" he asked.

"I'm not going to tell you," she said, "You will have to wait for your master."

Undeterred, the magistrate persisted, "Why three?" he asked.

"Three minds," repeated the mistress, "Three points of view. In order."

"Why?" asked Dashi

"These are the three minds that facilitate integration. The sequence acts as a healing key," she said.

"What is being healed?" he asked.

She replied. "The rise, the fall, the return. To refine, to integrate, to become whole."

"This is achieved by the meditations?" he asked.

She twirled the flower between her fingers. "Life itself is the meditation."

Dashi nodded and waited.

Finally she said, "The explication of the seed from which you came."

"What seed?" said Dashi.

The mistress smiled at him in a peculiar way, and then her face came over a little wistful. "When a baby is made..."

"I know where babies come from," stated the magistrate.

"Oh," she replied. "-Good. In that case consider... a crow, who finds an acorn for its dinner... in a woods, and flies away carrying it in his claws. The acorn pipes up in small voice saying: 'I'm an oak tree.'

"The crow says to the acorn in his claws, 'You're not an oak tree. You might have been, but you're going to be my sustenance. I won't say, I'm sorry. That's just the way it is.'

" 'I've grown wide and tall,' insisted the acorn.

"The crow laughed, and almost dropped it. 'Away from the place where you might have done, I have carried you. And even should I drop you, below me are rocks upon which I sharpen my beak - and where they are not - are thorns.'

" 'I am making many acorns,' it replied.

"The crow set down, dropping the acorn at his feet. 'Foolish acorn,' said the shadowy bird of its fate, 'there is only one outcome, and that is death.' And so saying the crow took it in his beak and tossed the acorn up in the air, swallowing it whole.

"But, the acorn got stuck in his throat. Try as he might to dislodge it, he could not. Choking - because he could neither swallow it down, nor spit it out - the crow died.

"There the oak tree grew - wide and tall, making many acorns."

"I'm a nut, you mean," said Dashi, "Fertilised by a rotting crow carcass."

"You possess a flair for the prosaic, My Lord," she said.

"I understood the story, Mistress," he protested. "The crow stands for tribulations, the acorn for potential and plucky drive. My nature, the acorn, therefore has a destiny.

"Clearly, however, the message is: a seed that falls on ground it doesn't like will be stunted. The same seed in conditions it likes, grows well – if it doesn't get eaten. So it's all a matter of luck," he said.

"Perhaps," she said, "You just think the crow understood. I think otherwise," she said. "Where an acorn likes to be, makes the difference – a point of view that arises from its self nature."

"But the story suggests foreknowing," said Dashi.

"It seems that way," she said.

"Don't you know? It's your story," Dashi said.

"Stories have more than you put in them," she replied.

"So was I destined to be this?" said Dashi looking about at the garden and his robes.

Said the mistress nodding to herself, "Self nature has a point of view. The acorn in the story was sure of its fate because the oak tree it would become already existed in future possibility. You think that time only moves from this to that, and that is all you can know. But minds see the patterns that portend. Maturation is integration and the gift of maturity is therefore perspicacity.

"The acorn merely knew what it was. Minds aren't there for your understanding. Who you are is your fate."

"Who am I? – My fate seems to be that of an outsider," said Dashi.

"Perhaps," she replied, "But then no one is interested in a tree all twisted and turned – until needing its shade, and are glad to find it still there. Long after the straight tree has been made into something useful."

"Exactly, you agree. Because I am considered useless, I remain," said Dashi.

"What you are is what you see," said the mistress, "That is why you meditate."

Dashi sighed, "To change what I am."

"To become yourself more deeply," she said.

Dashi said, "The two deeper levels of meditation that you won't tell me, you mean."

"Correct," she said, "Towards awareness of the whole."

"The acorn," he said.

"An oak tree would say, 'This has always been me.' That is the potential. The seed unfolds, long gone."

"Ah, the oak, then," he said.

"But *that* is the form that becomes, what of its origin?" she asked.

"Both," he said and Dashi thought a moment, "These are different points of view of the same thing. The whole."

"Two parts. Yes," she said, "All your points of view, your many minds, are within self nature. That is, what they see. Although the individual appearances are different, improving the awareness of minds is achieved by improving the awareness of self nature from which they arise."

Dashi furrowed his brow, "I don't understand what my self nature is though," he said.

"Then you had best maintain your practice," she said rising from the bench, "You seek to understand. You seek always with understanding. You are more like me than your master in this.

"Understand then my meaning: if you are counting the same fish over and over again, it is not because you do not know how many fish there are, but because of the depth of the water." So saying, the mistress walked away.

The mistress finished reading aloud a statute. She placed in on the pile with the others. This one on the usage of dung as fuel within the city during summer. Perhaps it was the subject matter that got to Dashi. Perhaps it was the heat. Perhaps it was his wanting to retire to bed for the evening. Perhaps it was that they'd proceeded like this for the past three nights.

"I am losing my ability to concentrate," he said, "Can't we stop?"

"Only five more tonight, My Lord," said the mistress, "then we can both sleep."

She began anew, this one a complex legal argument on trade and the weights for measurement, or some such.

"If I could think like you can, then this would be much easier," interrupted Dashi, looking over the reams of paper.

"Not at all," said the mistress. "People often say this, but they do not understand. If they're exhorting someone to cook, they will say, 'think like a chef.' Everyone then imagines how they think a chef thinks is how a chef thinks. But a chef does not think *like* a chef - they *are* a chef. Or they are not. Like means similar to, not of the same identity. So this is an error."

A pedantic one Dashi felt, replying, "You tell me to be more myself."

"I tell you to continue your practice," said the mistress. "If someone tells you to be more yourself - they usually mean more like yourself. Act like Dashi. Think like Dashi would.

Look outside yourself for someone named Dashi and what you'll find is the mask one uses to talk to others. A simplified version of yourself. Easy to take, with only the most popular qualities – mostly behind which is vanity, among other desires. And that's what we all do, until we grow up – if we do."

"And if we don't?" asked Dashi.

"Then they will be uninterested by what I just said," And she unrolled another scroll, "Though it will make them feel they are getting somewhere. Which might be true, but probably not. More likely they just like the feeling of power it gives them. Also should you gain any real wisdom, distinctions and arguments will be unnecessary filigree."

This annoyed Dashi, "Isn't that the point of reading all these scrolls? I still need to be able to think like a real magistrate would think."

"You are a real magistrate," she said.

"A trained magistrate," he replied.

"The position is the training," she retorted.

"Well, even though I am magistrate, I have to be able to distinguish when I judge as the magistrate that I am," he countered.

"Knowledge of law is important. Knowledge of people is better. Knowledge of self is best," she said. "That way, your judgements aren't just imitations of being a magistrate."

This response irked Dashi. "Like your sister," he said.

She opened her eyes a little wider, "Yes, her," said the mistress.

"I saw you wave at her," said Dashi peevishly.

"Oh," said the mistress. "Did you see that?" She allowed the scroll to roll back into itself. "At the moment, it was how I felt."

"But she's not your enemy then?" he pressed.

"No, she is who she is," said the mistress.

"Could you explain that?" asked Dashi.

"Her nature was what it was, and she did what she did. But I never condoned her actions. It seems to me a waste, and a sadness. A shame really," said the mistress.

"Do you forgive her?" asked Dashi.

"I forgave her many times," said the mistress, "Then she murdered my only child, and the desire for my son continues to exist within me. I have burned it, I have absolved, but it lingers yet. I accept that. I had a part to play in it, and I embrace that as well.

"Occasionally, I will find some loose thread to forgive still." She waved her hand as if to shoo a gnat, "Most are mere correctives. Some, it is good to sit down for," She closed her eyes, "There can be a lot of thread to follow to be free."

"I'm sorry," said Dashi, having led her into a painful conversation – realising he'd do anything to escape the mounds of papers. "Do you hate her?"

"No, I feel sorry for her. Like you feel sorry for the people," she said.

"Sorry for them?" said Dashi.

"You want to help them. But they are stuck. You're sorry for the state of their lives. Likely you are annoyed they're so stuck.

"Many years ago I was like you. I found the people contemptible. I was angry. Angry at them for what? What was I accusing them of? Of being stupid peasants. That was what I found contemptible. Why didn't they do something?

"Because I was from a family with a good name. I had been raised to consider the family as noble. We had hon-

118

our. We maintained it. These people had no honour. They lived hand to mouth, so they took to whatever bit was put between their teeth.

"I came to feel the people of this city, of every city, were the same. Acting like they deserved to be treated badly. No wonder the street were full of operators and thieves."

Dashi held his lips tight.

She continued, "I felt that way then, because it was less painful than seeing them ground under, and feeling desperate. And this was during the time when your gentle master was trying to help them. Just like you are now."

"Because they are stuck we cannot help them?" appealed Dashi.

"Because you are stuck you cannot help them," she replied.

"Could you help them?" he asked.

"I am," she replied, "I am helping their magistrate understand the difference between making his judgments out of his true self versus what he imagines himself to be. No prescriptions. No shoulds. Being – not pretending."

"Am I not to render impartial judgements? Can I afford the conceit of being pleased with myself? Do I not need to put my own feelings aside?" Dashi challenged.

A lock of the mistress's hair had come loose from her hair comb and she brushed it back from her forehead. "When someone who has done a great injustice meets their just end can there be a moment of happiness? Is this a habit of cruelty? Does it mean you are fundamentally a bad person? My answer is: you forgive it as fully as you can, and move on.

"But then every once in a while a little sneaks in. Perhaps it is part of the habit you didn't see. So again you forgive the habit. The stickiness.

"But maybe you find that you feel how you feel. Freeing a habit does not mean you will never react in that way – it only means it isn't a habit. To be unstuck, to live without the pretence, and shoulds, means to live the full range of human feelings.

"You wear the robes," she said looking him up and down, "The great pretence is stubbornly insisting, in this case, that you know what a magistrate should think like – instead of allowing yourself to be the magistrate you are," she said.

"But if you know you're not making good decisions...?" he began.

"–Then refine your consciousness and apply yourself to the task at hand," she replied.

"What if one isn't suited to making decisions?" countered Dashi.

The mistress re-unrolled the scroll and cast her eyes down upon it. "You say you don't know how to make decisions well, but when I tell you how you can, then you decide you aren't interested. Truly, you are the magistrate," she said and began to read the next statute.

"Captain," said the magistrate, as the captain bowed. The captain carried a lidded basket.

"My Lord," he said, "I have uncovered evidence that I believe warrants inquiry."

Dashi looked at the basket. "Let's see then," he said and the captain opened the small basket

Three Skulls. Tiny skulls.

"Monkey skulls?" asked Dashi.

The captain, with grave exaggerated slowness, shook

his head. "One of the farmers spotted one sticking out of the mud after the last rains. We dug and found more bones and skulls."

"In one of the fields?" said Dashi.

"Along one of the ditches. I thought they must have been disturbed when the field was recently ploughed, except..." said the Captain, "except it hadn't been ploughed."

"The farmers aren't ploughing anymore, I'm given to understand," said the magistrate.

"Oh? Why not?" asked the captain.

"None of the ones I spoke with knew," said Dashi. "Farmers do leave fields fallow from time to time."

"But all the other fields were ploughed year after year?" said the captain.

"True," said Dashi

The captain stated, "Except this one. On the orders of the previous magistrate."

Dashi looked into the basket. One of the skulls was larger. "Most farm children don't live to adulthood," he said, "Could this just be a burial ground?"

The captain said simply, "Farmers do not bury bodies in fields meant for food, My Lord."

"No," he said, "True. So could be an old unmarked graveyard?

"But why not mark them? And the bones are too new," said the captain.

Dashi said, "Captain, are you thinking the last magistrate had these children killed and secretly buried?"

"That would have been me carrying it out, My Lord," said the captain. "I would have remembered."

"Ah, yes," said Dashi, "Still - a secret burial ground."

The captain said, "It appears so."

"And along a ditch you say," said the magistrate.

"Someone knew the ground wouldn't be disturbed, but took the extra precaution of walking in the ditch anyway," the captain paused, "That is too secret, My Lord. I would like to ask permission to investigate."

"And you have it," said Dashi. "Let us pray it is nothing."

"I already have," said the captain.

"The deal was for five!"

"The deal was for four! Why would I give you five? That'd cost me more than you're to pay."

"Well I'm not paying until I get my five," said one.

"It was only for four," said the other

"It was five. Five, My Lord, he promised..." said one of the other.

Slouching sullenly in his chair, the magistrate, Dashi, raised his hand. He hadn't had any lunch and he'd heard another three cases more or less just like this one. All this morning. "The deal is invalidated," he said.

One man smiled, the other frowned.

"But he promised me-" began one.

"I'll promise both of you a flogging bringing this kind of ridiculous case before me. Work it out yourselves, or..." Dashi thought, "I will appoint an arbitrar. I have real cases to attend to. Good day!"

The two merchants scurried back from whence they came and once out of sight fell to complaining about the government, and then, to their quarrel about whether it was four or five.

The day was again rainy, but at least there were no court cases. This, because Dashi had forbid it.

Instead he walked the streets of his town. His wide brim magistrate's hat doing an admiral job to keep off the downpour. Behind him walked, at a little distance, two guards. The captain strongly suggested this, and Dashi admitted he might be right.

As they entered the darkened dumpling shop, everyone seated at the long wooden tables looked around and the room fell quiet. Immediately one of the guards went up to the small window between the patron's area and kitchen, to ward off the approaching waiter.

There were two steaming bowls ready to be picked up. Dashi removed his hat, showering his boots with rain water, and looked over the two. The first, long silky flat noodles in a milky white broth, dotted with blossoming, glistening fat, curling green onions and a yolk-still-runny-inside egg; and the second, plump dumplings scattered with red pepper oil and mushrooms, overnight roasted barbecue shreds and topped with slivers of caramelised garlic.

"The one on the left," he said. And the guard, put down a coin and taking the bowl, placed it on the table at which Dashi seated himself. It wasn't his favourite. But it was unlikely to be poisoned – and that *was* his new favourite.

The guards would go hungry until they returned to the palace, at which point Dashi would give them coin to go back. It only seemed fair.

Some people returned to their soups, but others, heads together, spoke in low voices. They'd glance towards him and away. Their postures stiffened and pulled in, like snails into their shells. He looked out the small grimy window at the continuing rain. Dashi wondered what they were afraid of. Perhaps they thought he was about to steal their soup.

Truth told, this soup was not as good as his chef's. But it was away from the dreaded chair. It was out from the palace walls. It was with the everyday sounds of the people, chatter and laughter and squabble.

But none were bothering him for a judgement. With or without him there, they just wanted to eat their soup. And so did he. In peace. It was his irrelevance to their meal that was his pleasure, where once it had been a source of loneliness. He realised he did not then know what loneliness was.

"I burn what is in front of me," said Dashi sitting in meditation in front of the others, eyes closed. "What is in front of me is a reflection in the other minds, of the mind I am in. If I do not change minds then I will have purified one point of view, but not the others." He thought a moment and said, "Meditating mind is comfortable. Like counting the same fish over and over again."

During meditation he'd moved from the comforting, wrists resting atop his knees, and drew his hands into his lap. His index fingers of each hand continued making a circle with their thumbs, but now interlocked so that a tiny space opened between them. Left over right palm, right thumb on top. It was into this natural space he breathed. He didn't know why.

Dashi shifted his focus between the two fingers touching and the centre space. The joins of the circles together seemed insufficient and naive, where the centre space felt tiresome. After a time he found he could focus on all three. This felt like an offering.

When the other sitters peeked at him, as they would from time to time, as they shifted posture, they saw. And they copied. And when asked after, he spoke about the three, and they nodded.

"Allow yourself to be in different minds," he said. "In different feelings. This is not about pretending we are at peace."

"I want to divorce him, My Lord," said the woman again, squaring her jaw.

"Please," said the man, still miserably pleading, "She didn't mean anything to me."

"And now you don't mean anything to me either," she said, and put her hands on her hips.

Dashi cleared his throat, and then said, "Yes, I can understand why you'd want to be rid of a worm like this."

"You see," she said to her husband, "the magistrate can see you are useless," her eyes and face in a squint.

"Useless, exactly," said the magistrate, "If fact worse than that - stupid. Look at him hardly able to hold up his worthless pathetic head. Mooning over *you*, begging for forgiveness - no sense in him whatsoever. Hardly a man at all.

"If he had any boldness in him, or sense, he would've run off years ago. Instead here he is - fawning at your feet. Why would any woman want that? He's not a husband, he's a melon."

"See here, now," said the wife, annoyed. "I didn't come

to hear this!" And she grabbed her husband by his collar and hauled him away. Dashi smiled behind their retreating backs, as she said, "Did you hear what he called you?"

One day the magistrate was out walking the streets talking to the people when he came across some of his guards, with buckets and brushes, scrubbing a red smeared wall. "Why are you scrubbing walls?" the magistrate asked.

"The captain told us to, Da... My Lord," said the one guard.

"And why did he do that?" asked the magistrate.

They looked at each other, "Something bad written on the wall, M'Lord?" one replied.

"What did they write?" asked the magistrate.

"I don't know, My Lord," said the guard, "I can't read."

"Me neither, M'Lord," said the other guard.

"Ah," said the magistrate.

"He chose us because," the second added nodding. "M'Lord."

" 'He?' – the captain?" asked the magistrate.

"Yes, My Lord. We scrub all the walls," said the first.

" 'Walls?' " quoted Dashi. "Plural? There are many walls to scrub?" And they nodded, not liking the position in which they found themselves.

Dashi looked into the red water bucket of slaughtered words.

"Captain!" said the magistrate, hailing his head guard from his horseback patrol.

The captain trotted the horse over and dismounted, "Yes, My Lord," said the captain.

"You've ordered your guard to scrub writing off the walls of my city. What are they scrubbing away?" he asked.

"Just the scrawlings of malingerers, My Lord. Some people feel everyone needs to hear what they want to say," said the captain.

"I see," said Dashi, and then pressed on, "What in particular were they expressing?"

"What? Oh, just... different things," he said.

"Discontent - with the current magistrate, perhaps?" asked Dashi.

"I think, some had some of that... yes, My Lord," answered the captain

"'Some...'" repeated Dashi. "How many walls have been scrubbed to this point?"

"A few."

"Please stop being evasive Captain."

"At last count, I believe... eleven, My Lord," he said.

"Eleven," repeated Dashi.

"This week, My Lord," said the captain.

Dashi blinked, "All right. What did they say?"

"O, I didn't see all of them, My Lord. I dispatched a couple of the guard to deal with it," said the captain.

"I met them. They can't read," countered Dashi.

"Yes, My Lord," said the captain, "Better not to put ideas into their heads."

"Of the ones that you did personally see, can you recall or express generally the sentiment?" asked Dashi, and added, "I won't hold it against you personally."

The captain stood at attention, "My Lord. Some question your parentage, referring to your initial social status, your mother's... line of work, and your father's method of attaining money after he left the army."

Dashi replied, "Bastard, country clod, son of a whore and thief? Is that the gist, captain?"

"About that, My Lord," he said.

"That's a lot of red paint," said Dashi.

"Red? No, My Lord, just black," said the captain.

"The one I came to was obviously in red."

" 'Red,' " repeated the captain, concerned "What did it say?"

"I couldn't tell," said the magistrate, explaining, "because the guards..."

"Yes, of course, My Lord..."

Dashi continued, "...had scrubbed away all the words."

"I'm sorry..."

"And I couldn't ask..." Dashi added.

"...yes."

"...because they can't read," finished the magistrate.

"I am diligently investigating, My Lord. I'm confident the perpetrators will be captured soon," said the captain, stiffening even more.

"At ease captain," said Dashi. "I understand we don't want these to be seen as... worrying us. Thank you for dealing with this tactfully."

Dashi took a breath and exhaled. "They are hard to please, the people, aren't they captain?"

"If you say so, My Lord," the captain replied, still at attention.

"As you were, captain," said the magistrate, "However before the slander is scrubbed away, I think it would be prudent to know what was there - should the slogans deviate from telling unpleasant truths into outright lies."

"Prudent, My Lord," said the captain, a titch more relaxed.

"Report them to the mistress. Thank you, captain. Oh, and since we've already the buckets out, have them wash any dirty windows too," said the magistrate and continued on his way.

"Where is this plaintiff?" asked the magistrate from his chair to the court clerk.

"He is missing, My Lord," said the clerk.

"I can see that. Send someone to fetch him too," said Dashi. "If we have to be here, then they need to appear. I'm told they've been waiting years to have these cases heard, and now they can't bother to show?"

"It is how the people are, My Lord," said the clerk.

"Meaning?" said Dashi, because if he was waiting anyway he felt he might as well know the mind of his clerk.

"My Lord, they are fickle," he said. "It would seem as though your hearing their case should be seen as a boon, but they are just as likely to see it as an imposition."

"Imposition? Why should they feel that? It was they who asked for the hearing," objected Dashi.

"Even though it was they who asked for it, My Lord, now that you are to hear it, they are commanded to appear, and it is that command which now makes them not want it."

"You mean to say they want what they want, when they want it, but if you were to ask them to want it, they would cease," said Dashi.

"It is true, My Lord," said the clerk.

"Let us see," said the magistrate looking up towards the door waiting for it to open. "I will ask him when he appears if this is so."

"You mean, My Lord, when he is dragged into court before your judgement?" asked the clerk.

Dashi thought about that, "I see what you mean," he said and regarded the defendant who they had managed to find and who'd seated himself on the court floor. "You. What do you think? Do people only want to do something when they feel it was their idea?"

The defendant looked up in dismay that he was being consulted. "My lordship," he said, stammering, "I don't know."

"You must have some opinion," replied Dashi.

The man shook his head vigorously.

This annoyed the magistrate, "Fine let us hear the case without the plaintiff. What are the charges?"

"No charges, My Lord," said the clerk, "This is the settlement of a dispute."

"Thank you for clarifying, clerk," said Dashi, "A dispute about what?"

"The plaintiff accuses the defendant of whistling," said the clerk.

"Whistling? ...Unless there is more to it I will dismiss this case," said Dashi unbelieving, "Defendant!" he shouted, and the man winced and cringed "Why are you being brought here for whistling?"

The man opened his mouth, but no sound exited.

"Come on," said Dashi, "I won't bite... hard," he joked. And at that the man burst into tears. Dashi looked up disgusted. He caught the gaze of the court clerk.

"My Lord, if I may," said the clerk.

"Please," said the magistrate.

"This man is accused of whistling at night," said the clerk.

"Ha!" laughed Dashi, "Because he thought it called a

burglar?" Dashi smiled.

"Or snakes," said the clerk.

"Oh that," dismissed Dashi, "Lots of burglars, not many snakes here."

"Or demons," said the clerk, "– ghosts and devils."

Dashi sighed and looked down at the man now cowering in a puddle on his courtroom floor. "I've never believed in superstition," said Dashi, "And this is why."

"The people are that way, My Lord," said the clerk, "That's why it's better that the wise and expert run everything. They have to or... we get, as you say, superstition run amok."

"I hear you," said the magistrate, his hand up to end the clerk pressing his case.

The magistrate, Dashi thought. He called over his runner and whispered in his ear. The runner whisked away, as the magistrate said, "Court will pause for a few minutes until my runner returns with evidence. If you require me I will be stretching my legs in the hallway."

"Evidence, My Lord?" said clerk.

Dashi merely nodded and left the court to stand in the empty adjoining hallway.

"Why would someone believe in demons?" wondered Dashi. "What does that mean that they do? What contortion of a mind, at what layer, becomes the idea that... well I suppose we ascribe character to people, and also to animals, and you can say a thing has a certain spirit about it, so why not consider a mere idea as having a spirit of sorts. It does have a flavour to it. Ideas can imply things of a certain nature, so a mind could imagine that to be a personality. But still..." and he mused about the strange nature of minds applying themselves where another mind might typically go, even if with less interesting effect.

The clerk appeared. "My Lord the runner has returned," he said and left.

The magistrate waited a few moments, and then he too re-entered the court room to the usual standing. And after he had seated himself did he turn his eyes upon what his nose had already told him was present. "You brought the fish?" he said.

"Yes, My Lord," said the runner lifting the cover from the tray where a plate with a small fish lay.

Dashi reached out and took the fish by the tail. "Governing is said to be like cooking a small fish. Isn't that right, clerk?" said Dashi.

"I have heard it said so, My Lord. One must be careful," he said.

"Indeed, care is what is needed," said Dashi. "Defendant," Dashi said, "Do you see what this is?"

He nodded.

"Can you say what it is?" pressed Dashi in his own case.

"A... a... a fish," the defendant said at last.

"Good," said Dashi, as a noise at the door saw the plaintiff, red and puffy about the face, literally dragged into the room by the guard. "Ah, your accuser. At least I think he is accusing you," said Dashi, "You see this fish?"

The plaintiff landing beside the defendant in the puddle looked up at and locked eyes upon the fish.

"Do you?" queried the magistrate

"I uh er-yah yah," fumbled forth out of the mouth of the shaking man.

"Good enough. Let the record show he agrees it's a fish," said the magistrate, "The smallest that the cook could find, but nevertheless a fish. And we all know that demons hate fish, right?" said Dashi, and he put the whole thing in his mouth, chewed and swallowed. It had been smoked, but was still kind of crunchy.

"Not my favourite, true, but I think this concludes this case. Defendant I ask you not to whistle at night as it further disturbs your neighbour's minds. Plaintiff..." said Dashi, looking down at the superstitious wretch lying at the bottom of the stairs, and considering what he could say to dissuade him from his delusion, "Just... grow up. Please."

Retreating to his chambers, Dashi sat down hard.

He just needed, for a moment, to close his eyes.

He relaxed his breathing.

He imagined being back in the mountains, at the cabin with the master, a small fire in front of him, smoking happily, and he breathed out into the coals to make them dance. He breathed on them again, relaxing. He watched the smoke go out from the fire into the mountain air, whirling with leaves.

Shielded from the rain by the small cave opening, he considered the line of trees, twisting, turning, ravaged by the invisible wind. A tall stack of bowls sat beside him on the rock upon which he was seated. He looked down at the large stock pot in the crackling fire, its water bubbling madly – steam rising in billows.

He drew out his knife, and cutting towards himself, cleanly cut off each of his fingers which dropped into the clear, slowly swirling soup like curled carrots. The scent rose sweet as flowers.

Then he put the knife to his wrist, simply slicing away his left hand. He noted that there was no pain, and looking to see why he saw the bone exposed concentric circles, like the rings of a tree, and the hand fell to the bottom of the water with a bloodless splash - awakening Dashi, disturbed and annoyed that his rest had been taken advantaged of by one of his minds speaking riddles.

"Master, but what if the people just don't like me?" asked Dashi.

No doubt they won't. Who is it that you would have over you? said the master.

"O, I don't fear the emperor and his laws. They could be better it's true, but... they keep us safe. Just as the garrison here protects us from the northern tribes," said Dashi, "Without the emperor we would have no roads, no walls, no order."

True, said the master, *Well said.*

"Indeed," said Dashi with pride.

I wouldn't say that, said the master, *If you're going to put words in my mouth at least make them the right ones– Oh, and I'd burn that vanity.*

Dashi said, "Uh... Sorry master, I was..."

If there were no emperors and empresses and warlords and chiefs then we wouldn't need the walls. Roads would be horse tracks. Order is a trumped up word for serenity – which is what you really want, and would mostly have if those stuck on power weren't stuck.

"Yes, master," said Dashi.

As for not fearing the rule of the emperor, you do not know the noose of war, said the master, *And now I'm too preachy,* he said, *I'm never this preachy, Dashi. You know that.*

Dashi said, "Again master, I'm sorry. Only I wish you

were around to talk to. You made things make sense somehow."

And I still would, if you didn't insist on being clever.

Sometimes, the magistrate, Dashi, when seated in the courtyard, breathing, feeling the group was breathing too - he would feel they were breathing together.

At times like this, it seemed as though, he didn't have to breathe on his own.

"I don't quite understand," said Dashi, "are they accusing me of something?"

"Well not accusing you exactly," said the mistress, and then quoted again, holding up the report to her eyes, "Thunder dragon's son," she said, and looked down the list, "Actually most scrawlings are about being on the look out for demons without mentioning any by name."

"Then what does that mean?" asked Dashi.

"It means they believe in the thunder dragon," she said reappearing from behind the paper.

"You mean they really believe?" asked Dashi.

"Oh, no, not real belief," she said, "They just really want it to be true. The more people in the group, the more true it must be."

"What?" said Dashi.

"I may realise great compassion," she said, with a rising hand gesture, "But if I tell people that - they'll think they should be compassionate, because people say it's good. They'll imagine themselves wandering about in robes with a pious look on their face, blessing small animals and flowers."

Dashi shook his head, "I... understand?" said the dubious magistrate, "You mean they're pretending?"

"More like dreaming," said the mistress. "They are unaware they are pretending."

"Because," explained Dashi triumphantly, holding up a finger, "they are not whole."

The mistress said, "Being whole, what is that? Why should you want it? Is it a good thing? Is compassion a *good* thing? *Should* you want good things? There are those who say you *shouldn't.*

"What is definitive at the deepest level is nothing – but what is that to the crowd requiring reassurance?" she said.

"I do not understand what you are trying to teach me," said Dashi.

"Indeed," she said, and patted his arm, "There was once a student, *who didn't understand,* who travelled a long way to an ancient school, high in the mountains, run by a great master. When the master granted him an audience the student said, 'Great master I have come from the southern school where my master taught me of the way. I did not comprehend an answer he gave, so he has sent me to you.'

"'Your master was wise in sending you to me. Tell me, what was the teaching?'

"The student said, 'When I asked him what the essence of the teaching was, he replied: Eating apricots.'

"The master upon hearing this said, 'Yes, that is a very good teaching. But they in the southern school do not quite understand the full nature of true essence. Ask me the same question.'

"So the student said, 'Master, what is the essence of the

teaching?'

"To which he replied, 'Eating apricots'."

The magistrate sat at the table with an empty bowl before him.

The fines levied against those who had conspired with the false magistrate allowed Dashi to order a lessening of taxes. In addition, food had been purchased for the stores. The people would not go hungry. And the new convivial nature of the city had led to a surge in trade. And that – to another noodle house. All which put Dashi in a philosophical mood.

Having now partaken of their fare the magistrate conceded the integrity of their broth, and the delicacy of their preserved plums, however their dumplings... although good, were insufficiently springy compared to his own chef's. Nevertheless, he consumed it all to the last drop. To do otherwise he thought was sign of a wasteful and wayward society. "Through contentment: gratitude," thought Dashi pushing the empty bowl away. A physical necessity was made by moral virtue, sweet.

Dashi gathered up his robes. However, he mused, morality needs to be come by without moralising. Without shoulds. Dashi felt to give second chances, to be charitable, was a virtue, just as long as it wasn't to be done *because* it was a virtue.

So given the broth had integrity, he would try the noodles next time – just to be fair. But not as a should. With thoughts of this in his head, and his belly full of dumplings, he ate a last plum and he pulled himself up to leave. The two guards parted as he stood, reforming to flank him as he drifted towards the door.

A drunk, head down in the corner, leapt from his table, blundered past, hurrying for unreasons and pushed past – jostling, out through the noodle house door first, effectively evading both guards.

Thus – when the tiny black arrow struck, it hit the side of the door. And the next thing Dashi knew, he was on the ground, guard atop of him, with his overly soft belly, full of integrity, being unpleasantly squished. Dashi observed from ground level the second guard's boots disappearing, running after someone. The heavy guard unsquished the magistrate and pulled him up. Dashi looked at the tiny black metal arrow wedged into the doorway. He went to touch it.

"No, My Lord," said the guard, "– probably poisoned."

Dashi drew his hand back.

They didn't wait for the second guard but quickly retreated, running a gauntlet of dark corners, doorways, windows, uneven passages. They took not the usual route, but a circuitous one. Weaving out towards the grand houses and minor palaces – and then back through the surrounding criss-crossing haphazard warren of tunnels. Only the indifferent river of sky, its continuous branching narrow strip of pale grey above the walls unbroken. Dashi felt displaced: a foreigner. "What is this city?" thought Dashi.

Those cast in doorways squabbling, those who hung from windows calling down into the narrow streets – their mutual mingled mad clamouring of leverage – they all slowly shifted their predatory gaze to meet Dashi as he passed.

He met their stares. Their eyes held pretence. Practiced mannerism without meaning. Masks with empty sockets.

And as the escaping magistrate and guard rushed away on their course, their wake closed behind, renewed in eternal dispute.

"What mind is this? What mind?" thought Dashi, "Threatened. Hunted." And although hard to fire breathe while walking smartly, he attempted it.

The open square yawned and they hurried across without cover, retreating through the heavy gates to safety. Dashi noted the suspicious looks of the bureaucrats.

They all seemed to know.

The captain, upon hearing of the attempt on the magistrate's life insisted Dashi from now on, carry a sword.

Dashi with folded arms asked, "What good will a sword do against poison tipped arrows?"

"Due diligence," replied the captain.

Upon her hearing, the granddaughter nervously hand clutched, while the mistress merely commented of Dashi's experience: "A good opportunity for practice."

"Master," said Dashi to his minds.

He lay in bed. The room was dark. Someone had tried to kill him today. Not that no one had never tried that before. Once, robbing the caravan as it came back to the city loaded with food. They were fighting. Everyone was fighting. It was dusty and hot. The guards tried to make the horses run, the guards who rode the caravan. They got pulled off. So they fought.

Dashi saw. That one - he turned, Dashi could still see

his eyes - and the newest one, the young one who'd just joined, and Dashi didn't even know his name, he crumpled under the guard's sword - the one who turned - saw Dashi, and advanced.

And there was his brother. The knife went in and out. A flicker. Had Dashi even seen? He was standing aside himself watching. The man dropped. Murderous arms, lying in the dust, held out toward him.

His brother called and they all loaded up and ran away back to the forest. It wasn't too long after that they caught him. Although Dashi was his brother's favourite successor - for devils in disarray, the contested leader could only be the strongest, wiliest of scrounging villains.

Dashi ran. Exiled, untouchable - outcast from even amongst thieves. He walked up the mountain.

"Master," said Dashi again into the darkness of his minds, of the room. "Why did they fight that day? They'd never done more than a token. It was understood, between us. We needed the food. They needed a black eye to let us have it.

"Were they not the people's thieves? - Now made murderers."

There are times and seasons of action, interjected the master.

Dashi asked, "What do you mean?"

To which the master replied, *That day the guard fought. You don't know why and neither did they. I mean, an action repeated tomorrow, is not the same action as done today. Because the day is different. Because you are different. And to be as sensitive to that as walking among tree roots is not to stumble.*

"I see," said Dashi out into the dark.

"The captain trains his men hard," the mistress mentioned to the magistrate as she mixed his morning medicine.

"He has all those new recruits he has to integrate," suggested Dashi, not looking forward to drinking the foul liquid. "Though I never hear them doing rifle practice."

"Yes - years of my sister - it left them flabby and demoralised. Why bother training to fight? Against whom?" she added, "And now he has to train you too."

Dashi who was self conscious about the sword said, "I can fight. I learned, thank you."

"Oh, I'm sure," she said and went back to grinding.

"You think I should train more?" he said.

She emptied the paste into another vessel and added some hot brown liquid. "Only if you want to," she said, and after a few minutes waiting for the brew, "If you think it might be of some use." And then she poured it and looked at him. Just a little longer than she needed.

"Fine, I'll ask the captain," said the magistrate.

"I'm sure he'll be as thrilled as I am. Now drink up," she said sliding across the table the small cup of yellow molten disgust.

It was unseasonably cold. The wind gusted and whistled chill obscenities through the door. A brazier had been set up in front of the chair, as well as to both sides, so Dashi sat amid flames, looking out over smoke and fire, down the steps, at the prisoners. A man, middle aged, who miserably wept. And a woman, who stood dumb and motionless, staring past fate.

The court officers, bureaucrats in black, each indistinguishable from the other, sat, having done their ceremony, the magic law spell, and the people had stood and sat and bowed and knelt.

"My Lord," said the officer, "The two, taken into custody today, and who stand before you are charged with taking money on false pretence."

Dashi noted the captain and his guard present. He held up his hand. "Captain, that is the charge?"

Like a hangman, he said "It is, My Lord."

"Continue," said Dashi to the court officer.

"The two did, with malice of forethought, receive into their care numbers of infants and small children from women in the farming community, promising that the children would be given a better life by being placed with couples who desired a child but could not have one of their own. This was not done. Instead the couple took the children and... allowed them to perish."

Dashi looked at the woman. He recognised her. His stomach filled with black cold. "They were paying for the infants to be adopted?" asked the magistrate.

"I fed them..." she mumbled to herself. Dashi glanced.

"Yes, My Lord," said the officer surprised, looking though his notes.

Dashi sat back, aghast, "What evidence have you?"

At this the captain made a motion with his hand and several guards, in a column of two, with large baskets held between them approached the centre floor. The same style basket that Dashi had hurled, months ago, to bring some feeling of gratitude to the merchants. Baskets now counting four... six, now eight, ten, plus one, in total eleven of them were aligned against him.

Dashi sat forward; he gripped the arms of his chair. "What have you found?" he breathed out.

At a wave from the captain, the line of guards upended their baskets in front of the prisoners. Bones and skulls clattered on the stone floor. Clattered against each other as they fell out. Clattered away as if to hide in their naked shame. The man wept even more piteously. The woman looked down at the pile before her feet. Basket after basket emptied, until it lay half the hall's width. A barricade between Dashi and everyone else.

Dashi stood, and those seated, those who wrote out what was said, those who waited to speak, stood also. He descended the stairs with feet of clay. The magistrate, Dashi, gazed from one side of the pile to the other, little brown skulls, and tiny brown bones, arm bones, legs, pelvises, tiny shoulder blades. "How many?" he managed at last to the captain.

"Over a thousand, My Lord," said the captain, "We are still finding them. Many old, some new."

Dashi breathed out long and hard. His ears rang. He bent over and picked from the top of the pile a little light brown skull. So light, so fragile. He walked to the woman who now stared at her feet and turned the skull around to face her.

The captain approached, "My Lord," said the captain quietly to Dashi so the court could not hear, "I have to report. The mottled colouration of the bones is due to... heating."

Dashi dropped his hands. The skull jumped away. 'Heating?' he repeated slowly, and then shaking his head "Cremation you mean."

The captain shook his head "Then why are there bones to bury at all?"

"Partial cremation...?" said Dashi.

The captain shook his head.

Dashi closed his eyes to the weary sigh that came from his lips.

He took a deep breath to push down, but found rising within him a fire. Dashi opened his eyes and looked into the faces of those present, the court officers and clerks who watched with a look of paralysed tension, the open mouthed bailiff, the guards who barely held their disgust at bay, the face of the captain of the guards, outwardly set in stone, but inwardly evading contemplating this tragedy. The only eyes that would meet his were those of the accused woman. She who looked on him as if he could not be real, and this was not happening.

"I..." said Dashi. He began to pace, but bones blocked his way - he needed to move, but what he really wanted was to run. "I cannot express, my... disgust."

He walked away, stroking his chin, touching his mouth. He walked back. "I won't ask you why. I don't want to know. And even then I would hope it wouldn't mean anything to me." He lowered his head.

"Fed them... I washed them..." she said, not in defence, but as to herself.

Dashi knew, there was nothing he could do. The power of the magistrate now seemed a different kind of being from him. The robes animated in of themselves. Trapped inside them, swept along in their movements, manifesting the office's true power: suffocation. Now he knew. The robes drew him into the sadness of the world and used him, as a puppet messenger, to speak at their bidding.

The court clerk cowered forward. Full of whisperings, he spoke quickly between his teeth, "My Lord, this must be suppressed! The madness of the crowds - they talk of demons, they are spooked by every shadow.

"If they find out they will hound you, and worse - they will come for them. One night. They will drag them away, and inflict inventive pains - they will cut them apart before they tie a rope to their necks and haul them, dangling, into a tree. Or if they really think they are demons... then nothing but burning will do." The court clerk bowed and retreated back to his position.

Dashi was plunged under. There was no reform possible here, no rehabilitation. He struggled to rise within the dark. Even life imprisonment was impossible for the two. Down, further he sank from the chance of light. If they knew, if the crowd knew, they would go mad. The weight of the entire empire pressed his will under, his held breath dissipating into the chill depths, until only the magistrate broke the surface, gasping.

He stood to his full height, drawing out the words like a sword from his mouth: "I sentence you to death."

When the door was closed Dashi would respect the mistress's privacy. When the door was open he would just go in. As he marched down the corridor he didn't care. He had just set in motion the commission of a great sin. The greatest sin. That it was lesser numerically than those now sentenced to die was immaterial.

"If compassion has run to its end and this needs to be so, then at least I can make their ends compassionate. Execution need not be an afflicting of prolonged suffering," he thought, "Remember what the court clerk said, we need to keep this quiet or the people will be afraid-"

Of demons, concluded a mind.

"This is a catastrophe. I'm in over my head," thought Dashi.

As magistrate he'd ordered the court records sealed and forbade any of those present to speak about this.

His minds echoed, *They'll hunger for blood,* equally with "I need to keep my dark feelings under control."

Because, truth was, there was one mind howling for tormenting vengeance. "Am I becoming the monster? Is this how it happens?" Dashi dreaded, "I need to stop it."

The door was open and Dashi burst through. "Mistress can you make something to cause someone to sleep?"

"Hello Dashi," said the master.

"Master!" said Dashi, shocked, and he covered his mouth. And then he covered his eyes so the master could not see the shame there, and he knelt in front of his master in remorse and anguish, and wept tears, bitter as ashes, "Master, I've failed," choked Dashi.

"Why do you think that?" said the master.

"I've tried to be compassionate and fair," he blurted, "I've burned everything inside me. But... sometimes my thoughts," said Dashi, "master... I have just sentenced two to death."

"Compassionate you say... What did they do?" asked the master.

In a half-whisper, "They ate children," he said. "Several hundred, we think." The mistress made a noise of disgust.

"Rumours had been around for years..." said Dashi, "We were all so hungry..." he said. "But to actually... And now I've had to sentence them with... breach of contract, fraud, I don't even remember," he shook his head, "I have to keep it quiet or the whole town will explode."

"Ah," said the master and he raised up Dashi's face in his hands. "First, this is what it is, Dashi," said the master.

"The title Magistrate sounds lofty, but it means you clean up people's messes. Drafted into position like a soldier. And like a soldier - what in life before prepares you to don the heavy mantle others shrug off?"

"But I thought I could make things better," said Dashi.

"And strangely you are," said the master.

"No, I don't think..." began Dashi.

"Better is comprehension - you are slowly coming to one. Doing the best you can-"

"And failing," Dashi interrupted.

Said the master. "I'm glad you're maintaining your practice. Failing is how you learn."

Dashi nodded, "Becoming magistrate was a mistake."

"See? You've learned something already," said the master.

Dashi smiled slightly, another tear rolling down his cheek, "I've made hundreds of judgements. I thought I could do good. I now doubt every one of them."

"Ah... when most people talk about the good they mean comparison. They mean to say, better than all of them," the master said.

"The greater good, then," said Dashi.

"Even worse," said the master. "The real good is in your bones and in the ground."

"Bones? The ground is churning up bones at my feet!" he started to argue. Stilling himself, Dashi said, "The feeling in my bones?" he looked to his master "- all I desired was to help."

"You have run into a burning building," said the master.

Dashi closed his eyes, "Then, as you said they would, they will eat me, skin and bones."

The master sighed. "Then why are you in pain? You throw yourself on a sacrificial fire that doesn't consume you, but only blisters."

"You mean I resent it," said Dashi, frowning wiping his face.

"That - and you're acting out heroic drama," said the master, "Real heroes die - a lot of foolish boys pretending, march off to die right along with them, because they've been made to feel they should. Pity."

This made Dashi bristle, "I'm not asking people to march for me."

The master as gently as he could, "No, but you did mention something about a couple dying."

That stung, and Dashi deflated again. "Not much of a hero... without ever risking battle."

The master nodded at Dashi's admission, "Hero is just another word for should," he said. "It means you don't feel it inside. You are watching yourself, rather than truly being in that mind. Real heroes don't know they are being heroes at the time, any more than the truly good know they are being good. It's who they are being. It's in their bones. Like yours."

"If you know my bones, do you know who am I?" asked Dashi.

"I know exactly who you are. I know the seed and I know the tree. My question is whether blustering winds will knock it down before it matures enough to endure the winter storms."

The magistrate sat on the floor. "I had a dream once where there was a great storm," said Dashi, "and you asked me who I was. But by that time you'd turned into a dragon."

The master taken aback chuckled, "What colour?" he asked.

"A green one," answered Dashi.

"That's very kind of you, Dashi. Thank you," he said. "Dragons don't ask questions for them to be answered, but for their meaning to be known."

"I don't know what you mean," said Dashi.

"Indeed," said the master, who folded his robes and winked at the mistress. "Dreams and stories are the young person's guide for maturing, not theatrical direction. If you are hunting the mountains for a literal dragon you don't understand where you need to hunt for dragons. Stories present one thing to mean another.

"The sacrificial hero of story, is not the same person at all in the world. *The Noble Sacrifice*, is a play, staged by every tyrant, precisely because they know youth don't always make the distinction. Pretending you're in the story just means you're enchanted," said the master and wiggled his fingers in suggestion.

Dashi shook his head, "No, master I still don't understand."

"Allow me," said the mistress, "There's a story called, *A Great Heart and a Little Sense*. Once there was a noble man, strong like an ox, who worked so hard plowing and planting the fields by himself that one day his great heart burst and he died, thus sacrificed himself for the good of his family.

"The people talked about how *good* he was, how *noble*, and made up songs to venerate him, thus his family felt gratified," said the mistress.

"Another man, who was not so strong, figured out a way to plant without an ox, or even turning the soil so that he could just watch from the side, only occasionally having to add to the soil or harvest the fruits of nature; thus, he could plant many times more. The people called him lazy, and made up jokes about him. Thus his family was ashamed.

"When drought came, the great man's family all starved. But the lazy man's family had enough food stored away to share even with the people who had called him lazy." The mistress paused, looked up, then added, "And because they owed him a debt of gratitude they felt resentful and called him greedy – the end."

Dashi eyed the mistress, "I don't think it will find popularity in the oral tradition."

"Truth seldom does," said the mistress, "As for tradition, once vital stories have been told too often, the cloth is worn to transparency so that even scholars can comment on them. I prefer to tailor my own clothing."

The master held up his finger, "Sacrifice is not noble. Noble is noble, and sacrifice is just sacrifice. Why sacrifice? Because you should? For what? Because the stories say so? Are they the stories of the wise? Have those stories been altered? What is their supposed meaning? Can you trust this commentary? How would you know?"

Dashi said, "Well..."

"To know, you must be wise. Then the story serves to merely point to what you already have, but perhaps hadn't realised. This wisdom you already have and call meaning. It is the willingness to look deep within."

"To trust," said Dashi.

"Yes, "said the master, "Stuckness usually comes with some sad tale. Of why you can't let go. Why you can't grow up. Why you don't do something about what bothers you. Or can't do what you want."

Dashi nodded, "This is why it's important what stories are told to the people."

"Always 'the people'... always about them..." said the master, "immature minds make immature stories make immature civilizations with immature ends," and added, "However, you can lend credence to any old yarn by forbidding it. Enforcement is dangerous. Tell of inescapable deep water wells and there will be those who'll say they come to quench their thirst but lean over to peer into the depths."

"What wells?" asked Dashi.

"Exactly," said the master, "What advantage is advantage if it's not clear what for?"

"For those who have to drink from mud puddles it would be clear," commented Dashi.

"'Mud puddles'," said the mistress scathingly.

"Dashi," said the master, "The people already have stories aplenty. You can see it in the unknowing way they sabotage their lives. Pray they can come to forgive themselves, and move toward their true nature,' said the master.

"You mean, value the people who..."

"That's right," said the master.

Dashi, said, "But wouldn't the stuck just value the stuck? If they weren't free?"

The master shrugged, "Of course," he said.

"Then how do I know I'm not stuck?" asked Dashi.

"Well there are many ways to be stuck and many minds to be stuck in. Have you looked at them all?" the master asked.

"No," said Dashi.

"Good answer," said the master, "The stuck seem sure of themselves. They pretend to emulate the sureness of mastery without the practice - but they are loathe to trust.

"To trust yourself is to look, is to be willing to put your values to the test. To let another mind respond. Stuck people could be so much more if they but had the strength to trust. Holding fast to their nightmare's tether, they fear it will escape them."

"Because they are cowards," said Dashi.

"They are afraid," said the master, "Fear has overcome them instead of them overcoming their fear," said the master. "Ironically, the stories they tell to protect themselves will destroy them."

"Because they live in fear," said Dashi.

"Because they live in a story made up to protect them from their fear," answered the master.

"Then they build that story into everything," added the mistress.

"Is there a way to help them?" asked Dashi.

"Of course," said the master, "For a start, teach them to grieve as I have shown you."

Dashi held up his palms in supplication, "But as I said, I have burned everything and I am still..."

"Pretending," said the mistress. "Trust is what makes you able to look again. When clearly you are still suffering, have you burned everything?"

"Yes," said Dashi.

The master said, "Then you'd best burn it again. And again. When done deeply, grief begins a rebirth. You are seeking true nature not a storybook about true nature. The end of grief is to grieve the grieving, to let it go too."

"To fully mature," said Dashi.

"That, and even beyond that," said the master.

"What do I...?"

Just then a couple guards came to the doorway. "My Lord, there's an angry mob outside the palace gate! They're calling for someone's death."

"Oh no..." groaned Dashi, his chin dropping, "Damn!"

He leapt up, "I'll be right back," and wrapping his cloak around himself, hurried to the hallway. There he turned,

"Master I have missed you," he said.

"I've been here every week," laughed the master, "You weren't paying attention."

"I agree," said Dashi, and disappeared into the dark hall, running towards the gate.

The shouts of the mob were loud. Even from inside the gate where the captain and his guards assembled, swords and spears and lit torches. They spoke in raised voices just to be heard.

Dashi marched angry into their midst. "Open the gate!" he ordered.

The captain looked at Dashi, and then made the motion. The gate began to open, and suddenly what was loud was deafening.

"Back, back," shouted the guards, using spears held between them to push the crush of screaming faces into retreat.

"Murderers!" shouted voices. They keened, "Kill them!... Burn them!... Baby eater!... Demon!... Vermin!"

Dashi held up his hands. And they just kept screaming.

"Quiet!" he shouted. And they just kept screaming, at him.

"This is your fault!... supposed to protect us!... why didn't you stop them?!... kill them!..." The mob grappled with the guards pushing them backwards, and lashed out their grasping hands, forcing the other guards behind them to also scuffle with the raving.

"Please!" Dashi implored. And they kept on wailing and shrieking. Dashi could see behind the crowd guard moving into position surrounding them, swords drawn.

Dashi looked back at the captain. He knew the captain would put down the mob in moments if he couldn't get them under control. He didn't want to have to beat his people into submission. That was what the last magistrate would have done.

"What would the master do?!" he asked himself, and the answer came, "– I don't know. I'm not the master."

Instead, somewhere from deep inside, Dashi let out a roar, "Sit down!" It was so loud the crowd was shocked. And they fell into silence. Dashi himself was rather shocked. But they were for the moment stunned. "Sit!" he commanded. And some did immediately. Then others joined them. And those late to sit received encouragement from the blades of the guards.

Dashi stood hands on hips, he thought, "Only one chance," searching for an answer, "What to say?"

How about, you're all a bunch of bloody ingrates? said a mind.

He agreed, "Why didn't *you* catch them? You're telling me you didn't notice? It was happening in right front of you! Someone knew something – or had an inkling what was going on – knew the magistrate's power had corrupted!" But what could any of them have done?

Nothing. They were just trying to survive. And in their bellies must turn the worm of self disgust, the hurt of grief from swallowed tears.

Dashi was angry too. Angry this played to his fear: that people were fundamentally cowards – that they were weak – that no amount of assistance would ever change them – that you might as well rule over them with an iron fist. Worse, that it became a logical necessity.

As he looked over the now suppressed rabble, of upper class, mid and low station all, he saw that a few of them had their eyes closed, sitting cross legged, their mouth forming a tiny circle. Like a kiss. And they were breathing.

He saw it. They were fire breathing to clear away their pain, and anger, and distress.

Dashi overcome, sank, and sat.

He assumed the posture. In through the nose, out through the mouth, held just as they did. He forced the air down, burning the hot coal of this anger, exhaling for as long as he could before drawing another breath for the bellows of fire.

He realised his resentment towards all of them. Dashi focused on that. Again expelling the grief. Again, came the tears. And drawing in, just as the master said could happen, he felt the little gratitude.

He said to the congregated, "Although we grieve, each in our hearts alone, we grieve together," he said.

Somehow they had learned the breath. Listening to him over the wall, they'd practiced in secret. Any still standing, out of reach of the guard, nervously sat and copied the others. Dashi thanked whatever allowed for this miracle. From now on he vowed the gate would remain open. Breathing... breathing... breathing.

Then, a thought.

The captain had confided to him in the court room, in hushed tones, about the truly horrific nature of the crime. A secret.

Dashi opened his eyes upon the people. Someone had screamed out: 'Baby eaters.' And the question appeared unbidden, and unwanted – *Who told them?*

Dashi rushed back to the mistress's room, and finding

the door closed knocked respectfully. In a moment the mistress appeared, poking her head out, "Your master has left," she said.

Breathing hard, Dashi said, "Did he say when he'll return."

She smiled. "He never does. He'll be back at the right time."

"Oh," said Dashi. He was irritated the master would go. He hadn't finished telling Dashi what he needed to know. People's lives were at stake when Dashi made a decision. Did the master not think it important that he should know best how to do so? It seemed, though, he did not like to think of his master this way, irresponsible. His forehead was lined with concern.

"I can tell you," said the mistress, intuiting the cause of his disappointment.

Dashi jerked his head up, not realising he had put his head down in the first place. The mistress reached out and put her thumb on Dashi's furrowed brow slowly smoothing it out. Dashi made himself relax.

"I'm not as eloquent though," she said, adding, in the way of someone of long acquaintance, "He does like to talk." She opened the door fully. "Come in," and then closed it behind him.

The mistress was in her bed robes and a small quilted jacket. She glided her way to one of the pillow strewn couches and sat down facing him. Dashi noted that she was relaxed, that she was always relaxed. Nothing seemed to phase her much, aside from an occasional disapproval for poisoned chefs and cannibals, which Dashi felt legitimate.

"Maturation," she said.

"Yes," replied Dashi.

"It comes when one decides to grow up and stop getting stuck," she said.

"Yes," said Dashi and waited for her to go on. And having waited, he said, "Mistress?"

"My Lord?" she replied.

"Is there more?" he asked.

"No, not really," she said, "Just release the blocks and you'll get there eventually."

Dashi smiled, "Where is there, mistress?"

"Ah, well... One might be... for example, afraid of spiders. You'd rather not spend time with them. This is fine. But to say spiders are frightening is incorrect. Rather you are frightened by spiders. You see?"

"Yes. You mean I should... That when I think something for which I am frightened–" he said.

"Or other exaggerated feelings," she said.

"... that I have a lot of feelings about..." said Dashi.

"Which is why your master taught you the fire breath. But ultimately they're not a problem because of the fear," she said.

"Yes, that should I... No, I'm confused," said Dashi. "Not because... You mean because I ascribe the fear to the object and not myself."

"You misplace it," she said, "You take it out of yourself, the only place any emotion will ever be, and pretend it is out there. That is why you symbolically burn away the residual feelings. Then you are free to think without their interference, symbolically. Then a spider may stand for fear, but it is not the fear."

"Ah, this is like should. But instead of 'have to,' I attach too much to a thing."

"It's emotionally exaggerated," she clarified.

"And if I'm emotionally exaggerated, that's when I

should things, and they get sticky. I get it," said Dashi and paused. "Is the goal to be unemotional?" asked Dashi.

"Not at all," she said, with her eyebrows raised, "Feelings are feelings. Know them. Acknowledge them. But if you muddle them up with other things..."

"Such as spiders," he said.

"Such as an object. Such as pain..." she said.

"Pain?" he said.

"Suffering," she replied.

"What about it?" he said.

"Don't muddle it," she sighed.

"Muddle it with what?" asked Dashi creasing his brow.

She cleared her throat. "In conversational speech, when you speak of things not being there anymore, you are clear in your mind that you don't mean the things are unthings," she said.

"As the master says," said Dashi.

"As your master says," she repeated. "Just so, when you speak of the feeling of pain, there is an associated emotion of distress. Or it could be anger, or sorrow."

"Ah, so to distinguish the two," said Dashi.

"In conversation we say feeling and emotion interchangeably. Because the association is frequent we assume they are bound together, but they're not," she said.

"Isn't that... muddled?" said the magistrate.

"Hopelessly," she replied, "But just as I'm *not* going to stop using the word *not*, despite the fact that nothing is not-a-thing, and so on... I will relate bodily feelings with conscious emotions. I will relate physical states with mental ones. I will relate the sensory minds with the temporal ones.

"In description, and pedagogy I delineate, but in practice I comprehend the whole. Just as I can speak of the purpose of each mind, but they are inexorably one."

"Because of feeling?" asked Dashi.

"The minds' purposes are half feeling," she replied.

"Half?" he said.

"The first half," she responded.

"Why the first half?" he said.

"Because it comes first," she said.

Dashi imagined for just a moment what a conversation between the master and the mistress might be like and why they spent most of their time apart. "Mistress, why does it come first?"

"Because things start subtly, and then through stages come to being able to be expressed with the languages of the minds," she said as if it were self evident.

Apparently the magistrate looked less than convinced because she went on without prompting. "However that doesn't help you if you muddle things. Especially if you do it on purpose. The mind that observes time, sequence, and is the ancestor of all the other temporal minds – in a way *is* time for the other minds, by that which they measure their progress, through its connection to the body, the somatic minds – reaches down to being itself. Thus awareness is of what is, not just some illusion. Although it is that too."

Dashi unconsciously slumped his shoulders. "What?" said Dashi who then began to gesticulate with exaggerated emotion, "I have a city full of angry people. And thousands of dead babies. And I've got them doing the fire breath – but don't ask me how *that* happened... and they're going to want something done – by me – soon!" said the magistrate and then went back to his slump.

The mistress looked perfectly annoyed at his claim to not comprehend her perfectly lucid explanation. She spoke slowly, "Human minds are temporal. It is our seeing of alternatives that defines us." She placed her hand on her chest. "But it's what we define ourselves *out of* that's important. Stuckness rejects this for a projection. – And, don't slouch... My Lord."

Dashi straightened his back, "You mean... we first experience time with our bodies?" he said, "And only come to be able to talk about time, about what is and could be, as we mature into who we are?"

"Indeed," she said, surprised.

"Otherwise it's..." he said.

"A muddle," she finished. "That's why feelings come first."

"Ah," he said, "So... do animals think of time?"

She looked up, and sighed, "I should think monkeys may. They seem to plan somewhat. Not being one, I cannot say."

"Hmmm... And these stages, mistress..." said Dashi.

"First you experience, as you indicated, naively. Then there is some complication that alerts you it."

"But didn't..."

"An experience without contrast tends to be invisible," she said, "Like a story without dynamic. There is the fall and the return to greater wholeness."

"Without change... Um... like without wind, you wouldn't know there was air," he said.

"There's wind all right," she replied folding her arms. "Ends depend on what is being contrasted. Time is change, but of what? Does that answer all your questions?"

"Mmm, one more," he said, "I meditate to remove my exaggerated emotions, so that I do not tell myself sad tales–"

"'Sad tales' being your master's way of saying distorted

thinking," she interjected. "You burn to empty the grief and release the tales."

"Yes," Dashi said. "Empty grief, release distorted thinking, make people mature, and–"

"And they will know beauty," she said.

"Beauty," he repeated, "Beauty? – really?"

"Yes." she stated flatly.

"Why?" said Dashi.

"Who can see your wholeness, your confidence, or compassion, or joy? Even humour is too ephemeral, changes too fast for any communing of the minds. A painting, a sculpture, or a story, or a building can last for hundreds of years – thousands of years. Naming things too, is important..." she mused.

"What about values?" he said

"Can't see them, can't touch them. Important, but sharing them mostly leads to arguing," she replied. "They can't understand art either but its ambiguity makes their self-righteousness less violent."

"Is that what the master wants me to understand for freeing the people? – beauty?"

"He wants you to embrace your inner impulse and its resistance. But this now is breaching into his domain of your instruction. I was only to teach you politics," she said, "Beauty is my way of the way. As an artist it is my personal perspective. And I am guessing it is also yours."

He wasn't quite sure what she meant by that. "Well if beauty is the measure – I have a long way to go with this town," said Dashi.

"Politically speaking," she said, "One has to raise one's head to beauty. People keep their heads down if you make them fear loss. Like my sister, it's the foolish despot who leaves the people nothing but sad stories and their humiliating lives to lose. Eventually they will fight."

"That's what I've been thinking," said Dashi nodding, "It's poverty that is the problem of the people."

"Of every kind. Of every mind," she added. "People possessed by wealth find loss a hidden obsession. Their fear is a poverty. So they project. Embroiling others to fight: for moralities, and shoulds, to keep the truth hidden within.

"Songs of freedom will echo fear's voice. They will light the sacred brasiers to dispel evil while sharpening the darkness with their words and swords - and the people will choke from the smoke of the wolf. What is going on in this town is not of your making," the mistress said, "Indeed, it is the times for the whole of the world, of which you are unaware. What you'd best do - not what you should, is to attend the ripening of your own awareness."

Dashi nodded his head, then shook his head. "I don't know exactly what you mean by that."

The mistress patted her hair, "Just as your master was explaining. I say ripening, to mean maturing."

"Then I must still be pretty green," said Dashi.

The mistress laughed. Dashi hadn't heard her laugh before. It was a knowing laugh. The laugh of a woman who had seen much.

"All right, Dashi," said the mistress using his name, "I like you."

"I also like you, mistress," Dashi returned.

"You're like your master: you like everyone," she said, shaking her head.

"Not everyone apparently likes me," said Dashi.

"This is a good thing," said the mistress, "But you are thinking of something particular?"

"The chef."

The mistress shrugged slightly, "That comes with the

position."

"What about the would be assassin in the street?"

"The guards dealt with it."

"But how did they know I'd be there?" said Dashi. "I didn't know I was going until I decided."

"It may have been random. Or someone could have seen you leave the palace in search of noodles and run ahead to hide in wait," she said as if talking about how to arrange flowers most pleasingly in a vase.

"Or how about just now, when a raving mob appeared outside my gates and they knew all about the dead children, which the captain had only told me... in secret."

"Oh," said the mistress. "I didn't know that," and added cryptically, "Or at least I didn't know that I knew." She immediately got up and rang a bell. Within moments her granddaughter appeared in the room. Dashi turned around. The door to the room was still as it had been, closed.

"Dear," said the mistress, "the magistrate tells me that the crowd outside knew about the unreleased particulars of the case being heard – and this agitated them – greatly."

"Oh," her granddaughter replied, "What did they know?"

"They knew about their..." Dashi thought of a nice way to say it to her, "diet."

"Cannibals," said the mistress.

"I see," said the granddaughter frowning, but nodding, "And that's why you sentenced them to death."

The news had traveled. Dashi interjected, "Actually, that is why I came... in the first place... to see your grandmother... to ask for a poison that would put them to sleep. Painlessly."

"He is nice," said the mistress.

"Yes," said the granddaughter in what Dashi thought a

funny way. "How many did they eat?" she asked.

"Hundreds and hundreds," replied Dashi.

"Were they well fed?" she asked.

Dashi scoffed, "If you were just going to eat them you wouldn't bother with that. It's been near starvation here for nearly everyone," He'd not previously considered the hunger as driving them to this terrible act. A creeping madness coming, slowly taking them over. "Although she did keep repeating... she'd fed them..." He put his hand to his mouth, and Dashi began to think something was amiss.

"I mean... were the couple well fed?" asked the granddaughter.

"Skinny," said Dashi, shaking his head, imagining them standing in court before him. A terrible feeling crept upon him, "No... emaciated," his hand sliding to cover his mouth entirely, "I've sentenced the wrong people – or for the wrong crime." He looked up into their eyes, his hand fell to his side. "This is exactly what I most feared. Sentencing someone to death and then finding I've had innocents murdered."

"Innocent of that, at least," said the mistress.

"Thank goodness," said Dashi, putting his palms together.

"It stands to reason then, they were the hands to the mouth but not the teeth," the young woman said to her grandmother.

"The teeth surround the tongue that tells tales," the mistress replied.

"So that eyes are averted to what the ear hears," said the granddaughter.

Dashi stood up. Their conversation, played to be over his head, was irksome. "So that feet go running in the wrong direction. I get it: someone is pulling my strings, manipulating events. I'm not a dummy."

"Then where ought you be running right now?" asked the mistress.

All of the slander, all of the belittling – by all the people he knew, was nothing to being played a fool by a hidden spider, some infuriating coward. Someone who thought the new magistrate was too stupid to even notice what was happening.

Dashi may not have been bred for the position – maybe he wasn't even deserving of it, but he was, nevertheless, the magistrate. That he almost had been manipulated to kill two people galled him to his very moral core.

A mind said, *But why whip up a mob?*

Distraction, replied another.

"Excuse me ladies," said Dashi, and was out the door, away to the dungeon to question the prisoners.

"That got him going," said the granddaughter.

The mistress moved her fingers in silent reply.

As he descended the stairs downward he thought, "Perhaps it's best that whoever's responsible believe these two will be punished. So they'll become complacent. So we can catch them."

Dashi began to formulate a plan: after questioning the two and finding out who was behind this atrocity, he would fake their deaths... –Ah! poison... it need not kill them – and then he'd have them spirited away. The true culprits would then be relieved and not expect he was still looking for them. Indeed, with the couple out of the way, they may return to their evil. Most likely. For the desire that created that mound of death poured forth into his courtroom was no idle fancy, but a driving need – an addiction.

At the bottom stair he stopped, the jailer, alerted by his footsteps, greeted him at their end. Dashi had not been here since the night he'd become magistrate. Perhaps this night too, he was becoming magistrate.

The bored jailer pointed to two far cells. Dashi strode over and looked in. They were sleeping. How cruel in their last hours to even deprive them of each other's company and comfort. "Open them," he said. And this was done.

Dashi entered carefully the cell of the man, not wishing to shock him. He put his hand on the man's shoulder and gently shook to rouse him. The man did not stir. Dashi shook him harder, but the man didn't wake. Dashi ran to the cell of the woman, grabbing hold of her shoulders and turned her towards him. But she too was dead. Her skin flushed. Her last meal still partially held in her open mouth, as if having just uttered her final word. As for their guilt: who knew what they took with them.

However, they answered one question with their silence: the mob was a distraction. Dashi stepped back, and crushed beneath his heel some object. A plate.

Dashi turned on the jailer, who accustomed as he was with others' deaths was sweating cold with fright. The magistrate spat out the words like thunder, "Who brought their food?"

The chef was awakened not softly. The door to his room burst open and a demon, with sword drawn, was upon his chest. "Who? – made the meal given to the prisoners?"

spoke the magistrate. "Speak truly and simply – without disassembly. Your life hangs in the balance."

"I've been asleep, My Lord. I retired after..."

"-If not you, then who? Quickly," articulated Dashi, leaning hard upon the man.

"Prisoners' meals don't come from the kitchen. They're sent from the barracks," squeaked the chef.

"The guards make their meals?!"

"Yes, My Lord," said the chef, his eyes shut tight.

"Yet another indignity," said the vengeful demon, vanishing with the slamming of a door.

"Inspection!" shouted Dashi, as he brought the lamp into the room.

The captain looked up from his gambling, and swiftly stood straight up like an arrow hitting a tree.

"Attention!" he shouted. And all the guards sitting at the table bolted upright. All of them with swords. All of them proficient in the arts of killing. And one of them a traitor, thought Dashi.

He glanced past the rows of rumpled beds and guard, to the back of the barracks where a small stove sat. A basin of unwashed dishes nearby it. Dashi confidently paraded down the line of rod straight soldiers towards the basin. He looked at their faces for clues. None looked him in the eye, as was deference, but also in this case hampered his hunt.

"My Lord?" said the captain. But Dashi put up his hand for the captain to be silent. Dashi walked over to the basin and kneeling down, pawed through the pans. Eyeing one especially old and unsavoury one, he lifted it out of the basin by its loose handle. It was heavily crusted with some dried porridge that had changed colour. He walked over to the captain. There was no point in being secretive. Everyone in the palace would know if they didn't already. If they hadn't known, that is, beforehand.

"The two prisoners are dead," said the magistrate, "They were poisoned."

What passed over the captain's face was the briefest of sadness. "My Lord," was all he said.

"Their meals are made here, I am to understand. I take it in this beyond-filthy pot which looks if it rarely sees a cleaning." The captain nodded, and Dashi proceeded to bang the pot hard against the side of the table until a part of the dried crust on the side broke partially away. "Take some," Dashi said, offering the pot up to the captain.

The captain reached in an took a piece. The magistrate then passed it around for all to take. As he did so he looked each in the eye and held their gaze.

"Are we all accounted for?" The magistrate asked.

"Yes, My Lord," answered the captain.

Dashi took a piece, throwing the pot on the floor. He placed it in his own mouth. And then the captain did the same, and his men followed him, and so too Dashi's brother's men. Dashi chewed and swallowed. The captain's eyes went wide as he watched the district magistrate swallow a loathsome crust of molding porridge. And then they likewise.

"Who delivered the porridge?" the magistrate said, looking along the line of the gambling guards, wondering if their weakness could be bought off to allow another to deliver it for them, for by their eyes he knew no poison had touched the pot.

"My Lord, the prisoners' meals are delivered by runner,"

said the captain.

"Do you know who it was?"

"Yes, My Lord. But what you tell me makes me fear for him."

Wild tall flames, and spiralling soot upwards flew against the clear blue – the mountains, stone-black and shrouded beyond.

Because he was so young, he'd no children to pay respect, to give a last caring for the body that had been his. Meaning this body, lips blackened with the poison he'd been forced to drink, found lying in the meat cooler, near the kitchen, would be made ashes and interred without ceremony. This, Dashi could not abide.

Enrobed as magistrate, Dashi had praised his bravery – as former food taster, and as his trusted honourable servant. His service, his lord magistrate likened to a warrior. Lying upon the pyre, onto his breast, the magistrate had laid his own sword. And when it was lit; Dashi walked around the outside of the pyre, touching it with fire.

The magistrate stood and watched as the fire crept slowly into the centre. The hours came to twilight and to darkness. And Dashi's sword, impotent to fend away both poison and grief, glowed red.

In silent promise, Dashi's reforging his heart in the fire, raising it with the smoke as an offering to any gods who would hear it. When Dashi turned from the fire at last, his smoke red eyes passed over the assembled: guard and servant and bureaucrat, for surely among them the murderer stood. In this midst, Dashi saw himself surrounded. For whom power was everything – what was kindness, but weakness?

"Go," he ordered.

Later, Dashi would retrieve from the ashes the boy's bones, his blackened sword.

"Who? Who are they?" asked Dashi rubbing his sore eyes.

Said the mistress, "The ones we are looking for have lost their faith and serve now only their self-image. I know this because they've no mercy. Also they're hot headed. Which we can now infer, when they became blocked, by the captain cutting off their supply..." – Dashi tightened his brow, but said nothing – "...they instantly angered and reacted. Thus they have an overblown sense of their own importance. Meaning it is probable they will overreact like this to any opposition, and My Lord, try not to rub your eyes."

"It's a they then?" said Dashi, ignoring her admonition.

"I should say so, yes, they," she replied. "If it were only one..."

Dashi put up his hand for silence when just then a servant came in with a dish of rice and vegetables for the mistress. Dashi felt the side of the bowl. If it had come straight from the kitchen it should have been piping hot. It was merely warm.

Warm as if it had lost much of its heat, perhaps due to standing out in the corridor while someone was eavesdropping. Perhaps due to it being passed on first to those whose pockets concealed small vials of death.

"The rice is not hot," Dashi glowered.

The boy looked at him, "My Lord?"

"What is the meaning, bringing this lukewarm dish?"

demanded Dashi, "I think someone ought to taste it. Apparently I need the whole kitchen staff to attend my every meal. Get the chef!"

The boy nodded and turned to go.

"Stay right where you are!" barked Dashi, "If I give you leave-"

The mistress put a hand on Dashi's arm, "My Lord, I ask them to bring it less warm. I prefer it that way," she explained.

"Oh..." said Dashi, his taut face now sapped of passion, "I'm... We'll ring to have the dishes removed," he said, "You can go."

"Yes, My Lord," said the boy and retreated immediately.

Dashi took a deep breath, and speaking soft said, "How many are they?"

"I don't know," she said under her breath.

"Are they spying on me?" he whispered back.

"I should think so," she replied.

He looked about the room, "Are they listening as we speak?"

The mistress looked from one side to the other, "Let's find out," she said, then raising her voice, "What is important is how they swayed the people. If they can raise a mob in minutes then our position is perilous," she said.

"It's because they're baby eaters," commented Dashi, resting head in hand. "I'd be outside the gates trying to break in too."

"Ah, but that is only the half of it," said the mistress, "I've had reports of the incident. What incited the mob was- There was some suggestion of... of their being demons-"

"What?!" said Dashi.

"-And should you have protected them- Well, you, yourself, could very well be a demon as... " She could see he was getting very angry. "Calm yourself, My Lord. That's only if you hadn't sentenced the couple to-"

"Then I'd be a demon," he said.

"But you did," countered the mistress, "And that, I suspect, the poisoners did not expect you to do."

"Expected me to be merciful, so they could tar me with... that?" he exclaimed.

"Exactly," she said putting a calming hand on his arm, "They seek to own your identity. We will say the two committed suicide. No one will believe that."

"Then why say it?" asked Dashi.

"Because the people will conclude that you are decisive but also wish to be seen as benign. They will understand that you understand, that they won't believe such a flimsy official story. Therefore to them you are both cunning, and by signalling to them your true intentions, while also being indifferent to their conclusions, you are therefore self-assured and strong in your pursuit of your ends," she said.

Dashi's head spun. "Is there a more tangled word than tangled?"

"Politics," she replied.

Dashi merely grunted recognition of that truth. "But... if I hadn't chosen to sentence them to death, as they expected, I would now have two prisoners who I could question about what the poisoners are up to."

"No, My Lord," she replied, voice steady, "Once they realised who'd been taken into custody, and what the couple knew, they were marked for death, whatever sentence you decreed."

"Doesn't saying they committed suicide imply I was lenient and therefore implicated?" he asked.

"But you did sentence them to death. So saying they

killed themselves–"

"If they were co-conspirators, perhaps I gave them an honourable way out," suggested Dashi.

"But why bring them in at all?" she asked.

"I didn't. The captain did," replied Dashi thinking about that.

"We are getting off topic, as usual," said the mistress, changing the subject.

"As usual?" said the magistrate.

The mistress adjusted one sleeve and said, "What is important, as I said, is why the people reacted, your personal reaction notwithstanding."

"The people, outraged supernatural-irrationality aside, are obviously moral, and this is an abomination! What more do you need?" said the cross magistrate.

"More," said the mistress. "The people don't just rise to anger so quickly, else they'd be night and day rampaging at every whispered rumour. The poisoners understand what is already dark within the hearts of the people. What is already seething to escape. Stories of demons acted as the catalyst to something they already fear – the darkness that clings to their heart."

Dashi said, "Ah... Demons. Of course. I see that now. What must we do?"

"We must make sure we're the ones who control what story is believed," the mistress said.

"Story? Why not just tell them the truth?' said Dashi.

"For the purposes of keeping power, that is not enough," she replied, keeping her voice soft. "Not unless your people are sages, each and every one. They can only believe what point of view they inhabit. Trying to tell them about truth is like telling them about transcendence. They will not be able to understand it."

"So you lie?" asked Dashi.

"So you save your neck by speaking to them about things they will comprehend. Even if you are not implying anything of the sort, talking over their heads will just make them think you're stupid, or make them feel stupid. And both will make them angry."

"You're saying they weren't at my gates because they're moral but because they're hysterical?" said Dashi.

"Yes," she replied. "That is what stuck means – in action. A point of view that is incomplete, tainted, mad, vain, superstitious – and ten thousand denials and self-delusions I can barely imagine. I'm not saying there is no one in the city who is sane." She adjusted the other sleeve. "Only they're unlikely to having been part of the mob baying at your front door."

The magistrate considered this. "Point taken," he replied. "What next?"

"First we must understand what mind the mob is stuck in," she said.

"To help them be free," suggested Dashi.

"To protect ourselves," she replied. "They don't want your good advice. No matter how badly you think they are suffering. It is only when they themselves have suffered enough to want it, that you may give it. As I have mentioned before."

"I know you have," said Dashi, "I find it a hard lesson to remember."

"To be an effective reformer one has to abandon thinking one knows better," she said. "The people, each individual, has their own way. Who are you, for them to heed your dictates?"

"Am I not already doing that as a magistrate of the empire?" Dashi asked.

"You are," she said, "A mountain of edicts have become accepted in their life. Just try to give them one more. Already they are shifty, trying to squirm out from under the weight of so much law. Do not use it capriciously."

"I don't think I would-" started Dashi.

"I misspoke, let's say... incautiously," she interjected. "You need to use the powers of the office that are not the legal ones. The benevolent, but just ruler, this is what you must create for their minds' understanding."

"It will give them a feeling of security?" said Dashi.

"And *you*," she replied. "An out of control ruler is frightening. And a frightened populous turns ugly." Then dropping her voice and without moving her lips, "Now, I lay my trap."

"Ah," said Dashi, having found himself caught up in her words, only now remembering why she spun them.

"Let me explain it a different way," she said, her eyes shining - benign and sincere. "First, understanding what seems the straight way is the reverse of the true path. The difficulty is based on seeing the world one way, where the better is the reverse. For example, politically you wish to provide the people with goodness. But goodness can only be effectively provided if the community chooses the good. And that can only be so if the individuals seek mature minds because the ideals of good are not the good."

When she paused Dashi answered, "I understand," though he most certainly did not.

She nodded. "The people do not trust themselves because they're afraid and they know it. They know themselves to be unworthy, and most do nothing when malevolence walks the dark, past their door... except draw the blinds tighter. Each blind, being another small step to evil walking, openly, out in the daylight. Then they'll know what fear really is–"

"Because they make themselves blind?" joked Dashi.

"Your wit improves," she said.

"I have need of it," replied Dashi.

"No – because they focus on ends. They neglect what is most important as the means to those ends. They seek to be gratified with cheap sustenance rather than facilitating nourishment. A bowl of rice to eat now, but they shun planting the fields.

"But to achieve this nourishment – how many things are necessary? More than physical things. The heart must intend for success. It must tend the world with care. So the question is: which way?"

Dashi just shrugged.

"The way progresses by reversal. For the complex ends must be achieved by simple means. For the people of would-be mobs, it must be as simple as a bowl of rice ready to eat. By these simple means, the people can feel worthy and stand with a leader against tyranny while it is still small and hiding. This makes them the leader's allies. A leader should court the love of his people, and do nothing to weaken that. Right?"

"Bowls of rice!" said Dashi, not knowing what else to say. "Nourishment... requires right power, which requires right community, which requires right justice, which requires right truth."

She smirked. "A worthy plan. The greatest idea I have ever heard," she said. "We must provide the trodden path – a course to our own becoming."

"We will march the path together!" said Dashi enjoying this ad lib play.

"Some of the young however are impatient," she said critically appraising Dashi with her eyes.

He said nothing.

"The thing that is necessary is obviously right there," she said her finger subtly pointing.

"The bowl of rice?" Dashi asked looking at the table.

"All the longings of the minds," she replied, her eyes slowly shifting to the door ajar. "A mind is not just a simple seeker. It learns. It looks to gain what it needs most effectively. Power, however, is subordinate to the more encompassing levels of maturation that come after. In this we are lucky because those who seek it are inferior. In fact lazy. They have played this game so long against the witless, they feel overconfident they will win."

"You're going to outwit them," said Dashi, low, following her gaze to watch the door.

"Easily," she whispered back, and then in full voice, "Focusing on the ends of power, you become enmeshed at the level of power's ends accomplished by the perfection of means – which are the ends, but perfected by ignorant aim. Of the true target of your power you do not even have an inkling."

"No, not one," said Dashi slowly rising reaching for his sword.

She put her hand to his arm, and lowered her tone, "Your master, I know, has told you, be humble, to see the enormity of the heavens: sublime, beyond truth, seducing lifelong scholars to gaze at its greater meaning. Realise as all the minds mature they speak of the same thing along the way. Though it is not initially realised. But then!–" she shouted, clapping her hands, and the door trembled slightly. She continued in hushed tones, "–by naming, they lift themselves into the next level. Nourishment – then their skill, and power, and so on, understand?"

"Can you tell me the simple way?" said Dashi.

"Feed their bellies, let them have their fill. They will come back for more. And they will choose you as their leader," she said looking up at the walls. Then, with her eyes, she indicated for him sit next to her.

Dashi nodded. "That is enough politics for tonight," he said loudly, "I wish you to eat your dinner while it is at least a little warm." He sat beside her. "Well?" he whispered.

"We'll see what they can make of *that*," she said removing the top from the dish, and a last small wisp of steam escaped. "They won't have understood a word."

"Me too," Dashi whispered back.

"You wonder why I tell you stories?" she said.

The next morning after meditation Dashi met the mistress in the garden.

"Can you explain what you were explaining to me last night, when we were trying to confuse, or ensnare, those who were listening... other than me?"

The mistress pointed to a flower off the tree beside the one Dashi said she could not pick. He picked a flower off the tree for her, and she put it behind her ear.

"To ensnare," she said, "Beyond words of truth, minds come to the edge of the mystery. The great power. The sublime and the beautiful. And each mind will experience its own beauty - a word I use, that you think you understand, but whose depth leads all the way to the roots of the one." She ran her hands through the pink petals of the blooming tree, gathering them in her hands. "Do not try to prove the beautiful with the language of truths. Beauty is beyond true. If you embrace your full consciousness you can come out to its limits, and look over the edge at the unknowable. The limit of the minds – here truth will not guide you."

Dashi said, "Then I should call for artists and architects, and have them create great works for the people to appreciate."

"Perish the thought," said the mistress, "All that money would only make the thieves crawl out of the woods."

Dashi spread his hands out.

Regarding him without even an eyebrow raise, she continued, "Praise the beauty of the wind in the tree, the cloud upon the mountain. Those enduring things that no one can buy or proclaim by fashion. Praise artists as you would nature. It is by not what they create that they're important, but the creation that flows through them, that is their soul.

"Then listen," she said, cupping a hand behind her ear. "If the people praise it, you are a decent leader. If you would, however, be a great leader, then you will need the level after that."

"I thought you said this was the limit to the minds. How can there be another level after that?"

"Indeed," said the mistress.

Dashi smiled, "That's what the master says too."

"He took it from me and uses it sarcastically. He thinks it's funny," she remarked and let the petals cascade out of her hands. She took Dashi's arm.

"Oh," said Dashi.

Evening, alone in his study, Dashi consumed a large bowl, of large dumplings, in a golden broth. A dinner of comfort. His afternoon – he, long-sitting in the red chair, passed out fines and rulings like sweet-buns. But the one image his minds kept seeing was of two fat women – arguing about who stole whose laundry; and, as it became more heated, slapping each other. Right in the courtroom, right under the eyes of him, the magistrate, they began to slap each other's faces. Dashi slurped down a dumpling, shaking his head.

"Remarkable," he said out loud.

"Are they? I ought to try some," said the mistress. Dashi spun around. She was seated. The young woman standing beside her, who Dashi initially thought the granddaughter attending, was instead one of the other women. A singer. She smiled captivatingly at him. He smiled back.

Then Dashi, broth on his chin, quickly wiped his mouth with his sleeve, then regretted that by the mistress's look, "How'd you get–"

"Dumplings," she said.

Dashi looked back at the dumplings. "Are they all right?" he asked, wondering if she were here to warn him of poison.

"You said they were remarkable," she replied.

"Did I?" Dashi said, "No, I was talking out loud about a case, this afternoon." Dashi regarded the woman, who he thought looked nervous, but stood perfectly postured.

"Interesting case?" asked the mistress.

"Not really," said Dashi, "Just pathetically violent."

"Ah," she replied.

He said, "What I don't understand is what they could possibly be thinking."

"What level," she stated.

"Meaning?" he said, wondering why she was here, with this girl in tow.

"We didn't finish our conversation in the garden about

what makes for a great leader, than a merely competent one. And what that level is," she replied.

"By level I mean that everything is understood as a kind of food," she said. Dashi nodded his head considering the sagacity of the statement.

"Then everything becomes about power," she said. And again he considered this wisdom.

The mistress said, "Then everything is understood as about identity. And so on. Revising what life is all about, in stages. Each is characterised by the language of one of the minds, the way of that stage of maturation. It is from the final cultivated stage that the great leader comes."

"I see," said Dashi, "this is my goal."

"No," she said, "I suggested a level beyond that."

"And it's this that I seek?" asked Dashi.

The mistress looked up at the woman beside her. "The level beyond levels. The true gold. So deep within, that you, being in the very consciousness, are not able to express objectively its truths. At the source of the minds is unspeakability - but not inexperiencability. It is from this vantage point, that of nothingness, the great leader comes."

Dashi, thinking this sounded difficult, asked, "Couldn't the people just lead themselves?"

"No doubt they could, but they do not," she replied. "Asking the immature concerned only with material goods and power to lead, is like asking children to raise themselves." The mistress looked to the girl.

"Well..." began Dashi.

"Those nans," asserted the mistress, "and the grand-fathers. They all know your name, Dashi. You think they remember every urchin who crosses their path?"

Again Dashi realised his indebtedness.

"What I mean is those who choose not to mature, will be like children forever. And not nice ones," she said, "However, a mature populace can contend with overgrown adolescents."

"Many hands," said Dashi.

She nodded. "And if they really get out of hand, there will be those who can deal with them. Like magistrates," she said, looking at the young woman who squirmed under her gaze.

"Master said no one should have to be magistrate," said Dashi. "That the people need to take responsibility for themselves."

"I agree," said the mistress, "For much of what is necessary, people can take responsibility. But if they can't, their responsibility is to abdicate their decision to those who can. That is – it's part of maturity to recognise who to trust."

Dashi sat again. His students – merchants and nans, and everyone just outside the gate, appeared to be burning away their sticky feelings.

In his own mind, he was trying to burn the disunity of the minds. "But they could be thinking anything," thought Dashi.

In court, just the day previous, two men and a woman told various stories about who did what to whom and when and under what agreement or lack thereof. By what they said, their ambiguous assertions and contradictory contentions, it was impossible for Dashi to determine what, if anything, had occurred.

Fortunately their neighbours were nosy and had watched

the one man, not being the husband, climb over the wall and up to a window on several regular occasions. If individual minds were like this, then the reason for second opinions became apparent. Many second opinions.

As for burning disunity, as to what that may be, within him there seemed no consensus.

The day began. Dashi dutifully drank his yellow tea medicine. Dutifully made his way to the courtroom hall. Dutifully sat in his chair, arranged his robes, and thanked his new runner for the tea she had brought.

"My Lord," said the clerk, "A word?"

"Of course," said the magistrate wishing for nothing less than a word with his clerk.

"My Lord, this is not my place but it seems the harvest is in question," said the clerk.

"What do you mean?" asked Dashi.

"It would seem," said the clerk, "that the methods employed are most... unorthodox."

"From the previous methods that kept us in starvation year after year?" said the magistrate, "Yes, I understand the farmers having regained ground, are using a different method, as you say. But then as I had no faith in what came before – whatever the harvest, it can hardly be worse."

"But if it is, My Lord," said the clerk, "with such large families, they will be very hard put to feed any additional mouths."

"The point?" said the magistrate.

"Just to suggest it's better to shepherd their appetites a little until after the harvest is actually in," said the clerk smiling. "I'm merely expressing a concern I think they should consider."

Dashi thought about the conversation he'd had with the mistress about urges. "I am a magistrate," said Dashi, "not a god. People will do what they do. I'm here only to deal with those who do it in public."

"I understand you," said the clerk nodding.

The magistrate, Dashi came into the yard. The new guards, former highway robbers all, were training. A sergeant barked out instructions as they fought. Standing off to one side was the captain with some of his higher level officers. Their relaxed posture and smiles vanishing as they came to attention with Dashi's approach.

"My Lord," said the captain.

"Captain," said Dashi, "A word." And he walked away expecting the captain to follow. Dashi continued until he was out of earshot of the others. The marching footsteps of the captain behind his. The magistrate turned.

The captain stopped. The magistrate eyed him critically. Then Dashi drew his sword. "When I asked for your sword on that first day, and you gave it to me, you wondered if I was going to kill you," said Dashi.

The captain's eyes remained open and calm, his body relaxed and ready. "It crossed my mind," he said.

"I felt it cross your mind," said Dashi. "My master thought you a man of intelligence. I think the same."

"It is an honour to serve, My Lord," said the captain but continued his wary stance.

"Just accept the compliment. When I learned to fight I learned among the robbers in the forest," said Dashi looking at the blade of the sword, "I know a few things, but my technique is I'm sure... unorthodox."

"That can be an advantage," stated the captain.

"I need you to train me," said Dashi. "Draw your weapon."

The captain looked Dashi in the eye and then slowly drew his own sword. "It will be harder for you to fight in that robe," he said.

The magistrate replied, "But it is in this robe that I am likely to be forced to fight. So be it."

The captain changed his stance. He smiled, "Stand like this," he said, "Many fighters lose because they topple over. They lose their balance, overextend. It's a common mistake that allows me to cut off their arm, or their head."

Dashi adopted the pose.

Immediately the captain advanced, "Begin!" he said.

Dashi grabbed the back of his robe with his free hand, and retreated sideways, circling the captain until his shadow fell in front of him.

"Good," said the captain, squinting. "I'll pretend I don't know for now." And the captain came forward with a blow

"What do you know captain?" said Dashi slamming his blade flat against the captain's swing – the force echoing through his arm and shoulder.

"The sun is in my eyes," he said.

"And what else?" prompted Dashi.

"About what My Lord?" queried the captain backhanding a second stroke.

A stroke which Dashi met but was pushed back by its force. "About the mob at my gates last night. About the dead prisoners. About the babies," said Dashi with effort.

"Ah, that..." said the captain again advancing.

Dashi raised his blade in expectation to block. "Yes, that," he said. And the captain swung up flat to hit Dashi's blade and at the same time hooked his leg behind the magistrate's, tripping him and knocking him down. Dashi rolled away.

"You expected me to do something. Don't," said the captain turning, "-You have to double back before you can respond," he said, swinging hard over Dashi's head. "That gives me all the opportunity I need," he said, offering the magistrate his hand, but Dashi was already rising.

"You mean: be bold, act!" said Dashi, his sword moving without forethought. He struck at the captain, who moved back, knocking the blow aside.

"Traitors," said the captain, who circled the magistrate. "The children are a key. You need to build up your arms," he said.

"It's been a while since I chopped wood and carried buckets of water," remarked Dashi.

"It shows," said the captain who came on with a flurry of attacks ending with the magistrate being once again in a sprawl on the ground. Dashi tried to kick away but his boot was caught in his robe, tearing. The captain said, "That robe will be the death of you."

Dashi kicked it away with the one foot. "I've thought that." And again he rose up, ready.

"Too much fine food," stated the captain.

"You know, as well as I do, I eat with the chef," he replied, wary.

"I was joking, My Lord," said the captain.

"Who are the traitors?" asked Dashi and he lunged forward.

"I can't prove any of it," said the captain knocking the blow away, but Dashi came full on with his shoulder, driving his leg behind the captain's. The captain stumbled backwards and Dashi came on with another swing. The captain again knocked it away while pivoting, and then running, Dashi in pursuit.

His arms may have somewhat weakened by sitting in that damned chair for months but his legs still could leap mountains, and he caught the captain by his collar, and simultaneously caught his foot in his robe's tear, tripping him forward, knocking over the captain. Dashi swore, and the captain, ridden by the magistrate, let out a mighty "Whoosh," as he hit the ground, beneath him in a pile.

Dashi rolled off, cutting at the tear with his sword. The captain struggled to his hands and knees, and then up he came. His face was bloodied where bits of pebbles stuck into his forehead and right cheek. They regarded each other.

"I think that's enough orthodox training for today," said the captain, picking out the rocks.

"You haven't answered me," said Dashi, looking at the captain, and noticing the rest of the guard, standing, watching at a distance, agape.

The captain coughed, "Maybe, My Lord, we should speak over dinner."

After sunset, a figure in a dark cloak walked the narrow streets of the town, far away from the safety of his palace. He came to the lane that ran between two buildings and opened to a doorless dead end courtyard whose back wall abutted the outer wall battlement. Or so it would seem. Dashi walked to the outer wall and looking back to his left saw a narrow passageway between the building and a freestanding courtyard wall. Looking down it, again a seeming dead end. Merely a storage area leading to the outer wall. But as instructed, he carefully picked his way forward, his ears attuned to any clink of steel or the whiz of black arrows out of the dark. The passage turned left and two strides forward revealed a door.

Dashi knocked once. Moments later the captain opened the door and he bade his Lord enter the small room. A single candle burned in the middle of the table. The quarters were cramped, dusty and unkempt. A broken ceramic pot lay crumbled on the uneven floor from where it had apparently been knocked from its shelf.

"Not yours?" said Dashi disbelieving.

"No, My Lord, this is the home of the couple who took in the babies," said the captain.

"Here?" said Dashi looking around.

"Here," said the captain.

Dashi breathed out. "Where were the babies kept?"

"Upstairs, mostly," said the captain and indicated a twisting near vertical staircase in one dark corner.

"Mostly?"

"For the live ones," said the captain.

"And the others?" asked the magistrate.

The captain took up the candle and passed it over the floor, reaching a knot hole and lifting up a section of floor to reveal a ladder into an even tinier room below, with a bucket in its centre. "We found quite a few molding down here, stacked up around the floor like wood. I saw to their internment."

"And the bucket?" said Dashi.

"Baby water," said the captain.

Dashi looked to the captain, "Meaning?"

"It's where you drown them," the captain replied, and then added, "That's how it's usually done."

"What do you mean 'usually'?" asked Dashi.

"My Lord?" said the captain, "This is how it's done. When it's done. How women do it."

"What women?" said Dashi beginning to be annoyed at the circularity of the conversation.

"Many women, My Lord," he said. "Farm women keep only one or two sons. Female children are more often than not killed here because there isn't enough food and they can't labour in the fields as well."

"This didn't happen in my day," stated the shocked magistrate.

"I'm afraid so," said the captain, "My own wife..." he said, "...former wife. She wanted a son. So I threw her out," explained the captain.

"I'm sorry," said Dashi, both shocked and dismayed, "I didn't know."

"It's mostly babies. The unwanted older ones are usually just abandoned," said the captain and then realised what he'd said. "Apologies, My Lord."

"Go on," said the magistrate.

"...Boys usually. And girls may only be kept to sell off at a later time."

Nothing came forth from Dashi's mouth.

"It's not what you think," said the captain, "Most of the time they end up in factories. Making cloth because of their small hands or dipping matches. Sending back money – though it's often stolen. This is how things are, and have been – for ever," said the captain. "I thought you knew."

Dashi scratched the back of his head, "I think my captain, there is more than one kind of cannibal among us." He ceased his scratching and gazed upon his hand, "If this is how things are, apparently I fared far better than I had thought."

"Yes, My Lord," said the captain.

The magistrate mulled over the past for just a moment. "Do you remember when my master was magistrate?" asked Dashi.

"No, I joined the guard later in the rule of last magistrate- the real one before yourself," said the captain.

"The second husband," said Dashi.

"No, the next one," said the captain, "the one who wasn't interested in her aging charms. He didn't last long due to his fatal immunity."

"I forget about him," said Dashi, thinking it was little wonder the character of his city could use some improvement. "Now, the two who lived here," he said, "What do you know?"

A stern look crossed the captain's face, "It is true that they took babies in. For those who couldn't bear killing, they paid to have the babies fostered out. In practice it usually meant slavery."

Dashi simply noted the horror in the string of horrors. "Go on," he said.

The captain said, "Often they died in their care. I think that much was true. But I suspect also there are children who were taken away..." The captain looked at the magistrate and shone the light towards the trapdoor.

"The stories – we all heard them, but I thought... It kind of made sense, making the hunger itself a devouring monster... we were all so hungry," said Dashi. "It was always said as a kind of joke – the rich eating the poor."

"Come," said the captain and led the way down the ladder.

"We are under the battlement," said the captain.

"I noticed," said the magistrate looking around at the narrow space dug out of rock and earth, with only the bucket in the centre and a crate against the far wall to sit on. The captain handed the magistrate the candle, and then he pulled aside the crate, revealing a dark space. Dashi put the candle nearer and it flickered in the draft arising from the black space below.

"A tunnel?" asked the magistrate.

"It runs under the wall," said the captain. "It comes out behind trees, so it is not easily seen. Indeed one has to crawl to get in or out, but it borders the woods on the outer wall."

"And those woods border the fields," said Dashi nodding. "This is how they removed the babies without being seen."

"They followed the ditches," said the captain as he pulled the crate back into place. "The real mystery was that the remains were found in two burial places. Why, I thought, would they bury them in two places so far apart? That's when I looked at the skeletons and noticed that they were of two kinds, normal and–"

"Cooked," finished Dashi.

"Yes," said the captain, "I hadn't realised it before we'd already taken the remains, jumbling the two kinds. So I went back to see if there were any left in their original location, and I found two at the second site, both cooked. Further, by their depth, I was pretty sure we should have found them."

Dashi blinked, "Someone buried them after you had removed the others?"

"It would appear. And either they didn't notice the disturbed soil because of all the rain, or they didn't see because they buried them in the dark, under the cover of night," said the captain who abruptly turned his head, cocking his ear.

Dashi did likewise. The lock on the door above was being opened. The captain quickly snuffed out the candle Dashi held and they stood still in the darkness. The door-hinges whispered and footfalls softly creaked the floorboards above. Dashi could hear the sound of the captain, very slowly, drawing his sword. Presently the feet stopped. Dashi, heard the sound of his own breathing, and tried to breathe more shallowly. The feet began to move again, coming closer. Closer. The hair rose on the back of Dashi's neck. Whoever or whatever was hovering over them, poised, listening – peering down into the dark where they hid.

The trap door shut, with an angry, heavy slam.

For a long time they remained silent in the darkness. Above no one moved. Dashi whispered, "Now what? Do we escape or attack?"

The captain, who had probably been wondering the same, having the question put to him, saw the correct answer, "We attack," he said. And no sooner had he said that, than he had grabbed a rung of the ladder – silently climbing until he was bent up just under the trap door.

Bursting open, the trap door slammed back and out flew the captain like a demon released from hell, his sword swinging wildly out into the darkness. Dashi hurried up the ladder and remained crouched down under the captain's wild swings, pulling his own sword, spying into the darkness for the intruder.

Chill wind blew in from the open door, the outlines of which Dashi could see. A logical mind said, the door was not properly latched and the wind had blown the hatch shut. The footfalls were just the creaking of the buckling floor under the wind. Indeed the door continued to move on its hinges, now slowly shutting.

Presently, by the now closed door, the captain had struck another match and in its flaring light the room reappeared, with its forlorn table, dust, and debris. He turned about in a circle. Dashi offered him the candle to light. The captain did so right away and set it on the table. Without a word he dashed up the narrow stairway.

Dashi backed away from the opening in the floor and dropped the trap door back into place. The floor showed him nothing. No footprints in the muddled dust other than his and the captain's. Creaking of the floor above sent Dashi jerking his head to look at the ceiling.

An assassin?

"Just the captain," he thought calming himself.

There was nothing here, and he stood listening, feeling as perplexed as the captain looked, having now descended the stairs. Still listening to the quiet, Dashi turned his attention to the table and the noisily hissing, guttering candle the captain had placed there. The captain looked into the eyes of the magistrate, who felt a shiver run down his spine.

Dashi said, "I believe you mentioned dinner?"

"The best," said the captain rubbing his belly.

"Thank you," said the chef, who was still eating his meal. As usual, Dashi was already finished.

"You eat like a wolf, My Lord," commented the captain, pouring himself another cup.

Dashi was not listening but staring at nothing. He brought his eyes up from his thoughts. "I am," he said, though if you had asked him why he said that he wouldn't have known. "In strictest confidence," he said, "I do not think I am doing a very good job of being magistrate."

The two other men looked at each other over the oil lamp, across the enormous table that served as middle for the kitchen, whose baskets, strainers, spoons and pots hung in shadow, cleaned and ready for the next day. "My Lord," said his chef, "You treat us much better than she did."

Dashi half smiled, "Anything would be better I suppose," he said. "Assassins stalk me in my own hallways and I'm lashing out at shadows-"

"That is my failing, My Lord," said the captain, "I take full respon-"

"You interrupted captain," said Dashi, and he absently rubbed the stubble of his chin.

"Sorry, My Lord."

Dashi continued to rub his chin. "Oh," he said, realising, "Captain, please feel free to speak. It was the robes talking. I find they do that from time to time"

"My Lord," said the captain.

"As you were saying," said Dashi.

"I was taking responsibility for my inability to keep you safe," he said.

Dashi said, "That's because I want more to my life than safety." Dashi held out his cup to be filled and the captain obliged.

He drank. Maybe he would grow a beard, he thought. Would it make him appear more dangerous? Why were they trying to kill him? Were they still trying? "Poisoners," said Dashi, at last.

"They're cowards," said the captain.

"They only attack from a distance, never directly," said Dashi more precisely.

"My Lord," said the chef, "What about my predecessor?"

Dashi said, "I forced his hand... I think... It seemed personal, his hatred of me."

"Or what you stood for, My Lord," said the captain, "A change of power. A change of *access*."

"Could be," said Dashi, "But they've always used poison. Even the arrow."

The chef's eyebrow went up in curiosity.

"Then why not attack like that again?" asked Dashi.

"My Lord, the tiny arrow was actually a bolt. It came from a crossbow, such as one might hide under one's sleeve. A one shot device such as that – they may not have another. Or..." the captain began, "We assume that the man the guard ran after was the assassin escaping. But that may merely have been a ruse. Such devices have a very short range. The killer may have been standing right there, with you."

"But the drunk got in the way and ruined his shot," said Dashi remembering.

"Unless the drunk, only was a pretending to be a drunk, My Lord," said the captain.

Dashi quipped, "Then he's a terrible shot."

"That's why you use poison," said the chef, and the two looked at him, "...My Lord," he said humbly.

Dashi said, "Every morning I sit in the courtyard. Why not just fire an arrow through my heart?"

"Perhaps they cannot use a bow," suggested the chef.

"Why not send someone who can?" said Dashi.

"Yet they do not send in more..." the captain said thinking, "Because if he were caught?"

"He'd apparently have to kill himself, than give them up," said Dashi, "and they aren't willing to be discovered any more than they've already been."

"Secret," said the captain, "Very secret."

Dashi said, "Maybe because there are no others they trust to hire, they poison," he considered his next words, "because they're frightened."

"Cowards," said the captain again.

Dashi looked at the captain who'd just had the same thought.

"Not professionals," stated the captain, "I've been looking in the wrong places. The attempt, even if it failed–"

"Which it did," said the magistrate.

"–which it did – made me believe it was someone trained," said the captain.

"But they're not trained killers," said Dashi.

"No," said the captain, "Hence the poison."

"It's someone in the palace," said Dashi.

"Someone who knew the last chef," said the chef.

"Most anyone then," said the captain.

Dashi pulled the sheets up and he lay in bed. Then he kicked them off because he felt hot. The room was dark and still. His mind was not.

His belly growled. Formerly he would have gotten up and gone down to get something soothing. He missed the warmth of kitchen and the honest folk there. The ones still there.

Of everything, that returned to his minds, it was the bucket. He oscillated between wondering how – considering them beyond callous – and wondering at the dire circumstance, that despite his being brought up in, he was never privy to.

He and his brother ran, fought – ate when they could – when his brother brought food from somewhere. Dashi knew. He stole it. If not the emperor, if not the magistrate and her court, if not the merchants who could buy up sustenance out of the people's mouths, the rats stole the food.

Any extra mouth had just that much less. And so there was the bucket. And so there was a woman who would buy the unwanted children. Dashi felt sad to his very soul, like being doomed to die in a cage.

He tried to imagine his mother had left them because she had no choice. But could she not have taken them along? Did she even ask anyone to watch over them? Or was it as Dashi remembered: one morning she was gone.

He breathed in a great gulping breath and burned away this worst betrayal. He burned and he burned and he burned. While all around was blackness, inside he was on fire. He would rid himself of her, grieve this, and move on. He had responsibilities to the living. These old feelings were nothing but rocks in his pack.

Although hidden, they kept him from experiencing with the full force of his presence. How could he trust himself now, if parts of him were still stuck grieving the past, colouring his judgements? Good riddance.

And his father too, thought Dashi, though he didn't remember him. And his brother, though it was obvious he owed him a debt of gratitude. Well let the gratitude remain, it was the grievance he burned with a vengeance. And he laughed at the thought of holding on to them. And when he had finished with his family, although quite exhausted, he turned back to the bucket of baby water.

What cries that water knew; what poisoned water had been made. Even if she and her husband hadn't been the ones who'd were the baby eaters, nonetheless they took the babies and children, for the cannibals who in turn paid. And by their poverty, they were sold for a pittance.

So the couple had to increase the supply just to survive themselves, Dashi thought. That was why they sought out the poorest, the farm folk. But even then. That was why she paid the women to give up their children. Things were bad, but they still needed persuading. Or the mothers were unsure, and the lure of money convinced. "I may have sentenced them to death for just that," thought Dashi.

The next thought, the one that kept sleep away from Dashi, was that this meant the one who paid the couple, who in turn paid the women, was wealthy enough to do this.

Even at the low cost fostered by the previous magistrate by keeping the farmers on the edge of starvation, the skulls on the floor of his court room stared back in his imagination – to do this frequently enough to pile up bones in the fields – it still cost a fair amount of money. His coming to power probably significantly raised the price.

Dashi wondered on the use of the power of the office he now held. What suggestion for a law might he create, that hid inside it the seed of an evil? Perhaps all laws were thus. Was the taxation *meant* to produce starvation and therefore unwanted babies for cheap? Defacto.

Did it mean the previous magistrate indulged? Or was it someone close to her that she needed, and whose favour she curried? Or did she even know, but did as advised without knowing the ultimate ends? Dashi imagined a black robe – up ahead in the hallway, turning a corner just as the magistrate approached and finding upon his also turning the corner – had vanished.

It was apparent that even the couple employed as accomplices had no idea of these crimes. Secret, unnatural crimes. The babyeaters dared not reveal to anyone their beastly appetite. And who, with their supply cut off, must be getting hungry.

"To the best of my recollection. I was just making things even," he said.

"Why did you beat the maid then? She's not rich," asked the magistrate.

"She worked for them. She's a turncoat and a snitch. Proof is my being here. I shouldn't have let her go," he explained.

"You mean after you entered their home, and broke her nose with a bat? – I want to make sure you are making your case," said the magistrate.

"That's right. She deserved it, for being a collaborator. Obviously, I was too lenient," he clarified.

"I see," said the magistrate, "You then proceeded to go upstairs and beat the husband unconscious, splitting open the back of his head and blinding him, whereupon you strangled his wife, and then when she regained consciousness, you tied her to the bed and beat and raped her. This is correct?"

"To the best of my recollection," intoned the accused, smiling.

"Clerk can you read again the injuries sustained by the wife during her ordeal after she regained consciousness."

"My Lord," said the clerk, rising from where he was seated upon the bench beside the captain of the guard, "After the woman of the house regaining consciousness, the accused used the aforementioned bat, breaking the woman's jaw, nose, and cheek. She has subsequently lost sight in her left eye. He then used a hot iron from the fire to brand an obscene image upon her forehead." The captain, who was in charge of the prisoner, further clenched his jaw.

"It's payback," said the thief, "This is what they did to us," he sneered, "whip us and brand us. "

"You think about this quite a bit don't you?" enquired the magistrate.

"Only every moment of every day," he said.

"And where've these thoughts brought you?" asked the magistrate.

"That we need justice!" he barked. "I know you understand, Dashi. Your brother hated them more than anyone."

"I know my brother," said Dashi, "Currently we're speaking about you," said the magistrate. "Justice, yes. It's a state of mind you ought to have cultivated. Problem is you kept thinking about it when you already had your answer." Dashi leaned forward. "You cooked it too long. The bottom of your pot got stuck with vengeance, and it burned black."

The astonished accused lunged forward in his chains. "They tortured your brother to death! How can you back them?"

Dashi said, "You will recall, as I do, my brother dealing with errant thieves. Those who threatened exposing our position by their–"

200

"This is the position you're trying to protect! Yegg magistrate! Betraying your own kind for-" the man in chains condemned with unalterable hatred.

"Save for my elder brother, and what protection that afforded me, I was never anyone's *kind*," scoffed Dashi. "Without him I would've certainly been the target of one such as you.

"As it so happens - I am now in just such a position as he - instead of just letting the captain and his guard slaughter you all, which would have been much less effort on his part, I've given you shelter and a new life. Just as my brother had the intelligence to keep all of you from getting picked off one by one. As my brother said what to do, and when to do it - I now I say what to do."

The thief barked out a laugh. "Sitting pretty on your precious throne - you think we won't come for you little snitch?" he snarled.

"You aren't threatening this," seethed the magistrate, indicating the great red carved chair upon which he sat, "You aren't threatening me. You're threatening the safety of all of my brother's men - who under my protection - are now *my* men.

Dashi banged the chair's arm with his hand, "Did you think my making you part of my guard was just a cover? A joke? I was pulling your ass out of the fire! And here, as thanks, to me, you've put it right back in so we can all smell your rank shit - Imbecile!" said the magistrate shaking with fury.

He readjusted his robes. "It saddens me..." he said, "Captain, take this traitor to his fate. Have those from the thieves' forest carry it out. They know the punishment for betrayal."

"Yes, My Lord," said the captain, and two of his guard

took each an arm of the prisoner to remove him from the courtroom.

The man protested, yelling and cursing, turning back his head as he was dragged away, screaming, "If your brother could see you!" howled the rebellious guardsman.

"If he were here," shot Dashi, "he'd stab you in the neck like a pig."

"My Lord, Mistress," said the captain bowing. "The matter is taken care of."

Dashi sighed, "I apologise for foisting this idiot into your guard."

"Don't apologise, My Lord," reminded the mistress, and she played with a square ring upon her finger.

"Yes," said Dashi, reminded. "I am however sorry, this idiot happened to end up in your guard, captain."

"It actually is of benefit," said the captain. "Some people have the discipline to keep themselves in line. Your brother's men were made up of the surly and unruly."

"The dregs," said Dashi.

The captain checked himself from a nod, "-Unless they have a leader who makes them snap to attention, and get in line. Proving their loyalty makes them more cohesive as a unit, and happier with their new identity."

Dashi reflected, tilted his head slightly, "Loyalty, identity, leader..." he said, "I think it's not loyalty, but belonging. It's with each other they see themselves. By action, they prove they belong. It seems..." he conjectured, looking to the mistress, "I wonder if some part of him knew he sacrificed himself for the cohesion of the group? Mistress? - what do you think?"

"What the heart needs, only the heart knows," she said.

Dashi nodded, but she knew he didn't fully understand.

"The heart is a bird," he said, and looked heavenward at the painted birds. "Even if it has what it needs, if you put in a closed cage, it wants to flee. Leave the cage door open and it will stay."

The mistress said, "You have to choose to stay. If you give a bird what it needs, it will stay for a time, and then leave."

"Flighty," said the captain.

"Arrows find me everywhere in my life," Dashi said, in mock pain. "I was just telling her of our theory that the poisoners are amateurs. Tell the captain what you think."

"Of course they're amateurs," said the mistress. "I knew that from the moment the chef attacked us," she said, "He put enough poison in that pig to kill everyone in the palace. Whatever supply he had, he must have just dumped the whole thing in. I can't imagine he was following orders. But his death must have also served the function of keeping the others in line."

"We're redundant," said the captain to the magistrate.

"Just your thinking," said the mistress, "But maintain your practice."

Dashi suppressed the urge to roll his eyes.

"Who is leader then, mistress?" asked the captain.

The mistress said, "Something is cooking. Soon the smell will reveal the dish."

The last of the winter food stores dwindled in the granary - the ebbing of the previous year's harvest. The city ate the last of the last. But spring, although cool this year, had already given a modicum of greens – some peas, some cabbages. It was enough. With the warmer weather right around the corner, the undercurrent of the main crops began to flow. And the spring-moon rose high, and wide and beautiful, bright.

Spring, when the minds' thoughts turned to mischief. Perhaps it was the scented air, that brought forth exuberance. Perhaps they were just now realising the relief they felt, having an oppressor thrown off. Whatever it was, everyone seemed to be getting into everyone else's business.

No matter where one went, there were earnest and animated discussions, if not outright squabbles. The air was full of babble. Soon, there were contentions. They pontificated for the right way. They argued the good. All hubbub and self-righteousness, because the stakes were just that low.

Returning from his morning patrol the captain reported to the magistrate. Dashi and his guard went outside the palace to look at the writing on the outer palace wall.

The captain held up his chin, "It says 'Magistrate of the mud,' My Lord."

"Right on my wall... Cheeky," said Dashi, in good humour.

"We will station guards outside to stop this from happening again," the captain said.

But Dashi said, "No. They've given me a better idea."

When Dashi told the mistress of his orders to make a wall for the people to write upon, she smiled quietly, and nodded. This, he assumed, meant she approved.

Black message gone, two weeks later the white of the writing wall mud was dry. The mistress asked if she could be the first to write upon it. The magistrate of course granted this and she gathered some special materials he'd not seen her use and she went to the wall and right in its centre she painted a large beautiful scene of mystic mountains with a gnarled ancient pine tree, and a river; and in the river stood a black crane, and there seemed a deer hidden in a grove of bamboo – it all seemed to appear by magic, she painted it so quickly, as if she had left normal time and moved through a different one. Finally finished, she drew out a small brush and wrote: 'Among a thousand sorrows, I stand alone.'

Pleased it was easy enough for him to read, Dashi assumed it was a line from a poem he did not know. A sombre feeling appeared in his heart, which coalesced into thoughts of his poisoned young friend.

The mistress finished painting, retired, but the magistrate attended, watching, hands on his hips. People bowed to him as they paraded past one by one to see. Then they just stood there. They gathered. They marvelled at her writing. More than one person pausing to look at her painting, for reasons unknown to them, wept a tear.

Dashi was sure it would please the mistress to know.

The mistress painted. She painted a bird. Her brush

moved of itself.

When she had finished she said, "The minds accept the brush as their tool. It is brought in, via the minds of the body."

"Why that brush?" Dashi asked, looking at all the others hanging on the rack.

She looked at it, "It was chosen because it was apt. It is as language. As in the choice of words, it expresses the minds' general intents most appositely."

"A tool is a language, you mean," he said.

"Yes. An inappropriate tool makes for poor language. It hacks the world apart rather than letting you express the shapes you intend. That is why there are so many minds."

"How many?" tried Dashi again.

"Indeed," she said.

"Indeed," he repeated, "Then if beauty is a mind, a language, so it is a tool. It inspires the people to freedom, and wholeness. Can the tool be used for ill as well?" he asked.

"Each mind has its layers of maturity, it's the culmination by which we name them. Beauty mind, it has its immaturity – vanity. The reason that despots everywhere surround themselves with beauty is to honour themselves. To prop up their mere humanness with glitter."

"Why do artists make things for them, then?" he asked

"Most don't," she said, "The truest go live in the forests. For those artists who stay, they allow tyrants to flatter themselves, and get on with making. In truth artists create for the glory of no mere ruler but for that which moves their hand to art in the first place. The merest presence of the dialects of beauty emphasise the order rulers crave, while simultaneously freeing the mind from accepting their arbitrary rules."

"Art undermines authority by contrast," said Dashi, understanding.

"This is why when a dynasty changes, the artists are the first to be executed," she said, "But it does no good. True artists all serve higher being. Their art will continue. Their legacy will be passed from hand to hand. To the hand that is impelled to risk, that is, called to make, even a dead hand will be clasped. They will revive the forbidden masters.

"What is truly dire though, is when bureaucrats who understand this are in charge. They find intellectuals who will banish art all together by clever argument. The transcendent replaced, by what they are capable of – the merely intellectual."

"To take the place of artists in the culture?" asked Dashi.

"Not just there. They apply their theories everywhere. If an empire is in need of soldiers, they will explain how to condition growing youth in ugliness and deprivation – to create surroundings without visual succour. Make sure to remove all beauty, all nature, all art. By starving essential nature, why wouldn't they embrace offers of fame and power and money? That way, what motive could they have to not do as you ask? That way what higher nature inside them is lost should they kill another?"

"These intellectuals, they do this because they want power?" said Dashi.

"Not usually," said the mistress, "They just want to see if their theories work. It's the bureaucrats that desire control."

"That's even worse," he said, and paused, thinking about being so stuck.

The mistress looked up from dabbing her brush. "Those who would destroy beauty are those most in need of it.

Artists seem unimportant, but ironically, when you remove higher vision to secure your rule, the space is filled by low level obscenity that surely dissolves any ability to rule.

"Beauty however, does not itself make for maturity. A beautiful city will certainly house a people who don't want war to take place there. They think the works of beauty give them some unearned identity. They are smug.

"If those who create the beauty are merely thought of as conduits for the people's vainglory, they'll just prefer wars that are fought *over there*. Where it is ugly. Ugly because other places are meaningless. Because they themselves are not there to bestow it any meaning.

"And when the territory is conquered, after the looting, any unique beauty remaining will be pasted over with mundane order to normalise passivity. To remove the nature from the people. To enrage local artists to identify themselves, in order to be dispatched. Those biddable to justification, will be given the whip."

"It's a jaundiced view of humanity," said Dashi.

"Reality is often at the point of a sword," she said, and executed a deft stroke.

"So my palace should be without art, then," said Dashi.

She dipped the brush. "Art is borrowed from the artist. Although it points toward something greater, it can only resonate what's inside you – just as the robes you wear present formal powers, but to be a leader you must find that within. Your surroundings are a relationship to the world, the context by which your minds express.

"Some things are made by innumerable hands. Some by just one. Some by no hand at all. What does any of it have to do with you? You sleep in a bed made by others, and live in a palace built by others, surrounded by walls built by others, hung with paintings created by others. What kinds of tools are these? Will they serve your purpose?

"If what flows through the maker is not simply of the maker, but of greater being, then so too your experience of what is made from that union. When you behold a beautiful cloud you sign your name in the air with your joy.

"One's identity of the teenage years is just for socialisation. The true identity is the whole of you. Which is the whole of everything, just from your point of view."

"Ah, so you can see what your part in the whole is," concluded Dashi.

The mistress picked her brush off the paper, "There are no parts in a whole," she said. "Like talking about not-things is convenient as a shorthand, but error prone if you pursue it as a line of thought – what we call a part actually contains the whole to some degree. Otherwise it wouldn't be whole, would it?" she said, and added her signature in a flourish.

At first Dashi thought the idea of making a writing wall was a good one. Then when no one wrote anything he thought it was foolish. Then after a time, some people began drawing on the wall. And soon after more elaborate drawings. Then the writing began.

Heartfelt writing from people who had never been asked. Then arguing appeared and spread out, threatening to engulf the wall. Until the artists reappeared, drawing funny pictures, taunting the debaters. From then on it was wave upon wave of change, tides breaking upon the wall – foaming, crashing and receding, ebbing and flowing.

And Dashi gave up trying to decide if the idea were good or bad.

"All over my wall," said Dashi, "I wondered what the enemy would write, and now we know."

"No enemy," she said.

"Fine, not my enemy. How can I defeat a foe that won't ever face me?" said Dashi frustrated.

"Foe is just another word for enemy," she said.

"Indirect opposition?" suggested Dashi, "spreaders of rumour, and offal, perhaps?"

The mistress made an ever so slightly sour face. She paused looking down and within.

"You're going to tell me a parable? Aren't you," said Dashi.

The mistress merely met his eyes.

Dashi said, "Please mistress, couldn't we just review what is actually happening, here and now?"

"Fine," the mistress said, "Now, in your position, and as you now are realising, a kind of secret order exists, they are unknown, invisible, but everywhere. They go everywhere, and they organise. A secret order that wants to rule the world.

"They consider themselves the true power, and leaders are just there as a show, as a target for public anger, but it is they who decide the fate of civilization. No matter how strong the tyrant, it is they who pull the strings. Indeed tyrants, being fools, are preferred and therefore elevated."

"The organisation is made up of the kind of person whose nature has certain minds emphasised – minds that make them suited to organising. Therefore they are present in every institution of society. The people who run the institution are a certain kind of people. And it is their opinion that those are the ones that matter, versus not." And she folded her arms for emphasis. "The bureaucrats," she said, nodding gravely.

"Them?" scoffed Dashi, "They're just there to follow my orders,' he said.

The mistress smiled and sighed. "And do they? Who follows who? Does being magistrate not come with prescribed etiquette? You as the ruler of this town – you have a crown of sorts, and a special throne. Those are just symbols of the office, not you. Why conform to expectations?"

"Ah, but why does the magistrate follow expectations?" he said, "He follows a procedure for the fairness of the court."

"He'd like to think so," she said. "But it is because he is tamed."

"Who by?" he said, annoyed.

"The culture around him," she said.

"Which is?" he said.

"Created by bureaucrats," she said, "Civilization is domestication. And there is good and bad to that. Civilization is a trance. Culture is a story that everyone knows so well, they don't even see it anymore. It is just how things are. That is when it works the best. It is tacitly agreed upon."

"Defacto," he said.

"Just like the minds, indeed because of them, a society only reflects the level of the minds of its people. The self-reliant hunter becomes a warrior with a code. The mystic on the mountain becomes the head of a temple. A leader of hearts becomes a lineage of emperors. The poet becomes a judge in a system of law."

"Each of these is reinforced by repetition. By expectation. Each is transformed from inside-out to outside-in. True good is transformed from a joy to a job. Each one with ceremonies, licenses, examinations, and tests – and administered by...?" she asked.

"Deception," said Dashi.

"Bureaucrats know that one can lead people around by the nose if you create the right stories. Compartmentalised self-serving stories, that only fit together into the larger story of domesticated consciousness. They understand how to lie to achieve their ends. What they do not understand is that they are not as clever as they believe, and that in lying they expose their soft underbelly. Because they do not understand human beings have a nature, and that nature cannot be led about forever."

"The oppressed people will rise up?" said Dashi.

"The oppressed people will excrete the poison from their souls into the world. Most won't even know they are doing it. Unhappy, they'll obsessively gnaw, like mice, at every foundation, until nothing works."

"I know how they feel," said Dashi, "If I could chew off my leg to escape hearing another report I would."

She pursed her lips. "Society becomes unmanageable because it is managed, where it needs to be led – something no bureaucrat understands. It is at those junctions of failure that those who possess leadership facilities can wrest control. However, if they do not comprehend the danger that the obliging bureaucrat represents, they will allow them to return. Which they do not. So the cycle tends to repeat every few generations."

"What makes them so dangerous?"

"Individually, nothing," she said, "By themselves they

are of no more threat than any other halfwit – what makes them exceptional is the way they organise."

"Aren't the minds supposed to come to organisation? Isn't this just an external form of that?" said Dashi.

"One of them, absolutely," said the mistress, "but the level they serve is immature. Armies kill, pillage and plunder, and are also organised. It's not so much that they work together in tandem – but they are mutually non-aggressive. Unless they stand in the way."

"In the way of what?" he asked.

"To rule the world, as usual," said the mistress. "Unlike the despot, they are only concerned that their side wins. Their way. Their principles. Not understanding that anybody's way at the level of principle will never work. There will be cracks you can neither see nor fix. It is only a matter of time before the pressures exerted by the rulers will cause them to break their own principles. That is the beginning of the end."

"Because they don't really believe their own principles." said Dashi.

"Oh they believe. But they do not comprehend there is more to them than ideas in their heads. Indeed they refuse it. They can stand neither the body, and its ultimate death, nor the inspiration that transforms that fear by faith. A human is, by their definition, fragmented. It lacks a wholeness, or as I say, beauty."

"They've chosen to be fractured then," said Dashi.

"They've chosen a future," said the mistress, "fracturing is the result of what they have chosen."

Dashi said, "They didn't choose to fracture, but chose something that has fractured them."

"They imagined freedom to be in the future," she said, "So they toil towards this goal. But by the time things appear in the moment they may have sought, they merely execute them by rote," she said, "Having broken themselves from their own immediate experiencing."

"They've made themselves predictable," he said.

"Indeed," she replied. "Once the arrow leaves your hands can you help yourself? Isn't it just how you are? How you have altered yourself to be? To choose otherwise is a trajectory of alteration not an immediate act of choice. This is why a wise ruler needs to be compassionate for the difficult situation that people get themselves into, but also recognise the grim rigidity of their choices."

"So it is up to the wise ruler to help them see the right way," said Dashi, realising the trap too late.

"Why would they want that?" she said, "Do you think some wise words will effect the ambitions of yes-men, blood-suckers and operators? If you are soft then the system is overwhelmed by opportunists. Make it strict and opportunists invade the system itself.

"Learn from the mistakes of your master. He became convinced that being lenient and making benevolent laws in this northern frontier town of banished cast offs and drug-addled, bitter formerly-powerful, would bring them around. These spoiled entitled children! Instead things fell into chaos and the replacement magistrate reintroduced order under their boot.

"Those who would overstep boundaries in their bid for power are only stopped by a greater power willing to overstep boundaries. We are not speaking of those who keep fairness as an option. They already test you every day, to see if you will bend.

If through your actions you make the city uncontrollable, you create the conditions for another tyrant to be heralded by the people – who merely go where they can best achieve *their* ends. Each mind has its desire - fractured, stuck minds included," she said, in a tone of leading him on.

"Ah," he said, "But... as long as the majority wanted wholeness things would work."

"How much time your master and I have devoted just to you Dashi - and your master believes *you* have potential," she said fiddling with her square ring.

Dashi replied, "Well, we'll all have to - for each other. Isn't that how what civilization we have came about?"

"Once-" she said, and Dashi sighed. "There were four bulls who pastured together for a long time. They would swat the flies off each other with their tails. Then would take turns standing up wind or blocking the blazing sun, when one of them wanted to lie on the ground to rest. They huddled together in the winter for warmth. And offered space under the small tree that shielded them from most of the winter's rain.

"Unknown to them a lioness watched them. She would lie hiding in the tall grass. She wanted to eat one of them, but she was afraid to attack while they were with each other. When in the past she'd tried to attack them, the fast friends turned their tails to one another, so that whichever way she approached she was met by sharp horns.

"The lioness therefore considered long how best to break their friendship. They are big, she thought, but not very smart. So one by one, she snuck as close as she could and whispered to each, 'They are secretly finding the best grass and keeping it for themselves, how greedy,' and 'There's taller greener grass all for you to be found just on the other side of the pasture.'

"Pretty soon the bulls began to quarrel. And soon after that they left each other's company to look for taller grass in the separate corners of the field.

"That is how the clever lioness ate them one by one without fear - feasting until all four were gone and their carcasses made the grass grow taller and greener."

"Meaning? said Dashi.

"That is how they defeat us," she said, "and also how we defeat them."

Dashi sat day after day in that red chair. But instead of despising the boredom of it, he chose to go into the minds of the accusers and accused.

"In what layer, of what mind, are they getting stuck?" he asked himself. How could he suggest a verdict that might raise their awareness? As the mistress had said to him: it is the fall of our civilization that the people stay as children for their entire lives. The only way out is to give them back their minds. He wondered how interaction with him might ameliorate a piece of their puzzle.

He saw the same usual cases. People stole things from under each other's noses. Nothing left unattended was there for long. Those who did the taking felt others had it better. They justified they were only getting their fair share. Their piece of the cake.

At first he thought this was for survival. But many of the thieves, Dashi was surprised to find, were wealthier than those from which they stole. Often taking something worth very little, as if pretending they didn't have as much. He found a strange kind of envious, resentful, jealousy percolating within the city.

Over and over what Dashi really saw was that even people's good intentions were foiled by an inability to rise to their own maturity. And they knew it. Haunted by the ghost of their wiser character, they stole as retaliation against themselves.

Soon Dashi was fascinated. Often he couldn't wait to return to court to see what kind of case came before him. The practical trials of living: mouths to feed, things to attain, morality, truth, kindness and bravery, couldn't compete with aggrandisement, prestige, status, and adolescent bids for sympathy.

Manipulation and fraud for the covert, fighting and mugging for the extraverted. In time Dashi related this to what the master had said about the use of creative mind to get something for nothing. Dashi saw how you could sway people with offers of easy-to-come-by-wealth. That is, other people's wealth. Dashi considered whether this wasn't the basis for invading armies.

Importantly he realised, it wasn't that people were stupid. It was that they didn't believe they could do, and create, what they needed. So in their immaturity, they'd give themselves permission to have to take it. It became a necessity, a justified reason, an imperative – a should.

Hence invading armies. Give the people an enemy and they will strive for being the best at hatred, or for the extraction of their enemy's undeserved wealth. The ready justification for taking from some tribe worthy of spite, and therefore not worthy of having material wealth, was convenient. And if someone of authority said they could, then that was even better. An authority legitimised by them – someone who promised free goods.

Whether in secret or openly, obeying government was only done because it was in the people's own interest. Follow whoever there is to follow, and make up excuses for why as you go. When they said one must obey, it was justified as for one's own good – this appeal to mock goodness only serving to reveal they'd no real discernment. That they had desires to fulfill was a given. That they cared not for any but themselves was a recipe for mayhem. And that like immature leaders, immature followers presented exactly the same hazards.

When not in court, when not invested in the documents of government, or the lessons of poetry, the delights of soup or the frustration of evasive sleep, Dashi sat outside the palace. The firebreath had left him feeling strangely yearning. For what? – he did not know. So now the act of sitting was peppered with endless, tiresome questions of himself. Therefore Dashi's minds thought:

"Consider, what is the problem?"

They all need to grow up!

"Is that the real problem? What do I even want to happen? And how would I know it had happened if it did?"

They need to stop doing what keeps them from growing up.

"Which is?"

If they were adults – they'd be able to talk about things instead of attacking each other.

Ahh...

"Who would that benefit?"

Everyone.

Everyone?

"Who would it hurt?"

Anyone who makes wealth off others' immaturity.

Them.

"What would they do to counter my plan?"

By stirring up immaturity.

Those who remain stuck.

Induce disorder.

Don't forget those who oppose what we represent.
"Which is?"
Power
"Authority you mean?"
Are you their superior?
A target for resentment.
Is that the real problem?

The mistress had effectively sequestered him from the crows, directly. That was the good part. The bad was when he wasn't in court, or learning to read court documents, he was pestered by bureaucratic notes and missives.

Dashi quashed a spontaneous effort by the crows to issue licenses to write on the wall. They also petitioned to do inspections. Dashi countered he already had the guard to do this. They counter-countered that the guard couldn't possibly be expected to make decisions on so delicate a matter. Dashi replied that the guards sent all messages to the mistress and they could take it up with her.

Usually the conversation would end at her formidable mention. Occasionally she would need to consider the request, and so discuss it with him. Such as when he tried to move a farmer's market within the walls of the city. The functionaries suggested it was unhygienic. Dashi replied that people threw their waste water out their windows, which he'd asked them to deal with, and that there were rats aplenty. But those are city rats, they replied, side-stepping the night-soil issue entirely. At this point Dashi referred them to the mistress.

Undaunted, they pressed on with their concern of having field workers inside the city walls. Dashi began to feel this was not about rats at all. Finally, after several long and wearisome exchanges, Dashi outright ordered them to put the market in the town.

They capitulated, but weeks passed and still no market appeared. Dashi sent a runner with a note through the mistress to ask what the delay was. The response was that there was no delay and they were working as hard and fast as they could to plan for the new market. They added, uncharacteristically, thought Dashi, that they were indeed excited about its prospects. Further weeks past and some lumber was piled in the square nearest the north gate, where outside the farmers had set up.

It was when a drawing came, detailing the wall that would enclose the market, that Dashi became angry, telling them to set it up today. Another note came reporting that all the lumber had been stolen. Dashi shot back they could use old boxes if they had to. A note returned suggesting that would be unhygienic.

"We could hold it for time, but the garrison isn't manned as it once was, even counting the new men. Not to mention the bullet issue," said the captain to the mistress, as Dashi came in.

"We'll discuss this later captain, you're dismissed," she said.

And he departed with a "My Lord," as he passed Dashi.

One day, after a hot dry spell, there came lightning. And then quickly came the rains. It was only the next day when sun shone again the farmers found the wide scorch mark on the edge of the grain field, by the ditch.

When the crops came in it was a miracle. Even though much of the rice went south to the capitals there was still abundance. At market the magistrate, with his nervous guard in tow, walked and chatted with the people amidst the stands of vegetables and fruit - in the town! Their smiles meant everything to Dashi.

"Well done," said the master who appeared at Dashi's left shoulder, making the guards jump. Dashi put up his hands to stop them from tackling his teacher.

"It wasn't my doing," said Dashi, "just good luck, and good weather."

"Actually it is," said the master, "You ordered the removal of all the interfering officials. Thus I could help the farmers, which is what I've been doing, and why I haven't been around."

"Does this mean you will be appearing more frequently?" asked Dashi smiling, "I have some questions."

"When don't you have questions... My Lord," said the master.

"I have some rather pressing ones," said the magistrate.

"Ask my new wife," he said.

"Did you marry?" asked Dashi.

"Finally," said the master, "A couple months past."

"You didn't want me to preside?" asked Dashi, saddened.

"At this point- all that ceremony- I just asked her," said the master, "That's good enough for us."

"I rejoice in your good fortune," said Dashi.

The master acknowledged the blessing. "Now about

your questions. I still have work to do with the farmers. As I have indicated, ask her."

"But she is too smart for me to understand," said Dashi, and then thought of what he'd just said, "Not that I mean that you're not as smart, master."

The master said nothing. "She is very educated," he said at last, examining a radish, "And she has a complex mind. It's a difficulty for her, but also a source of pleasure. Thus she remains here painting and I upon the hill." The master smiled. "What question is pressing you?"

"I want to know about the poison," said Dashi quietly.

"That, she knows," said the master, "I assume you think it will lead you to those who are responsible for the murder of your food taster."

"Yes," said Dashi.

"It's a rat poison," said the master, "It is easily available."

"That's too bad," said Dashi.

"It is odd, actually," said the master.

"Why odd?" asked Dashi keeping up.

"Because in the palace, those who might wish you dead should have access to better poisons. Why choose such a common one?" asked the master.

Dashi joked, "Maybe they're cheap. Or think I'm a rat."

The master regarded Dashi, "Clever," he said finally, and then pointing, "Look over there!"

Dashi turned his head. But there was nothing unusual he could see. "Master what are you pointing at?" Dashi asked looking back to the empty place where the master had stood.

Dashi looked around and sighed.

"I'm behind you," said the master.

Dashi turned to his left, but no one was there.

"You have a habit of turning left," said the master.

Dashi turned right and there was the master smiling, leaning upon his staff.

He said, "One does not become a poisoner because one has means of force. It is exactly because they are in a weak position they use these means. Further, you cannot see them because they see you. Knowing where you are looking, they simply slip behind you. Always at your back, where you are most vulnerable, making their relative position more even."

"I can't always be looking over my shoulders," said Dashi, "Living like that would make me feel paranoid."

To which the master replied, "Those who would have power would have targets painted on their backs."

The warm light reflected off the grey paving stones, dully illuminating even the deepest shadows thrown into the alley by buildings in the lee of the sun. While the hat served to shield the magistrate from the glare above, his black coat was stifling with so many layers, even of cool silk. But Dashi walked through the town, four guards trudging behind him in the heat.

"Now the crops are in," thought Dashi, "The taxes have been collected, and they'll have noticed they're reduced. Now we will see how the people feel."

But everywhere he saw sullen faces. Their burden lifted, if it had been lifted, imperceptibly.

"You," said the magistrate to a man pulling cart of pots and pans for sale.

The man stopped, and shielded his eyes against the sun, "My Lord?"

"Are you happy?" asked Dashi.

"Happy, My Lord?" said the man in such a way Dashi thought he was wondering if this was a trick.

"Too general... Are conditions better for you, now?" he asked.

The man thought a moment and said, "Everything is fine."

The magistrate looked at him. "And your taxes?"

"Paid in full, My Lord, on time," he said.

"The amount," prompted Dashi.

"A fine amount," said the man in the street.

"Are you not surprised?" asked Dashi annoyed that this man hadn't even noticed. Perhaps this was not something people cared about.

"No surprise, My Lord. Same as last year," and he re-adjusted his hands on the cart handle to balance.

"Less," said the magistrate.

"Less?" asked the working man.

"It should be less. Less taxes," said Dashi, perturbed. Again the man looked at the magistrate as if this might be a trick. Dashi therefore added, "Please speak freely. I give you assurance that I will take no action..." The man's eyes darted to the guards. "Nor my guard," Dashi added.

The man nodded slowly, "That would be nice," he said. And that was all he would say.

"They told you," stated the mistress, brush tracing over paper.

"They didn't tell me," avowed Dashi.

The mistress looked quizzical. "I will look into it, and if action is necessary we will undertake it. However, they report that they told you," she said indicating some official papers on a distant table.

"But they didn't," said Dashi.

The mistress raised her brush. The granddaughter picked up that painting, replacing it with a new piece of paper, "Maybe they showed you something in writing," she suggested, immediately regretting saying it, as it made Dashi glance darkly at her.

"I realise that I do not have any way to know anything of what is going on," said Dashi. "I give orders, but are they followed? Are they changed? Now perhaps there are false documents saying what I was told – that I was told. Are there papers saying I have done things I have not done?

"You ask me if they showed me something but I did not know what it said. I would remember that also. I don't need the librarian's book. Nothing of the sort has happened."

"What book?" asked the mistress, and, "You've been to the library?"

"Yes," said Dashi, "I was at the library. I was exploring," he explained.

"I do not mean offence, My Lord," said the mistress, "What book was this that the librarian mentioned?"

"It was a book on how to remember things. Something I don't require," said Dashi.

The mistress and her granddaughter looked at each other. The mistress raised her eyebrows, looked at the granddaughter and glanced towards the door. The granddaughter bowed and left immediately.

"Is it important? - the book," asked Dashi.

"I don't know, My Lord," said the mistress adjusting the paper herself. "Every bureaucrat is trained to remember, aside from having that aptitude to begin with, needing it to survive. There is no one here who can read the book, that would need to read the book. This is not a book of remembering. Therefore something is being hidden."

"Something in the book," said Dashi.

The mistress said, "Perhaps. Or just the book itself."

"In a library? It is hidden in plain sight, then," said Dashi.

"They may have come across it, or had reason to investigate it. But that doesn't mean whoever took it knows what was hidden there," she said.

"I think there is a more obvious reason to hide it. If a book contains something... better that the blind librarian is caught with it," he said.

"I fear this may be correct," said the mistress, "But all we know is that the book has been retrieved. What we want to know is what was inside? "

"What if the book is to help other people to remember?" suggested Dashi.

The mistress nodded, "Or forget. It makes things simpler."

"A map," said Dashi.

"Just so!" said the mistress.

"To a lost gold mine," conjectured Dashi.

The mistress said, "That kind of a map you keep with you even as you slumber. This is one that you fear being found in your possession. Meaning what it tells you, if you have any sense, you fear."

"What could that be?" asked Dashi.

"Some books purport to tell how to raise spirits, demons and the dead," she said.

Dashi said, "Do you think that–"

"Don't be absurd... My Lord. Those are ideas that people will act upon, but there are a thousand such books. One of my minds is using that image as a way of telling me what to look for. But now I must interpret. A book as dangerous, that raises something thought dead..." she mused.

"Ah, or makes you dead," said Dashi, catching on.

"A poison," she said, nodding.

Dashi said, "One certainly would not want to be caught with a recipe book of poisons in my palace."

"Every medicine book is a recipe book of poisons, My Lord. I have many. It depends only on dosage. No," said the mistress, "that may be why they went looking. But I doubt they understand what they've found. I believe it is the book itself that is the poison."

It was not too long after that the granddaughter returned, "The librarian says it was taken out by someone in the treasury. And something curious," she said, "He said it was a new book."

"New? why is that–" asked Dashi.

"There are no new books in that library, My Lord," said the mistress.

The granddaughter replied, "Except this one."

"When did it arrive?" asked Dashi.

She said, "Five years ago."

"Hardly new," said Dashi.

"In comparison," said the mistress, "very new."

"The question is why the interest now?" said Dashi.

"The question is why he answered our question," she said.

When the mistress had confirmed the taxes were not being reduced as ordered, "Come," she said, "We cross the river."

"What river?" asked Dashi taking her proffered arm.

"The one that runs under the palace." And to his look of incredulity. "Have you never wondered why, here, at the end of the empire, at the end of the road, there is a palace within in a walled city?"

Dashi hadn't truly, but now that she mentioned it, it did seem a curious fact. "All right," he said at last, "Why is there a city here?"

"Gold," said the mistress. "They found gold. A lot of it. Long ago, the mountains had many mines, and they teemed with men like ants. So much gold, it was necessary to garrison an army to protect the mines, so that was built first. To keep the men, stores were built, and water they drew from the river.

"A treasury was built on the other side of the river from the garrison. Now to defend the treasury against invading armies – a wall was placed around the treasury. The administration required lodging, and the area was important enough to warrant an emperor's magistrate, so a palace was built with its own wall around the garrison, the treasury, the stores and the palace.

All on the small hill before the golden mountain, they brought nobles and servants, and rank. And the great houses were built by princes requiring lodgings from which they could oversee and defend their mines, mostly from all the other princes, but as well from the northern tribes. So about the whole city they built yet a final great wall.

The golden princes, traded with far kingdoms, furs and cloth, steel and horses, wine and exotic delights. These poured in and gold poured out: north and west and east, and eventually, after many wars to the south to the emperor. "

"And then?" asked Dashi.

"Then one day the gold ran out. Somewhere became nowhere and was no longer important," she said. "The trading routes stopped coming. The princes, that were left after the wars, the nobles, and their servants relinquished their holdings. The imperial buildings remained, a few unimportant bureaucrats left here and there, but this was an outpost to empty wilderness. For almost a century it sat mostly abandoned, the palace still off limits of course, but all the great houses filled with rough men from beyond the roads. Fur trappers and their many dogs inhabited the halls of nobility. I suspect doing what came naturally to them wherever it seemed most convenient.

"Eventually they brought their women and children. But it never left the grip of the empire, so it became, after a time, a place to send people the powerful wanted to have vanish. The vanished and banished from one court or another, often generationally so, brought what wealth they could carry, reclaimed the flea infested dog houses, and immediately proclaimed each other as the city's nobility."

"And the river?" he asked.

"The river too vanished." She dipped her brush in water and drew upon the flat stone on her table. "Forgotten. The river everyone knows about, comes down from the mountain, onto the upper finger of the valley, moves south past the fields and west around the city wall to Long Pool, before it heads south over Beginning Inch Waterfall," she smiled, "A smaller tributary, just before the falls, divides at a rock, on which the wall now sits. It takes a small detour before rejoining the falls to the west. It was on this rocky island that the garrison was first built, as the river surrounding it made for a moat.

"Long ago, when the river was open to the air, it ran between the magistrate's court with the army garrison behind that on one side, where the law and army were kept – and the other wing, that of the emperor's treasurer, where the gold was kept. This separation was by design.

"After a mysterious fire that burned everything except the garrison, the palaces were rebuilt, and the palace wall was extended to surround them, the river was eventually covered from the sight of day. The outer wall of the city being created later. But before that, in-between the two palaces, part of the river was crossed by way of a covered bridge. Although the river now lies beneath the ground, that is still the only way into the treasury from the palace of the magistrate."

"How do they get their food in?" asked Dashi.

"Through the door to the kitchens," she explained, "but that's surrounded by high walls."

"That doesn't sound very hard to breach. Over the wall and just go in through the kitchen door?" he said.

"If you can get across the second wall," she said.

"Another one?" he said.

"Yes, with archers," she said, "You'll find the kitchen doors behind the portcullis, and through the tunnel, also with archers."

"I was thinking I'd have to ask the librarian for a map, but here you have made me one," said Dashi.

"So when I say, we are crossing the river, I mean that we are to visit the treasurer who has not implemented your reduction of taxes."

"I understand," said Dashi.

"What you *need to understand* is that although you can increase or decrease your own levy, imperial taxes are levied by the emperor, administered by treasurers and collected by magistrates. You are the law and in this you rule. However in the treasury, the treasurer reigns. He will offer you wine but under no circumstance should you accept."

"Why not?" asked Dashi, "Is it poisoned?"

"Just don't drink it," she said, "I call him the golden caterpillar. I'll explain later."

They left her quarters, and walked the corridors Dashi knew, but then passed through a pair of large doors he'd never taken and walked down a long corridor. "Do you think he has the book?" he asked the mistress.

"Potentially," she evaded, "My granddaughter found out something from the librarian. Or I should say, she discerned when visiting the librarian."

"What's that?" asked Dashi, "He's not blind?" he guessed.

"No, he's blind. I never met the man myself, but he uses a fragrance. Did you notice it?" she asked.

"Woody," said Dashi, "...and sweet."

"I had her walk me by his door. It's a distinctly warm scent. It's an aphrodisiac."

"That doesn't surprise me," said Dashi.

"Really?" said the mistress.

"He lewdly informed me he had picture books that–"

"I understand. Thank you, My Lord," she said.

The magistrate tilted his hat and asked, "Why are you thanking me?" At the same time he noticed the floor had changed beneath them to a polished wide and dark wood.

"Because you have told me something important," she said. "How does a blind man know what is in picture books?"

Dashi thought, and said, "How does he know what is in any of the books? Someone must describe them to him."

She said, "But his interest in the picture books was more *personal*, you would say?"

"Rather apparently," said Dashi, looking ahead to a pair of grey-black double doors at the end of the corridor, flanked by guards, not in palace dress.

"Librarians merely memorise a description of what is in all the books. Hardly anything to become excited about. You will have noted his professional disinterest in their contents."

"Ind... Yes, yes I did," said Dashi, glancing up at the slit that ran along near the ceiling.

She paused. "So as you say someone is describing the books to him. Rather explicitly. Who do you think that is?" she asked.

"I have no idea, do you?" he asked in return.

"Someone with access to beautiful and expensive things, perfumes, who needs favour from a blind librarian" she said as they approached the doors. "Allow me to speak for you, My Lord."

The guards looked ahead, their unmoving gaze, unwavering. Still as statues. The mistress stepped forward and removed a tiny golden key from its place hanging on the door and put it in an equally tiny keyhole. Immediately the doors began to move. Albeit slowly, and only after it had well opened did he realise why: the door was made of iron, like the palace gates, and as thick as Dashi's forearm. Once fully opened, two inner guards moved to stand facing each other on the golden carpet, which continued down a red and gold corridor as long as the one they had just left.

"The golden key can open any gate," she said, as the mistress and the magistrate entered to see the treasurer.

"Or a couple pieces of good stiff wire," said Dashi, as they entered the gilded passage. Dashi noticed between each red post, upon which were embossed golden florets, there were long silk paintings, themselves hung on golden backgrounds, draped from red tiled floor to carved decorative ceiling, where the golden embellishments continued. Dashi could see the mistress's eyes furtively dart to the paintings which looked quite ancient.

"Are they any good?" asked Dashi.

"They're copies. Ostentatious counterfeits," she replied, rolling her eyes, and, added with a snide smile, "No doubt, bought as originals."

Dashi looked around him at the depictions of peacocks and dragons, pine trees and chrysanthemums, and down the hall at the great gold doors at the end.

Dashi looked at the two standing guard at the door, whose uniforms were so embroidered with golden thread Dashi wondered if they could even move in them. Clearly no one had attempted to steal what was locked in the treasury vaults for hundreds of years.

"If all the gold is gone from the mines, what's in the treasury?" asked Dashi as they slow walked forward.

"Gold," she answered.

"I don't–"

"As the banished nobles arrived, the magistrates taxed their gold at a rate higher than even the emperor. Where else could they go? What else could they do? After many years some trade reopened. In fact the descendants of the first nobles, became quite adept as mercenaries. In peace time, merchants of grain, and other rare items," she said, "You might think with money they would leave this place, but given its location, it provides a surprisingly inaccessible refuge. Over the centuries several wars have raged, some for a decade, but never having touched this valley."

"It provides a good hideout for thieves," said Dashi.

"Ones much more so than yourself, despite their clothing," she said. "Now we come to the caterpillar," she said quietly, "If you allow me to speak, it is because this matter is too trivial, and so I am handling it. He will look at you and speak but won't address you directly." At the door she bowed to him.

"Why?" he said.

"It's not done," she said bowing again.

"Then I leave it to your capabilities," said Dashi.

On his great golden cushioned throne, the treasurer sat, overstuffed as a pillow. He vainly whisked away tiny flies that returned. Red and gold beads hung to one side of his great belly which caused his court black robes to split the gold embroidered bird in two, revealing that he was not sitting crossed legged, as Dashi first assumed, but in fact had none, with only stumps remaining. The treasurer tipped the liquid contents of a goblet mostly into his mouth, as he eyed the approaching two. The smell was exactly that of the librarian.

A servant wiped the treasure's mouth, "You've come to see me. I've heard so much about you. I thought I'd perhaps been forgotten," drawled the treasurer looking directly at Dashi.

The mistress answered, "Previous situations left a terrible tangle. I am attending to every thread," she said, and added, "And I know *how to remember*."

The treasurer's left eye twitched stealing a glance at the mistress. He clapped his hands, "Wine," he said, and a wine glass was poured and brought to the magistrate on a golden tray inlayed in white with a crane. "For your health," he said.

Dashi moved only his eyes looking down at the wine. He returned his gaze to the treasurer.

The mistress said, "I must refuse."

"Your heart not for the cup?" said the treasurer leaning forward, and waved away the servant. "What then?" he sniffed.

"The taxes were to be lowered by a tenth. This has not been done. Why?" she said directly.

"That," he said, instantly bored, "The levy by the emperor is such that a reduction of a tenth would result in our not having the means to pay our land-fees." The treasurer smiled, "Are you sure you won't try the wine?"

Dashi knew this was a lie. They had more grain than since he was a boy. He crossed his arms.

"I can show you the figures," the treasurer said shooing a fly, and a man stepped forward with a book opening it in front of Dashi for him to look at. A slight twist appeared to one side of the treasurer's knowing smile.

Forgetting himself, Dashi's mouth slipped, "Worthless paper," he said.

"Then don't ask," said the treasurer squinting.

"I live up to my expectations," said Dashi.

"*My...*" The treasurer sat back, clearly amused. "I'd heard the mud monkey was a disciple of the master of birds and flowers," he said, and took a drink, and grinned, "You'll be gone by winter. Go to your mother." The treasurer looked away like they no longer existed to him. And at that the guards who'd been standing to either side of the treasurer's raised seat, took a single step forward.

Dashi put his arms down by his sword, ready, if they advanced, to make them take three steps back. "I will free the people," he said.

The treasurer exploded into laughter and held his ample belly, "That is the most amazing thing I've heard in years," he sneered, the sour smell of his body reaching Dashi's nostrils, "See the filthy ape leaves safely." And turning to the mistress, "My Lady," he said simply.

As the metal doors closed behind them Dashi turned to the mistress. "I apologize. I got angry. I shouldn't have spoken."

The mistress took his arm and led him away from listening ears. "Don't apologise. I already told you. You are magistrate," she said.

"I'm s... yes," said Dashi.

She said, "And as for shoulds you already know."

"Still, I forgot," he said,

"You reacted honestly, and with surprising eloquence. I might have prepared you better – he's a loathsome worm."

"Is that why you call him the golden caterpillar?" asked Dashi.

She paused. "For several reasons," she began. "The wine..."

"Was it poisoned?" he asked.

"Not poisoned, exactly, he..." she said, making a face, "He urinates into the wine," she revealed, "For his guests mind you."

Dashi looked affronted. "Disgusting."

She explained, "A witticism: treasurer – gold. It's his little joke."

"It isn't particularly funny," said Dashi.

"It is for him," she said.

"He's mad," said Dashi. "Makes him feel big I suppose. Next time, he will beg for mercy from me, and I'll crush the worm under my heel."

And the mistress, watchful, observed the magistrate's face, the subtle mouth corner twisting delight of imagined vengeance. "To him we are amateurs. That is partially why we went, to make the awful creature move. We'll see what comes of it. At any rate, at least he revealed two things."

"He did? What did he reveal?" asked Dashi.

"When I alluded to the title of the book, he twitched. "Meaning he knows about the book, and he believes that I know, and I know that he believes," she said. "I've sent a letter to my contacts asking if they too have had a new book about remembering that's been placed in, and then removed from, the library in the last five years."

"Ah," said Dashi. "But how can we catch anyone if their actions take place over five years?"

"My Lord, plans take time. Coordination takes time. Considering how hidden they have been, five years seems slow to act. This may have been in motion for decades, or even centuries, depending on how many are involved."

"I see," he said.

"The other thing he told us was that you would be gone by winter," said the mistress, "probably meaning they expect you to be dead by winter at the latest."

"That's rather more ominous," said the magistrate.

"Indeed."

Dashi sent word to the nans. Come to me. And he told them where – and they came.

"Captain, as you won't let me go about the city without

an escort, and I presently am in need of a guard that is inconspicuous, I choose you. You can put whoever you like on the periphery of the market – but give them something to do – eating is popular."

What else could the captain say except, "Yes, My Lord."

They, the nans, keepers of the city's mannerfulness, turned up behind the crowded stalls in the equally crowded market, dressed in rags, feet trailing earth, mud, and other. Completely invisible to any town dweller. Dashi only wished he could do what he was about to do and have them march through his halls to affront the tender sensibilities of the palace. But this needed to be their secret.

The nans cackled in rough laughter and clucked to each other. They were to meet by the broken brick. They all knew where. It was where a housekeeper would leave a copy of her keys when she wanted to teach her employers a lesson. Considering recent events, and out of some sense of respect, it was not, for the present, being used.

Dashi and his brother never bothered, they didn't need a cut key. As he and the captain peeked out from the hung canvas shading a stall, Dashi imagined that the second time they'd arrested his brother, they must have bound his hands, or stripped him... lest he escape again. When all the nans had assembled, he and the captain slipped out from hiding.

Dashi explained to them the third assistant chronicler's special arrangement. He needn't have, because they knew all about it, and approved of the turn he'd given him. Three close-by nans even patted his back, in pride. Then he explained.

He'd had an idea. An awful idea. A wonderful, awful idea. He told the nans, "I want you to tell the captain, every dirty little deal that you know of, or suspect." He turned to the captain. "And I want you," said Dashi, "to interrupt these arrangements. I don't want to see them in my courtroom. I don't care how. Just cut their supply lines. And humiliate them if you can."

The captain grinned. "I've already begun," he said, "It'll be my pleasure."

"Consider it a gift," said the magistrate.

The sun was set. The warm glow of diffused evening light ebbed and stars emerged. As the musicians left the harvest festival stage in the outer courtyard, all the gathered people, who'd moments ago had been vigorously dancing, spontaneously cheered. They cheered loudly because instead of the long customary speeches celebrating the rice harvest, the new magistrate had ordered the cellars to bring out barrels of newly distilled spirits, for which the crowd had heartily cheered the young magistrate's name.

Dashi sat with the other black clad officials at the front of the stage and looked behind him to see their happy reddened faces, field hands and townspeople alike. Many had removed ribbons from the banners decorating the walls and tied them to each other's wrists and ankles. He felt his own face flush with heat having much imbibed.

The festival to celebrate the great harvest was a brilliant idea, he thought to himself. A show of beauty and abundance brings everyone together. The walls were cleared of contentious squabbling. Released with forgiving white paint.

Suddenly, from behind the stage, strings and bells and flutes sounded in jolly cacophonous overture. Actors appeared upon the stage. Mock battles erupted, the clashing of swords came with exciting crashes from behind the stage. A dragon ran quickly through and disappeared. A dark figure, in a dark hood slunk slowly into view while behind him was pandemonium: men running to and fro, with flashes of light and real-sounding thunder rolled from beaten metal and drums. Then he picked something off the ground, carefully putting it under his cloak. He then drew his sword and slew everyone until he was the last standing and slowly he walked off stage.

The mistress leaned over to the magistrate, "They have not yet invited me to their table. We will see if this gets a reaction."

Dashi was about to say, "What?" when the play began.

A low black box covered in a grey blanket to make it look like a rock was placed centre stage. A single horn sounded. A young man came onto the stage dressed in rags eating a piece of fruit, smacking his lips. He looked at the audience side to side, still eating, until the audience laughed.

At the cue, right behind him waddled the dragon. And when the actor would look left, the dragon moved right, and when he looked right, the dragon would have already moved to his left. The dragon looked at the audience and jiggled up and down, laughing silently.

"I hear," the actor said out to the audience, "that it is said there are dragons in these parts." And the actor again looked in both directions for wily dragons, to the laughter of children and adults. "Don't worry. It's just a children's tale. Any adult knows there's no such thing as dragons." And hearing this, the dragon did a little victory dance and again laughed silently.

"I hear," the actor, said in hushed tones, "there's gold

to be found around here," and he threw the core of the fruit behind him, bouncing it off the head of the dragon, to great laughter. The annoyed dragon retreated. "I'm no fool. That's the real thing to be thinking about." And he crossed his arms.

Just then a woman came running on stage carrying a swaddled floppy doll, "Help, help," she cried, "There's a dragon trying to eat my baby."

The actor put his hands on his hips, "No, no it's all right," he said, "There are no dragons here."

"There are," she said.

"Aren't" said he.

"Yes," said she.

"No," he said.

"Ya-huh," she said.

"Nh-nh," he replied, shaking his head.

"But how do you know?" she implored.

"That's easy," he said, "I've looked."

At this the dragon popped his head over the back of the stage.

And the man looked to the right and she followed his gaze and so did the dragon, and then dragon moved left upstage, to get a better look at what they were seeing. All three of them staring together.

And the two of them then looked right and they looked the dragon right in the face.

"Nope, no..." he said, turning forward.

Then to be sure, he quickly turned right again, putting his hand over his eyes as if to look into the distance. But the dragon had receded. And the crowd had laughed. "Nope. No dragons whatsoever. Your baby is perfectly safe," he said.

"Thank the heavens," said the woman, and put her baby

down on the rock, and the two pantomimed they were talking, and she put her arm in his and flirted, and he took another fruit from his pocket, and she, taking the fruit from his hand, ate.

Meanwhile the dragon, eyeing the audience, snuck behind them. Scooping the baby up, it walked stage right and looked at the two, and then to audience again as if sharing a secret. A drumroll sounded and the dragon tossed the baby into the air and snap! – gobbled it up.

And then it laughed, "Hor hor hor hor!" to the sound of great booming thunder and exited the stage.

The two actors ran all about looking for its source. And then silence fell and they separated to stand to both sides of the rock – upon which their eyes fell simultaneously.

They jumped in shock. "My baby!" she cried.

"Your baby!" he shouted. And both of them ran about some more until exhausted they slumped onto the rock and against each other.

"It was the dragon," she said, and began to weep.

"There must be a logical explanation," he said.

"You're mean to say I am speaking nonsense!" she confronted.

"I confess I can make no sense of what you speak," he countered.

"But my baby is gone," she despaired, directing his gaze to the spot where it had been.

"I confess the dilemma," he admitted, "Even if dragons are nonsense, one need not focus on that to see there's been an affect. A real one."

"Will you get my baby back for me?" she pleaded.

"Well, I was going to get some of that gold I hear is around..." and he stopped. She was looking at him, her head tilted over, her hands clasped together, batting her eyes. "I guess I could see if I could do both at the same time. All right, sure, I'll get your baby back."

And again there was thunder and the laughing of the dragon from off stage and the two lovers departed to riotous music. The crowd clapped and in a few moments the two came back onto the stage followed by a line of searchers. It was clear they were looking for the baby.

"Ba-by..." called the actor.

"That's not a name," said the actress, "How will it know it's us?"

"It's a baby, it wouldn't recognise..." he began. But the woman looked weepy again and he said instead. "Of course, well, what's its name?" he said.

The searchers observed them and looked at each other, and put their hands up in disgust, as if having seen it before. They sat hard upon the ground, looking instantly dishevelled and bored.

"I hadn't given it one yet," she replied.

"Fine then what do you suggest?" he said in curt manner, "Name-less..." he called out. "Form-less..." he did likewise.

The music began to rise and out of the shadows came the dragon. It came up behind the first searcher sitting on the ground, who turned to see, and drew his sword, but too late, legs kicking, it ate him. The sword fallen from his hand.

"You mock my pain," she said.

"I mark my sore feet," he replied, lifting up his foot. They eyed each other and turned their backs – with stolen hurtful glances.

By this time the dragon had eaten half of the seated search crew, who entered the mouth, flailing, and then could barely be seen crawling quietly out the back side of the laughing dragon, which happily continued its devouring the entire crew.

The man turned around to face her. "Look you have to calmly face reality, to get a grip of the situation, to be effective. Yes, we've been searching for your baby for three days, but rationally speaking, even though he's lost, he's probably not yet perished from hunger or cold-"

At this she cried, taking out a cloth and blew on it noisily.

"Howev-" he started to say, but again she blew her nose. And each time he tried to continue, she would do so, making the audience laugh.

The man put his hands on his hips, pontificating, shouting, "However if there are dragons, which I doubt - then he's most certainly been eaten."

At this she fell to full weeping and he instinctually went to comfort her, but she took to blowing her nose like a strangled trumpet - and he, disgusted, thought better of it - retracting his hands, and sidled off to put some distance between them. She noticed this and stopped crying. What she didn't notice was the dragon creeping up behind her.

"Whooop!" she exclaimed, as she too was eaten by the dragon.

"What did you say?" he enquired, not turning back to see. Arms crossed, he said, "I've been considering this dragon business of yours. I think many people have this delusion. It seems to me some disavowal of the self that one makes to walk the stage of our internal theatre," he said to the audience, as the dragon approached. "Our time in this world is given to flights of excited fantasy - to chase after insubstantial dream, for with a little drama we may chase away boredom's dire doldrum. And what better than a ghost, a nothing, our imagination's puppet - which we hold completely in control? But this life of make-believe – at what cost do we but close our eyes – to slumber a moment longer in our illusion?

"Failing – to see what's right in front of us," he said waggling his admonishing finger at the crowd. The dragon was behind him. "When enlightenment is just in trusting what's rational." And the dragon reared over his head, with its mouth ready to swallow him up. "What do you thiiii...?" he said turning around, looking up, "Ah... ya... ya...!"

And then he ran about the stage shrieking, the dragon in pursuit. At first the dragon chased the youth, but behind the rock the youth found the sword, and the youth chased the dragon. The dragon spun around and around the rock until the youth was dizzy and confused, and the dragon laughed, making him jump and look this way and that. Meanwhile the dragon hid, covering itself with the grey blanket to pretend it was just a stone, while the youth, with his sword, ran about but couldn't find it.

But behold, where the old rock had been, now uncovered, was a great stack of gold bars within. The youth rubbed his eyes. Marvelling he picked them all up in his arms, occasionally dropping one and rescuing it, until, weighed down, he held them all.

"Now I know why the dragon is eating everyone!" he exclaimed straining, and then speaking the secret with a guttural hiss, "It's guarding its hoard of gold... sssss..." And then he straightened himself, vain and foolish. "But when I catch up with him, it's going to be my gold." And he winked with exaggeration.

So he marched off stage to search for the dragon to the sound of clanging marching music, but after a few moments' pause he came back.

"Oh, I've searched everywhere for that dragon. I can't find it anywhere. Maybe... I don't know. Maybe there was no dragon. I just imagined it and I've been chasing my own tail. But there was that gold- and all those people disappeared," pondered the actor, sitting down upon the rock.

The rock began to move, carrying him, sitting on the back of it. The menacing shape of the dragons head, still beneath the blanket appeared. The crowd laughed.

"What's so funny?" he said to the crowd. "I could enjoy a hearty laugh about now. What's so funny?" he said as the blanket's shape changed, and dragon's mouth opened and its head turned to stare at the youth. And then it ate him, and the actor put up a terrific fight, his legs sticking straight up in the air, but the blanketed dragon ate him all up.

The musician's played, thundering and boisterous, as the dragon in the blanket twirled around and around and around - and then whoosh! - the blanket fell to the stage, empty - everyone had vanished. The crowd erupted in great applause.

Dashi leaned over to the mistress, "I thought it was going to be about me at first," he said with drunken candour.

"Conceited to think, humble to admit," the mistress said with a hardly discernible slur.

"Yes, well despite not having the advantage of me as the main character, your play seems to have done all right with the public," joked Dashi.

Then the long ceremony began - giving thanks to ensure good harvest for next year, with the high bureaucrat priests sitting in golden chairs, as one of them droned, flailing a flail, made of woven rice, and droned, making the offering of burning rice, and there also was the swinging of a censor, and smokey cloying incense which made Dashi feel woozy, and it just seemed to feel as if it would go on and on interminably. Finally, with some small difficulty, a bureaucrat stood – although the droner didn't seem to have finished – and began the concluding clap. All standing.

Everyone clapped in unison and then cheered, "Long live the Magistrate! Long live Dashi!" During which all the drunken bureaucrats retreated to their thrones. The droner just collapsing himself in a heap near the guards at the side of the stage, fiddling about with his garment, and coughing in the smoke.

Dashi glanced at the mistress sitting beside him bobbing her head. He wondered where her granddaughter was. It was their idea to throw this festival for the people. Perhaps now the ceremony was done he might get to dance.

It was then a man in a mask, dressed in red silk with black trim staggered on the stage, dragging a chair with him. He clapped sloppily and everyone laughed.

The drunken man spoke in a silly high voice, "Thank you. Now I will really show you something!" he chimed, barely able to stand, and the crowd egged him on. "How about you madame," he said, holding out his hand to the mistress.

The mistress, with one eye closed looked at him long and hard. Slowly, she rose. And with Dashi's help, though he had to sit back down first she stepped up onto the low wide stage.

"Now if you would put out your hands, back to back. Just like that yes," he said as she complied. "Now focus on your hands. Really focus."

And the mistress looked intently at her hands.

Suddenly he pushed them down, "You're asleep!" he

commanded and she fell back into the chair. A gasp of alarm went up.

"No need to be afraid," he assured the crowd and alerted Magistrate. "She's just... taking a nap. But... wait, wait... Mistress, if you would, bark like a dog," he said.

To the surprise of the crowd she began to bark.

"Now, crow like a crow," he commanded.

Out of her mouth came the sounds of a cawing crow.

"A chicken... cluck like a chicken," he said and even though he wore a mask his voice said he was smiling. "You will now awake, and remember nothing, princess, you may return to your seat."

Everyone clapped.

"Would another like to try? You?" he said aiming his hand towards Dashi as he helped the mistress down.

The crowd rewarded him with spontaneous clapping as Dashi took to the stage.

"Look at your feet," he said. Dashi did, and the man pushed him backwards into the chair, yelling, "Sleep!"

Dashi, drunk, wheeled back, falling into the chair, his head hanging down. He laughed, but didn't feel any different.

"Now Magistrate Dashi, lets hear some poetry. Recite the children's verse, *The Farmer's Toil*."

The magistrate stayed silent. He didn't know the poem. Though he knew it was children's verse. "Farmers toiling..." he began gamely, not wanting to disappoint, "Toiling in the fields..." The people tittered.

"Hmm, no no," said the masked man, "Let's try another. How about *Goose, goose, goose*."

Another child's verse. Dashi felt his face flushing even more.

"All right," said the masked man in the high voice moving around to the back of the chair. "Something easier - count backwards from 500."

"500, 499, 498, 497, 4...95, no, 496," Dashi said flustered.

"Ha! How about from 250 then," and the crowd laughed. He spoke again right in Dashi's ear, low, without trace of slur, "Perhaps you should stick to animal sounds. The sound of a turtle... or its egg."

Dashi stood up, angry, and wheeling around advanced, pointing to the masked, red man. "From your mouth come the sounds of worms!" Dashi motioned to the guards. "Who are you? A ghost? Reveal yourself! Don't be timid now..." And Dashi drew his sword.

The man fetched from a pocket a glass flask, throwing it upon the ground, from which a billowing, poisonous stinking cloud of smoke arose. Dashi swung his sword.

Quick as a rabbit, the masked man had lunged off the platform and through the crowd, throwing a few flasks upon the ground behind him, dodging the stumbling guards. Many festival goers were instantly ill, causing the rest to panic to escape, scattering chairs, further hindering the guard, as the man slipped into the labyrinth of dark streets at the edge of the crowd who now blocked the way.

Dashi's eyes stung with tears. "After him!" bellowed the magistrate, coughing. The guard, fought their way forward, and disappeared into the dark with everyone else, leaving the courtyard empty save those who were vomiting.

"Give the sick pickled ginger," said the mistress, to one of her women who had appeared at her side. Dashi turned to look at her, standing perfectly straight and sober, gripping the point of a dagger in her hand, "Now I have met the poisoner," she said.

And then she coughed.

"Arrest him!" said Dashi

"Who, My Lord?" said the captain.

"That, second attendant to the historian-chronicler of the city with the horse. I remember his high voice. Why didn't you just stab him?" argued Dashi, pacing between the captain and the mistress.

"Because until you came up on the stage I didn't know it was him, and my first responsibility is to your safety. Your master would be cross if I let your throat be slit," said the mistress facing him, "You were in the way. And then because of the smoke, and your standing, the archers couldn't fire without potentially hitting you."

"Archers?" slurred Dashi.

"Awaiting my word," said the mistress.

Dashi covered his face. "This was a trap. You set a trap with me as the bait."

The mistress's face was calm as ice. "You've been a target from the moment you became magistrate, My Lord."

"How'd you know he wouldn't just fire his poison arrows - right in me?" said Dashi pointing to his chest.

"If he'd any more bolts he's had plenty of chance to use them. Every time you have a yearning for noodles and dumplings you go wandering-"

"Yes, I like soup. We all know," Dashi sat down. "You pretended to sleep," said Dashi.

"I did," she said.

Dashi said "But you knew it was him."

"I knew that he was rude: dog, crow, chicken," she snorted indignant, "That didn't mean he was our poison-

250

er. And if I had stabbed him, that would have driven any real poisoner away."

"I'd like it if he was driven away," said Dashi.

"There are hundreds of people in the palace," the mistress said, "Too many," she explained. "There could be several co-conspirators. But we need only find one trail of paw prints to learn the location of the warren. Now we know something," she said tucking her hands into her sleeves "He said, 'princess'."

Dashi, rubbing his face, thought about that, "Why?" he said.

"Why indeed," said she, "Who here appreciates my rank?"

"You're a princess?" said Dashi.

"It is said in the capital there are more princesses than mice," she replied. "My point is it speaks to his station."

Dashi suggested, "Obviously the worm knows. He's told everyone."

"Why would he do that?" she said, "No, this man is so very careful about everything, he makes no mistakes. But in this charade, this impromptu review of my play, he was pretending to be someone he is not, you see? He must have been furious to risk telling me I've guessed his operation and exposed it.

"So he had his fun with me, and as I was leaving he slipped when he called me that. Meaning it's so ingrained he doesn't even notice it."

"What about me?" asked Dashi.

"Toying with you in front of the crowd was apparently important enough to risk death. Why? To prove he was better?" she pondered. "My theory is they've decided not to kill you – at least yet."

"Why aren't they trying to kill me yet?" interjected

Dashi.

"Because they don't want to bring a new magistrate," she postulated. "Someone competent - with experience."

Assassins lurked potentially everywhere, with no comprehendible motive. Dashi breathed in and then he gave it up, the scent of the foul gas still lingering in his nose.

"You're saying they've decided to not to kill me because I'm a bumbling idiot - which they've just demonstrated to the people - that I am an illiterate and bumbling idiot?" he said.

The mistress said, "I wouldn't have said it that way."

"Really?" said Dashi putting his head in his hands.

"The question is why," she said, "Why bother humiliating you? Why the writing on the walls? Perhaps they just hate you," she said shaking her head, "but there is more. If they were just doing this to get at me-"

"You?" said Dashi.

"Yes," she said, "Because you're my pu... pupil, politically speaking. To go after you to humiliate me, I understand... but they're playing to the crowd..."

Dashi watched the mistress consider.

The festival she'd organised to bring everyone together to celebrate was a disaster, except for revealing his would-be masked assassin, "It wasn't quite the result I'd hoped," sighed Dashi, "Do you have anything to add captain?" he said, looking up, doubting the captain could make his face look any more stern.

"My Lord, we have the flask shards. That may lead us to them. We secured the perimeter-" said the captain.

"Apparently not," said Dashi. "He slipped through your men."

"Yes, My Lord. I take full responsibility. But the men couldn't see through the smoke, My Lord."

"I know. I can still taste it," said Dashi. "Somebody get me something to drink," and he scratched his head. He could think this through as well as anyone, "All right. If they're not trying to kill me – what're they doing? On stage, in front of everybody, just so they can humiliate me? Or you mistress. What good is that for them?" he said, adding, "I know," putting his palms to the sides of his head. "I think they're crazy." Rocking his head slowly side to side, "Crazy..." exaggerated the magistrate.

"Drink some water, My Lord," said the mistress, "You should probably rest. You'll feel more like yourself in the morning."

"Well, that's good," said Dashi, "I'd rather not be me right now."

His morning table, cup and teapot were in attendance, and even though he dutifully drank the mistress's cure, a dirt flavoured yellow tea, he felt surprisingly well. Tossing and turning all night, were by now usual. The hangover wasn't as bad as he imagined it would have been. The enemy had revealed himself. A phantom hiding in the shadows no longer. He could face these.

"My Lord," said the mistress's granddaughter as she put a piece of torn red silk down on the table in front of him.

Dashi looked up.

Her face was swollen on one side. Dashi looked down at the torn cloth. "You tried to catch him yourself," he said.

"He wasn't in the mood, apparently," she replied. "I was in the alley and tried to stop him."

"And he hit you to get past," Dashi nodded, "You did

better than the guard."

"Actually he just bowled me over. I thought I could trip him. It was the wall I hit," she said.

"Ah," said Dashi. "I am still sorry."

"Would you be sorry if the captain had been injured?" she asked standing straighter.

Dashi considered the question. "I'd rather no one is injured," he said. "Accept my compliment on your efforts."

She shifted her weight to one foot. "Thank you, My Lord," she said.

Dashi took a sip from his tea cup and was reminded again how it tasted. "Has anyone else seen this?" he said, and rubbed it between his thumb and fingers. It made that crunching sound, and it was very thick. "Silk armour," he said.

"Therefore he is wealthy," she said.

"Or steals only the finest," he countered.

"More likely the first," she counter-countered.

"You forget my former occupation," said the magistrate flourishing his embroidered sleeping robes. "I once walked in rags, until I stole this office – it may be I do so again."

"Black is not your colour," she said.

"Indeed," Dashi said and laughed. "I freely admit I enjoy not being hungry, but am also ready to move on when the winds of heaven will it," he said, "Presently, very ready."

"You are magistrate for another three and a half years," she reminded him.

He said, "I am magistrate until I am not."

She was about to argue, when the captain came to the door, bowing. He came forward when the magistrate waved him in.

"I am pleased to see My Lord well this morning," said

the captain.

"Can I offer you some tea, captain?" said Dashi gesturing to the pot, offering to pour him a cup.

"I have already had my fill, thank you My Lord," said the captain. "I have come to tell you about the writing on the wall."

"Which wall?" asked Dashi.

"The palace wall," said the captain. "You probably will want to see it."

"Let's go then," said Dashi, "I will dress."

The two retreated from the magistrate's chambers and then when he was ready, together, the three of them made their way to the middle of the outer courtyard to look at this writing the captain spoke of. Written in red, One large word, two men high: Dashi.

Dashi had a moment's consideration, "Why be so dramatic?" he said. "Surely shooting arrows at me, and trying to poison me directly communicates the threat more effectively."

"What was once private is now public," said the granddaughter.

"They are swearing that they will kill you," said the captain.

"By winter," said Dashi, "if that tea doesn't get me first." Dashi shook his head, "I was on the stage with one. He could have slit my throat right there and have been done with it."

"But he wouldn't have gotten away," said the captain.

"Wouldn't he?" said Dashi. "I don't mean to rub it in captain, but he evaded capture just fine last night."

"He couldn't be assured of it," said the captain. "It is one thing to be rude and caught. It is another to attempt murder and be caught. He could plead his drunkenness, and assume your mercifulness."

"Ah, but why would he assume that? My reputation is not for mercifulness, apparently, but for bizarre and cruel judgements," he said.

"That's not true," said the granddaughter.

"Not entirely true," said Dashi, "However the question remains how he knew that."

"What would you have me do about the writing, My Lord?" asked the captain.

"In this case," said Dashi, "remove it. No need for bad omens. However if someone is going to express themselves, anyway... my government ought to be seen as encouraging it, rather than its victim." Both captain and granddaughter widened their eyes. "See to it that a rectangle along the bottom of the wall is painted with a wide red border. If the people want to tell me they wish me dead, or tell each other to drop dead, or other foul things, then let this be the place. We will invite it. But if they write outside the lines, paint over it."

"Is that wise, My Lord," asked the captain, "They may say terrible things about you."

"We'll see if it's wise, captain... However," and he looked at the granddaughter, "I should think some will say good things of me. And, what's more, this will get lost amongst discussions of matters more important than me."

Dashi turned his gaze back to his name, in red, dripping down the wall like blood. "Messy. They must have used a broom," he laughed, and then the magistrate walked away. "I am cold – I'm going in now."

"My grandmother says I should continue your reading

lessons with poetry, My Lord," said the granddaughter.

"The one about the farmer?" asked Dashi with a wry smile.

She laughed, "That's just a children's poem."

Dashi, silent, looked down, and the granddaughter fled the room.

The mistress and granddaughter walked arm in arm.

A walk the grandmother had requested and the granddaughter had obeyed. The younger woman was, as indicated she should be: silent, as they wound through the maze of lane-ways outside the palace, but still inside the palace walls. Her grandmother moved her jaws very slightly, tapping her teeth together, something she did when she was thinking. Perhaps she was unaware she did it, and likely unaware that her granddaughter, watching her, noticed.

Just before their mysterious walk together, they had been speaking, and she had told her grandmother of the large letters written on the wall and how the magistrate seemed unconcerned, and had repeated what he'd said, and then, her grandmother put up her hand, rather in the same way the granddaughter had seen Dashi do, and together they went to see what was left of the red writing. Then, at her grandmother's insistence, they wound their way deep into the palace yard.

In this way they continued until they were well behind the garrison, approaching a large building with great doors carved with the figures of rats. Two workers at the grain storage parted the doors, letting them enter.

Immediately her grandmother seemed fixated upon something to the right, but all the granddaughter could see in the storehouse were stack upon stack of dusty bags. She followed the gaze of her grandmother and squinted, trying to determine what it was that had captured her interest so. Finally her curiosity was too much for her to be silent any more, "What do you see? What are we doing here?" she asked.

Her grandmother took her hand from her granddaughter's arm and walked over to the wall and she pointed. There hung, in a row, several red handled brooms for the workers to sweep up any fallen grain. She merely placed her hand upon one red wooden handle.

The granddaughter shrugged, so her grandmother looked up. As the granddaughter's eyes traveled up she realised the bristles of this one broom were also red.

"Then why not just paint the wall over and forbid anyone to write there anymore," said the frustrated magistrate.

"Because you have given it," said the mistress, "To take it away says you do not know what you are doing. If you leave it in place, despite the dissension, then you are stronger for it.

"Besides it keeps your opposition guessing. They threatened to kill you, and you've acted to give the people more freedom. They humiliate you, driving a wedge between you and the people – you act as if it's nothing. They will wonder why."

"Can we at least then have more poetry?" asked the magistrate.

The mistress nodded. "A very fine idea," she said, and "Indeed," and "I will arrange it, My Lord," and to her granddaughter, "You can stay," she said and unusual for her, she stood, bowed and left.

"That got her going," said Dashi.

"Poetry is important to her," said the granddaughter.

"Yes," said Dashi, who had been growing to appreciate the art of saying difficult things, with just the right words, in just the right order, and honestly done, rather than for the flattery of purists and quibblers.

There was silence then. Which Dashi realised had followed on his saying 'Yes,' and had been continuing for some time while he had been thinking to himself about poetry. "Should we read some then?" he inquired.

The granddaughter nodded emphatically. "Let's," she said. "What does My Lord suggest?"

"Let us begin with *The Farmer's Toil,* and *Goose, goose, goose.* I hear they are all the fashion with those under five years," he smiled. "I find the air holds the meaning better. Speaking the poems draws them off the page."

She returned a wan smile. "I will ask the librarian."

Dashi said, "If he offers to show you picture books - decline."

The librarian had never had so much activity in decades.

"We are to read the worthy classics," the granddaughter explained without saying who it was who was to be doing the reading.

"To be found on these shelves are only worthy classics," the blind librarian had responded, and began retrieving some books, muttering to himself, "Poets."

"Then we've a wealth of reading," she'd called, but he ignored her and her conversation.

"That's a good one," he said of one, and of another

grunted "Hm... too long," stacking the books on one practiced arm as he went.

"I require also books on politics."

"Eh?" he said stopping, "I thought you said you only wanted worthy classics," said the librarian, turning around and retrieving some books from the shelf behind him.

"Are they not?" she replied.

"Politicians are the handmaidens of deception, and warfare is based on deception," he said out loud. Touching the spines, he traced his way to another shelf, pulling off more volumes. The granddaughter could hear him whispering to himself, "It's a terrible thing. To lie, to have to lie. To obfuscate and deny. A tiresome, sticky darkness."

"To what lie specifically are you referring?" she called out.

Roused from reverie, he brought the collected books back, slamming them upon the table. He stared at her with his milky unseeing eyes, and he spat, "A book hides a hoard of gold!" dousing the light, disappearing again into darkness – like a crocodile slipping back into its pool.

The snow drifted down the mountain one day and decided to stay. It came in flurries and also in slow graceful lazy blankets, making the earth look simple and pure.

Some weeks later it warmed enough for rain, and for the roads to churn into rough mud. But by then the mountain pass that led south was already closed. The valley was its own world until spring thaw. If one had observed, smoke appeared briefly from the signal tower and was then extinguished.

Long icicles hung like glass daggers from the eaves,

and one had to watch one's feet for fear of slipping. On the palace wall people still wrote poetry. But read in the streets, someone wrote 'freedom' - in letters of red.

When the women played music, the mistress' granddaughter would teach the important dances to the magistrate. Sometimes other women would dance with him too - the granddaughter cutting in, better to instruct. Other times, when he was tired, Dashi would just sit amongst the coloured cushions and watch, or listen, often to find himself awakening, a blanket having appeared over him in his slumber.

Today the women quietly read in the room of birds. The granddaughter sat beside Dashi. Her hands were being kept warm between them. He was concentrating on the book. Sometimes he forgot and moved his mouth silently over the words, "That is a beautiful poem - but very sad," he said at last.

"War time is sad," she stated.

"And the losses of age," he said "- Perhaps another losing battle," and she nodded.

The granddaughter smiled at her pupil. "Indeed," she said. "Maybe we should switch to a writer with more of a sense of charm." She reached over to the table aside the sitting couch and retrieved another volume from one of the piles of books.

Empty
my heart is empty
my cup is empty
for filling is not what I desire

let my left foot follow my right
as day follows after night

in spring they will meet again
and bloom

"What do you think?" said Dashi, noting the other women made sounds of muffled tittering.

The granddaughter smiled. "Lovely. But it seems to me your feet will meet in spring."

Dashi looked over what he'd written. "I imagined it as the merger of opposites: left, right, day and night."

"Without the empty cup part then," and she read just the ending to herself. "No, I still see feet - blossoming. I feel the beginning part is better."

"I will rewrite it," he said.

"Cook a new dish rather than reheat a burned one," she said.

And he nodded. Then he watched her walk, to get another book.

A stack of books grew out in the hall, carried by the granddaughter, without the help of the other women.

Breakfast at the palace.

"Why?" asked Dashi.

"Because to the people, you are the power behind these walls," the mistress said raising her arms, "Not just your power, but a chain of power all the way to the emperor – those that hold *your* fate in their hands. You are not just you anymore. Not Dashi – the magistrate."

"But I am the last link in the chain," said Dashi, eyeing his tea bowl.

"No, not the last. Think about the captain. Or any one of the guards beneath him. Or the scribes and bureaucrats who run this outpost. Believe me, if we were not so out of the way, you'd have to contend with every petty official, trying to make a name for himself, butting his way into every detail of your policies. To gain power. To become indispensable," said the mistress.

"Shouldn't one want to be useful?" asked Dashi.

"I've seen quite a few heads of indispensable men on poles," replied the mistress. "This is no game. Most people surrounding you do not consider right governance. They follow because they wish to advance. Which in the case of this place – is to leave forever."

"I told them they should leave, those who had sided with the previous magistrate."

"Acting magistrate–" corrected the mistress, "False magistrate," she corrected herself. "If they're here: they have nowhere else to go. This is the end of the road. What you told them, in effect, was that they were worse than useless, and they'd best become peasants working the fields." The mistress smiled. "That is quite funny."

She retrieved the bowl and placed it on the tray to be

removed. "I've been spending much time with your nans. A field worker is a fine thing," she said. "But the ambitious desire for usefulness is another stuckness. You can tell because they're forever comparing themselves to others. The fact that they're not at one of the capitols accentuates how they feel their lives have been ruined. Not by them, of course."

"It makes them contemptuous," said Dashi.

"It makes them dangerous," said the mistress. "And don't think the common people don't know they too are living at the end of the road. It is only fortunate for them they've never been anywhere."

"Why?"

"Because if they saw the riches, delights, majesty of even the regional capitol, let alone city of the emperor, they'd never be content. Except if they knew better," said the mistress.

Dashi smiled. "Mistress," he said, "what is the better?"

The corner of her mouth turned up. "Firstly let me say what it is not."

"Of course," he said.

She said, "It is not the pursuit of survival, nor the power. It is not the pursuit of togetherness, nor justice. It is not even the true. But as those are, it is an agreement for the minds."

"An agreement?" said Dashi.

"Each mind mirrors another. That is why there is a duality. A part that is the initial desire that motivates and the part that's motivated into a formed action. First the inner, then the outer. So for each mind there can be many different ways to create action attempting to fulfill a desire.

"Some ways work more than others. Desires don't necessarily translate as well from mind to mind. However some minds, having learned a way, can translate it for the other minds. It so happens that some very good strategies are ones that all the minds can use. Any average child should be able to absorb their meaning, in sequence, by the time they are twenty-eight or so."

He suspected she was alluding to him. "And how many are there mistress?" asked Dashi.

"Six."

"Oh," said Dashi, "I didn't think you'd answer that."

"Why not?" asked the mistress.

"Because you won't tell me how many minds there are," he replied.

"That would be a problem for you to get tangled in. This is not that," said the mistress. "The six levels are: nourishment, skill, identity, reciprocity, truth and beauty. These words do not do them justice, but are reasonable placeholders. Every mind contains these agreements in potential. From bare necessity, through mutual relations, to the subtle comprehension of what is better."

"Beauty," said Dashi.

"Indeed," said the mistress, and smiled.

"Shouldn't I just make everything beautiful?" then preempted her correction saying, "Should," himself.

"Is that your centre?" said the mistress, "At any rate it will not work by itself. Beauty can be presented, but that doesn't mean it is appreciated. If you insist on spoon feeding the people, who have no inclination to gratitude, do not be surprised when they act carelessly with your beauty. Yes, one mind may be able to see it, but what of the others? It has not become a way of being because the minds continue with immature agreements.

"Remaining immature, one can conceive of power as the greatest good. Stuckness has advantage – lack of any other consideration makes one very effective at dispatching competitors. That is the lure of stuckness. But then many a warlord has destroyed countless things of beauty in their lust for greater status."

"Do you not mean power?" Dashi asked.

"I do not," she replied, "In one's childhood, nourishment is initially given. Then one requires facility, power, to take it – feeding yourself. Then you gain your identity within the family and tribe. This identity condones your use of power to acquire, by each mind, its individual ends, its nourishment. The position in the clan is all important to those stuck at the level of their status. Especially for the leader.

"After that, the undeveloped levels: every manner of horse trader, and truth's lesser aspect of rules, and of course beauty. Anyone who plunders and destroys beauty does not appreciate, or consider it for itself, but only because it is valuable to bolster the status, that lends itself to power and their minds' infantile desires."

"Stuck," said Dashi.

"Very stuck," she replied, "Their development has halted in the wounded image of themselves. They do not compromise, nor bargain; they attack. Consider a terrible teenager. Giving is only utilised for taking. Its true meaning they do not grasp."

"So that is what stuckness is," said Dashi. "Not wanting to grow up."

"Yes," said the mistress. "This, as I have said, does not mean they do not have rudimentary conceptions of these things, of truth or beauty. And because we have many minds some will grow up while others atrophy. Their minds fixated on desire for significance, until the blockage is eliminated."

"By using the firebreath," added Dashi.

"Or through pain," said the mistress.

"And by significance you mean comparison," said Dashi.

"Yes," said the mistress.

Dashi nodded. "Mistress, you mentioned rules. Do you mean a map?"

"Maps are useful. Truths are useful. Rules are useful. But those are shallows, shores to the apprehension of meaning," the mistress said.

"Would you care to explain that further?" Dashi asked.

"You, Dashi, are searching for overarching principles. You are that age where many become stuck at truth."

"Stuck at truth?" said Dashi, "That doesn't seem so bad."

"No? You are magistrate. For justice to work there needs to be rules. Agreed upon truths. But what is true? *Truth is a game of adversaries.*"

"The real truth," said Dashi.

"The real truth is a yet deeper tangling. And the more stuck you are, the more tangled it will become. A safe haven for career soothsayers and salaried sages. The discernment you require is deeper than truth.

"Words that are truth words become inadequate. Language is full of truth words because that's where many people end their maturity. But the truth about the deep truth is we can at best point to it. And to comprehend, we must transcend its easy categories.

"The reason one clears all the emotional and intellectual conditioning, is so that one can even see your nature to embrace it. What is our nature, human nature, the way we are, the way it is? Look, fundamental being is right in front of you."

Dashi stood in a dark forest, unafraid, "Brother wolf," he called out, spying a grey slinking beast weaving among the far trunks.

The wolf turned to face Dashi, and the forest began to glow and dance in shifting shadow as if a fire were suddenly raging behind the magistrate. "Monster, I know you not," said the wolf, eyes glaring with red flame, and darted away as fast as he could run.

Dashi awakened in darkness.

"Captain," said the mistress, "I want you to go this morning to investigate if the tower at the pass has been compromised."

Round and around and around. Feet stepping lightly. Flowing like water. Concentration unnecessary. The mistress nodding with the music, and clapping with the other women who weren't dancing or playing instruments. A moment to simply enjoy. The dancing of teacher and Dashi. In front of the window they could be seen dancing by those watching in the courtyard outside. The light of warmth set against the blue-lit numbing sleet-soaked winter's day.

When the song ended they parted with style still holding one hand. They bowed to the appreciative spectators. Their time alone had now borne its fruits, and this coming out, its confirmation. One by one the other women took their turn dancing with the young magistrate. The granddaughter looked on, and then sat down by her grandmother who patted her hand.

The mistress said, "Well done." They watched Dashi dancing in a red silk robe the mistress had procured from somewhere in the palace. It had slits down the sides and a wide belt which made it suitable for this modern style of dancing as well as wearing a sword, the black sword normally left behind in his chambers – which the mistress had insisted upon – as well as his hat, as was proper befitting his rank. She thought it charming.

The granddaughter however thought it looked hopelessly old fashioned, comical even. "He didn't step on my feet once," she joked to her grandmother.

The mistress said, without eye contact, "Yes, he's become quite agile. It doesn't even look like he's having to evade them."

The granddaughter held her face tight and only turned her head away to look out the cold window. It was then she saw, shooting skyward, a tiny red glow trailing a snake of smoke. Someone had just sent up a flare. She touched the arm of her grandmother. "Someone has fired a flare," she said.

Her grandmother reacted like she'd been bitten. "What?!"

The granddaughter pointed out the window. "See?"

The music began to falter as the women stopped to look.

"Keep playing," she said to the musicians, "Keep playing." And so they did. "Dashi, we must get you out." She grabbed a throw that was roughly the colour of Dashi's robes and threw it around the tallest girl's shoulders.

"You two keep dancing and making noise until we're gone. Give us a few minutes and then follow," she said, "Weapons out!" She grabbed Dashi's arm and led him to the passage way behind a wallhanging that was being held back by her granddaughter.

"What's happened?" asked the magistrate.

"No time to explain, and keep quiet until you get away," she said.

And the magistrate glanced back just long enough to see the women he had been dancing with, pull knives from their dresses and fighting spears from beneath the cushions in the couch.

The mistress closed the passage door behind them. "This is the last thing I'm going to say. I'm slow - so don't wait for me. Get him to safety. Now go!"

The granddaughter grabbed Dashi's hand and pulled him onward in the dark narrow passage. He had to crouch. This had not be designed for someone of his size to be moving through stealthily at speed. But he managed not to trip. Nor did he careen into a wall and come tumbling out somewhere in the palace.

As they passed slits of light, where secret doors and peepholes looked in on every office, most of which were uncustomarily deserted, he occasioned to hear a repeated muffled phrase: "Time to act."

Soon they came to a ladder through a narrow hole in the floor. Dashi looked up, and looked down. The granddaughter eyes flitted back and forth between the two, she bit her lower lip. "Down," she whispered.

So together they descended in silence, rung upon rung, disappearing into the darkness below.

Dashi would have liked to ask what was at the bottom, or how far the bottom was, but then again, looking down, perhaps he didn't want to know. If one thought that he was merely climbing to the next floor, then one kept moving. Rather, if one imagined just how far one could fall, a fearing mind might grip a rung and not be able to let go.

Or he realised, in this case if he slipped, because she went first in this narrow shaft, he would take her with him; plummeting together. He felt there was a philosophical premise here, but couldn't say what. This secret descent into shadow - as shadows. In the underworld, even with your eyes wide open, you were as blind as if they were shut tight.

Dashi felt a hand upon his back. And then his foot came down onto the ground. And her hand touched his mouth to signal that he keep quiet in this empty void. But her hand smelled of jasmine. "Follow me," she said in his ear, and took his left hand.

The passage was also narrow. They turned three corners and then slowly moved along towards a pale ghost of light. Dashi could hear water flowing. And its presence became louder, until its reflections dominated his senses. A wet chill aching into his skin. They came out onto short and wide platform, a ledge built over the natural rock, the river rushing beneath it.

He smelled smoke. He realised they were standing under the foundations of the palace. Above his head, stone arches crossed the river to the source of light - some opening in the ceiling on the far side reflecting off the rocks that jutted out of the churning noisy water - such that a small cavern existed between the two sides, a wide cleft in the natural stone over which the original builders had spanned. It was this that reflected the sound - the sound of the river, that here made him as deaf as the narrow passage had made him blind. Looking upstream he could just make out a dot of pale daylight.

To the right, at the edge of the ledge there was a metal ladder going up to a trapdoor in the ceiling that overhung the river. She pointed up the ladder. Dashi followed her example, as she took hold of the ladder and swung from the ledge to climb the ladder on its outside over the river. When she reached the trapdoor she hesitated.

Slowly she edged the trapdoor open and after a few moments, she pushed it back and climbed up through. Dashi did likewise. They were in a large stone room, and she closed the trapdoor quietly. Dashi looked about and all around them great dripping carcasses hung on hooks. Near the trapdoor a bucket sat, attached to a rope, and also a filled trough. He could see the large hole in the floor on the other side of these. A source for the water, and the cold of the room. Dashi knew therefore what rooms in the palace were above him, but he didn't think he'd have time for something to eat.

As they climbed the stairs to the kitchens they could hear a distant ruckus. They opened the meat cellar door and heard feet running above and the din of shouts. Entering the kitchen, they passed through the big washing area, and past the large ovens, to the one Dashi most frequented. They found the floor caked with mud, and trampled noodles, the table overturned and the room empty, save only for two kitchen maids weeping together in the corner by the stove. Not one pot was left on the walls. Dashi went over and touched their shoulders.

"No time for that. We have to go," said the granddaughter pulling him away. "All this commotion is perfect cover," she said running to the doorway leading up into the palace. "The way out of the fire is through the fire."

And now they too were running. They ran into a hall-

272

way full of rain-sodden shouting looters, tearing at everything they could get their hands on.

How many times Dashi had dreamed of this? – the people, storming the palace. For the common good. For justice. But here were no people, no common good, no cries for justice, just a raging blind beast, a mob, a plague of insects devouring. Still holding hands, the two waded to their necks in the greedy panic of humanity packing the hallways with their human stink, their fear, their hot foul breath and sweat.

The granddaughter made for the outer yard of the kitchens where the butchers killed the animals and threw out the scraps. Dashi pushed them through at the door against the throng pushing to get in. Immediately the two cleaved to the outer wall to allow the rushing inundation to flood past, frothing and spitting. Striking at each other. Tearing at each other's clothing. Dashi and the granddaughter shoved their way to an inside corner by a shattered and empty chicken coop, away from the convulsing pillage. Out in the yard the rain fell; they drew their first breaths. The smell of smoke, stronger. The sound of the pounding rain only barely heard.

The granddaughter pointed to the gate. They needed to wade through the streaming people. "Take off your sword!" she said, in his ear, "We have to be seen with something or they'll know we're not pillagers." Then she looked him in the eyes and kissed him. "For luck," she said, and she took his hat and the rain began to pour on his head. Dashi nodded, removing his scabbard and belt, gripping it with his left hand and holding it above his head, he dragged her behind with his right hand, bullying his way through the rain-soaked hoard to the gate.

Once out at the gate, they dropped hands, running

down the causeway between buildings leading toward the main gates. Again the granddaughter who was fleeter of foot took the lead, always checking for Dashi behind her. As they neared the arch closest to the main gate she checked again, running into a woman, and they tumbled together. Dashi reached down mid-stride and grabbed her up, off the other woman, who in that split second looked up into his face, with recognition. She began to wail and pointed.

The granddaughter regaining her feet, ran beside him, as they crested through the, now always open by magisterial decree, main gate. People were streaming in on one side and at the back of the square he saw others wringing their hands and huddled in numb commiseration. Some familiar faces he recognised.

Here, where he had once protested for the cowardly magistrate, a self appointed dispenser of justice, to face him – here he, duly appointed, escaped, stealing into the gutter like a rat from a fire. He held his sword aloft. Perhaps those friendly faces saw him also. Someone did.

And they made a grab for his sword. And then another meaty hand joined it, and another – pulling and pushing to wrest the scabbard away. Holding onto it with both hands the magistrate hit back with his elbows and knees. Knocking one back, only to be assaulted from another side. Someone grabbed his neck from behind and the force of them began to take them down. But the granddaughter was upon their backs, circling and plunging, a dagger thrust in where an opening was revealed, thus they peeled away. Dashi threw off the last attacker and grabbing her slick hand they ran for their lives as the people looted the palace.

It was then that someone grabbed the hat. The granddaughter fell backwards, onto the ground, kicking off the greedy hands that snatched at her. Dashi burst into the fray and pushed them away and grabbed her hand but it was so slick she fell back again. Another jumped Dashi from behind and held up a dagger to strike.

"Dashi!" cried the granddaughter as the magistrate threw the attacker into the crowd.

Everything went slow. She covered her mouth, in disbelief of what had just come out of it. Dashi just stared into her eyes. The crowd stopped moving in towards the gate, and turned – to face him.

The master's pupil, at the centre of a churning storm of unseeing hatred. An eye opened around him. Dashi drew the black sword. He slashed out, and a greasy fat man fell back. He swung out with his scabbard in the other hand and connected with the dry hard skull of a thin man. They lunged at his back and he turned. Again. And again. And they began to laugh. A giddy, disconnected unbidden laugh.

This was play to them, he realised. Wolves circling, waiting for a weakness. Someone pushed a small man forward, who received a slash to his thigh, at their urging.

Someone further back had bent down and picking up a handful of mud, flung it at the magistrate, splattering his rent, red, silk robe, as well as the heads of those at the front.

Dashi hadn't really realised no word had yet been said by the tense pack but now it began, along with a rain of thrown wet slops of earth: "Mud clod! Dirt! Filth! Monster! Savage!" they yelled, as Dashi turned and turned striking at hands and pelts of mud. Slipping on the stone, and regaining his balance only to lash out again.

"Throw him out! Out the earth gate! – Throw out the

mudman!" some woman shrieked above the din, and it caught the mob, and soon they joined in the last part as a ragged chant, and when Dashi finally slipped and fell, they were upon him. They grabbed him and beat him, and they held him aloft, and he tried to attack with his left but they caught his belt and pulled away the scabbard, and they grabbed too at the hilt – but Dashi now held it with both hands.

Dashi raised the sword to strike, but a hornet sting ran through the centre of his left hand and he felt it shock all the way up his shoulder, and his left hand fell away in pain and they lunged to get the sword, but he held on still, and striking him head and body, they dragged him through streets he had walked that first day as magistrate, to the gate he'd entered as a thief in the night to reclaim his master, and depose and free the people from a false judge.

And when they had arrived, at the gate, they threw him from it bodily so that he landed square in the wet mud which splashed and oozed and he tried to stand but slipped and fell back into it on his face and they laughed, and Dashi got up on his knees and tried to wipe the slop from his eyes but his left hand had been injured, and the blade he could feel was still in it, so he used his sword hand and with one eye clear, he could see they were beginning to fan out around him in a large circle.

As the outer doors were closing, the first clump of mud came with a rock. And another. And he could see those who were weaker searching the ground for stones that the strong might liberate from their hands upon the tyrant. Another stone flew, with the word, "Demon!" and Dashi stood half blind, advancing to one edge, slashing, and these tormentors fled, while those behind bombarded him with stones. And the shouting began in earnest. "Kill it!"

He could hear the sounds of blades being pulled. "Gut it!" some ill-bred yawled over the din as if they were about to butcher a pig. He swung his sword around, and a rock caught him full in the face, and he went down on his knees. And they all began to shout, chanting, "Kill it! - Kill it! - Kill it!"

The pounding blackness in his head drowned out the shouts, and the thudding of the ground, the crowd bursting into screams and mayhem. And then suddenly it went quiet and Dashi heard a friendly voice.

"My Lord," said the captain kneeling by the bleeding magistrate. Dashi put his arm on the captain's shoulder, avoiding the hand as the captain raised him to his feet. Dashi wiped the filth from his face with his left forearm. And there was the face of the captain. A beautiful face thought Dashi, only the captain wasn't looking at him, but stared at his hand. Dashi raised his left hand to see protruding through the centre a small black double-headed arrow. And now he knew why his heart was beating so.

"My Lord," said the captain again, standing in front of this man, and he pulled the bolt from Dashi's cold hand. Dashi hardly felt it. The captain's face fell and Dashi's face reflected the knowing.

Dashi began to cough. "Not here," he said, blood pouring from his mouth with both words - his judgement. Every mind that broke faith from unity, abandoning levels hard gained, left his body ringing with alarms. "The people have swallowed a venomous worm," he said, and wiped the blood from his lips.

The captain said, "The mistress-"

"Captain, the gate's been closed against us," said a guard who came running.

"Order it open! – the magistrate is wounded!" the captain shouted.

"They're treasury guard and they're refusing," replied the guard.

"What?!" said the captain. "My Lord, be strong," he said, allowing Dashi to stand free, and the captain marched through the mud to the gate. But instead of heeding his command to open, they threw whatever refuse they had upon the wall down, and the re-agitated rabble hurled some mud for good measure, while those restrained began to scuffle anew with the distracted guard, whipping the whole uproar into shouting, screaming, fighting, brawling, yelling, and bellowing.

The deposed Magistrate, Dashi – stumbled away, from the city full of fear and trembling, away from its walls, away down the rutted road – and no one saw him veer right, doubled over, fleeing into his beloved forest, to die.

III
The Butterfly

Lying down to die.

*We lie, in our ability to accept that which
is –
in that we accept our ability: which is to
lie.*

*This is no dream and its awakening is final.
Without awakening the snow descends
upon the body,*

*one gentle whisper after whisper after...
in deep layers, glacier slow as forgetting.*

*This stuckness of the living dream. Falling
down and dying.*

*The emptying, the falling out, the walls
crumbled and flowing
away into being... and before we were this
being.*

Where is that?

*Only in our roots, the most tenuous fila-
ments, and tiniest fascicles
surrounded by motes of presence, reach
into the void.*

There, it is too much to say we are ignorant.

Lying and down falling,
a white cloth draped over two faces in
reflection,

of heaven and earth, in oneness –

where there is seen no division between.
Where everything could be.

Where the bird of dream carries you to the
river of immortality.
Where all that ever is, is the golden river.

And where from before – this – this pre-
sumptuous before,
where no before can possibly be,

here spring is its death.
A feather, falling, mirrors the leaf arising.

Life is the death of death.

He gasped for breath. On all fours, he didn't remember kneeling down, he stared at the sick beneath him. He didn't remember being sick. He crawled away.

He was crawling, on all fours. He didn't remember deciding to crawl. His hands made lopsided red stars in the snow. His hand hurt. It was red. He looked at it. He felt unwell. His stomach hurt. He felt he was going to be sick.

Lying on his back, the snow drifting down into his blinking eyes. He didn't know...

He blinked into the white sky.
Trees – anchored through him, like ladders, five left, five right – piercing his body. Nurturing him as themselves. He drank as one with them, their winter sap. He felt at peace being a tree.

"Who am I?"
First answer appeared, most subtle:
Dragon.
"Ah," he thought, not expecting that reply.
"What does it mean?"
The second answer spoke:
Why.
He understood this was meant not as the question, but to say: meaning.

Mystery within mystery.

...And then, he had the thought – that when he'd thought he was alive – he'd apparently been dead – and that now that he was dead, was he finally alive?

It was night when the magistrate awoke. The snow was blue in the overcast light, the face of the moon hidden from the face of the valley.

He had forgotten who he was.

magistrate...

Slowly he remembered as he awoke. As did his anger also awaken.

"Why didn't they listen to me? Why wouldn't they let me help them?"

Because they're ungrateful. They see kindness only as a weakness. No wonder anyone in power treats them like cattle.

The magistrate looked at his dirtied hands.

"How dare they... treat me... how weak you must take me for-"

and stupid... a failure...

"Push me out... to die? No, no..."

rejected... sacrificed...

Mortifying!

worthless...

"Discarded like trash, filth..."

Demeaned! Disgraced!

alone...

He closed his eyes - the people shouting, ransacking his palace. A mob, fighting itself.

He looked then at his wounded hand. He seethed, "If the people would bite the hand that feeds them - then they tell me how to rule them - *with sharpened teeth.*"

He struggled up and cast about immediately for his sword. The magistrate stumbled around between the thin trees, searching with no plan, crisscrossing his own path.

blood... like mud...

The black sword lay on the snow. He grasped at the hilt. His hands fumbled and dropped it, so that it stuck up out of the ground. Clenching his numb fist in rage, he drew up his sword.

An impact of will reverberates being like a stone breaks ripples onto the waters. The rising sword - a dark echo - from when animals ruled the world, and the first sorcerer-king, cloaked only in the hides of wolves, and only whose madness kept him from perishing - gazed, communing with deceitful spirits of fire - grasped the desecrating spell - to erect walls, by the point of a blade.

In silent shock the woods made witness, held their breath. The magistrate gazed into the empty woods. His own breath rising from his mouth like smoke.

It was in the exact centre of the woods. He knew this because looking around from where he found himself - there was nothing but woods. A sign. He was the centre - from which all power flowed. The solution clear - go back to the city, and together with the captain and his guard, track down the humiliating pillagers.

Steal from my palace!
like... like mud, like garbage...

Reascending his throne - all clenched fist and dire gaze - this magistrate would remake law to *keep* the people in order. If they couldn't be peaceful in their hearts, then by force they'd be silent. Or else! And the magistrate clenched his bared teeth.

He would let no one escape. Truth would be his sword, dividing innocent from damned. The high from the low. Over all! All would kneel in respect.

now we'll see who laughs...

The magistrate sloughed towards the hidden threshold, to recapture his city. The sword taking the lead; Dashi trailing behind.

He staggered under the dense trees, low along the outer wall, feeling the shadow for a gap. Now he understood why previous magistrates had ruled with an iron fist. These rabble, these monkeys. That he, a monkey king thought he could tame them! They were humiliating. Unforgiving. Then so too would he be.

He slapped his hand onto the bitter stone he could not see, again and again. He crawled in the underbrush that girded the wall's base. The cold made his hand ring with ache each time he flung it out to break against the darkness

His hand missed the wall and fell into the secret space. He pawed at the hole. Pushing his sword ahead of him, he pushed his way through to the greater blackness of the hidden chamber.

But, once in, it was not pitch black. He could see above his head the flickering outline of the trap door. A candle lit. Then the floor squeaked and a chair was moved. Someone, with a candle.

He crept. He gripped his sword and slowly climbed the ladder. He climbed all the way until he was pressed up against the hatch.

In one movement, thrusting it open, he attacked from below, swinging his black sword wide with a battle cry, aiming it at the heart of the intruder sitting at the table.

The sword spun out of Dashi's hand, clanking against the wall, and lay in the corner.

"Hello Dashi," said the master.

The master sat at the table, turning to prop his staff against the wall behind him.

"Master!" said Dashi, "I'm sorry - I didn't know it was you."

"Who did you think it was?"

"I didn't know."

"Do you swing your sword at people you don't know? You won't get on very well like that..."

"I was sneaking in..." Dashi began.

"Really," said the master, "from the sound of it I thought a company of baboons had taken up residence under the floor."

"I mean... I thought you were possibly an enemy."

"Enemy?" said the master arching his eyebrows.

"No, not an enemy," Dashi corrected.

"There are no enemies," said the master, "That's an illusion, Dashi. You know that."

"Some illusion," said Dashi, rubbing his hand.

"They can be very persistent," said the master, "Especially when one is enraged... apparently at someone you don't even know."

"I wasn't... sorry master, I was," admitted Dashi.

"About time too," said the master, "We were talking about when you'd finally get mad."

"They threw me out of the town."

"They? Who're they?"

"The people did. I don't know. But they shot an arrow at me," he said and held out his hand to show.

"The people?"

"Just one of them..." said Dashi.

"Who?"

"I don't know," said Dashi.

"Them again," said the master.

"But it was a poison arrow!" said Dashi.

The master brought the candle to look at the wound, "Lucky," he quietly, nodded. "It wasn't very good poison," said the master looking Dashi up and down. "Unless you're a ghost."

Dashi looked annoyed. "It was raining - maybe it got washed off," he suggested.

"Perhaps," said the master returning to the table.

"Or when they threw me into the mud," said Dashi, glancing down at himself.

"Apparently," the master said taking out his long pipe, "And so," he said putting the pipe in front of him on the table, "you were coming back to have a chat with them?" asked the master taking out his smoking pouch. "Set some boundaries?" He stuffed a pinch into his pipe. "Ask them never throw you out of the town again?" He put the pipe between his lips. "- and into the mud... apparently."

"Something like that," said Dashi, "I have to get back." He went to retrieve his sword.

Swift as an arrow the master retrieved his staff and held it out, blocking his student. "To join the fighting?" asked the master with gravity, striking a match with the other hand.

"Are they still fighting?" Dashi asked.

"Everyone is. They've taken over most of the city while you were away," said the master. "An embarrassing rout by the sounds of it." He leaned his staff in its place again.

Dashi felt so sad. Like something precious had been broken. It was not an emotion he would have expected for news such as this. Anger, horror, shock, but not a sorrow like that which follows the destruction of something irreplaceable.

A new mind shifted into place. "Your granddaughter!

The mistress!" he expelled.

"Probably fine," said the master, in the midst of lighting the pipe. "They're sneaky, if you hadn't noticed."

"Do they know you're here?" Dashi asked.

"My wife, or the insurgency?" asked the master back, haloed by smoke.

"Well... either," said Dashi turning to look at the front door.

"Neither, I should think," said the master, puffing, "Though she may."

"What are you doing here then?"asked Dashi.

"Oh, I came to clear away a few things," said the master, "Since you told me about this place I've used it as a home away from home."

"I have to..."

"Have to?" interrupted the master.

"Need to... I feel a need to," countered Dashi.

"You think you must," said the master.

"I do," said Dashi.

"Why do you?" the master said.

"I do, because they need me to," asserted Dashi.

"Do they?" the master asked, "Who are they?"

"The people who believed in me," he said, "I've seen their comments on the wall."

"Your side?" the master sighed. He changed the subject. "I've heard you're reading pretty well now."

"In this situation I think they've need of my sword not my poetry," said Dashi.

"You've been writing poetry?" asked the master surprised.

"It's terrible poetry," responded Dashi.

"Of those who've ever heard truly terrible poetry many would prefer the sword," replied the master, and he smiled. "As for your side – they've already lost."

Dashi felt pressure building in his chest. Despite all his good intentions, he'd failed.

"There were too many looters. They trapped most of your guard by barricading their barracks before the fighting even began. While the captain and his best guard are locked outside the gate. Good plan that," said the master, poking at the contents of the pipe. The master asked, looking up, smoke issuing from his lips, "What need is there, for them, of you?"

"But I'm the magistrate. I swore an oath–"

"Who are you??" exaggerated the master, his eyebrows raised.

Dashi gave up, "I'm Dashi." he said, "Just Dashi."

"Sit down just Dashi," the master said, "Stay a while with me. The battle is over and the war can wait for a plan. If you are to return at all, you will need that."

Dashi reluctantly sat at the table.

"Now that you can read, there's a book – about governing. It's very old, but I think you'll find it enlightening," said the master. "In a form rather like poetry."

Dashi closed his eyes and thought of the people. The stupid people. The people who were at this moment destroying not only a chance for their own freedom but his home. Not the palace. The city itself. After this it would never be home again.

The smoke hung around their heads. Dashi rubbed his forehead. He thought about all things he'd tried to make better, up in flames. The master just sat and smoked his pipe.

Finally Dashi said, "I'm used to it – people saying..." he paused, looked away, looked back, "It only gets me mad when they rub it in my face... Treating me with..." he trailed off.

The master pulled the pipe from his lips, "Contempt," he said, and replaced the pipe.

"...yeah," said Dashi, both elbows on the table.

"Your problem, young Dashi," said the master removing his pipe once again, "is the people frighten you," he said, waggling it at him, "yet that's only because they're so violent and crazy."

Dashi looked up, with a wan smile. "Then I guess it won't matter how many books I've read."

Smoke flowed around, and rose over the master's head. *"Driven by hunger, driven by fear,"* the master quoted, and added, "A book means nothing, worse than nothing, unless the reader is in the right mind to receive it."

"And the right mind's more sophisticated than any I've got," said Dashi, "I just wanted people to be... happy and... how stupid is that?" he said. "I understand now."

"What do you understand?" asked the master.

Dashi shook his head, "That I can't do what's necessary. To play politics. I'm not educated enough to govern."

The master made a noise, *"Pff...* Schooling is overrated – mostly by those who have it or sell it. You don't comprehend how what they would call your ignorance serves you, because just as the eye does not see itself, the minds we use are invisible to us. It's just who we are. It's the others in our lives that hold up the mirror.

"What I can see is, it's exactly because you're an outsider that change is possible. A thousand books won't tell a bureaucrat what it's like to live off the land. O, they know much about stealing – but they know nothing of what it is to hold up a supply caravan, because you are hungry, with bullets being fired, and blood being spilled. They know no compassion for those suffering in impoverishment –

they've never known it. Nor are they interested. Any principle beyond regulations and rules which concern and benefit them are... irrational, emotionalistic, superstition.

"Generation after generation things stay the same not because of laws and armies and tyrants and emperors. They come and go – but the hidden minds who run the invisible empire, stay."

"The crows," grasped Dashi. "Is that then not an enemy?"

"No," said the master, "We cannot allow ourselves that conceit," he said, and blew pretty smoke rings into the air, "What kind of person wants to be a bureaucrat? Who could do this deadening work? Is this their original nature? If no, then they are stuck. If stuck, they are underdeveloped, and quite possibly gone mad."

"Why mad?"

"Because of the things they've done. The bridges to their own humanity which they've burned. All with should, must and had to. A thousand lies fester within. A great deception they perpetrate upon themselves by deciding against their own minds – they shun their freedom to decide. They tell themselves they are not free. And so no one else ought to be either.

"Hence the endless paper. The endless tightening. Bureaucrats would, bit by bit, close the noose, secretly ruling the world, until no one is free. That is the way they have made for themselves. Useful. Indispensable. If we wish to dispel it from the world, we need first to remove it from our own minds."

Dashi said, "The one's I've met are of the quiet sort. I hardly ever have to deal with them. Mad drunks, frauds and liars – they're found in plenty in my courtroom."

The master said, "I will explain. There are as many

ways to be stuck as there are minds. But drunks do not organise – bureaucrats do. That's why your city is being sacked," he said.

"By the bureaucrats?" asked Dashi trying to imagine the crows getting up much of a steam to lift anything heavier that a pen, and only then to make a list.

The master said:

> *He was a quiet sort,*
> *often begins the report,*
> *of a class of crimes most horrific,*
>
> *The denial of the passions,*
> *to emotional rations,*
> *engorges ruptures-sadistic.*

The master puffed his pipe, a little curl of a smile at the corner of his mouth. Dashi wondered how it was the master could stay so happy.

"Very well, master, if this is inside, if it is one of my minds, may I enquire as to which mind that is?" asked Dashi.

"Of course," said the master.

The magistrate ruffled, but Dashi dutifully asked, "Master, please tell me which mind it is."

"The one I've spoken to you about most," came the master's reply.

Dashi thought for a moment. He thought first that the master and mistress made him think, instead of just telling him, because they were the sort that liked to do that kind of thing. Second, he thought he was being childish to question the methods of those that got nothing from trying to help him. Third, he actually thought about the question, turning it over in his memory.

"Map making mind," he said.

"Good," said the master, "Why?"

"Well," started Dashi, "If you are stuck in making maps then you never look up from the maps. Or you think the map is all there is," he thought for moment and said, "Perhaps even all that *should* be."

"There's that word again," said the master, and Dashi nodded.

When Dashi awoke it was still night. Before sleep he'd washed himself with the cloth in the basin, turning the water brown. He saw that the master had obviously replaced it with clean water, and he'd been so sound asleep, gladly fallen into the rough bed with its ripped worn dirty bare covers, that he hadn't even heard him. Although brief, he'd not had sleep like that in his own bed; that is, the magistrate's, with the softest sheets and warmest of quilts.

He looked about for his clothes, but they too had been taken away in his sleep. So he padded downstairs in search of them and his master. He found both, at the table. His master sewing the tears.

"Thank you," said Dashi.

"Oh, you're up," said the master.

"It's still night," said Dashi," I haven't slept that long."

"You slept all day," said the master.

Dashi took that in, "Hard day," he said at last.

"Hard day," repeated the master, tying off and handing the naked magistrate his trousers, "Would you like some food?"

Before Dashi had in one leg, "Oh, yes," he said.

"Rice porridge, on the stove," said the master pointing with his thumb and forefinger to the stove as he threaded another needle.

Dashi found the oblong pot of hot porridge and then looked for a bowl.

"This is the only bowl," said the master indicating the one in front of him on the table. So Dashi retrieved it. Then looked for a serving spoon.

"Use the lid," said the master.

Dashi spooned out some thick paste. He looked about for something to eat it with.

"I didn't trust any of the implements here. With the babies..."

"Hmm, yeah," agreed Dashi.

"I just used my fingers," said the master.

"But it's hot," protested the hungry Dashi.

"Wait 'til it cools," said the master, pushing the needle and rough thread in and out of the silk garment.

Dashi tried to wait but he was very hungry, scalding his fingers to get the flavourless mush to his mouth to burn his tongue."Ah!... Ahh!..." he said.

The master stopped sewing and just looked at him, Dashi, the magistrate, or former magistrate, sucking on his burned fingers.

Dashi looked back. "So... what were you doing while I slept?"

The master resumed his sewing. "I talked to people," he said.

"Ah..." said Dashi.

Not making eye contact the master said, "You say, 'Ah,' but what do you mean by it?"

"I mean, I understand what you said," he said.

"What did I say?" asked the master.

"That you talked to people," replied Dashi who was thinking about how comfortable and warm it had been in bed.

"And what did you infer I meant by that?" the master asked.

"Master, it's early," complained Dashi.

"No, it's late," the master observed correctly. "Almost too late I'd say."

Dashi sighed, "You were gathering information on the situation at hand and from that devising a course of action."

"That's a lot to mean by 'Ah...'," said the master.

"I can be surprisingly concise," explained Dashi.

The master smiled. "Ah," he said.

"Master do you mind if I change the subject?" Dashi asked.

"Ah," said the master, "Here, put this on," he said passing Dashi his red dancing costume, now criss crossed with broad sturdy stitches.

Dashi struggled into it. Sewing the rips had made it tighter, so that instead of flowing silk, his muscles were easily discernible. "It's kind of tight," he said.

"Indeed," said the master, "Old ways are constraining. For example: you've been practicing the firebreath, but still hard feelings remain. Why?"

Dashi said, "Because-"

"Because of thoughts," said the master. "Emptying is not enough if a shell is left behind to just fill up again. Feeling takes on the shape of thought."

"The firebreath doesn't get rid of thought?" asked Dashi.

"Often the thoughts will dissolve, but some are more stubborn," said the master, "especially the ones you enjoy."

"Stuck," said Dashi.

"Exactly," said the master, "An idea whose time has come and gone, but still it remains. Grasped because there is motivation to repeat it. That motivation is the same one that makes the grass grow, the birds fly, causes the animals to fight and mate and devour. It moves through everything.

"It is in all that you do, in every thought that you have, in every feeling that arises. It is a law and not a rule. That which is without it does not exist in this universe. That which loses it ceases to be. That is why the most devilish thing that can be done is to extinguish it."

"Is it trust?" asked Dashi.

"No," said the master

"IT?" Dashi asked.

"IT?!" said the master, and then he considered this, "Alright, not IT, but certainly a deep reflection of IT. That which corresponds within you, your body and mind. And that which you can come to in yourself."

Dashi thought and thought. He looked up and down. He looked from one side to the other. And finally he said, "Nope," and scratched the back of his head.

"It's Joy, Dashi," said the master.

"Did you really think I'd get that?" asked Dashi.

"I thought you might find your way there with some assistance," said the master.

"I thank you for your faith, master," said Dashi, "but people have said I am not the most clever."

"Do not lump me in with them, if you mind. I understand quite well your limitations, and what *they* think," said the master, "They call you foolish because you would benefit them for seemingly nothing – this they cannot understand. A call within you so strong that you foolishly accepted being magistrate of a town full of ungrateful people addicted to miserable Joys."

"Thank you, master," said Dashi, accepting as good a compliment as was likely coming his way.

The master said, "You are most welcome."

A silent moment descended. Dashi made nervous, prompted: "Joy?"

"And the problems therein," said the master.

"What possible problems could you have with Joy?" said Dashi.

"It's in all motivations. All of them," said the master in emphasis. "But the greater Joy – the heart of Joy, is made further distant by addiction to thoughts."

"Addiction to a mind?" clarified Dashi.

"What a mind can produce. Underlying all consciousness is Joy, but we think it's just this or that thought, so we pursue the minds," said the master, "But it's not necessarily a happy feeling. Solving a problem, squelching a fear, even pretending something isn't there, gives a ray of pleasure. We are speaking again of the why of stuckness."

"I see," said Dashi.

"What therefore is needed is a way, after the firebreath has removed the inflamed feelings, to remove the habitual thoughts," said the master, "One requires forgetfulness. For this there's a practice. A sequence of three minds that unlocks stubborn thoughts. The first mind of which, is trust. It's the same three minds incidentally as the firebreath just from the second point of view."

"The second as in power?" asked Dashi.

"No, the second mind in the sequence. You are thinking of levels."

"Oh," said Dashi.

"The firebreath comes from the mind of trust, and uses

297

the three," said the master. "Of which it is the first. And this practice also uses the same three but comes from the second mind," said the master.

"Is that mind forgetfulness?" asked Dashi.

"Perhaps it would be better called forgiveness," said the master.

"I was going to say: Ah," said Dashi,

The master laughed. "Ah."

"And the third after trust and forgiveness?" asked Dashi.

The master paused. "Call it freedom. But understand, these words are merely place holders. I could just as well have called the third mind faith instead, or confidence, or a kind of indifference to time beyond the moment.

"The point is to integrate your minds into the heart of Joy. To integrate yourself, such that there are no separations and therefore no technique necessary. It is to do without forcing. You may say you believe a rickety bridge is safe, but until you walk across, there is no real faith. Freedom is freedom to do."

"Yes, master, I see," said Dashi.

"Doubtful," said the master winding the thread tight on the spool and placed both needle and thread into a leather folder. "Regardless – to get to the third, first you practice some form of the second – in your case, a small prayer," said the master who folded his robes over himself and pronounced: "I embrace the joy in this... and I release it from everywhere it is stored within... now I am free," he said.

"That's it?" said Dashi.

The master replied, "Let's begin with the most difficult. The most hidden. Invisible barriers to the heart of joy."

"Good," said Dashi, "I'm ready, master."

"You need to find joy in the things you hate, things that

are painful," he said.

"Joy?" asked Dashi.

The master leaned forward and nodded slowly.

"About what?" asked Dashi.

"How about the thrill of being angry and playing martyr because they threw you out of your own city?" said the master. "That which threatens value, prompts a response."

"Joy?"Dashi asked again. "What about not wanting pain?"

"Not wanting?" said the master, "Unwanting, you mean. What is it that you wanted?"

"I wanted to get away from them," said Dashi.

"Exactly," the master said, "By joy I do not mean skipping about. Joy is the vital force. It is within all motivation. Why do you do anything? Why does a flower turn to the sun? Joy exists underneath all conscious experience. Even when something painful happens it is still there. It is with you always. It says, for example: your life is worth living, get up, fight, run! That is joy too," said the master, "Now, don't just mouth it - like with the firebreath, I want you to mean it."

Dashi scowled, he felt neither in the mood for the master's mysticism nor humour right now, "I, hmm, I embrace the people who threw me out of the city..."

"Stop." interrupted the master, "Not them - You."

"Me?"

"You," said the master.

"What about me?" Dashi asked.

"You're the one feeling humiliated. The old maps of the future you're holding onto, the things you wanted, gone. They remain because some joy remains caught up in a thought that needs to be forgiven. You're embracing your own motives, confessing to yourself. That's how forgiveness works. This isn't about changing *their* minds," he said. "– So don't try to make it about them," and the master sat back in his chair waiting.

"I thought this was about Joy," said Dashi.

"Joy is what you are releasing from addiction. Forgiveness is the way to free the joy from the thought that has surrounded it. Try, you'll see," said the master.

"But how does that work?" argued Dashi.

"It's magic," the master stated, "Just do it."

"But what about what they did?" asked Dashi, former magistrate.

The master sighed, "Mostly I would say, what is it to you? Get on with your life. Don't be distracted. If however, they'd done something truly terrible, then the first thing you need do is forgiving.

"It is only in forgiveness that we see truly. We untangle ourselves from our past reactions and thoughts. Trying to think our way to a solution only reinforces the thoughts we already have. We need to break with the thoughts. This is forgiveness. The most terrible people are our teachers provoking us to be able to forgive and clear our minds."

Dashi asked, "What about their responsibility for their actions?"

"You mean – what about the punishment? – that is a completely different thing from forgiveness."

"Not exactly that," said Dashi, in defence, "What if someone did something... and you couldn't release them because they would just hurt more people?"

"You will recall as a magistrate I was so lenient criminals laughed at my rules and did as they pleased, so my advice on this is hard won. Now I would look at the situation. Because I'd be able to forgive my own thoughts, my minds would be clear. What they have done is an excess, because of addictions. Hopefully we might help them, because justice need not be vengeful. I would talk to everyone, defendant included. If this person was dangerous to others, or they to him, I simply point out there are many ways to keep one individual away from the rest."

"But right and wrong," Dashi said, "Isn't there right and wrong?"

"Stalling won't help you," the master urged.

"No, master, I really want to know," said Dashi stalling.

"Alright," he said, "But then we will try to forgive, yes?"

Dashi bowed his head, "Yes, master."

"Very well," said the master, and he closed his eyes, gathering his thoughts. "Right and wrong aren't arbitrators of themselves," he began. "The question being: can the discernment of any particular right or wrong, know how right it is – or does it always need to refer to something else for its confirmation? If you say any particular right and wrong needs a separate confirmation then you have answered, 'no'. If you answer 'no,' however, this leads to an endless regression of confirmation. At best, after a few levels of right answers, you feel you have an adequate foundation. It is true enough.

"Whereas if we answer 'yes,' then we are left asking what mechanism is responsible to ascertain rightness internally. We will find ourselves asking about the totality of rightness itself, by which any particular right participates in this total rightness to some small degree.

"This only leads us to ask whether the degree of inclusion can be determined without knowing the totality, to which it is but a part? Can a rain drop know how big the ocean is?" said the master, opening his eyes again, "The answer is no – unless...

"In experiencing a totality, you aren't experiencing the

particular outside of its wholeness, or it isn't really experiencing a wholeness. Right?" said the master.

"I guess," said Dashi.

"How therefore can this be achieved? Self wholeness. You are you. By wholeness being experienced as the ground condition, a unity – both ground and figure, viewer and viewed. The mystery, both personal and transcendent! *The drop that swallowed the ocean.*

"Rightness, as such, therefore can either be experienced as the ground condition of meaning and not be divisible from what you are, and I assure you, you are something – or it is the afore mentioned lesser version, which is just the comparison of significant things. In my opinion, thinking about things, mapping things, trying to understand things, is important but subordinate to the totality. To wholeness. To what is."

"Which is IT?" Dashi asked.

"Which is Joy," rebutted the master, "And it is also you. That's why I teach you to clear yourself every day, instead of filling your head with doctrines and pointless arguments about right and wrong," said the master, "To understand is to be that which is understood."

"I don't understand," said Dashi.

"Excellent–" said the master, "It's completely meaningless chatter. Do you want to be able to live your life or give a lecture?" and he folded his arms. "Now," he said, "you were about to forgive."

It was Dashi's turn. "I, um, embrace being thrown out, of my own city," he said.

"Joy," said the master, "Embrace the Joy *in* – very important."

"All right... –Really?" said Dashi continuing. The master nodded. Dashi took a deep breath, "I embrace the joy in being thrown out- But why would someone get joy from humiliating someone else?"

"Maybe because they were humiliated themselves," the master said stretching, "Maybe living under autocratic rule made them feel small. Who better to take it out on than some magistrate outsider? With the support of the crowd around you... it isn't hate – it's justice."

Dashi got it.

"You can do their side after – but whatever your reaction was, what fuels the fire is Joy. That is nature," said the master.

Dashi centred himself, remembering how it felt, the hands grabbing, the mud, the stones striking him from every direction. "I embrace the joy in being thrown out of my own city," he said, and along with the pain there was a small thrill of battle in trying to save one's own life. He'd been cooped up in the palace so long, they even had him dancing. "And... I release it from everywhere it's stored within," said Dashi glancing at the painful hole in his left hand. This seemed pointless. "Now, I am free," he said, and no sooner had the words left his mouth than he felt a small relief rippling through his body, "...Oh," said Dashi surprised.

"You mean, 'Ah'," said the master.

"Put this on," said the master, handing Dashi a more modest cloak. He began to take off his red silk one. "No, just put it over top," said the master.

And Dashi did. "Are we going out, then?"

"We are," said the master.

"Why now?" asked Dashi.

"Because," the master said, "It is time."

"I wish I had my silk armour instead of this," said Dashi of his red robes, putting up the hood.

"Perhaps. If they are looking for you at all, they are looking for someone in magistrate's robes, not ancient rags," said the master, "consider it lucky."

Dashi did consider. He considered as he and the master slipped out into the night. It was the first time he'd been back in the city proper, the first time there was the potential for him to get something more than porridge to eat. They crept through alleyways towards the main square.

Before they got there they could see fireworks and heard loud brash music. Horns blared in earnest discord along with impassioned crashing of cymbals and random firecrackers banging. When they came out to the edge of the square in front of the palace, the tall brasiers were burning, and the coloured flags from the harvest festival reemployed. The stage had been raised, in front of the closed palace gate.

At the back of the stage, were persons occupying several large ornate chairs well behind the largest chair that sat in the centre – one that Dashi recognised, having sat in it for many long hours. And in this chair sat the golden caterpillar, gesticulating and shouting to the crowd, who responded with whoops and cheers.

"Let's see what he has to say," said the master, and moved into the crowd. Dashi hesitated and then plunged after him. Hesitated, he realised, because this crowd, this exact crowd had days before plundered his palace and been readying itself to kill him. How he felt about these dark warm figures that stood facing the fire spectacle? – he told himself to embrace, release, and be free. The shift was subtle but calming. He couldn't say what'd disappeared as he didn't know what he'd held in his heart. Something scathing, now meaningless. He realised a little more of what the master had said, that it wasn't about them at all, it was the inner self that gained, and that alone.

Dashi caught up with the master a few bodies shy from the front of the commotion. A cloud of alcohol went up in the steam of their breath. Dancers in front of the stage performed, some in unison, others in their own manner, laughing and singing, shouting and weeping, their costumes and masks improvised – men in women's dress, having exchanged presumably with women in men's, while some, both men and women, wore little at all, save the amulets which hung from their necks. These pieces of wood with writing, tied through with red string, then around the neck. They gyrated and jumped. Some swung their bodies and arms bent nearly backwards. Others, crouching low, spun, their hands held up behind their back as if they had wings. Their bare red feet pounding the snow and mud to grey slush. Another round of firecrackers exploded, competing in the din.

"Who are we?" shouted the caterpillar.

"Winners!" they shouted back, and Dashi saw the worm smirk. He smirked when they said that.

"That's what you are!" he shouted laughing, "I love each and every one of you. We cannot be stopped!" And again he laughed, and looked back at the ornate chairs for reaction. Then he said something that Dashi couldn't quite catch.

In the flickering light, looking along the back row of chairs Dashi's eye suddenly caught on a woman in a green dress with a hat.

The dancers threw themselves around ever more excited. "Who cares?" they called out, "Why not?" they answered, "Why can't I do whatever I want to? If we don't care, why should you? Who cares? Why not? If you dance nude or have sex on the ground, what's it to me? Be free!" and they chanted, "I won't care if you won't care. I won't care if you won't care. I won't care if you won't care."

"I need to see something," said Dashi, and he began to push his way through the crowd to one side, the master following in his wake. When Dashi was close enough to see the woman he was close enough to hear the finale of the caterpillar.

"Freedom is everything! No longer will we be the underclass. We who do the real work! We who love!" he bellowed. And they all applauded.

Dashi only vaguely noted the plagiarism, as he was looking up on the stage at the mistress, sitting with her hands folded in her lap. The magistrate's hat upon her head.

"Be as you are! Do as you like! Take what you want! Just follow freedom! Follow love and we will crush our enemies! The future will be free! Freedom is everything! This, I, the golden master declare!" And they cheered, as servants who Dashi recognised from the kitchen brought out more wine and steaming dishes of food and rice. Dashi thought the kitchen staff looked unkempt, harried, exhausted. The people around them pressed forward to get to the free food. The master tugged his sleeve, "Time to go," he said.

He saw others instead of going for the food, had opted for the wine and were gyrating about to the jolly tunes the out of sight musicians were playing. Two men were laughing, looking to each other, as the bare breasted woman between them, tilted up her head to receive the wine they were pouring into her. She screeched in drunken debauchery as it spilled down her breasts, and then spun herself in circles. The cacophony of the music rose. Dashi looking back, thought he saw treasury guards walk by where moments ago they'd stood.

They made away from the flickering fires, and back to the darkness of the streets, their eyes adjusting quickly with the aid of the moon. The din hiding their quick footsteps.

When they were back in the shadows the master said in Dashi's ear, "What do you think of your first political rally?"

"I think..." said Dashi, "that's my hat."

"She wears it better than her sister," joked the master, and he tugged on Dashi's sleeve again to lead him away down into the narrow alleyways. Dashi followed, and when they were back in the dark alleyways away from the revelry, the master said, "You don't think she's betrayed you?"

"No... of course not," said Dashi.

The master chuckled, "It's just a game to her. Let's go to a place I know where we can speak freely."

Outside it had begun to rain and the thin roof echoed with pittering splashes, while inside drops fell into pots set out to catch the leaks. The master put down his cup on the tavern table. "She's not much for running," said the master, "Too bad - she absolutely hates pompous officials. Especially the golden worm. Well, she's in for the duration."

"I call him that too," Dashi laughed. "The poor mistress," he said feeling bad about distrusting her. "And where?... I know some of the people can be rough - but all those... uh, – it was as they'd gone feral."

The master said, "They were always here. A constellation of minds from earlier layers, revealing a regression. It's inside everyone."

"And the dancing?" said Dashi.

"Hullaballoo," said the master, "The dance of the damned. That's what a physician from the south, I met visiting the court, called it. It's involuntary. You can think of it like a spell."

"The poor people," said Dashi, who's eyes kept darting to the far door to see who was coming in to this, the roughest place in town, from whence so many of his customers came to stand accused at his recently magisterial feet. "They don't know what they're doing."

"They did try to kill you," said the master.

"I thought we released that," said Dashi

"You released the joy you didn't think was there, making things sticky. You forgave. But that doesn't mean they didn't try to kill you," the master said.

"Even if they didn't understand?" asked Dashi, watching a dampened patron enter, his cloak dripping spots across the floor.

"Oh they understood enough," the master said, "and even if one could say they didn't, they were still getting ready to stone you."

"There is that," said Dashi, pensive. "And I don't forgive them for that? Is that right?"

"If they didn't understand then what would be there to forgive in the way you mean it. But that isn't even what forgiveness is," he said, "When people describe someone begging for forgiveness, and it being granted they are describing the pardoning of punishment. Nothing to do with forgiveness at all."

"I think I see that," said Dashi.

"You, for example, were set to go back into the city, and with your guard, butcher your way back to being magistrate. Thus Dashi the good would have become just another in a long line of self-serving magistrates the golden worm could do business with.

"That was another possible outcome of their plan – and they map many contingencies. The reason why they hide is so they can play it, whichever way it goes – which seems pretty smart. Actually they're just cowards, but they realise its advantages."

Dashi puffed himself slightly to protest his innocence saying, "If I were going to do that, why wouldn't I just have all the damn crows executed?"

The master said. "Because they run your city so you need some of them. And because you would have to deal with the rioters first. By the time that was done, you'd find the entire bureaucracy had ironclad alibis. O they might throw you one or two, who knew nothing enough to implicate anyone. But they'd have already been chosen for potential sacrifice.

"However, they believe their plan has succeeded in another way–"

"Because they think I'm dead," said Dashi realising.

"Indeed," said the master.

"So now we need a plan," Dashi said.

"Yes, a plan," said the master.

And Dashi waited. "All right, master," he said, "what is the plan?"

"Don't know," said the master.

"But you're thinking about it," said Dashi.

"No. I don't think. You're the one who thinks," he said and briefly scratched his chin.

"I need to let it come to me. I understand," Dashi said.

"Do you?" said the master, "I don't mean for you to come up with a plan – or me for that matter. The plan awaits us."

"But..." said Dashi.

"What has exceeded its bounds will be set back again. The mob is excessive already, so they will step over the boundaries that will weaken their position. Ones that will mean their failure. That is the nature of nature," said the master. "Not careful, they will leave openings in their armour. When there is a small opening there will be all the space in the world for us to move."

Dashi nodded.

The master said, "As for the crows, they have severed minds, they are therefore blind to them. Their blindness is our advantage. We can act in ways they can no longer understand – nor therefore map."

"They will interpret incorrectly," said Dashi.

"Yes. When you said to the treasurer that you wanted the people to be free, he *knew*... that you meant the people ought to think they are free, as a means to control them. That you were setting yourself as the people's general and that therefore you'd need an enemy to depose for show. He guessed that it was him. Who else was a greater target than himself?

"He knew whatever limitations you truly had, that you played the fool. So your game was hidden behind ridiculously brash journeys for *soup!* All calculated to let the people see you were not afraid – that the power was *yours*. He, who could not easily leave his gilded fortress, watched, as you plied the people not with gold, but with flattery. See how pleased he is with himself, having turned the tables on you?"

Dashi, emphasising each word, said, "That - is - completely - twisted."

"An addiction to the small Joy contained in a small thought," said the master.

"Twisted," repeated Dashi.

"Conflicted," the master said.

"More than that!" said Dashi.

"It all boils down to that though," the master said, "What all ideologies are ultimately about: a strategy to attain a broken joy. Broken because of inner conflict. Let me explain it externally. As a child maybe your brother did something you hated, so you felt that you want to kill your brother..."

"I loved my brother," protested Dashi, "mostly."

The master conceded, "But you also love your brother... What to do?" he said, "One philosophy says throw out the part of you that wants to kill. Just take that desire and put it behind you, push it out of awareness. However the desire remains. In fact, in the dark they become stronger.

"Another view focuses on the light and the dark saying: because love and hate are obviously opposites they cannot both exist simultaneously, therefore we need to find the one that is the more essential. Which is indeed love. However this merely places the feeling in a hierarchy. It doesn't help with the urge. And it tends to introduce an ideal good, that ultimately breaks the world into itself, as the good, and everything else being evil. We know where that leads.

"A third position then is to get rid of all desires. They pull and push you into every motivation. It's reasoned they're the problems. I have some sympathy for this, but obviously you need desires to operate in the world. Even the desire to be rid of desires is a desire – so really this is just a trap. One mind plays last man standing, while pretending to be impartial. Minds are never impartial," said the master.

"If you can't throw one, or all of them out, or put them in a hierarchy – you could just follow through with the desire. Slay your brother. That of course will have consequences. Probably unpleasant ones. And more important for us, it sets the minds against each other in competition.

"And if you say that the desire to love, and the desire to kill, are contextual to what is happening, that surely when he was kind you loved him, and when not, that's when you hated. Again, it has the same effect of making a competition. Only now you've externalized the choices into the environment as a way of escaping being responsible for making the decision," said the master, "So what to do?"

"We forgive?" guessed Dashi.

"Not as such," said the master, taking a drink, "Try again."

Dashi tried again, "We grow up?"

The master took another sip. "Good enough," he said, "We seek the natural way. We hear all minds' desires. But instead of pitting them against one another, we ask what is the quality of this urge? And we know from observation that the marker of quality for any mind is joy.

"As each mind rises to its joy it's also what we understand as maturing. Because as they rise to their individual joys, to be at their highest functionality, they also become able to function together, and together they are able to function even better than they can alone.

"Thus the joyful mind is the most powerful, the most able to survive, with the most worthy identity, the greatest ability to give and receive, with the greatest of understanding, and the greatest ease and simplicity. Which is the wisdom you expect from maturity.

"A desire to kill your brother, we would say, comes from the mind of a child. You need things to buoy you up: wisdom, beauty, inspiration. And people who know the difference between being adult and juvenile, and will tell you so. Or you'll be surrounded by fawners and liars. They'll tell you it's all right to kill - if that means they can go on stealing, and feeding on life's energy - yours.

"As the minds are connected, we are. If a child has no one, if they belong nowhere, then they will decide for themselves. A long journey. But even then people do not make decisions in an empty space. The world conditions your thinking without always your best interest at heart.

"Though it may seem, and some think this is the answer to answering rationally, perfectly, by doing so without regard for anything or anyone. That each should be their own isolated consciousness. What they do not take in to account is what it is that they are, and its connection to time. We have a nature. We will go through stages of integration. An action taken now in one stage will affect your future. The temporal minds connect us to time. We are physical beings. We are social beings."

"But if you have no one-" began Dashi.

"An abandoned child is extraordinarily lucky to have a nature that chooses blindly, but well, otherwise it will be a tragedy. That is why adults seek to help children," said the master, "It's so crucial, they will go out of their way to mother or father, or in my case to grandfather it. That is what true adults do. It is natural. How could we survive if our individual maturity didn't mean guiding a child to its own maturity? That's why it's so easy to exploit,

Dashi asked, "What then is this desire centred on the child? What mind is it that has come to joy? What mind loves a child?"

The master said, "The mate of the mind of freedom. Inspiration, like a star in the night. You do not know this yet, but when all the world is dark, a child is a glimmer of hope. It is for the future, where our children will walk, that we seek to make a better world today. At the highest level of integration what you do for yourself you do also for the world. That is what being an adult means."

Dashi asked "What does the individual receive?"

The master answered, "They receive the faith to go on."

"I understand, master. I'm ready to forgive," said Dashi.

The master looking up from his porridge pursed his lips in thought but said nothing.

"A donkey out of a ditch?" offered Dashi.

"A butterfly out of a caterpillar," said the master, who then continued to think and eat porridge.

"I don't know if I like the company," Dashi said who had already finished his.

"They also become moths," replied the master.

So Dashi waited. He gazed into his empty bowl. A crack ran down one side and so it would soon break and be useless he told himself. That what he told himself removing it from the tavern under his cloak. And the master was right: there was a small thrill. Still there was also a twinge inside him. His old ways returned with surprising ease. And if that, how far to sleeping outside in the forest, surrounded by the other rejected undesirables.

The spoon from the tavern however, felt more like an essential dignity and he therefore somehow felt more justified. But he knew justification was a trick of creative mind. It was just a challenge. And what did creative mind understand about being put to ill use? What mind was it that had asked for a believable story? One that was thinking about survival, he surmised.

It made him think differently of those who'd just ransacked his palace... the magistrate's palace, he corrected himself. Dashi didn't know if he'd be able to come up with a justification. As the master said, perhaps it was something else they needed.

Dashi was startled out of his reverie. The master was already speaking.

"Before civilisation, there were adults, they were whole, and they did what was most valuable to them, they were one with their heart of Joy. That was their contribution to the group. They did not do what others valued most. Just as each of the minds have interdependent natures but work best in concert, so too do people. Cooperation makes for a heart of Joy.

"Heart of Joy," repeated Dashi to sound as if he'd been following all along.

The master raised an eyebrow. "Because the minds begin in survival, wanting security, they do not always cooperate well. The child cannot coordinate many points of view simultaneously. They are drawn in many directions.

"When they are faced with a great difficulty, a great loss, they will do their best. The minds, unable to comprehend each other's language come to fighting. Learning is a long road. We learn by mistakes. We learn by making them and forgiving ourselves and trying again. Without forgiveness, learning stops and maturity arrests. It is in this manner that each mind must traverse all the levels, each more integrating than the last. And to speak to one another each level elects one mind to be the central language into which all the others are to be translated. This is how they find commonality.

"But what language is best? Which mind is to be the centre? Your strongest minds will inevitably come to stake their claim, but cooperation is not created by strength alone. Just as there are ways to every other potential, there is a way to the heart. The heart, is reached through maturity. It is the sequence of levels. That is the sequence of central minds: survival, power, identity–"

"Cake!" said Dashi recognising.

"Cake?" said the master, confused.

"The layers of the cake. The mistress... She said levels actually, but I thought cake..." Dashi trailed off.

"Cake, then," sighed the master. "Whose layers are?"

"Survival, power, identity, reciprocity, principle, and beauty," said Dashi.

"I say wholeness," said the master, "She says beauty."

"A disagreement?" asked Dashi.

"A difference in definition," replied the master, "Wholeness is the centre, the pinnacle of observing mind. Because when you reach wholeness it is of course the beginning of that level, or layer, so it is mysterious. The centre matures into Joy as its indicator – and your particular and personal heart of Joy, a stable pair of minds. If you want to know.

"Beauty is her heart of Joy, her particular version of wholeness, to which she would say that there are only particular wholenesses and so why talk about a general case. However, salient a wholeness as beauty is, I am continuing the sequence from the fifth to the sixth.

"Wholeness is recognised first as the inescapable maturation of principle, and *then* one gets to the heart of Joy, which is the individualised nature of it."

"Wait, there's more than one wholeness?" asked Dashi.

"No, just the one. But everything in the whole is reflected throughout the whole. The reason each specific mind is present in the first place is because it was naturally advantageous and harmonious as a family, both cognitively and tribally. The drop that swallows the ocean. It can be difficult to imagine it," admitted the master.

"IT?" asked Dashi joking.

The master ignored this, "An aesthetic... no, let's say a metaphysical identity. Wholeness has many faces. As many as there are minds."

Dashi interjected, "And who knows how many *that* might be."

The master stopped speaking and looked at his pupil.

"Sorry, master," said Dashi, "I'll be serious."

"Case and point," said the master, "Certain individuals with dark histories can find introspection into their own minds akin to speaking as family members whose characteristics correspond to some mind they naturally hold in common. Such as your brother's sarcastic sense of humour.

"As I said, children can only do their best. And I also said that mistakes are the road to learning and to maturity."

"If they can get there," Dashi said, looking around him to indicate the house of the dead children.

"Indeed," said the master, "Here there was no attempt by those without their own Joy to foster the flame of the soul. The couple who kept those children, fed them, kept them clean – but did not love them. Why?

"Because they had been instructed by authorities they feared. Why?

"They told them not to. Because they knew if one doesn't love a child, if there is no Joy, no flame to light its candle, it will die of despair. This being known, we can assume the buyers were seeking greater supply and a therefore a lower price."

"That's despicable," spat Dashi.

"You think one can chart a course based on right thinking. But that is your level. Every strategy subscribes to the current centre, the layer's motivation, or you don't continue it – good or bad. Even if that good is to be rational.

"At survival, a child can readily understand hurt for themselves. Show them their behaviour hurts you. They'll empathically understand that too. But they will chose their survival. Good and bad, right and wrong are abstract principles of morality, cohering to a different centre.

"When you tell a child it is wrong, and bad, the child takes it that you do not love it – and that only on the condition it is good and right – will you grant again the love the child needs. The child, who does not understand what they are doing, just learns to lie – to please. To survive.

"It puts on a mask to be acceptable to the bewildering constellation of seemingly ambiguous parental shoulds. The child mimics them. Creates within them a caricature of the adults and their motives. It pretends a false centre and steps off the path of its own Joy.

"Worse – punish a child for making mistakes, and they start looking over their shoulder, watching themselves being watched. They lose trust. Always questioning, never certain. They weigh everything against their fear. Between a right and wrong, a good and bad, they cannot divine – they are maddened.

"Minds don't tolerate confusion. To be confused is to become immobilised. To freeze is to become prey. Minds require a centre to harmonise. Made in confusion and fear, the false self, it has imagined a centre. One of the child's minds will answer to this. If making a mistake is forbidden - then the child will find an answer. The best being one that answers everything."

"A justification you mean," said Dashi.

The master nodded. "Thus a refined mask is created and put on over the previous. Soon the world will supply a reflection, created by others with the similar masks. The addiction to this little Joy they do not realise traps them in a strategy they will find hard to release. They cling to it with grim death and defend it with irrational fervour. A cause, a noble cause, and they are the hero. Even if a dark one," said the master.

"You are saying they need to forgive," said Dashi.

"They fear that to forgive, is to lose it all, and fall back into the chaos of ambiguity." The master smiled, "Only artists and gods can live in ambiguity... probably."

"All those people bellowing in the square are looking for something to hold themselves together, not realising that the strategy they've adopted is what makes them so miserable?" said Dashi.

The master nodded. "People need to believe in something deeper than their pain. Otherwise any half-wit cult leader can sway them to do anything, with a bit of over-excitement," said the master, "To be free you must come to maturity, to your heart of Joy, which is Joy in its wholeness. It is your natural mature state. But to get there you must let go of the Joy that has imagined itself separate from the whole."

"So if the people can come to their heart of Joy then they will be free?" said Dashi excitement building.

"If they come to themselves. Coming to yourself is coming to wholeness - and the way of wholeness is Joy - and that Joy, is your heart of Joy and no one else's. What matters is to speak the language of your Joy. Beauty is the way of the mistress, her heart of Joy, the language which she most naturally speaks. In her centre everything is about art because it translates the other minds best."

"Ah, bring the people to their own language," said Dashi.

"And how would you do that?" the master asked.

"You show people how to forgive?" suggested Dashi.

"To forgive is to become yourself again, true. But how?" asked the master.

"Teach them the firebreath?" said Dashi.

"To remove grief. A good beginning, but again, how?" said the master.

"Of course – you teach them to release, to forgive," Dashi said.

"I will teach them? Not I. But again, how, Dashi? What if they are resistant? Tell them it's good for them, and they will shy away. Tell them the greater glory awaits, and it sounds ingenuous. Tell them: to not do it is to remain in sorrow, denies the pleasure they know they receive from however they've chosen to be.

"All of theses are just sneakier ways to say they *should*. But do they need it from the inside? This isn't a proposition about value. This isn't a trinket in the market. Imagine that you are rich and that you have anything that you can desire. You have power, identity, money, standing. Perhaps you live in a palace," said the master.

"Yeah," said Dashi, understated.

"Even if it's all a fiction, an act, so what? The world just reflects our insides. The strongest in you is exalted, and what conflicts you debase. Why would you potentially give all that up to pursue some notion of true self?" asked the master.

320

"Because..." started Dashi, looking within, "there is part of them that desires to be whole. Even though that part has been shoved aside, its desire remains. Speak to that desire."

"What if you, offering the path to their freedom, wait, and they just go round and round arguing? Some minds want the change and others don't. Immature as it is, the only integration is a layer's centre," said the master.

"I guess they have to grow up," said Dashi disappointed.

"I guess they do," said the master, watching Dashi carefully. "And what do you feel about that? - about the people?"

Dashi felt within himself, "I'm disgusted by them," he said, "Perhaps I could be more compassionate but right now I feel used - except I know it was I who imposed myself," he turned his head away. "It seems so futile, and confusing - and sad."

Said the master, "Consider feeling to be like water. In grief one is crushed under an avalanche of ice. There is nothing to do except wait for spring thaw.

"Except if we learn to use the firebreath. Then we change the ice into flowing water. Now you feel as though you may drown, but you are swimming.

"As we continue our practice the water becomes a mist, and we stumble about not knowing where we are, yet the more we do, we are standing on solid ground. The water becomes then moisture in the air. Our tears just some more sorrow added to all the others in the background of being human. And we move on.

"What is a puddle or a lake but an impression in the ground? What is a thought but an impression on your minds? This is not about losing feelings but freeing them from stagnation. If reactions are based in the past then

321

you don't respond to the present and toward your future. A river is always in motion; the best a puddle can do is dry up. When your joy is in dirty puddles, it lessens the flow of your river.

"When you forgive, you release the thought. It will be like it'd never been there. Forgiving is the forgetting that a child does so easily, and we are taught not to. We regain ourselves by eliminating these channels and depressions in which we no longer wish to flow."

"I understand, master. In order to grow up you have to have forgiveness. That is what I'll teach when I return," said the magistrate.

"You assume," said the master.

Dashi realised, Dashi, the magistrate, had a map to a future that perhaps no longer existed. This was pretending.

"I embrace..." said the master, and Dashi silently removed the old shell of his thought so his energies could flow into new territory.

Dashi felt another thought lighter, "Master," he said, "after I have cultivated my self, will I then be able to release the people from their oppression? I mean, I know that part of it is in their own minds, so I will teach them to release what is stuck. But what about externally? What about tyrants?"

The master put his hands together and thought. "I have not gotten through... yet," said the master and he paused. "There are two things. One is that the process of forgiveness is the inherent process of learning from your mistakes. Children do it easily.

"The second, is that wholeness cannot be explained at a level below the level of wholeness. This means there is no procedure, codification or map; no deal, trade or exchange; no name, status, or identification; no force, facility, or skill; no endurance, sustenance, or nourishment, which will reproduce the effect of that very same thing given via a master of self. Even if they appear the same. Because the ends are different. Thus the means will diverge. The same object, given openly is a gift, given to manipulate you is a trap.

"Two problems. The first I have already spoken of. A child made afraid of not knowing what is right, of making mistakes, gains the fear of learning, and loses the ability to forgive. They take on the strategies to make themselves acceptable, to survive," the master raised his finger, "For being clever, for being nice, and being approved of. All tied up with this critic. This false serious mind, with its numbers and its maps. Do you understand?" said the master.

"All too well," said Dashi.

"Good, then we're getting somewhere," said the master, who again paused. "Without..." he began, "Without a true adult, there is no exemplar of wholeness. They are left relying on their inherent desire for wholeness - the mind of that will one day be their sixth centre. The entelechy that grows within them to bloom.

"But the child is dealing with flawed giants and that is so very far away. So for the potential of a future, it sacrifices its integrity. Just as their flawed parents did. And theirs. Grandparent to parent to child. All of them pretending to do what is right. Putting on the mask of the disapproving caricature they created, and didn't have the capacity to comprehend. The child pretends it understands why its parents are the way they are, when even they don't know. In fear, for that is the intention by which it was made, the mask takes on all the trappings of the authority it claims itself to be - wrapping a cloak around its denial spun in the garb of dream figments: emperor and empress. The mask becomes the terrible parent."

"Or magistrate," said Dashi.

The master nodded. "The mask, which is a constellation of minds, exists at the level of survival and will use the fear of death, from the language of survival, to drive all minds to comply. The brute at the root. 'Why am I being punished?' They imagine a reason. 'I must deserve to be punished.' Then a mind will create a voice saying: 'You do deserve to be punished, but listen to me and you shall be saved.'

"It will ride you, it will spur you in the most painful of places. Desiring to be free to live, you'll chose to be a willing slave. The mask forged at the level of safety will maintain itself to keep you safe forever. It will map hidden dangers, which will appear everywhere. Out of fear of death it will grip hard the reins of power. And that is why," said the master, "to remove the tyrant from the outside, you must first remove it from the inside."

Dashi drew in his breath, "Oh..." said Dashi, the long breath falling from his mouth. "Master," he said, and bowed.

The master returned the bow. "To forgive is to grow up. To remove the deadwood. To be done with the past. By embracing the Joy in the disciplinarian, by embracing the Joy in your inner tyrant that lives in fear of death, in the fear of being wrong, the mind that draws up pointless charts and makes foolish rules–"

"The crows," Dashi realised.

The master continued, "So why give up all that? Maybe you do, maybe you don't. However, now you understand, what you give to yourself in the spirit of wholeness is a gift, what is done in addiction is a trap. Always the severed minds will have their say. You will live knowing that inside you have created a false self image, and a false enemy image."

"I see," said Dashi.

"Almost," said the master, "What is stuck?"

"Mapping mind," said Dashi.

"Is it?" replied the master.

"Didn't you just say...?"

"Did I?" the master replied. "– Yet another twist."

Dashi furrowed his brow, hoping for the seed of inspiration.

The mind of inspiration, a mind corrected.

Which got Dashi to thinking about how mapping mind does that. Keeping things in little boxes. "But how then does in make the pretend mask?" he wondered.

"Oh! – mapping mind doesn't pretend, it makes maps..." said Dashi, "– that's pretending mind..." he said, the illumination dawning, "Master, pretending it's being mapping mind!" and he put his hand over his mouth.

"Or any other," said the master nodding slowly. "Remember I told you about leveraging creative mind?"

"Pretend maps, and pretend deals... and, and pretend empathy. Pretend confidence?" sputtered Dashi.

"Pretend Joy even. All of it," said the master.

"Master this is terrible," said Dashi. "How do you ever know if it's an illusion?"

"Give up the great pretence, and allow your creative mind to return to you. Embrace the joy of its adaptability. It may be, to mature, the mind of analysis must discern truth and illusion. See simple maps and accurate ones. Know between trivial and deep. This is my teaching. Forgive and be free."

The two lay in the small bed, in the small room at the top of the stairs. The sole window of the house cast a moonlit smear of itself upon the far wall. Dashi was abnormally aware of colours. The black night, the blue light, the orange flare of the master's pipe.

Dashi laughed in the dark. He felt excited, but he felt at peace. In a strange way he couldn't define either. He felt like he was somewhere between worlds. Thoughts he'd carried, known, used, everyday – now they were gone. More than that, it was hard to even remember what they'd been. He searched his minds for what wasn't there.

It was funny. Once he said he was free, the thoughts just vanished. Though sometimes with a little repetition. He couldn't recall the distinction he'd moments before felt certain was crucially important, and by tomorrow he'd have forgotten it'd ever been there. He confessed, he forgave, he gained he didn't know what.

With the master's guidance, Dashi had already acknowledged the joy in pettiness, in greed, in worrying, in being the sensible one, in the desire for popularity, in false humility, in self pity, and especially in anger. Dashi embraced his unacknowledged Joys. Where he thought to find himself indignant he found instead self-righteousness. Where he thought to find himself compassionate he found instead a veneer of hurt superiority. Naked self-justification hidden inside a character he'd thought was him, but was revealed as a kind of dream. An intention long forgotten. Creative mind just doing what it was asked.

He still struggled with anger. It lessened but it didn't leave. The master said there was more to embrace. More miserable Joy. Pull the energy from the masks of habit, release the little role that had forgotten it was a role. Forgive the monsters from under the bed. Better that than sleepwalking your life away.

Dashi imagined the mask suffocating him, with only the tiniest of holes to breathe through, and only a pinprick mouth with which to eat. His stomach growled and he wished for better than porridge. Then he forgave it. When his stomach growled again, he was a little more grateful for porridge, but he'd still like better.

Dashi looked out the small window sideways to see the moon just coming into view. It was big and fat and full. The moon changed. Dashi was changed. The moon was the moon, but who was he? The master had said the partner of creative mind was intuitive mind, and they shared the ability to fill in empty spaces – to guess. Eventually, even under uncertainty, one had to take action. Pretending you knew, helped. As long as you could remember when you were pretending.

"This is how we could free the people – isn't it?" he asked into the night.

The master smoked his pipe, "I don't care for the freedom of the people, just you," said the master, "But if this should happen, the people will require a leader who has become free. Only a few will follow at first, but then more, until eventually they'll agree it's just common wisdom."

"What wisdom is that?" asked Dashi.

"That in cultivating the self you add what is greatest to the world," said the master blowing a ring across the moon beam which illuminated it like a halo. "And that if people aren't actively looking for their own wholeness they will be driven by fear."

"O that," Dashi said, "So you explain to them why they don't have to be afraid."

"Telling people, 'don't be afraid,' doesn't make them any less afraid. It only tells them to hide their fear. Some ways move people towards their own blossoming, and others to rot in the ground. The way that does not contain the whole spirit becomes a mockery of itself. Good intentions are merely another kind of should, a joyless means to inauthentic ends.

"Your mistress would promote beauty. In public life to praise it, and to nurture great artists. But if a ruler does this because... it's a good idea... then they do not understand. Because they think they should, or worse, have to – these thoughts arise out of being good, doing right, making sure, and other disassociations of purpose.

"Real beauty opens you to the silence, to being. Real artists have difficult personalities because they are focused upon whole Joy, whole beauty, not vainglory and counterfeit goodness. Unlike politicians, what they express is self-originating, out of their being – imperfect as it is. Artists have better things to concern themselves with, than telling other people... what to do," said the master, letting the smoke drift up out of his mouth.

He said, "Whereas, an ideal of beauty will be perfected, enclosed and placed upon high. Operators will appear. They will leverage it. Liars and fawners, always charming and witty – they will define it. Pretenders will make it fashionable to desecrate, because that is all they can do. Because they have turned away from themselves. They have lost the way. Should you offer money, all of them will burrow into the carcass until any sense of beauty is hollowed.

"Thus the ruler who would foist what is good and beautiful upon the people, but does not care for it himself, will in the end only make the people despise it and him. Every advisor, who is themselves not free, that brings a proclaimed good to a ruler, only serves to entangle that good with madness. Theirs, the rulers, the people's – it's endless."

"This is evil then. This is what we must eliminate," said Dashi.

"No enemy," said the master, "Just a pretension, a charade. Evil shows up in the guise of good."

"They're pretending to be good?" asked Dashi.

"They pretend to be evil," replied the master, lighting another match, "Pretend they're not themselves." And with his breath he rekindled the embers. "Evil: is a thin gruel of miserly Joy," said the master and left off to puff his pipe.

Dashi looked out at the moon again.

One day the master said he had to attend to other matters. Dashi wanted to go with him, but the master insisted Dashi stay and concentrate on his cultivation. He acquiesced, doing as his master bid. Dashi watched the door close behind the master, leaving Dashi alone in the house of dead children.

Dashi ate some porridge. It was too cold. He could have reheated it, but he was keeping the fuel they'd collected for warmth. If he really needed to, he could crawl out through the hole in the wall and into the woods and gather more. Though truth be told, he didn't like going beneath the floor of the habitation. The cave beneath his feet he'd entered when he'd come out from the trees, felt like stepping back, and he wanted to move forward.

Dashi therefore spent the first day in bed, sitting, meditating, with all the rags of comfort wrapped around for warmth. As was his habit he did the firebreath. He wondered whether any of the others who'd sat with him still did. He hoped they were safe. He burned away rising fears.

After a time he switched to forgiving practice. He found in himself many irritations. So many things that irked him. Attitudes that other people had that really made him jump. Judgments covered in prickles.

Dashi realised two things that day. Firstly that Joy, despite appearances to the contrary, was indeed under everything. No matter how bothersome their actions, nor how justified his anger, or impeccably reasoned his self-righteousness, there lived underneath, the impulse of doing. All action, all thought, all feeling stemmed from saying yes. Even saying no required you say yes. A positive affirmation of will – whatever the object. What, in its tiniest shards was difficult to make out as Joy, but in quality, in feeling, was revealed as the wage one drew to bear witness against yourself. Self in abnegation.

The other thing he realised was all of the now invisible freedoms from forgiveness opened space in his heart for serenity. The constant whir of old feeling swarming beneath his awareness he could now hear. He could pick out one, and hold it in his attention.

He might begin on a first pass, by releasing 'this,' subsequently realising the little trapped joy's spiteful pleasure. What you get out of saying yes to your sense of separateness? One mind can lose, and another win. Then that one mind can be more important. Not just presently, in this circumstance, but just so. Dashi tried to argue for it, but he couldn't argue it.

A line of principle he imagined, greater to lesser. Outside of which was an emptiness. If he drew the ends of the line together, the circle was just the defined temporal importance, arising, reaching the peak, and falling. Comprehension existed in the judged domain within the circle. The focus. While outside was the extreme at which thought dissolved.

What previously was undifferentiated thought, because of a wall became a belonging. Like a house, or a city. A trick of focus. And without really changing anything, focus could make the background become foreground anchored but unbounded – the so called, everything else. Not an emptiness at all. Just the unknown world.

Which is more important? The city or the land? Beyond the cropland, where the enclosure was a mere ditch, there was more. And beyond this valley, more. No matter how far out he drew the bounding circle, there was more, all just as important to what was within the circle.

He wondered if this might apply to more than land. By this time, however, the day was becoming dark. It had been overcast and although nearly spring, winter held heaven and earth in its grip.

Dashi reheated the porridge too hot. He put out a bowl for the master. The master did not return. Dashi returned to the bed and cultivating his minds, fell asleep. In the morning he thomped downstairs expecting to see the master but was met only by the table, the chairs, and the bowl of porridge now gone cold.

On the second day, Dashi either sat at the table most of the day, or paced about it. He opened the hatch to the cave, thinking he might escape and go wandering about in the woods beyond but the master had asked him to clear his minds. Dashi closed the door to the forest.

As he walked the boards he became again magistrate

and pontificated, sometimes aloud, his opinions on statecraft and public welfare. "One pretends to be something one is not when one pretends to not be something one is," he said to the imagined crowd. They nodded.

"The seen is not separated from the seer. Nothing can be outside of the whole."

"*Ah...*" they replied.

"Our inherited longings, are chosen by nature – to drive you, to drive everyone. We cannot help but create them in our external world. In the desire's fulfillment you benefit the tribe, and its future generations. It is because of these conditions that the individual minds are the ones they are," he said to them, but really he was wondering where the granddaughter was. He hoped she was safe.

Someone in the crowd asked about stuckness. To which Dashi replied, "The single minded pursuit of any end will be its downfall. Even the consciousness which divides heaven and earth and thinks it understands something will be without recourse in the end."

Someone popped up in the back and said, *Recourse to what?*

Dashi didn't know. He went back to bed to think about it. "Sanity," he replied, lying there. "To hear only your own voice, to see only your own reflection, to be solitary is to go mad – for one mind, for one person, for an empire."

The crowd nodded. *Then why do people go along with the group?* said the same voice, popping up from the otherwise awed gathering. Annoyed, Dashi wondered, who was this?

He answered, "Groups of followers have leaders. A true leader comes out of the one within, becomes the many minds and returns to the one just as the oak grows from an acorn, and in its maturity it creates them.

"If you do not live your own nature it's just another game to win. Leadership will be filled with predators playing for power. Thus the followers - grovellers - echo whatever they see as powerful, cooperating only to maintain their supply. Truth becomes flexible. Understood as only a way to get what is desired. Thus when the powerful fail - their followers disavow.

"Everything is about their nourishment but nothing else is nourished, everything is about power, but nothing lasting is achieved. The small are crowded out, nature is abused, and under the regimes, food becomes scarce or tainted. Because they do not care. Because they have chosen the tactical means of a predator, and not the greater one."

Isn't a magistrate, a judge of life and death, also then a predator? asked Dashi's heckler.

"Absolutely," Dashi said to himself, "A predator of predators." That seemed to shut him up, finally. Dashi stared at the stained ceiling for awhile. Then he got up again.

He thought of leaving to look for food, but one mind pointed out he'd no money, and if spotted he'd be arrested and also the reason he wanted to defy the master's request was, he admitted to himself, to be a rebel - just for the fun of it.

He sat. "I embrace the Joy in being the defiant one," Dashi began his absolution. How many times he wondered had he made a decision that changed the destiny of his life because at the time he felt a tiny spark of spite. An attempt to regain some power. A mind remembering itself as a small child with the desire to choose its own way.

A wind blew the door open again, as it had when he and the captain had met here. Dashi got up and closed it tight, and then he wondered - how his friend was faring, a warrior, unable to hide like he, a thief in the night, with the ingrained instinct to run.

This Dashi realised was the humour in the tragedy – the compassion and the humanness of all evil – these natural childish desires. How could any of us know they would become mistakes? – a little decision – made in innocence – that dooms us. A perfection of means ending in an unseemly confusion of character. The only way to do better, to see further, was to cultivate the temporal minds, to free them to see over the horizon as they'd adapted to do. To open ourselves to our own Joy.

Dashi sat with his back against the wall. "I embrace... release... free... embrace... release... free... embrace... release... free... embrace... release... free..." he chanted sometimes aloud, sometimes within himself.

Dashi spent the next day removing more. And the next day after. And he only thought of soup and noodles and dumplings seven times.

The master returned three days later in a sombre mood. He was quiet. He greeted his student, handed him the book he'd recommended, but then said nothing for hours.

Dashi didn't feel like pestering him with questions.

Eventually the master said to Dashi, "In life, you may see something so terrible it will disturb you," he looked off. "It's hard to imagine the beginning mistake that ends in so malevolent an insanity," the master said, "and yet realise there are no enemies – that good and bad are ideals... But one can be put on the spot to choose to champion nature, when others have chosen to play monster." And the master spoke no more, and they remained in silence together until late when the master said, "I'm tired of porridge."

Thudding thunder spilled down the streets. Stomp. Stomp. Stomp-stomp-stomp! And again – Stomp. Stomp. Stomp-stomp-stomp! And again.

When Dashi and the master arrived, the square was a smoke-filled gyre. Whizzing pinwheels were being set off, sparks firing with swelling plumes. Their faces painted, masked with mud, and blood – the crowd circled – from just in front of the stage, all the way to the outer buildings. As they completed their orbit around the fuming fire surrounded by rocks, at the centre, they spun themselves around. They flopped their red rag limbs and legs. They lolled their heads. They gaped and gasped and muttered and mouthed.

The master and he stood behind a small immobile group holding vigil agape. They wound their way past. Looking to the side, Dashi noted bored treasury guards leaning against the walls, their rifles asleep in their hands, only rousing themselves to push away those bodies reeling back onto the wheel.

He could also see those slumped against the wall, not seated, nor fallen over in exhaustion, nor even as if they'd been dragged or dumped there, but rather kicked to the side of the great gyre by the stomping swarm. Not far, a woman had fallen in such a position that the dancers, as they passed, kicked her in the face. Dashi, eyeing the indifferent guard warily, waded in and pulled her into the street. The angle of her head slumped unusually as he eased her to the ground. The master knelt down, touching her neck.

She was dead.

Dashi closed her bloodied staring eyes, "Master, what

is happening?"

"They are sleepwalking. Or rather – sleepdancing," the master said.

"But how? Master?" said Dashi desperate to understand, turning his face from the in-repose corpse to the ones still twirling. From beyond the stomping he could hear the voice calling out to them. A hoarse, howling yelling, bellowing.

"Be you! – So whatever you're doing... it's you... doing it... for free-eee!" said the caterpillar, extending the word in giddy laughter, "'Cause the future is e-v-e-r-y-thing!" he growled and anticlimactically complaining into his cup, "Wretches... I never...get anything I want... I don't care," and sloughing back into his chair, he drank, spilling wine from the goblet over himself, then held it out briefly toasting the dancers, before drinking it dry and banging it on the armrest to be refilled, in a tantrum of rage.

Dashi could just make out the sound of polite applause. Peering over the crush, he saw the thrashing caterpillar was back in his palanquin, rushing attendants seeking to mollify, the magistrate's chair beside him, empty.

It was then he realised the crowd was chanting with their breathing, whispered so low and drowned by their thudding feet he hadn't heard. Droning, "share... unfair... share..." and so on, they made their procession.

Another came into view on the stage. It was the court clerk pulling a stand, a megaphone affixed to its top, to the front of the stage before the red chair. Then he retreated. Another came and adjusted it. Then the stage was empty. Some small movement caught his eye. Dashi went on his toes to see. Barely could he make out the bobbing heads of what appeared to be naked forms, fornicating en masse up against one side of the stage. Aside from that, and for a time, nothing seemed to be happening, until, from out of the back, she came. The mistress - in a yellow dress, with a gold embroidered dragon winging around her middle baring its teeth from her heart - slowly walked to the front, to stand behind the stand.

"We who live inside the walls," she intoned, "the middle path between the too low and the too high. How perfect we are. How noble in our self-sacrifice. We who humbly keep the world turning," she said as the human whirlpool churned before her feet.

The crowd responded in monotone, "Unfair."

"What good are rulers? - what good ignorant peasants? - without us to keep things running, to make everything work. Not the unwashed uneducated farmers, the courtiers, no not even the emperor, have even a conception of the real understanding."

"Unfair," they mumbled.

"Those who rule are imbeciles. Showmen and actors who entertain you with empty grand gestures, ceremonies and speeches. And that is at their best. At worst they are mere puppets of the emperor who would keep you in servitude.

"But it is we who understand the issues. We who know the facts. It is we the righteous. The majority who seek only the good and the best. Only we know the shining truth. Only we know true golden love."

They stomped, leaden. "Love."

"That is why we chased the dirty farmers out of the city."

They half-cheered.

"Their demon leader, so bold as to take the seat of the magistrate, by our superior virtue was disposed of like garbage!"

"Garbage," they babbled.

"Thrown from the gate! Slain with a magic poison arrow." She paused looking over the crowd, sensing their reaction. "It is our purity, our righteousness that banished his evil magic. This is our home – these mighty walls. It belongs to us.

"Those kinds of people – need to stay where they belong – in the mud!" A swaying murmur of rabble agreement rippled through. The dancers kept stomping to music unheard. The musicians having long ago fled.

"We who have been unfairly persecuted through-out history, mistreated and helpless – judged by ignorant liars."

"Unfair! Unfair! Unfair!" they chanted.

"Inferiors! – who cannot comprehend our innate rightness. How you, the good ones, have suffered. No longer," she paused, "submissive – we will not yield. But yet, they may try to enslave us. They watch for any moment of weakness. Will you be the one who is the weak link who breaks the chain of our freedom? Shame!"

"Shame," they cried out.

"Why settle for our share when with an invincible army we can take it all? For too long we have been kept within these walls. But soon we will break free. No longer suppressed by society. Our proper place as heroes – with statues to honour our greater good is assured. And those who have tyrannised us will find how it feels underfoot. Unfair!"

"Unfair! Unfair! Unfair!" they growled.

"We will rule the empire! We will rise up!" she raised both arms.

And the, until then disordered, mob all raised their arms.

"Rise up!" she said again, raising her arms once more,

and Dashi noticed in her right hand she held aloft a red book.

"Rise up!" the throng aped, their arms flopping ungainly over their heads. The dance of the dead continuing nonetheless, churning the mud and straw beneath their feet.

"Transcend the inferiors, transcend the lesser, transcend the second class. Be and have whatever you desire. Embrace the lie," she said, "Embrace all the beautiful lies. Everything is false. Nothing is forbidden. Rise up!" she said, and the multitude echoed her.

"Rise up!" she said again, and the congregation chanted.

"End the lie. Know the lie. Tell the lie. Believe the lie - then it is no longer a lie - it is truth! Rise up!" she commanded.

"Rise up!" they barked.

"Freedom!!" she unleashed through the whistling megaphone.

"Freedom!!" the mass howled in union.

The mistress brought her arms slowly down, and sat in the red chair. The treasurer, having forgotten his tantrum, transfixed by her oratory could be seen clapping, soon joined by the court clerk. She bowed her head. Polite applause followed from the other chairs.

The masses kept churning. Around the cinders burning, still smouldering, their remains danced.

"Rice!" someone shouted, as fireworks crackled and a red flare shot up into the sky, bathing everything in an ember glow. At once the dancers spun towards the wooden tubs of cooked steaming rice and herbs set upon the stage. As they passed, plunging their hands into scalding

grain with no apparent discomfort. More was brought before one tub emptied. They gorged. They writhed. Their
carcasses gambolled and bound. Spinning outward to
the walls where Dashi and his master stood witness, the
nightmare cavorted by, grains of sustenance lost upon
their heads – up into their hair, as though infested by huge
parasitic lice.

A group of servants stood by with brooms to sweep up
the mess after, as did a few who licked the fallen rice off
the ground.

"Master, I need to go," said Dashi his palm on his forehead, "or I will go mad."

"All right," said the master, and he led Dashi away, holding his sleeve, Dashi following like a child.

It was the best thing about it – the roof didn't leak.
Which was good because the floor was bare earth, and
whatever had spilled on to it for as many years as the tavern had stood – its musty scent filled the air. Hanging oil-
lamps added smoke and soot to the dark-yellowed ceiling
and the pall which hung at head height.

Dashi had never been into this tavern, though he remembered standing outside while his brother collected a
debt. He had however sentenced many who frequented it.
As then it was full of noisy bluster. He tilted his head away
from the light and into the shadows of the corner table at
which he and the master sat. Dashi could see his breath.
He warmed his hands against his cup of hot rotgut. The
heated rock in the bottom shifted and scraped when he
put the vessel to his lips. The mere fumes intoxicating. It
was his third. "Does one not have a responsibility to their

welfare?" he half-shouted.

"If one is whole? – yes. One may take on responsibility and it will be true and genuine. But there is no have to. Just as those who reject the way, do not have to listen," the master said, leaning forward, "But if they are stuck at the level of power... pardon me, power layer, of the cake, they will say that I am the one only interested in power. And if I say they are immature, they hear patronising: you don't understand... you'll understand later."

Dashi had felt that. He said, voice raised higher to cut through the drunken singing that'd erupted, "Are they not just being careful? Aren't there manipulators and thieves?"

"Indeed. It's a gamble. Believe and quickly move forward. Disbelieve and have to go the long way around. A good liar you'll believe and never catch. The second best you'll realise only much too late.

"Whereas predators have simple effective short term lies, parasites engage in long term entanglement. While the third type, regurgitators - not clever enough to form a lie, conspire. The worst of them don't even know they're lying - true believers. They infect others, but receive only a meagre payoff - the tiny Joy of thinking oneself in the right. Its enough however to incentivise them to repeat the lie as often as possible and spread it widely as possible."

"Then how can I possibly be of any help at all?" asked Dashi, dark images of gyrating ghouls still dancing in his head.

"The only solution I know for this is wholeness. You can't fool all of your minds all of the time. Now you either trust what your master is telling you or you're going the long way of finding out for yourself. Which, even with my assistance, is ultimately true, because it's yourself you need to trust," he said gesturing with his cup. "Firebreathing is emotional absolution. Just as releasing thought allows forgiveness in yourself. A self in which you must find faith if you are to dream. Do you understand?" the master said, dropping volume, realising the singing had ended but he was still yelling.

"But – what about their welfare?" demanded Dashi waving his hand.

"That's no, then," sighed the master, "I have no interest in chasing after the self-infantilising. Because I have no interest, it is also best for them that I not do so. I would only make things worse by my pretence. Nothing fails like fixing, and nothing fixes like failure."

Dashi said, "So do nothing?"

The master looked at him. "As I have said, do what your own heart tells you, if you can hear it – over your pretending to be someone else."

"I forgot," admitted Dashi.

"This juncture in your maturing is difficult," said the master, "The way is confusing. You want to make sense. So you turn back to what you know worked before. But what worked describes an area of thought which you must transcend to view the new layer. A new world requires a new set of tools, and within the relation, a new self. The new self has new horizons, previously inaccessible. The different self creates the different path to the different future.

"While they in festive noise cavort, you drift, seeming lost. They believe more than anything in trying to control what cannot be controlled. So they deny their greater selves. Better to reign in feigned perfection than to serve imperfectly. Divining one's joy will align you with the world. Not an idea, but a path that appears under your feet leading to... you know not where. In unknowing, cross the bridge.

"Ironically this greater self is the original self. That is why it seems too simple, too easy, or too fundamental to do. As if I am asking the impossible. Far from it. This is just being yourself.

"Being yourself is not doing anything special. Special is fascinating, significant, rare. You can impress other people with that. Special finds its way to positions of importance, acclaim, honour - and therefore great pretence.

"The way of you in contrast is made of private meaning. There is no audience. Only another who holds dear in their hearts similar lights will delight in your delight," the master said, "The pretenders will label you a useless idiot. If they didn't, then the way would not be the way."

"How then is the mistress helping by making up new beguilements?" asked Dashi.

"How much easier to hook these fish who cannot feel the hook in their mouths," said the master, his voice low and grim, "If you can see where the hole in the wall is, you can just walk right past the minds they deny - their blind spots. How can they avoid being manipulated? Don't have blind spots others can exploit. And if the predator is already inside the wall? How do you get rid of them? - because they've manipulating your opinions... of what's real... of whom to trust... and you don't have those critical facilities anymore. You threw them away when you abandoned yourself."

Dashi looked in several directions inside his skull to see if the answer might be there. It wasn't.

"Do you want me to answer?" asked the master.

"Please," said Dashi.

"It is the same answer: to forgive. Only that will bring

back the minds that have been banished. Only then can you have the tools to see if you are being manipulated. In summary, if you have rejected your own consciousness then you are vulnerable to attack, and many attacks are designed to further weaken, so the attacker can feed upon you at will."

"Blood drinkers," said Dashi symbolically, but then realised what he'd said.

"As within so without," said the master.

"So how could she?" Dashi asked rhetorically.

"You assume," said the master.

"Can you not see?" asked Dashi?

"Oh, I see," said he master, "What do you think you see?"

"She has them all bewitched. She's made them dance with that book!" said Dashi a little too loudly causing heads to turn. His condensed breath rising.

The master brought his hand down flat to suggest inconspicuousness. "Why?" asked the master.

"Obviously to control them," said the impassioned Dashi - now quietly.

"Why?" asked master.

"To... to... use them," Dashi responded.

The master rejoined. "Those idiots wandering in a circle, useful? - for what purpose?"

Dashi couldn't think. "I don't know, " he hissed, shaking, "I only know it's wrong."

"Do you?" asked the master, "Tell me what you weigh it against? You pressed to ask about right and wrong, if you recall," pressed the master, "You fall back on your own principles and rules of how things should be. The ideal. This is a fantasy of perfection. It's just a map: flat, and abstract. Simplified.

"In the real world there are curves and bumps. Everything is subtly unique; nothing remains the same. We cultivate ourselves to attunement. With our whole selves we apprehend. Thus the inferior way is straight and confident, and the superior way crooked and unsure."

"But you always seem so sure," Dashi said unsure.

The master laughed, "Not sure. When I act - I do not know," he said, "Knowing would mean I am apart. I'm not only in the stream, I am the stream. I follow the impulse of that moment. If I let it go by, then that impulse will have already changed, because the river has changed. You need to flow with the heart."

"The heart of Joy, you mean?" said Dashi trying to comprehend.

"Seems that way to me," said the master and he drank, and Dashi seeing, did likewise.

"Do not try to understand what cannot be understood. Rise up," said the master smiling, "Come to yourself."

Dashi closed his eyes. He felt he was making such good progress, and now it was so hard. He believed in the master - but what he said just sounded like riddles. The mistress was fanning the flames of the enemy image. 'No enemy' - but even baby eaters? And the dancing - Dashi thought he knew how foolish people could be, but those half naked, half alive creatures... They had gone beyond what he knew of being human. If he was one of them - then what kind of being was he?

All of this rattled in his head like it was an empty creaking vessel, a listing ship with shifting ballast. He wanted to forgive; he truly did. But how could he move forward when every mistake he corrected became invisible? When he'd found something that fit, but it became so easily comfortable, he forgot it?

How could he find the right path through the forest when it kept growing over instantly behind him? Without looking back to see the line of the way, how was one to know the direction in which one was travelling? Paths appeared, and when you strode forward they vanished in your wake. Like water, thought Dashi.

"Master, does the... when I move, the path disappears behind me. Is the path that appears before me, the wake that I will make if I move on that path?"

The master smiled and nodded. "The temporal minds," he said.

Added Dashi, "So the future wake fades and a new one appears?"

"Yes," said the master, "It becomes lucid."

Dashi nodded. "It's a kind of dreaming your way forward," he said. "I can see why rules are unhelpful in this."

"Indeed," the master said, "One does not awaken from the dream, but in the dream. The will of heaven. What is. The river. There are many ways to see it – the whole. To see there are no rules outside. The universe is its own law. That this self is one with its design, brings one a sense of faith and confidence in acting out of one's integrated being. Being is sovereign."

Dashi bobbed his head. "How... What happened that we forgot?"

"You mean the cataclysm, I surmise?" said the master, "When all the adults perished, and the children who survived did their best not to think about it, the eldest pretending to be adults to keep everyone safe," he said, and Dashi winced inside, "And that's the real reason it has all slid into brutality. It's the tool and seeds of the minds that they had not yet received. Something like that?" The master smiled. "How dramatic."

"Unfortunately I'd say it's just because most people are weak," he said, "They give up to get along. And its generational. What parents hid from in themselves they'll make their children hide from too. Lest they reveal the truth. That's why the old stories begin with the child who has no parents. This is the spirit finding its own way, beginning with truth. To go off your path is easy; to find it again requires a mountain of courage."

"But if, even slowly, someone forgives themself," said Dashi, "then society can come back?"

"It can," said the master, "But you still have all those people who've lived their entire lives sleepwalking. Looking but never seeing. Defining but never integrating. Adding but never absorbing. One may be lost, but in essence one is total. My being is as true as a tree, as the sky, as the moon," said the master. "But some do not want to listen, Dashi."

The master gathered his robes. "Those who achieve their ends by being unaware, especially. Who can blame them? They think: why would anyone want to be whole, to be an adult? Indeed, if you see them as children, if they awaken the parent inside, you will be constantly chasing after people who get themselves into trouble opposing the ways of the universe.

"Everyone thinks being the one who gets to say: 'do this,' is powerful. But mostly you say: 'stop doing that!' And are thought tyrannical. A thankless burden. Especially if you try to keep the sheep away from friendly seeming wolves," said the master, who took a sip of his tea and put it back onto the dark table. "So are you drunk yet?" he said.

"A little," Dashi admitted.

To which the master responded, "Then that makes it time to go."

As they left, they stepped over the snow pushing against the building sides, and into the centre of the street where it was clear. Outside it felt less cold. As they walked along, Dashi following to a destination unknown, he had time to release his thinking and just look at the stars twinkling in the clear sky. Dashi, letting his head fall backwards, looked up, his breath illuminated with moonlight. The master must have noticed because he said, "Ah, that pink one? It's a planet. Wonder, beauty, laughter, compassion – we are given all the gifts worth receiving if we can but unwrap them."

"You're unwrapping them for me," said Dashi.

Said the master, "I answer your questions because I want to."

"But master, you have such wisdom, do you truly not feel a need to pass it on to everyone?" asked Dashi.

"Which I'm apparently doing through you," said the master.

"Oh," said Dashi, and later, "Ah," and still further, "Hmm..."

"We are here," said the master, but before they walked down the stairway into the dark, the master said, "I want to show you something young Dashi," and he pushed his staff into a pile of snow. "Temporal minds each track a different kind of changing in the world. Nature is what you begin with, and also what is affecting you as the time changes. You understand this?"

"Yes, master," said Dashi.

Continuing, the master said, "When, as I have said, you come to your joy, the minds work cooperatively."

"As you have said, master," answered Dashi.

"But that one has a central focus, and everything else is also there, this is unity within, and that is why grasping at it with your thoughts stops you from being able to flow. Agreed?" he said.

"Again, master this is what you have taught me," Dashi replied.

"Uh-huh," said the master and then, "Good snow for this," and crossing to the other side of the empty street reach down into the snow and between his hands formed it into a ball. "Watch," said the master over his shoulder – and still facing the wall, threw the ball up into the air behind him.

Dashi watched the white ball arch up into the starry sky like a tiny moon, and come down onto the point of the master's staff and perch.

Dashi opened his mouth. The master retrieved his staff, handing the ball to Dashi for inspection, "I have no idea how that's done," said the master, bursting into laughter, "Come on," he said, and he descended down the steps, disappearing into blackness, for Dashi to follow.

At the bottom, the master opened a door to no light. When they were inside he shut the door and Dashi could see the outline of a door at the end of a corridor. They opened the door quietly and the corridor continued for a short way beyond. At its end there was a candle sconce lit room, and around the room were blankets and buckets and shoes, jackets and bags. From two of the walls a seating bench extended outward, meeting in the corner, built out of the same plaster material. There, a few young men and women sat around a slightly older young man who was speaking, "...when you have transcended to the extent that I have, you will be able to see IT – then all will become clear." And they nodded and said 'Ahh,' and 'Ohh,' impressed, "Master Dashi, confided this to me himself," he added piously.

"Pff," said Dashi to the master.

"Ring the small bell," said the master and Dashi seeing a bell pull did as he asked, though yanking it harder then he'd intended. Instantly, came the sound of feet running. One after another, they burst into the room with knives and stout cudgels to face the hooded strangers. Old women, and young, men and boys. And Dashi recognised some.

As he put back his hood the frightened but beautiful faces of his students lit up in seeing him, "Master!" each cried as more came in and knelt, including the young man.

"Dashi!" came a voice and an embrace. The master's granddaughter kissed Dashi on the lips, "You're not dead," she said.

"Yes," he said, "I'm alive. And that's the second time, you've..."

"But the arrow..." she interjected.

"Inferior poison," he replied. "Isn't that right master?" Dashi turned around. "Master?" he said.

Dashi thought, he'd probably gone to the kitchen to get something to eat, because that was what Dashi wanted to do right about now.

"Forgive us master but who is this other master? We've never seen him," asked one man.

"I'm not surprised, he's like a cloud," said Dashi annoyed but with a smirk at the joy of it, "It's her grandfather."

"So the treasurer isn't your master?" asked one of the young women.

"Ugh... No!" said Dashi, "What made you think that?"

"That's what he's been telling everyone. That you were his disciple, but became possessed so he had to send you away," said one of the nans.

"That's crazy," said Dashi, and he meant it. "Even for him."

"He says he told you about freedom..." said another.

"No... I was speaking to him about freedom – because he hadn't lowered the taxes," explained Dashi.

"Have you ever spoken to us, of freedom? – My Lord... master," said a boy, no more than twelve.

"Uh," Dashi said, "I am about to, apparently." He looked about and chose the corner bench, pushing aside a blanket, as the young man crouching there gave way. "It's unnecessary to call me master," said Dashi, "or rather unwarranted. If I achieve great attainment I will tell you then."

"What should we call you then?" the young man asked.

"Dashi is my name," he said, but none looked pleased with that.

"You are still legally magistrate," said the master's granddaughter, "You're used to being called My Lord, My Lord. How about that?"

And there was suddenly a discussion about the merits of one over the other. With some beginning to take sides. Dashi held out his hands.

"Wait, wait," he said, "I am not here to argue about titles and names. It is your relationship to me that you are creating, call me what you wish that to be.

A frightened looking woman spoke, "Master," she began, "How can we be free?"

Dashi folded the mended red silk of his robe into his lap. "All right. First we have to know what it is, and is not.

Freedom is found in here," and he touched his head, "and in here," he touched his chest. "What people call freedom in the world is not what it is. Freedom comes from you freeing yourself, and becoming whole."

Anxious, "That's all they talk about – being free," one woman said.

"We need to stop them," chimed an older man, one of the merchants, who looked to Dashi as though he'd been in a fight. And soon the room was a buzz and a murmur of whispering fears.

Dashi cleared his magisterial throat, and silence settled. "To be free is to be whole. A whole person is decent and joyous – but not by observing correct social relationships, but from within. While a fragmented person is full of self-loathing and violence, also from within. It is by cultivation that one becomes the other.

"And it is understood that those of both kinds operate within their perspectives. As such, all actions will arise from these states. Indeed, what law could stop those whose inner freedom is injured, from seeking to injure yours? What law could stop those who are whole... from seeking to make others whole?"

The woman said, "We seek to free ourselves in order to free the others?"

And Dashi smiled. "They are not tied together. We free ourselves in order to free ourselves. If we choose to assist others in freeing themselves, then we choose that. But we cannot do it for them, and only choose this because it is your joy. Otherwise you're just getting stuck alongside them being something you think you should."

"How, My Lord?" said a man.

"Because you have an intention that is not your joy," said Dashi.

"I mean, how do we help if we choose to," he corrected.

"Ah," said Dashi, wishing the bench would stop swaying. "Well, they tell me that beauty is the most easily visible representative to wholeness. If we value beauty, if we make beauty, we demonstrate our care. We therefore hold a value of wholeness out to minds of the people in order that they value outward wholeness and therefore their own inside. However... it is easy to become false, by pretending you value something when you don't. Leave art to the artists. There is a way already in you.

"Clear away the debris of the minds. Then you will truly know. This is the heart of joy. Your heart of joy knows, and the rest follows. Joy will find a way."

They all made nice sounds at this and bobbed their heads.

"Dashi, is that why you asked the people for poetry?" queried the master's granddaughter, "- to write on the wall?"

Dashi appreciated her help. But he didn't know. Within him a mind stepped forward and said, "A wall is a surface of interpretation. It is the structure of a shelter. It is a border of protection. It is a demarkation of separation, and a barrier of imprisonment. We live inside every kind of wall. But the kind of wall depends on us. A wall of poetry is therefore a space of expression. A fortress is a facade of stone, nothing more, unless we seed the mortar with our thoughts."

Again the approving noises, and Dashi who thought that had sounded good also nodded to whichever mind had said that.

"Also, because of the nature of people. Survival being the beginning level of the minds' maturation. If one can supply abundance..."

"Which they are doing," stated the young man in challenge, "They gorge themselves on rice day and night... master..." he said extending the vowels.

"And when they run out?" asked Dashi. The young man had no reply. "The problem is they think all this comes from, I don't know... that farmers are magicians and just make it appear. Or that it is easy. Or they think they can force nature to make more, which will only get them less.

"They do not value those who make their sustenance," he said, "because they fear death and want to control death. Those who bring food, bring life. This generosity doesn't matter to them because the intensity of their fear is so great. It desires to control life, but as it cannot, to control those who can."

"So you're saying that farmers should run everything?" the youth sniggered.

Silently embracing and releasing his reaction, Dashi realised he no longer felt like he deserved to be talked to in this manner, as though he was an idiot. He silently thanked the young man. "No," he said, "I mean, if there is always desire to control, because you are afraid of not being in control, then you never value them in the first place."

"So no matter what's happening, we never take control?" said the youth.

Dashi breathed out, to several smiles around the room, "What I mean is, if the way someone is acting is irksome to you, you may lose your sense of humour, and there may arise a desire to control them. Your centre becomes unbalanced and you slide into one of the minds. Regain your centre. Act from your whole being. With practice it gets easier I hear."

Dashi continued, "But if you've become stuck, the minds

act as adversaries. Even though truly there is no enemy. Those who cannot abide the differences even in their own minds will end up by becoming afraid of their own fear, and avoiding it. As their minds are at the layer of survival, or power, they will preemptively take too much, to feel secure. They therefore stuff themselves like wolves. Burning through resources meant for everyone. But that will not stop them from being afraid.

"And the worst of it – is they assume others can be simply ordered to make more, like magic. It's not magic, it's an understanding of the land, what it needs and what we need, and they know nothing about it. We see this by how they treat the land without reverence.

"They lack reverence because they are lacking wholeness. Lacking wholeness they do not see the beauty. Not seeing the beauty they pillage the earth like vandals.

"What is more beautiful than nature? What is more abundant? What is greater poetry than a field in flower? If we are whole enough to not act out of our fear, but our joy, only then can we be filled."

"Ah," said one.

"I see," said another.

"Farmers," said the young man.

Dashi wondered what there might be to eat.

"The dancers?" asked another woman.

"I have seen them," said Dashi.

"Master they attack and loot, should we not respond?" said one of the older men, who came with knife ready, which now he'd sheathed.

"Should?" said Dashi, enjoying the other side. "I cannot say we should or shouldn't. Only that if things do come to violence it is as a regrettable necessity. When faced with the petty, one can become petty. When faced with complaining, one can find one's own lips issue complaint against them. Upon hearing of evil, or of having evil done you, you may be filled with rancour, and a desire to hurt, as they have hurt. These constellations of minds, are but an act – sweet revenge. In whole mind the sweet and the bitter are drunk together."

"Master, you mean they are pretending?" said a voice from the back.

"They are stuck. It's an act they no longer know how to escape. No longer realise they are performing. They are puppets being jerked along by their own hands. They're sleepwalking," said Dashi, "Casting off a mind they do not like, pretending it isn't there, like how one dismisses the message of a dream. What they refuse to hear, they are deaf to. Yet that mind exists, speaking at their back.

"It is the whole that gives you the best perspective. They resist it. They have broken themselves. By casting out one part, they have cast out the whole. And by doing so cast themselves out. Because the whole – it is you."

"So, My Lord, we should not pretend," said another man.

"Should?" replied Dashi with humour.

Rectifying the question, "Pretending is sticky?"

Dashi said, "To put yourself in another's place, to reflect them, you will... constellate. You pretend you are them. But you remember who you are. It is the quality of pretending that is important. Is it playful, spontaneous? My master contrasts pretending with pretence. Costume or uniform? If you can put it on and take it off, it's a tool. If it sticks to you, it's a disease."

They nodded.

"I do not understand how the many minds become a whole," said a man.

Dashi replied, "As you mature your minds choose a series of central languages. First you're a survivalist, then a powerist, followed by an identitist... in your teenage years," said Dashi thinking there might be a better word, "This then leads to you being a reciprocalist and a principlist and by the time you are cresting thirty you've become a holist. If – you do not get stuck."

"If," said the young man mostly to himself.

"In each layer of maturity you are, in a way, already whole. A very divisive and argumentative whole," said Dashi joking, and they laughed along. He liked that. "In each successive layer the minds learn to work together, such that in the last layer they not only act together, they recognise themselves in each other. Seeking then not just their own fulfillment but of each. What goes on inside us is the template for the society we make outside ourselves. If our thoughts are full of anger, we will make an angry society. If they are sad, then society will reflect that."

"How?" said the young man.

Dashi raised one eyebrow, "How specifically, or how does it reflect externally?"

"Either," he said, "master..."

"Well," began Dashi, "These layers become associated with feelings. If you fall back into the patterns of power, then you are likely to be angry. If you are sad then you allow yourself to long for security like a child. Those centres seeing things in the way that they do. They have a language. And if for example, in that language if there is no word for fairness, then there won't be any considered."

"So we have to make a better system at the highest level," the young man said.

"More fair, you mean," said Dashi intuiting.

"Yes, fair," said the youth.

"Ah," said Dashi, "but even if a whole system is created – it can only be done by those who've achieved that layer of maturation. If the system is then run by those who do not understand wholeness, they will translate it into the layer they do understand: principle, reciprocity, identity, power, or – survival."

"So only those who have reached this layer of wholeness can be allowed to create the rules, and run things?" said the young man, "master..."

Dashi gathered some thoughts from his minds for potential usage, "Those of wholeness will primarily speak to principle. Those at principle will speak to reciprocity. Those at reciprocity–"

"will talk about identity. I get it," the young man said.

Dashi thought to say something curt, but then realised in fielding this endless barrage of questions was how he himself had changed, and inwardly thanked the boy again for showing him the mirror, "Obviously those who have achieved their own maturity will, from time to time, have an opinion."

"Obviously," said the young man, and few people in the room stiffened, "But how do you test everyone?"

"You just clean away the old," said Dashi, "There is no test."

"Then anyone could just say they were mature," he objected, "master..."

"They could say that. But to those who are mature, the behaviour of immaturity is transparent," said Dashi. "The deeper your maturity, the deeper your ability to see. The greater your freedom."

"Now you're saying you're omniscient," scoffed the boy.

Dashi drew a breath, "I never said that. I have been asked about freedom and what I say is my present point of view. I know am still not as free as I could be."

"The golden master says: 'Only true freedom is freedom'," said the young man.

"What does that even mean?" asked Dashi, adding, "Is that quoting the caterpillar?"

"How would you know? - you admit you don't know what freedom is? So why should we call you master?" he demanded.

"No should. And I've said it's your choice to call me that," replied Dashi.

"But you also let people," said the boy.

Dashi said, "I don't let people anything. I already have enough titles. Fool is one. They write them on the wall - and for helping me be more indifferent to their slander, I thank them. For now I am still finding my way. When I find it, if I can tell you what it is, I will. If I have a change of heart about any kind of title, it will be because of what I find. What I do understand now is that wholeness gives best judgement, not perfection. It is the expression of what is centred in oneself and humanly meaningful."

The young man thought about that, and said, "But why do you get to define what's better?" the boy interrogated.

"Not better, mature," responded Dashi.

"Fine... who's mature and who's immature?" he replied.

One of the women moved to intervene, but Dashi raised his hand.

"I'm not defining. Maturing is a natural process. Animals mature, trees mature, and so do we. It is. But for people, a process that can become stuck. I seek to free myself and others from stuckness so the natural process resumes. Maturation I can do nothing about," Dashi said, his right eyebrow moving up.

"Sighting its naturalness is no proof. Call it what you

like, it is still a hierarchy. With you on top," accused the young man.

"Any hierarchy is based on some value. Each mind is just such a value, and yes, I will say they are natural. Nevertheless these natural values must then coordinate or there is an endless confusion of fighting. Each mind goes through a series of maturations to bring them into alignment. This does not mean however you get a hierarchy of hierarchies. As I have said, the goal is the whole. Identity isn't better than power, nor that better than survival. They build upon one another. The latter cannot exist without the former. The whole does not dismiss hierarchy but contains all hierarchies. It however no longer plays that game, else it would be inside the category of itself," said Dashi.

The young man said, "That seems like sophisticated..."

"...babble?" suggested Dashi.

"Something like that," he said, "...misdirection."

"Then try this. Stuckness is caused by your becoming attached to some thought or feeling. You find some tiny piece of joy – like the joy of arguing," Dashi said, "But this little joy then becomes the object of your efforts while the greater joy of your whole self is unrealised. Your attachment becomes a way of life, a mask you put on, and the destination of your actions.

"Alternatively, in every moment, in all conscious being, underlying every impulse, is a feeling of joy. And this is no figment of the imagination but a direct experience, such as you have with your own ears. But not hearing with the ears, but with the minds; not hearing with the minds, but with life's fire."

He said, "Joy?" unconvinced.

"Joy is how we are connected. Joy is what makes the grass grow. It is what we call it, how we experience it. It's true nature, I do not know," he said.

"So what you're saying is... That all of those crazy people doing terrible things are driven by joy? And that they need to just find a bigger one? And that if they just cleanse themselves?"

"If," echoed Dashi.

"And that if... when they're whole – then they can just do whatever they want? How is that any different?" the young man stammered, his arms extended.

Dashi tilted his head slightly, "It is important to understand what is happening for them. It is important that as many people as possible become whole so that the society has a centre from which to orient."

"So they can just go on dancing? Doing terrible evil things?" he accused.

"They are free – even to enslave themselves," said Dashi.

"We can't make them better?" appealed the youth.

"No. Not directly," responded Dashi, "and you were just complaining about hierarchies of better."

"Ah, but the whole is better than the hierarchies," he counterclaimed.

"The whole is identical to the hierarchies. To be whole means there is nowhere else to go. You're it. What you see is what it is," said Dashi.

"If it's all just there, then why do I need to listen to you?" dismissed the boy.

"You don't," said Dashi, "But I have heard it is a long journey, alone. Assuming you get there."

The master never returned as Dashi expected, but hoped otherwise. As consolation there was no porridge.

There was rice, and some preserved vegetables and eggs. He ate with the others and they all told their harrowing tales. Anyone who didn't denounce the old regime was shouted down and chased by the mob while being pelted with mud. All farmers had been expelled from the city. Save those that were in hiding.

They knew there were several safe houses but they didn't know where. As they suspected at each, there was a store of rice and other grains, as well as a pump for water. There was also a store of straw.

When Dashi asked what it was for, a silence dropped. The master's granddaughter nudged the former magistrate and mimed putting straw on top of something and then more straw. Dashi laughed. Then everyone smiled.

"It would be a problem otherwise," she said. "All these people eat a lot of rice and that... It would be easy to know we're here if not for the straw."

"That's good planning," said Dashi, asking who it was that had the foresight to make sure everything was in place, but no one knew. Dashi had an idea who.

There followed an amusing discussion of the new law – forbidding people from gathering in groups of more than four.

"And no dancing," said Dashi, and they laughed.

"Master, you haven't told us your story," said a young woman with long black hair.

"No, he hasn't," agreed a nan, who'd apparently escaped the expulsion.

Dashi held up his hands, and was of a mind to try to beg off telling the tale, but their eyes, greedy for the hope of a dead man come back to life story – and his belly full of more than just food – he chose to fill their cups to the brim.

"It begins with dancing," he said, and getting up form the table beckoned the master's daughter. He put his hand around her waist and they danced the new dance he'd just learned. She held herself close. And as they spun around Dashi began to tell of his adventure. "The flare went up and next thing I knew the master's granddaughter and I were sneaking along secret passages..."

The grand tale twisted on. The listeners sat back when the crowd surrounded him. They leaned forward when the mob grabbed him bodily, he was struck with the arrow, and they were about to stone him. And the listening became as quiet as death he described his journey to, and back again, in the woods.

Dashi held nothing back, and they cowered, at the poison's anger. From that, back to his master, and then nodded at his return to the way. He told them of the absolution prayer. And how it was through this forgiveness of the little broken joys, that one made joy whole again.

Some were skeptical. That then was the topic for the rest of the evening. Even for the sleeping dancers? they asked.

Dashi said, "When I first began this, these joys seemed to me not like joys at all, and I only said the absolution because my master bade it. Now I can see the mischievous joy in pretending, The act is a game. I embrace the joy in this little game I play with myself, pretending not to notice I'm fudging the rules. I am fibbing. See even in talking about it I do not come right out and say I am lying. I want my advantage. And I justify why I deserve it. But I see them now, where before I could see no game – what I was doing was reacting appropriately to what was really happening. I just happened to get something out of it.

"What I mean then is just push through these with the

prayer. Don't stop to wonder whether this one or that one is or isn't a lie. If you are half-adept at lying to yourself you won't be able to tell."

Later in the evening when most everyone had gone to sleep, Dashi tried to slip out but the master's granddaughter caught him and insisted on coming as well. They carefully left the hide out, making sure no one saw them, and then snuck their way back to the house on the wall. The master had gone, but he'd left Dashi's sword on the table.

"Does he mean he wants me to fight?" he said out loud.

"He will mean that he wants you to decide," said the master's granddaughter.

Dashi nodded and closed his eyes only for a moment. When he opened them he took up the sword and it's sheath, and tied them around his centre. "Let us hope that you will sleep sheathed. It will not be I who awakens you."

"Even if another provokes, it is you who unsheathes," countered the granddaughter

Dashi nodded at the truth of this. "Then hopefully no one will provoke me," he said.

So midwinter passed with his students. One by one they came and sat by him, and asked him to speak to them.

The first was a wealthy man, one who'd been thrown down by the magistrate Dashi, and then made to sit every morning. He came to Dashi.

"I am glad you chose to stay with us," said Dashi, "I'm sure you have a fine house you could hide in."

The man said, "My Lord, They have taken my house, but I would choose to be with the people who value what I value."

This made Dashi smile, but he addressed the confiscation, "Who is it who has taken your house?"

"The treasury guards came and said that it'd been forfeited because of my association with you, My Lord," he said.

"I am no longer your lord as I have been deposed. And your association to me is hardly a crime. We were very careful to make sure any reparations that were made were based upon your profiteering from the false magistrate – which under imperial law was a crime," said Dashi.

"Yes, My Lord," said the man.

"And given that you have already paid, I consider the commandeering of your home to be theft and should I rise back to power, will seek to reinstate you there," he said.

"Thank you, My Lord – but, My Lord, I'm actually happier here," he said. "I have a family, I have a community of people who believe what I do."

"If you had your house back is there any reason you couldn't invite them over?" asked Dashi.

"Oh," said the man, "all my neighbours... I don't think they'd like that."

"Do you enjoy pleasing the neighbours?" said Dashi.

The man breathed a sign of recognition and went away happy.

"Speaking is different from asking," thought Dashi. When Dashi asked the master a question, he had the impression that his minds were just an empty bucket the forthcoming answer fell into. When he was asked these same question however, he answered in a way he thought was better than he knew. Obviously, he thought, he didn't really know what he knew until a mind had to speak it. This made him ponder how the minds were invisible when you used them. But it didn't get him anywhere. At least not anywhere he was aware of.

The young man returned. He argued that new perfected procedures and laws could be built that would make everyone happy. Dashi admitted he'd previously thought so as well, but had been disabused of the notion.

"While you certainly can make very poor laws that are detrimental, and I will speak in a moment about who it is who is passing these laws, I have thought long about procedure and I find that by itself it's woefully insufficient.

"The example my minds considered was how to make a decision. First there is a problem – is it a problem? – is it the problem you think it is? – is this only a symptom of something much deeper? But given that you have identified a problem and propose a solution, or solutions, then you will need to think about who it is who will benefit and who not. And therefore who will seek to undermine the law. And before you say that the guard will see to it that the law is obeyed, you will have all the other laws they need to enforce and the whole question of whether you want your city to be civil only because armed brutes patrol the streets," said Dashi.

"But it would work," said the young man.

"That's just it – it doesn't really," said Dashi, "You can't reform a government, formed around power, to exemplify reciprocity, without passing through identity. And then it's not going to be sages and artists who tell the tale – it's horse traders and dealmakers. Should you get to principle, arguers will come. They'll prove why, what you think is the problem, isn't the *real* problem – or even that there's a problem at all. And they'll have their own-"

"Then we must pick who is to define the laws. Only the smartest, and the best, and the most noble," interjected the young man.

"And who can be trusted to choose the choosers?" asked Dashi, "Who will then be in positions of influence – and can trade this for that?"

"We will make the punishment for such traitors severe," said the young man.

Dashi said, "It only moves the problem. For each one you catch, there will be seven who slip by. For a sufficient prize – any odds a gambler will play against their life. Besides, get enough gold and one can turn an investigator's eye away."

The young man made an awful face while thinking but couldn't come up with any response.

Dashi said, "Imagine a cake."

The young man looked dubious

"There is a shipwreck and there is no food for the survivors except a cake. How shall they divide it? To the strongest? To those most in need? To those most able to get them out of being stranded? Or those most capable of helping them to survive beyond the cake? Or they could divide it equally. But... whatever they choose is the value. When I answered this question I was thinking of fairness because that was the value I sought. As I believe you do.

"In a shipwreck, people will pull together because of survival. But in better conditions they will have their own priority they are seeking. Thus you would not, even in principle, get a consensus as to how to divide the cake. Everyone will argue for their benefit because that's what the minds do. And minds are not equal at convincing. The arguers will win, and they will make of your and my perfect systems whatever they can interpret it to be. There is no system so perfect that it cannot be captured."

"And so what is the answer?" the young man asked.

"To return to human nature," said Dashi.

The young man scoffed, "I thought you said people argue for their own benefit because of their minds."

"That is correct," said Dashi.

"Then it's not the right answer," said the young man.

"It is if you cultivate the six layers of the minds, to bring the individual to wholeness," said Dashi.

"How is that not just based in its own priorities? – leading to some other group being in power?" the young man challenged.

"Because everyone already has it. No one can have more of it. And we do not seek to add, but to remove something every day until there is nothing left but you," said Dashi.

"Me?" he said, "But how do we do anything for them?"

"That depends on who you are," said Dashi.

"Who am I?" said the young man.

"Indeed," said Dashi.

When Dashi had miraculously returned, arriving at their safe house, the students had given up one small room, in the already crowded cellar, for Dashi to have his own room, and would take no modesty for an answer. It was to this room later that the master's granddaughter came to Dashi. She was weeping.

When she could speak, she croaked, "They burned her."

They all sat together.

They breathed the fire of grief. Into their bellies they committed the dead woman's memory. But the question of why... why she had been out of hiding? It was obvious she was a country woman. One of the women who sat with the others outside the wall perhaps. Which one Dashi did not know. No one did. And the inattention to who this was while she lived - an uninterest in her presence - even as she sat arm lengths away - meditating with them - felt now like callous indifference.

Catching her, they'd madly beaten her, all the while ceaselessly dancing. Their own inner darkness spilled out into the world, they hunted the outsider like an animal. How terrifying her last moments - as the pack outran her - tearing at her with their clawed hands, striking with club fists, as she tried to escape - and then dragging her senseless body through the streets back to the square - where, they threw their prey into the flames.

Some wept, barely able to breathe. Others came to a deeper understanding of the firebreath, burning their coal of grief to cinders. With ferocious focus they let go. Feeling somehow responsible, Dashi embraced this grasping blame that came upon his heart, knowing if you can't put it down, you have to carry it.

Underground, they'd not smelled the smoke right away. Dashi and some others investigated, foolishly leaving their safe den to gaze at the haunted grey air over their heads. "It can't be their fire making all this smoke,"

thought Dashi, "They've set the palace alight." He and three of the others walked in stealth through the shadows and the sound of panicking people grew ominous.

One suggested they climb up to see, so they clambered over a low roof and by foothold and handhold they came to the building's top and there watched far away some structure within the palace walls erupt in sinister dark billows. Distant scream upon scream rose up to their ears, as some tiny far away figures tried to battle the flame.

Getting his bearings, Dashi said, "It's the granary," and although no one said a word after, they fell into agreement: this unlucky event presaged far worse. When there was no food left to eat, what then? A malefic flowering – this darkening cloud and leaping flame promised. Even those addled and giddy in their prances, slowed, heeding the mind that languaged the future rumbling of their own bellies, a beast reawakened.

So now they sat. And they hid from the panic that was gripping those above. Staying close to the store of food secreted from the abundant harvest, now lost. As they had done in the forest with his brother, Dashi ordered it be long cooked, over low heat, with clothes over the pots to dampen the smell of food that would lead the hungry right to them – so their subsistence might not tempt doom.

He spoke to them, "Free yourselves from fear," he said, "Do not turn away from terror, run towards life's ragged tatters with open arms and embrace. Then release what is in your minds. Although the world may be grim and heavy with heartbreak – free yourself – free your minds to not be pulled this way or that. Be in balance – in absolute balance. Neither pushed nor pulled. That is freedom. From freedom any direction is possible. Even the heart of Joy.

Gather it to yourself, as the best friend you will ever have."

So they burned within, and they released, cultivating freedom underground in silence. "It is not easy, I know," he said, "to turn away from your clever mind that tells you there is thinking to be done. That you need to analyse. All I ask is that do not let it argue it must come before release. Clear your mind. Clear the feelings that arise. Say the prayer. Say it three times even. Say each line three times. Whatever gives you room to breathe. If you have to think, then think with a mind cleared."

The master's granddaughter told Dashi later that this had moved many of his followers. He replied he had no followers. Then she told him what she had heard. They'd accused the nan of being a spy. A saboteur. "One who'd been working for... you," she said.

Dashi noticed. "They said 'demon,' didn't they?"

"Yes," she replied, "-But she wouldn't renounce you."

Dashi blanched. His city was heading towards famine but the fear tearing it apart was the hunting and unmasking of demons.

"Don't you see?" she said, "They believe in you."

Dashi groaned, "Just what I've always wanted."

With soft voice, removing the sting of the truth, she said, "It is what you've always wanted. People who believe in you."

"Who like what I like," quoted the rueful Dashi. "I also once wished I were magistrate. That the power be mine." He looked away.

And then he looked back at her. "I embrace..." he began. And she spoke it with him.

They were depending on him. So he became dependable.

Every moment was another opportunity to shed a deeper or more subtle stuck thought. He felt a clarity inside. A deep strength. But in removing, there also came a new sense of emptiness. Different from the one that came with the firebreath. Another layer, another stage.

He felt he was becoming less of what he wasn't, but not necessarily more of what he was.

"Well, it'll move things along," said Dashi.

And they waited for him to explain.

"They will have no food, but we do. Their advantage is the ferocity of the mob. But things that are out of balance eventually reverse. When they can't feed them anymore, their control will end – abruptly. Then it will be our advantage," he said.

"Are you going to share our food with them?" they asked in so many words.

Dashi pulled up a chair and sat mid table. He spread his hands out wide. "If they will sit at my table they will eat. If they choose to not to sit, then that is their choice.

"What do I mean by sit at my table? It means to choose to practice forgiving themselves. To speak that intention. It means to choose to care. To choose to be free. To want the whole cake. Their cake. It's their choice to make. If they would make themselves slaves – they sit at another's table."

"But master," said an older man, Dashi recognised as one of the merchants, "We need to have money to sustain ourselves."

"Money?" said Dashi, "To buy what?"

"You said, 'make themselves slaves,'" he quoted, "I exchange my labour for pay. Those in my hire do likewise. We are not free."

Dashi said, "Ah, but trade and service, and yes, gain, evolve from fair dealing, and concerns for right action. It doesn't mean you fall asleep. Reciprocity, and principle proceed wholeness.

"Let your values be your values. Have your own minds and do not pretend for another's sake. The more you're yourself, the less willing you'll be, to become what someone else wants you to be. To serve another, if that's your path, is as noble as any other exactly because it is chosen freely."

"Because your will is strong? - So you can choose your own path?" said the young man who argued, who'd come into the room.

"No, not will," said Dashi, "Nor is it *what* you are willing either - or willing anything at all," he said, "To be who you are takes no force of will. In fact the will obstructs." Dashi opened his hands out. "When forced-will vanishes, natural-will appears."

"What you mean by that is - do nothing?!" charged the arguer.

"You can only flow with your judgement. What the future holds we but guess at. Still there is the presence of our whole consciousness that we may cultivate. A unity in which we no longer push or pull ourselves - as in unity there is no one to act, or be acted upon, there is only the whole flowing through its motions. And as each mind in its use is invisible to us, to flow is to be invisible to ourselves. If we can go with ourselves faithfully, then we have guided ourselves best without knowing that we know."

"That just seems like some sort of game too," refuted the young man, "What proof is there, following this way of yours, leads to anything but navel gazing inaction?"

Dashi was about to join battle again with the youth when another voice spoke.

A large man entered behind the arguer, raising a stout wooden cudgel in one hand, with the other lifting the stump of his leg upon the table with a thud, "I have something to say."

At once Dashi recognised him. He'd married him.

By Dashi's decision he'd forced him chained to his hated rival - who he'd likely murdered, and it was said he dragged the putrefying corpse with him - rotting his own leg in the process. Dashi's hand dropped beneath the table's surface to his sword.

"YOU!" he bellowed pointing, but not to Dashi, but the youth. "You fight too much," he said. "You want will? I'd a belly full of will. Was born that way.

"I's your age - I'd been a soldier. Killed thirty-six men... two women... animals - lots," he said, shaking his head, "I was sent north here, because I was too wild even for war. Because I liked to drink, I fought everyone. All comers.

"Their side, our side. Didn't care. I had hate for everyone," he spat. And then he looked right at Dashi. "But then I went before this magistrate, he... he bound me to my hate. Made me look at it," and the man began to choke-up. "To see it - You bound me to that man I hated so much... who was just like me.

"The humiliation... I couldn't see he was like me. With combat in his veins."

Dashi swallowed.

"His foot got infected and I laughed. I chained us to

374

a post, so he couldn't get a doctor. I'm the strongest. I'd kick that damn foot - and he howled. Used the chains to break open the skin, so I could see the lovely red pour out of him. But he fought to get free. To live. And he was sweating from the fever," he smiled with a shake of his head, "Even all broken up - I broke his bones - my enemy, all swole, up and tried to get away," he said, gravel in his throat, "So, he just got weaker and weaker... and my smile got bigger and bigger. Until he was dead.

"Only then d'I unhook us from the post. Only then'd I realise I could not unhook myself from him - from death - and that his fate, by my hands, would become my fate, to drag me down, by me dragging him. And as his body peeled and stank and bloated I got all the measure of death I could take and more. My own leg began to rot and I lost my mind.

"I hid. Awaited my own death, like a soldier accepts. But in me there was something more. I'd lost the fight in me, I'd lost it, and I'd gained something else moving through me. I didn't want to fight no more - I wanted to live. Like him," he said tearing, "I wanted to live.

"So out I came. And the guard found me. And you didn't have me chained to a post to rot, to die like a murdering dog. You unshackled me. My leg was too far gone. My sacrifice. But the rest of me was healed. With my crutch I came to sit outside the wall. I sat with all the others." - and the man looked around the room - "And when the guard tried to send us away, you came out and told them to stop. I remember that so well. And I thought here's a man with heart.

"I'd felt what you did to me was wrong. I'd hated you. But it was you pushed me down this path. And I have done the firebreath every day since. I sit and I will forgive everything in me until I am clean and whole. And I hear what you're trying to get into the thick skull of this one," he said and knocked the youth's ample hair forward, "No thicker skull ever was than mine. You listen," he said to the boy, "The master's saying even though we make mistakes, it's our relation to the joy. That makes all the difference. Inside we have a compass to joy. So from even bad things can turn out good. But we have to choose. Is that right, master?" he asked.

Dashi choked out, "Indeed," and pulled out the chair beside him. "You – will dine with me at my table."

Each one, through out street and mansion, the innermost self within their body's solitude felt the tightening grip. A ghost had walked in into the room. The fear of famine so recently escaped, felt now a cruel deception as the greedy fire consumed all the food. Snow and rain without end, shepherded them into the enclosure of survival – a contract of clenched teeth. Soon they'd descend through the hidden layers of themselves.

Those who weren't caught in the dance, caught more sinners in their midst. Saboteurs of freedom. Impure haters. A movement in reverse. Strict laws were needed to protect the people's freedom. They needed to protect themselves from the others. Those who still walked free.

The treasury guard compelled, coerced, and enforced popular rule to quell stampeding hysteria, but swiftly it was followed on by more calls, for more laws, and more brutal arrests of those in league with the expelled mud demon Dashi. Too dangerous for their ranks, the palace guard were soon used for the worst work. Traitors who questioned, or anyone who might, were chased through the streets by frenzied former comrades - when they weren't a roving looting mob.

Those accused, as their crimes justified, found their way onto the fire.

When he heard, Dashi dashed out the door - and a few followed him on instinct. The elder merchant stayed, but tossed Dashi his own grey silk cloak as he sped past, better to hide the magistrate's identity.

When they arrived a pile of firewood had been added to the front of the fire, and despite the cold rain, a throng were throwing stones at the young woman bound with rags torn from her own dress to a stake in its smoking midst. The mob jeered and swore and spat. Occasionally a stone went awry and hit another of the soggy rabble, bringing indignant tears.

From out of the usual din Dashi could hear someone cackling a rhyme, "Dripping fat - imagine that! For her sin - crispy skin! Get the stake - give and take..." and so on, the chant repeated, worming its way into the mob mind, working their puppet mouths. His eyes fell upon the black robes of a bureaucrat in the dancer's midst, its normally camouflaging colour standing out against the dirty half naked bodies.

Dashi grabbed up a stone. "I will cut her ties. Move around to the sides. Make as though you are one of the mob, but when I signal lob stones upon their heads to make them clear a path for us to escape. Then scatter." And he was off.

Dashi circled the crowd towards the back of the fire -

seeing where the treasury guard stood distant, out of the eye stinging smoke, rubbing their hands together, talking – punctuated by the occasional cough. Halfway around, and hidden by the crowd, he let fly his stone, skillfully winging the crow in the head. It searched for the perpetrator in vain, Dashi having already moved on.

The rain increased, and big drops hissed as they died in the heat. Lucky timing, thought Dashi, as the wet but speedily drying wood began pouring off even more rescue-obscuring clouds of smoke and steam – before the heat caused the wood's incubating crackling flame within to burst forth.

Keeping the fire in between him and the guard in back – and him and the crowd in front, Dashi looked both ways. Then, knife in hand, he ran at the fire and up the pile to the woman he could no longer even see, closing his stinging eyes, holding his choking breath, fumbling for the rags that held her, cutting them. Fire below, water above – he grabbed her like a sack and ran down the pile, leaping out of the flame, knocking over a guard, who grunted hard as he hit the ground, as Dashi breathed out and kept running. The alarm raised, their sacrifice stolen, the mob turned as one and advanced.

"Now!" coughed Dashi, and a hail of rocks came upon the heads of the treacherous crowd, causing them to part. Dashi dodged up the middle of those unlucky enough to not have been hit, and thus moved, as a volley of arrows descended from heaven after the fleeing thief – felling those at his side and at his right hand, through the now panicking crowd.

Light blossomed behind him as the fire burst aflame, and as another joined him, "I'm with you my Lord," carrying the young woman away, like a bundle of sticks, and

Dashi was glad of the help because she was heavy enough to make Dashi's shoulder ache, and he feared he might drop her when he coughed.

Though the guard ran after, their eyes were blinded by the ignited pyre, and all Dashi's men scattered into the night and not one was caught.

Dashi lay down gingerly on the bed.

"Good thing it didn't hit you in the head," she stated, and the master's granddaughter removed a soft leather cloth from her cloak and gripped the slippery, blood stained shaft. With her other hand she pulled away at the many layered silk of the merchant's fine cloak and drew the arrowhead out of his shoulder.

"Wouldn't have hit anything import-!" he grunted as she pulled it free.

"That'd kill you. Take off your cloak and shirt, Dashi," she ordered pressing her fingers into the wound "I need to clean it."

Dashi did as he was told and bared his torso.

Meanwhile she carefully examined the lightly smeared tip and shaft. Holding it away, she tentatively sniffed it. "Lucky. No poison, just an arrow," and she chastised in disbelief, "And you don't even know when you've been hit?"

The former magistrate looking up to the ceiling simply replied, "Sarcasm strikes deeper than any arrow."

She turned sullen, "Ridiculous," she said at last, fussing about with a jar from the medical bag. Looking at him, a beautiful bruise blooming where the arrow struck. She poured liquid, into her hand, sat on the side of the bed, and spread it liberally on his shoulder. It stung.

She looked up toward the closed door. "It was raining when you escaped?" she asked.

"The rain poured off us," he said between his teeth.

"And their quivers," she said. "Also lucky for you – it's cold. In addition to having hands that were wet, they'd also be stiff. That's why their shots went wide."

"Except the one in my shoulder!" said Dashi.

"They were probably aiming for your head!" she chided, "Poison or not, head wounds are mostly fatal."

"You keep saying that," said Dashi.

"Yes," she said, "And what conclusion might you come to regarding the theme of my disquisition?"

"That I'm lucky," said Dashi.

"Indeed!" she said, walking to the end of the bed before turning back to face him.

"I don't feel lucky, I feel ill," Dashi said, putting his a hand to his pulsing wound.

"The fact that you are still alive to feel anything at all is my point! Heaven and earth conspire in your keeping," she said, angry, "Why do you think that is?"

Dashi said, "I have a feeling you will tell me."

"I don't know," she said, unsure, "But... I think you're destined for greatness." Dashi didn't know what to say to that, so they just looked in each other's eyes.

And then she took her clothes off. Defiantly. And now he really didn't know what to say.

"You keep running into battles. Lucky or not, you might get killed. And... and I like you," she said, shyly adding, if that, and her current state had not made it clear, "Very much."

"Well," said Dashi, nodding, "I like the kind of people who like me."

She nodded too, and her eyes looked around inside her head to see if knew what that meant. "My name is Li," she said.

"Ah. Would you like to join me on the bed... Li?" he asked. She did and he put his good arm around her, so that she put her head on his chest. Her hair was soft and pretty he thought. The skin of her back was silky under his caressing hand. "You're cold," he said, "Do you think we should get under the covers?" She nodded and slipped under. Dashi meanwhile sat up and struggled to remove his boots.

"Let me help," she said coming around to kneel in front of him. She removed one boot. And then the other. "You need someone to look after you," she said, and began tugging off his leggings.

"Doesn't everyone? Dashi asked.

"Some more than others," she replied, now, they were both naked. Nervous, she swallowed

"Come, let's get into bed," she said, and they did. And then they just lay together for some time. And then they faced each other's face. She looking to see what was turning in his mind. He, looking to see what she intended in her heart. Then they wrapped their legs together and moved closer. And they put their lips together. And moved their hands everywhere.

And Dashi and Li became one together.

When Li led him to her, she was in a corner bed - gripped by paroxysms of coughing. Her red watery eyes squinted and tears wept continuously from them. Dashi held her hand as she coughed - convulsing into the hem

of the shawl she'd wrapped around her. He hoped one day she'd be able to sing again, as she once had with the other women in the room of birds. For now her breath was queerly noisy and came in shallow gulps.

Wind rose in the night, chasing away the rain. Then it began to snow again. And the winds dropped down, before the snow ceased, and the rain once again resumed. The perfect day for a story. They gathered by the cook-stove fire.

"Master, why did people stop being whole?" said a young boy.

"You mean, how did we get here?" said Dashi.

"Yes, master," he said.

Dashi said, "By people not caring about what is most to be cared about."

"What's that?" he asked right away.

"Children," Dashi answered.

"I thought you said what was most important was to clear our insides?" said the woman stoking the quiet fire.

"That is the practice. Everything that is inside moves to the outside and then returns. We begin within, but our focus must eventually move outward knowing this will come back to us again. In being what we already are, and I have also said that is of a tribe – and so what is in us, is a tribe. The tribe of our minds. So concern with bringing all minds up to into joy is reflected in the that same desire for our children.

"Freedom is being able to be yourself. We want that for ourselves, so we want that for others. Just as the tribe is our outer mind to help us stay in balance, and likewise us toward the tribe, so the parent is the surrogate for young minds still growing.

"What is it to be an adult? To navigate the river of time. To have one's temporal minds unite, for our joy, which is made in us simultaneously for ourselves – and future continuity. Creativity begets creativity. Children grow up to raise children."

"Hmm," said the boy who'd first asked the question.

"If it is to go on, it must go on. Do you understand?" said Dashi. "It's a circle."

"Ah,"said the man restacking the sticks for the fire.

The boy said, "The minds are a circle?"

"You could arrange them in a circle," Dashi said, symbolising a flat disk with his two hands, "Then stuckness could be if a mind bends the circle down on one side, so that you slide towards it. That would be grasping. Or if you bend it up then everything rolls away from that mind. So that's rejecting," he said, gesturing.

"But if they're balanced, you never get too much, or too little. You can go right out to the edge and not fall off. And more important, you can stand at the point in the centre – here your will is free to choose," Dashi said, happy with this image having just magically appeared from out of his own mouth.

The boy looked up, and wrinkled his forehead.

"Look," Dashi rubbing together his hands for several moments, "Once," began Dashi, "there was magic in the world. The spirits of the trees and animals and fields knew us, and we knew them. We followed them. In times of want when we called out for food – and in their movement, they showed us where it could be found – by river, by the edges of the great forests, and even within their own bodies. This is how we survived, how we learned to survive – they taught us. And the circle of the world was heaven and earth.

"Then one day we made friends with fire. And we brought fire into the centre of our lives. But the animals weren't friends with fire, so while we were with it, they stayed away, and only when we left its circle did they greet us. Though now with some trepidation.

"Then came time. We learned that we could plant food ourselves – now – and reap later. And we learned the art of storing. Land was a plot we farmed, and the plough, a thing of our own making, became our powerful friend. Some of the animals we kept, but the others we cast out outside the circle, beyond the fire, beyond the fences we created, because they wanted to also eat our crops, and the animals we'd kept – and so they stopped talking to us.

"Now the world was split, and where before we knew the names of all our companions – even plants that we'd known, medicine and food, were names only remembered by elders and medicine women. Except for a handful of crops, everything else was a weed to be ploughed under.

"Along with the power to separate inside from outside, came the fear of the unknown – for all magics have two sides. But we didn't understand this. We were too excited with our new power to define. We had forgotten who we were in the world, because we forgot who they were outside the circle. For a circle describes the whole of being minus itself.

"And so we imagined ourselves to ourselves. We used its new power to define who we were, and who we were not. We used the magic to imagine who we were going to be, and simultaneously cast its opposite: what *they* were going to do to us unless we stopped them.

"Walls appeared. Powerful walls. And who we were, we

put inside the walls. And who we were not, we put out. And because we are of our tribe, we did this to our very minds as well.

"Then when we'd amassed enough wealth inside, there came those wanting to breech the wall, to eat the fruits harvested of our labour. At first they were wanderers, those who had but fire and tents, easily sent running. Then came those who's wealth had strengthened their defensive armies to the point they could extended themselves from their own walls. And even when these terrors were but imagined, our minds attacked themselves with its possibility in our nightmares. Time, which taught us to feed ourselves, now taunted us with our inevitable death.

"Some few then began to realise the other side of the magic we had learned. They began to teach those who would listen. But they were few.

"So we built a yet greater circle, of new greater definition. And in its centre we placed an emperor where before there were leaders who inspired us, and we defended it with soldiers where before our hunters brought us food, and the medicine men and women became priests of our new identity, a name chosen for us. And we became more resolute, and more divided within. We encompassed, from the city, a land around it, a territory, and by that new extension we now either fought - or traded.

"Because our remaining minds realised the future was safer if there were truce. Coins were struck. The circle increased again. And with these agreements came rules, and means of court, and law. The law of the land. The law between lands.

"Mystics appeared looking for the laws of heaven, philosophers sprang up looking for the laws of earth - ingratiating scholars reckoned the rules for ruling. Rules that advantaged those who made the rules. That separated by rules of usefulness, and productivity, for the benefit of the inner circle, who was to be lauded, within – and who to be shunned, on the out. Once we were one with the world, and then we called ourselves caretakers, and then guards, and now mere functionaries. At each step becoming less and less.

"Some realised every time we'd made the circle bigger on the inside, we made it smaller on the outside. The more we included, the more it distracted us from what exists beyond our bounded ideas. 'Til eventually, we'd have nowhere to go – not back to the land, nor even to nature itself – without the finite divisions that gave us our significance. We were lost inside a circle, inside the walls meant to protect us, a maze of boundaries indefinitely distant or hidden. Thus came the longing for outside, for our true selves, and the understanding of the duality of magic.

"Others realised this magic could create a new kind of lie – a circle without an outside. Without an outside, nothing is true and everything is permitted. Despite the contradiction, people believed, and wanted to believe, in any answer for everything. Endless loops were created to addict minds' desires to their most immature layers, rendering them unable to see through the enslaving magic.

"Thus did those stuck in power become the rulers. They who take advantage of the world, do this by first by taking advantage of themselves – by some minds ruling to the exclusion of others – minds they fear. Therefore to the exclusion of their true selves, to their heart of Joy. That's why cunning and guile are rewarded – to hide the truth from the rulers, that they too are enchanted. They are not free.

"The walls have come inside to divide us each from each other's hearts. Disconnected, the absence of the outside appears within. Grows until it is too terrible to not see. Until the choice is to face the abyss or to pluck out your own eyes.

"And the more people separated themselves, from themselves, the more desperate they became. Seeking the most extreme and debasing exploitation of the minds they had left - for any crumb of Joy. Unable to be adults, so turned away from their whole nature, so protected with wall after wall, they even hurt their children.

"Self-justifying, self-rationalising, self-obsessive, self-righteous, self-aggrandising - traps created by the maddened and shunned minds, left to die in darkness, whose seductive whisperings float over the walls of consciousness. Those whom the maddened would destroy - they first make gods.

"You are perfect," they say. "Everything is permitted." Bedazzled, the bloated self wanders unaware of the dark, sticky pools awaiting to reunite the halves.

"By just starting small, people who self-justify can be led by the nose into atrocities," said Dashi with an ending flourish.

"But why?" said the boy.

"The foolishness of youth," Dashi said, "It's a trick, by those caught up in their own trickery."

The boy wrinkled his forehead further.

"I think my story wandered," Dashi said.

"Children," the boy said.

"Children are the deepest of Joys," said Dashi.

"Seems complicated," said the boy.

"It's not," Dashi replied, "It's pretty simple: get rid of the garbage, then forget yourself and be free. The firebreath releases the feelings that you don't want to go into. The prayer allows you to escape minds you go into too much.

And then there's the thing about wholeness..."

"Wholeness," said the boy.

"Wholeness is the return to the infinite circle of the ancients, from the merest dot, that of ourselves," said Dashi.

"Hmm," said the boy.

"In all of our acquisitions of power we were invisible to ourselves, and acted as if the world was given. But it was our creation, a myth we created – created from our depths. And so by plumbing those depths we come to ourselves and the world simultaneously, the created and creator – only to find we did not create ourselves – that being hubris.

"Which means that at the point of life, there is a rock to stand upon. That being life itself, its nature. To grow to be that which one already is, and to want that more than anything else, not because it is good, or the best, but because that Joy is who we are."

"What about planning?" said the man.

Dashi said, "That can be an inspiration too."

Just then... the young man ran into the room, "They're coming! Soldiers – they're coming!" he yelled.

The moment of silent fright. Then the arising of noisy panic. The screams drawing the predator in on target. Dashi remained seated.

Some might make it away, he thought, more likely we are already surrounded. A few remained with him, apparently ready to fight, including the young man who ran into the room, the one who argued with him, though he stood apart from the others.

Then the room was full of soldiers. His former guard in black first, then treasury guard in red. Followed by the red guard's commander and finally the captain. The former magistrate's eyes met the captain's, which were as open wide as a cat's.

"My Lord," said his lips silently.

"Arrest him!" shouted their gold tasselled commander, and promptly two of the black guard had Dashi up on his feet, his arms pinned.

"Sorry, My Lord," they whispered out of the corner of their mouths.

Dashi offered no resistance.

"I thought to just find a nest of vipers, but here I find an eagle," he said.

"That is a poor metaphor," said the former magistrate.

Indignant, their leader came forward and slapped Dashi across his face. "No one gave you leave to speak - mud boy!" he said, putting his face into Dashi's - trying to burrow dominating eyes into the eyes of calm.

Dashi turned his head and looked to the captain, causing the lead soldier to spin around to follow his gaze.

He grabbed Dashi by his hair, put his mouth to his ear, "You think your former lackey will save you?" he spat, and as thoughts began to crawl out of their hiding places of his minds, mounding up like corpses, he deeply - slowly - grinned, stretching his lips backward as if those muscles, long stagnant, had forgotten how.

Dashi had never seen such shameless wicked malignancy.

"Let's go then," said Dashi.

"I'm giving the orders," sneered the tasseled commander.

"Well?" said the former magistrate.

The commander looked perturbed. "You're nothing now."

Dashi replied, "And yet you chase my people. If you'd known I yet lived, I have no doubt the city would have been torn apart to find me. Rather extreme measures for a nobody," he said, "Do you really suppose I have nothing?

They knew I was here all along. You know how we at the top stick together – because they know, I know."

Fuming he slapped Dashi again, "Take him away," said the commander, and marched out of the room ahead of Dashi, "Captain, throw the others you find in prison."

"Yes, commander," said the captain, as Dashi passed by.

And as he left through the dark corridor, "Good-bye – master..." said the young man.

Dashi looked directly into his eyes, smiling – completely unnerving the boy, "No enemy" said Dashi.

As the guard dragged Dashi through the alleys and then out into the brighter streets, he saw the people. Bells began to ring.

"Getting it now!" a man jeered from his painted doorway.

"Now he'll see justice!" mocked another whose clear window was draped with one of the pulled down banners. They hooted and whistled.

"Take him to the magistrate!" hollered a woman with a small child hiding between her legs.

Dashi turned to look at the child, and she, or he, stuck out its tongue, like a snake.

Across the cold grey muddy square they paraded him to the gathering crowd. Yarding his shoulders as if he was putting up a fight, as if some common thief. They marched him through the gates. They marched him up the stairs. They marched him through the doors of his own court. And flung him down on his knees beneath the gaze of the red seat of the magistrate. The crowd pressed in at the door.

"Clear the courtroom," she said – the mistress said – the sitting magistrate said.

Dashi had been looking up at her. He glanced at her hat. All the black cloaked court bureaucrats skittered into their places. More who had heard of his arrest, had come to listen retreated into the hallways, out of sight but not hearing.

"The charge?" said the mistress.

The court clerk ascended the stairs handing the magistrate the charge he'd just written. She read it and handed him back the official document.

"You, Dashi, former magistrate to his imperial majesty, august-sovereign, of this, his fine, northernmost city are charged with desertion of your post, and dereliction of your duty to the Divine Emperor, ruler of all under heaven, how do you plead?"

"A handful of grapes," said Dashi.

"What do you mean by that?" asked the magistrate from her chair.

"What is meant by a wooden horse winning a race?" replied Dashi.

The mistress looked curiously down at Dashi. "Do you wish to plead innocent to the charges, young Dashi?" she said very slowly.

Dashi said nothing.

At once, there was a flurry, and on a golden palanquin, which ascended the steps under a strain of sweating bearers and came to rest beside the magistrate's chair – was the treasurer. He cooed and fidgeted with his many rings, in a state of excited delight. "I hope I haven't missed much," he said to the mistress. His entourage of deposed princelings and princesses, courtiers and courtesans, gaily dressed, attached themselves behind the throne and around the walls to watch. Dashi counted those that had collaborated with the last magistrate, those that he'd spared when first taking power.

"Not much at all," she said, turning back to look down upon Dashi, former magistrate. "Do you wish to make a defence?"

Again he was silent.

"Court clerk, it pleases the court that you represent the former magistrate as defence. It is unseemly, as he well knows, that he should be tried without giving an account. His imperial majesty's government has had quite enough of this city's method of magistrate removal. We must proceed by the rules, or else what have we?"

"Yes, My Lady," said the court clerk, and stepping out from behind the desk he advanced to Dashi's side. "My Lady magistrate and Lord treasurer, before you is a man unsuited to high position. This boy, this country waif, abandoned and illiterate has no place being thrust into the exalted position of magistrate.

"To have *him*," he said with disdain, "rule over *us?* – it's absurd. Regard his broad hands. His kind are suited best to digging. He should have been seated in the cow pasture, not an eminent seat of governance. His abandonment of his duty is without a doubt true. My contention to your Ladyship is only the defence, that he should never have been magistrate, should never have been given power and responsibilities beyond his capacity to grasp. Surely this boy is too stupid to have ever been considered for the appointment."

"Do you have anything to add to this?" asked the mistress of Dashi.

Dashi put his head up and answered, "I embrace it."

The mistress nodded, "If there is no objection then, I wish an accounting of his desertion," she said and bade a runner come to her with paper, where she wrote something, and giving instructions, sent the boy off. He crept down the side of the steps, delivering the message to the court desk to the nods of the bureaucrats who read it, and then he exited the courtroom.

"An accounting, My Lady?" said the court clerk.

"Couldn't we just..." said the treasurer, leaning on her chair to breathe into her ear.

She leaned away and forward, "The records will need to show it. Give us the tale of the young thief's flight."

"Yes, My Lady," said the clerk. "On the day of the twelfth full moon of the year, the then magistrate was seen fleeing from the palace and escaped into the wilderness through the northern gate."

"I see," she said, casting a stare upon the clerk, "Can you conjecture *why* he chose this particular day?" She leaned further forward.

The court clerk pursed his lips and nodded slowly, the once. "There was a... disturbance."

"Of what kind?" she inquired.

"Some of the people, apparently unhappy with the unfit magistrate's bizarre and incompetent rule entered the palace to challenge his power, and one can only assume, request the ousting of the bumpkin," he said matter of fact.

"Good," she nodded to him, "And he escaped before they arrived?"

"No, My Lady," said the clerk, now getting her gist, "This one confronted and threatened his own people, swinging his sword wildly at them."

"A sword?" she asked, aghast.

"Yes," he replied.

"They'd cornered him?" she asked.

"They tried to speak to him," answered the clerk, "But he is a wild man – a brute. Even his own kind shun him."

"This is grave indeed," she said, shaking her head, "He tried to harm his own people?"

"Yes, My Lady," he said.

"In order to escape," she prodded.

"Indeed," he said.

The mistress's face did not change save for her eyes. "And they gave way? Just like that."

"No, My Lady," said the clerk, "When they realized he was a savage they decided they'd have to use regrettable force to remove him lest he endanger everyone."

"In the opinion of the court is this man mad?" she asked.

The clerk considered, "I am not a physician, My Lady, you are better positioned to make this distinction, but from appearances it seems likely. Perhaps some worm has infested his insides and fills him with maddened rage. Who knows what he might be capable of now. I fear women and children may not be safe from one such as he." And this drew an inhalation from those pressed in at the door. "All the more reason to have him dealt with."

"Were there children present when he escaped?" she asked and observed the captain slipping though the door.

"No, My Lady, not to the best of my knowledge," said the clerk, "I only bring them up as there have been disturbing reports of... well, I do not wish to say – but out in the fields where this one prowled with his brother thief, some discoveries have been uncovered."

"I am aware of the discoveries," said the magistrate, placing her hand under her chin. "Already reports have made their way to the provincial court. You believe there is a connection?" she said. And then nodded to the clerk.

"I do," said the clerk with a slight turn to one corner of his mouth. "And I do not say this without mindful trepidation of my office. I believe we have captured a demon." There was a gasp that rose from the hallways and court, and then from the ajar door an echo of it upon the steps as the charge was relayed.

"Order! Close that door!" commanded the magistrate. "My bones in the ground will be warmer than here in this chair," she said, placing her hands into the sleeves of her robes, "A demon?"

"I believe so, My Lady," he said.

"I'll not have wild accusations made in my court. What proof have we?" the mistress demanded.

"Possessed by some unknown force, a demon, perhaps as a curse for his mother's indecent ways. His ability to defy death indicates this conclusion."

At this Dashi turned his head slowly and glared up at his defence.

The clerk shifted his eyes to the corner, and then gave it no thought, as none was necessary. "If you believe what some have suggested, this explains his whole sorry life story," the clerk said.

"A curse, court clerk?" asked the magistrate, "This situation becomes ever the more dark."

"Very dark," he agreed.

"All right, I am taken to agree with your assessment of the facts regarding the remains, "she said, "Continue now with your accounting. They had restrained him somehow, and he put up a fight?

"Oh, yes," said the clerk. "This creature has the strength of three, the good people fought hard to subdue him, but finally managed it."

"Bless us, for the righteous people of our city," said the mistress. "But how did they manage to subdue him, with the strength of three? Were any injured?" she raised an exaggerated eyebrow.

The clerk saw, and said "With great luck the people were spared from any fatal injuries. Strong men battered the beast into submission with rocks fortune had placed for their defence against this monster. They struck out at him with courage. Driving him from the city."

"Rocks," she said. "The brave people's heroes armed only with rocks?"

"Yes," he replied, excited, "many rocks. Others came, bringing their weapons when they heard the commotion and brandished their knives, saying 'Begone dark demon!' and someone very brave even shot him with an arrow, wounding the devil's hand. But even that didn't kill him!"

To which Dashi held up his left hand bearing the wound's deep scar.

"I am impressed," said the mistress, "That accounting will surely do for the imperial court records. It is clear now we have before us, if not a dangerous criminal, then some evil, a demon in the shape of a man. But which?" she said.

And she looked to the treasurer. "Do you have any of your special apricot wine, My Lord?" she said to him."If I am not mistaken, the one you receive from your connection in the divine court?"

A smile spread across his lumpen face. "I do indeed," he said, clapping his sweaty palms for it to be brought.

The mistress continued, "As one is well aware, that which is demonic is opposed to the divine will of heaven. The wine of your possession, made as it is under the aegis of the divine Emperor, must be of his divine nature, else it would be an affront to serve for his drink. Is this not so learned treasurer?" she asked.

"I am in agreement that it is," he exuded.

"We shall see then," she demurred.

And after some time a runner came with wine and cup. An attendant poured a liberal dose. The mistress rose from her seat, taking the cup.

Said the magistrate, "We shall see if we have mere mortal gone mad, or some demonic indignity, dishonouring his august sovereign."

If he drinks it and he be a madman he will find it to his liking. If he's a demon then its divine origin will disgust him - his ability to defy death will be defeated by the greater power of the divine emperor.

She walked slowly down the stairs until she stood above Dashi. "Who are you?" she asked offering him the cup, one hand held under and one over.

Dashi looked up and looked her in the eyes. He looked at her robe bearing an embroidered crane. And at her hands, the simple band ring showing atop her fingers. And again into her steady eyes.

"Drink, demon," she said softly, and handed Dashi the cup.

The treasurer, with eyes wide as a barrel, gripped the stumps of his legs.

Dashi looked into the cup. A crow cawed, and a princeling called: drink up! And then they all joined in - laughing and shouting and sneering - they beat the walls and desks. The joy of cornering an animal.

Dashi suddenly held the cup high as if for quiet, but there was only din. Then holding the cup out at arms length, and he turned, looking each and everyone in the eye. The whole hullaballoo. Saving his deepest stares for the treasurer, the court clerk and lastly their magistrate. The room fell silent.

He held her eyes as he crossed that bridge, upended the cup to its last drop. "It's sweet," he said, in surprise.

At which the treasurer and his mob howled in laughter. The whole court joined in on the joke. The supposed empty hallways reverberated with crowing. So loud their hilarity that they didn't hear the choking.

Dashi felt his body become stiff, his eyes began to swim, and soon drool was falling amply from his mouth, and with dizziness he fell to the ground and began to shake.

"Only a mad-man," commented the mistress, remounting the steps, "in the wrong place and time."

"Oh, My Lady," said the treasurer, "You are too kind."

Dashi's twitching was slowing. His consciousness ebbing and flowing black as ink.

Dashi's minds caught up in the last swirling darkness heard:

She, "Capta... this... bury..."

He, "No... example of... we burn..."

and thought, "Again?"

The treasurer clapped his flabby hands and his minions appeared. "Take this garbage out into the square to be incinerated," he said.

"And drag it in the mud," added the magistrate.

"Ah, I thought for moment you were being soft on him, your star pupil," the treasurer grinned.

"Let the mud return to the mud," said the magistrate, cryptically, and excusing herself left, her own attendants holding her arms so close they were shoulder to shoulder.

Again the treasurer clapped his hands. "You heard. Do it! - you idiots. Get moving!" a flurry of hands surrounded him and lifted him up, "I want to be there for the show. Hurry."

The treasury commander and his troop too busy receiving praise left the body where it lay for someone lesser to deal with. It was the captain who took charge of the body. He called for rope and a pole. He tied Dashi's hands and feet and hung him from the pole so that it could be shouldered, and ordered the men take him to the outer square.

As soon as the guard passed through the door the people were upon him, tearing at his clothes. For a memento, or to sell later, they fought over the scraps of him as dogs on a bone. It was only because of the additional guards who fell in beside to protect the bearers that those who produced knives didn't remove his fingers to sell as demon relics or to be ground into potions to enhance virility.

Between the door and the gate he was stripped naked. And then the captain did as asked - upon the appearance of a slough of dark muddy silt, he had the body dragged through. Three young women came to his side. Picking up clumps of mud, they threw it at his body. They threw another. And another. When briefly the bearers had to stop to move the rabble out of their path, they formed the muck around his head into the rough face of a monster. The captain ordered them away - Dashi's body becoming increasingly heavy. But others having seen, yet splattered the body and its attendants, laughing as they threw heavy globs of filth and wet straw.

The guards took him out the gate to the square, where the people shouted at the captured demon, and the dancers gyrated, and the banners that hadn't been pulled down snapped in the wind, and the wood was being piled, and the grimness of the late-day winter-sky, and the hunger in their bellies, and the fear that hunted them came together in a roiling entangled abnegation. Sovereignty failed, they stood with their dirty fists raised like burned-out stumps blackened by fire. They offered to the sky the unholy howls of the wind and the wolf. Spinning and stomping – a detonation of hammer heavy feet, they drummed an earthquake. Underneath their feet their shadows were no more than indistinct mist, because that was the time it was.

And the women came out with the mistress and they undid the ropes and they bound the clay monster to the post in white dressing, round and around until he was a silk cocoon. Then the wood was piled and the palace guards lashed him to the pole that stood up out of it, and they tied his hands in silk. Others ran from behind, crouching, dousing the wood with oil, as the mistress looked on with wide eyes.

In failing light the treasury guard, in their red uniforms, shouldering their rifles, marched in ceremonial single file – each marked with burning brand, held on high. The treasurer, in cushioned recline, borne aloft by servants and the ululations of the writhing mob, raised his fists in supremacy – then by gesture of his mortal hand gave sign – ignite the flame.

The fire that no one could extinguish began to burn. Its light making shadows evident. A sudden wind blasted the square like an omen. Because that was the time it was becoming.

Like coming up for air, Dashi eyes flew open and he drew breath. Everything was pale grey. He turned full around. No matter which way he looked, it was all light grey. A mist. And so he stopped looking and listened. He made himself open and quiet. Emptying himself, he honed in. Like a pulse in the air, something so subtle. He felt it more in his skin. That way.

So Dashi followed that way. Through the mist he advanced. It reminded him of climbing the mountain. Only the ground here was level, spongy soft, nearly bouncy, and he bent down to look, but again, it was just that uniform colour – of no colour.

After a time Dashi could hear high voices. Closer still, it was the sound of children. Slowly appearing in the mist, forms, what Dashi assumed were children running about, laughing. A child ran right out of the mist towards Dashi and stopped in front of him. A boy dressed in old rags. He stared at Dashi who bent down to speak to the boy. Dashi held out his hand and the boy fled; he disappeared back into the mist.

Dashi could now see a larger form ahead. The form appeared to turn, someone was sitting there. So Dashi walked forward saying, "Hello?"

"Hel?... Dashi?" said the master's voice.

Dashi came closer and there was the master. The master was holding his hand to his heart. "What are you doing here?" he said with alarm.

"Your wife poisoned me," said Dashi.

The master reached out and pinched Dashi's arm.

"Ow!" said Dashi.

"Ah," the master said, "All right." He relaxed and sighed, "I was wondering for a moment."

"Where are we?" asked Dashi, rubbing his arm, and

noticing childlike forms hovering just out of sight in the mist.

"Exactly," said the master. "I didn't realize you could... oh, no, you said something about being poisoned."

"Again," said Dashi.

"Ah yes, exactly, again," said the master, "It's that time," he said as if it explained something, and he coughed.

And Dashi noticed for the first time the master had a mirror he held at his side.

"What's the mirror for?" asked Dashi.

"I'll show you," said the master, "Stay still," and he called to the children with what sounded like the call of a bird. At first they hesitated but one cautiously crept forward. The child's hair was bald in patches. It had sickly blotchy red skin, and its movements were jerky. The master turned the mirror to the child who stared into its reflection. And then something. The child was healthy. Dashi remembered he'd always been so – but he also remembered him sickly – that memory now rapidly fading, a dream forgotten.

"What?" said Dashi. "They look in the mirror?" He could see now it was a little boy, who had never been anything but whole. Dashi wondered why he had this thought. And what deeply echoed in Dashi was – this boy was beautiful. And also: what kind of person was it who'd dared strike the sublime?

"Exactly," said the master.

Riddles, thought Dashi. He'd try again. "Master, where are we? And why is there this mist?" Dashi asked, noting it was getting thicker.

"Not where Dashi," said the master, "When," he said.

More riddles. "All right..." Dashi began.

"And there isn't any mist," the master said.

"Of course not," thought Dashi.

"It's smoke," said the master, waving his hand through it.

"Smoke?" said Dashi.

"Yes. You're probably on fire," he said.

Dashi said, "Fire?"

"See, look," said the master who turned and held the mirror to Dashi's face.

Only what Dashi saw was a golden dragon surrounded by flames. And the dragon began to laugh.

Down from the mountain snows came a whirlwind. The whirlwind came to the fire. It twisted the flame into a cyclone that spiralled up into the night and bent fiery tongues outward, that no one dared near. Even at the back where the wet wood had been stacked by the guard, the oil flared up in wild excitement. The dancers wheeled a ring around the rosy light, aping the would-be rescuers who chased each other helplessly around the fire. Their plan: the captain, his men, the mistress and most of all Li – to secret away the body, dashed by the wind. Their desperation mocked and mimicked by the chittering deranged.

The captain ran in and grabbed a burning log at the base, throwing it away toward the crowd. His men seeing this did likewise, trying to make the whole pile tumble over. Soon the treasury guard approached. Half the men stopped throwing burning brands and drew their swords to protect the rescuers from the advancing bayonets. The guard attacked the guard.

"Dashi!" Li wailed, trying to rush the flame, her dress

catching fire. She escaped the now unbearable heat, the women grabbing and extinguishing her, holding her back. The captain stood watching, his face and eyes glaring in mirror reflection. The end of what they could have been. Burning in their minds. Loss, and welling shame, he thought, "He would have run in to save any of us." A whistling scream sounded out of the pyre's dying wood.

It was the mistress who began it – waving her hands for everyone to join her – in whistling. Soon all the would-be rescuers were whistling in the dark. Ceasing pursuit of the retreating treasury guard.

The crowd became frantic. They writhed like venomous snakes roiled in their bellies. They hissed and stuck out their tongues – and turned their dead black eyes to the women whistling. They advanced on them in deepest darkest madness. The sharpest sword brandished meaningless to them.

The feeling of a spider's web fell across their faces; the hair prickled at the back of their necks. Beyond all the screeching, above all the din – an incongruous laughter. The corpse. The burning man.

Piercing each heart, thrust a sword of ice which no inferno could melt. The mourners numbed and weeping tears ceased flowing, the dancers froze. And yet he kept on laughing.

Breaking clay shards shattering, stiff-legged and tumbling upright the man of mud clambered down out of the flames and stood there, arms upraised, wafts of burning white silk dancing about his head like a crown, his eggshell of clay falling away from his naked skin, "I'm a dragon!" he shouted in jubilation. "I am free!"

And those who had danced uncontrollably now fell uncontrollably. All together – they all came tumbling down.

By the same power that caused them to dance, they fell to their faces, locked in sheer terror and submission.

Even those who knew him, fell to their knees and covered their faces. Only the treasurer and the some red coated guard kept to their feet, and they ran.

Dashi looked out over the cowered, "Captain?" shouted Dashi.

"My Lord, I am here," said the captain nearby, putting up his head like a turtle.

"Get your men ready. And bring rope. I mean to cross the river to catch a caterpillar," he commanded. And the captain jumped. Literally he jumped. He roused his men. The men roused, roused yet others to fight, so what was moments ago the bitter poison of defeat became a surging intoxicating in their veins.

Dashi looked around the square, at the cowering people and the mess.

Beautiful, a mind thought.

I feel taller...

The treasury guard gone - the citizens flooded back into their square, they poured in and began shouting at and pushing at the prostrate revellers, tearing at their clothes, if they had any, and cutting off chunks of their hair.

"Stop that!" said Dashi to the crowd, and some of them listened.

Suddenly the mistress appeared at Dashi's side with a dagger. He turned.

Turning it to hold by the tip of the blade, she slowly offered the handle to him. "If you'd become power mad, I'd kept this for you," she said. "Now I ask your forgiveness."

Dashi laughed at her. "Do you think I would've drunk your poison If I didn't trust you? - Good plan," the naked magistrate said, pointing to atop her head, "My hat?"

"Ah, yes. It turned out better than I expected," she admitted, passing it to him, looking upward and uncharacteristically humble, thought Dashi – like he was seeing her properly for the first time.

Dashi bent down and picked up one of the shards of mud that had fallen off him, "Nothing wrong with a little mud clod," he said laughing. "Li!" the magistrate called out donning his hat and turning back to the mistress, "I was just talking to your husband," he said. "Li!" he called again looking about. "He's somewhere in a mist – hm... Do you know where Li is?"

"I'm here," came a shaky voice from a crouching kneeler.

"There you are," said Dashi, "Come on, stand up."

"I can't," she said.

sweet...

Dashi laughed, "You most certainly can. I've seen you."

"I'm afraid," she said.

Dashi crouched down beside her so that his face met hers. "There's nothing to fear," he said.

"I'm still afraid," she replied, adding, "You're different now."

She's right.

"I think I always was," said Dashi. "Now get up."

"I can't," she reaffirmed.

He stood scratching the side of his neck, which hurt because it was a little burned, and he looked at the blood on his hands – they too being a little burned. "As magistrate, I order you to get up."

ah...

"You said you didn't want me to treat you like that. See, you've already changed," she said, sad hearted, "Now you'll leave, now that you're..."

Whole.

"... a dragon?" said Dashi.

"Yes," she said and looked up at him.

"How do you know you're not a dragon?" he said. "Maybe we can start a dragon family." Knocking the last sticking clumps of mud off his thighs. "You've seen this before. Has it changed?" he said.

She laughed at that. She wiped her face and got up. She brushed the mud off her. "Sorry," she said.

The captain appeared, snapping-to like an earnest cadet, "My Lord, ready to take the battle to the enemy."

"No enemy," said the magistrate offhanded, still focusing on Li, who was looking into his eyes.

Dashi's gaze broke away, "All right captain, let's go."

"Yes, My Lord," he answered.

To which the magistrate inquired, "How is our supply of gunpowder?"

"See for yourself," said the captain, and he dug out a couple barrels tucked far under the stage. "My back-up plan," he explained, "They used up the rest for fireworks."

"*That's* why they didn't shoot," realised Dashi.

"That," said the captain, "and maybe the treasury confiscated all their bullets too."

In burned tatters, and trousers pulled off a dead treasury guard, and his magnificent wide brimmed hat, the magistrate led his guard through the palace maze to the bridge's entrance. His sword returned, to his side. Several carried burning oily brands from Dashi's would be pyre. Beyond, the impregnable fortress, beyond this small corridor, beyond the iron gate at its end, beyond those who awaited them in ambush, was the unassailable throne of the golden caterpillar – the worm.

Dashi liked the superior confidence this would give the treasurer. It gave him time to think, to plan his escape, time therefore to waste. Or for those more wily, to implement the plan they'd already conceived. Speed was therefore the magistrate's chosen weapon.

"Careless of them to leave that lying about," said Dashi, indicating the gunpowder, "You could say they have a flare for mistakes," he joked.

"How shall we proceed, My Lord?" asked the captain without humour.

"We knock on the door," said the magistrate, pointing to their rear, where, slung with a strap, a young man carried a small barrel of gunpowder whose bunghole had been stuffed with an oil soaked cloth. "That's the civilized thing to do," he said, "I wouldn't want to be accused of being some country rube without manners."

"Yes, My Lord," said the captain smiling, "That iron is thick, My Lord. Do you think that will be enough to break it?"

"Just the hinges," said Dashi.

The captain beckoned the young man bring the keg forward, and another who carried fire, "Put it in front of the hinges, light it, and run," he said. So the two march down the corridor to the solid iron gate. While they all stepped forward to watch.

Suddenly slits opened along the ceiling and Dashi saw protrude twenty arrowheads on each side.

"Archers!" he yelled, as arrow poured down. The two men dropped over, bodies filled with shafts.

And Dashi was running, "Before they can reload!" he shouted now, as his brother had shouted then. Dashi grabbed the one with the keg, and dragged him backwards. The captain right beside him, pulling the other to safety, the brand left burning and smoking on the wooden floor. Head down, the brim of his hat blinded Dashi to everything, save the boy in his arms. Without warning, a singe of feathers flew past him. As Dashi yarded the guard to safety, hands grabbed the body from him, pulling him into the palace corridor beyond.

Dashi looked down at himself. He took off his hat to check for arrows,

"You missed me," he taunted.

Then turned to see the captain, still on the bridge, covered in the blood that sprung from his neck. The body of the guard who'd carried the flame, the one he'd tried to save – now his protection, pinned under – as arrow shafts buried themselves into the corpse with shuddering force.

It seemed to take a long time for the last of the arrow volley to strike. Time became a slow trickling stream, a lazy river.

"Now," said Dashi. The magistrate first and another of the guard, one of his brother's men, moved slowly to the captain. Pulling him away from the fallen dead, whose open hand, Dashi noticed was pierced, and pinned to the floor, whose feet were likewise struck upon with some embedded into the wooden planks. The two of them hauled the captain from the bridge.

Dashi had his hand upon the wound giving pressure against the flow, which leaked from between his fingers. Hands came and lifted the captain's legs and arms, they bore him a safe distance. They propped him up. And then the hands came in with cloth, and needle and fire, and Dashi left the captain to their care. The captain grabbed his arm, and tried to speak, to say, "I searched for you," but blood poured out. Dashi looked into the self-accusing eyes of the captain.

Failure.

Coarse laughter and indiscernibly muffled taunts followed after the wounding arrows.

Dashi retrieved his hat where he'd dropped it. Returning to the captain's side, he bent over and kissing the captain's forehead, put his hat upon his head.

"Keep my hat safe," he said.

Dashi opened up his thoughts to all his minds, and his gaze moved to the slits, where behind, the archers must lie hidden upon some platform, arrows poised for flight.

Above what?

Dashi looked at the walls, imaging the tall decorative eaves that from outside below could be seen extending out from under the bridge's roof.

Another secret...

"... ah...Give me the barrel," said the magistrate.

Setting fire to the cloth, and using the strap, Dashi spun himself full around, hurling it as far onto the bridge as he could; it landed against the left wall. The muffled sounds of a retreat in panic emanated from the narrow passage way.

Blasting fire tore open the walls of the bridge. With concussive white smoke, flying shards of painted wood and scaffold, flung at their feet, the fireball consumed the airborne powder. And the smash of crashing debris and archers rained down onto the ground far below. As the smoke cleared Dashi saw through the broken wall the narrow passage which ran along side.

"Attack!" he cried, clambering over the still falling rubble and sprinted to the open passage on the right of the bridge, and along its narrow length with the sounds of wounded men above in their crawlway. The blades of the guard behind the magistrate thrust up into their former-ly hidden safe space. The guard came out into the treas-urer's golden and blood red hall, spattered in blood, like camouflage.

Aside from a few guards who'd been posted inside, and were taken easily, the hall was empty. So sure had the treasurer thought the iron gate would hold – and it had. It stood strong and solid as ever, locked, only Dashi's minds had just gone around it, opening it from the inside. The rest of his guard poured in.

Another explosion shook, from where, Dashi didn't know, but he ignored it for now. Dashi flew down the way, and they burst through the golden doors into the throne room, the cocoon of the worm. Surprised crows, still bearing scrolls and platters of treats, scattered in every direction. But the worm had slipped away. The lair was empty.

"Find him," said the magistrate, "Don't kill him, if you can. There's a judgement awaiting him." Dashi unexpect-edly felt glad that he was gone. Perhaps the golden cater-pillar would curl up and die and Dashi wouldn't have to worry about how to sentence him. Dashi breathed, he calmed himself, centred himself.

Don't think about the caterpillar...

Funny.

"My Lord," one of the guard roused, pointing up, "Smoke."

Dashi gazed up at the ceiling, as did they all – which hung heavy with a pale hued mist.

They've set the palace on fire.

A trap!

"Retreat!" Dashi shouted, and the men turned back the way they had come. Going up the counterfeit golden

411

hallway to the great doors, all around whose edge leaked with billows of smoke. Before any could stop him, one of the guard grabbed a handle and instantly pulled his hand back from its heat.

A trap, like I said.

I guess it's that time...

Yeah, funny – but how'd we get out?

A window?

"Find a window," the magistrate said, and he and the men ran back and through rooms to the outside of the treasury, to find barred windows, many smashed in, and out on the ground below people, torches held aloft, lobbed them up again and again, like a carnival game, trying to get them through the windows. While others amused themselves with burning the bridge, bringing fire to the carnival. Dashi could see more scrambling through a hole in the wall where the treasury gate had been. These were not the mad revellers. These were the citizens.

Un-believable...

Hey, we've rushed into a burning building!

Fool.

No – dragon!

"Dragon," thought Dashi searching from side to side. Below, he noted treasury guards stripping off their coats and running away through the crowd.

They've escaped! How?

Down!

Dashi looked down. "The basement, the cellars. There must be a way out," said the magistrate. "Stairs!" he said and the men needed no more instruction than that. They scattered. Soon shouts of discovery, followed by trumping feet, as all accounted they descended. Here they were met by the swords of the last loyal treasury guard lying in wait. They advanced. But Dashi knew, as they must, that the higher ground was his.

Defection...

"Stop!" said the magistrate, "Your master has left you to die: burned alive or by our swords. Join us and live!"

The commander, with the golden tassels and evil sneer, came out from behind and pointed his sword to the centre of Dashi's heart. "You! You son of a whore! We'd rather die than... uh... be ruled by filth... like you. You disgusting dung filled..." and he said no more, but looked down at his chest from which a sword protruded. Then he slipped off it to the ground.

The treasury guard in red, holding the blood covered blade, eyes cast upon the silenced carcass at his feet, "We don't want to die," he said, "Not for him." And he spat. "We pledge our allegiance... My Lord."

"Such as it is," said Dashi. "Accepted. How do we get out of here?" he said glancing back up the stairs where the glare and noise of the fire was increasing swiftly.

"This way," said the red guard, and they all ran after him, through stone archways and down to the level which led to the kitchens. The doors to the courtyard had been barricaded from the inside with tumbled shelves. Several guards, together, easily pushed this out of the way. But upon opening the door they found burning wreckage and smoke began to fill the room.

"Close it," Dashi ordered, "Where is the deep cellar?" he asked. The red guard immediately led them to a hallway where he opened a cellar door. The meat locker. The guard took the lantern that was there and lit it with a match. This gave a few guards the moment to glance towards the kitchens, always in search of food.

"My Lord," they said, "The kitchen will have more

matches. Just in case."

Dashi left those descending into the locker to enter the kitchen proper. Here lay what Dashi assumed were the kitchen staff, dead and bloody, on table and block, in the corner, by the stairs, and the ovens. Through-out every room, and into each far nook, blood and boot prints.

Why?

Dashi looked at the body of the man, who by his dress had chopped the wood and stoked the fire. Stabbed from behind, likely as he tried to flee. Others who perhaps had fought, whose wounds covered their front, had been hacked down. Their rough hands held to protect them ruined.

"This one, My Lord," said the guard, looking under the table.

Under the table there was a dead body, dressed in black. To get a better look, Dashi nudged the corpse's head with the toe of his boot, the head of the third assistant chronicler. His fingers cut away.

Remember...

"Matches," said a guard.

"My Lord," came a voice behind him. Dashi turned. The young man was looking round at the kitchen massacre, hand over his mouth, "You'd best come see this, My Lord."

The rest of them descended down the dark stairs, one hand upon the stone wall, with only the light from the open door above, a few guttering matches, and the lantern light beckoning from the depths. At its bottom, and off to right, the other guards stood, their lantern making their shadows stretch and shift upon the stone walls. They were standing about a hole in the floor beneath which Dashi could hear rushing water. He knew where this led

– and also that across the forgotten river, there was a platform, and a trapdoor through which to emerge back into the palace.

Secrets...

They stood motionless peering into its inky depths.

"My Lord," said the treasury guard who'd brought them here, "The ladder is gone." And he held out his lantern shining it down. Dashi coming to the hole's edge, knelt and saw, that like on the other side there was a platform far below. "And the rope," he said, holding it up. "And the other lantern." Dashi looked at the empty pulleys hanging above. He remembered when he and Li had escaped the palace riot how he'd seen the light streaming down upon the water. Someone had lit that lantern. Someone who'd been standing there.

"Tie your jackets together, sheet bend," said Dashi, knowing his brother thieves could tie an escape rope.

Where before the guard had been concentrating on the pit to escape, now they turned the lamp and their heads to the tying to see. Illuminating all the small animals skinned for meat on hooks.

"Look away!" Dashi ordered his men. "That's an order!"

Dashi breathed and centred as the golden feeling he held inside quivered. As his command echoed away, there came a noise. The magistrate listened, "Quiet!" he said aloud. And they heard the faint sound of a voice calling out. "Where's that coming from? Find it! Now!" And soon they stood in front of a wall. An empty wall. He looked all around it for a crack.

"It must be another damned door," he said.

Another.

No time. Just break it down!

Yeah...

"No time," he said, "Break it down!" and the men began hacking and prying at every niche they could find in the cunningly fashioned door. But there was no getting through. Only the pleading howls had become more urgent, as their swords clanged against its immovability. It was then that Dashi saw the smoke curling out of the wall. From a small hole.

The keyhole, I bet.

Good odds.

Be nice if we had a key...

A golden key.

Dashi stood there as the yells became more and more desperate. More frantic. High pitched. This didn't look like a keyhole. He put his ear to it, and clearly the voices were children. Dashi searched. What was he searching for? A mechanism? For a key could be lost, and whatever lay behind this door, who'd ever made it could not afford to be locked out. Or in. The fire above was breaking through their ceiling, and soon they would die, trapped, sealed in...

A vault?

He immediately thought of the light that had streamed down from the well onto the water below. The sounds of crashing wood up the stairs behind them told them they needed to soon be gone. The red de-robed guard were looking most nervous. The captain's guard stood firm.

"The rope better be ready soon," said Dashi.

"Here, My Lord," said a former thief, and Dashi lashed it around the waists of two of the largest guard and threw the free end into the hole. "Hold on to the anchors. The biggest go down first. Three on the bottom, then two, stand on each other's shoulders to get everybody down." One by one they followed into the shadowy din of the river.

Dashi, accustomed to thinking he didn't know, didn't know how to open the door. Maybe the dragon did. He didn't even know what that meant. So he breathed out, closed his eyes, releasing everywhere he was within.

Expectations-
Shhh.
Don't shhh me-
Shhh.

Dashi stood opening everything that was closed, every knot that was tied.

A good knot uses no rope and yet cannot be untied. A good door needs no lock yet no one can open it.

...A door need no lock if there's no door.

The magistrate laughed. He'd walked out from his own pyre, after being poisoned, and missed by flying arrows, and found the people who knew how to get down to this escape. Yet he hadn't figured out how to do any of that! It was done without thinking.

"Ah," he said, and he followed an inclination to look up. "Lantern. Show me the ceiling." The guard did as the magistrate asked and Dashi saw the bolts that held the kitchen chute on the other side.

Dashi lowered himself onto the rope of coats and climbed down, dropping to the platform. The churning river echoed, deafening. The last guard took the lantern down with him, clambering over them, dropping the coats to the ground. By the time the platform was full of guards, Dashi had moved, feeling his way, onto a narrow ledge that hugged the wall, and more importantly led to a recessed door with a short rounded ramp that led to it. Dashi shouted for the light.

Dashi banged on the door. After what sounded like

someone moving heavy sacks about, the pounding began on the other side. Dashi took the lantern, and looked around the door. First he eyed the lock, and regretted not bringing some wire. Looking further, he saw the bolt looked good - but the hinges were rusty - down here in the damp above the river. Plus with the mistress' dagger he could easily loosen the crumbling mortar around them.

He pointed to the hinges and made the gesture for digging it out and stood back as the two burliest guards dug their sword tips in behind the hinges like shovels. It didn't take long 'til they were bending them out of the wall and together they grabbed the door's exposed edge and wrenched it back from the wall. Dashi was illuminated by the light from within.

First a rank smell, then a gasp, then a high cry came tumbling out, "My saviour," said the treasurer, flopping forward into the door way, "I knew someone would rescue me- It's been terrible," he sobbed, his voice rising.

For a split second Dashi saw the treasurer for what he was - a weak, fragile creature wanting to be loved - hiding behind a facade of power - now bemoaning his self-fulfilling fate. An energy began rising up in Dashi - and his heart clenched.

"Ich... You?" said the revolted magistrate in disgust.

The treasurer blubbered, "...and they pushed *me*... down the garbage chute!"

Dashi tried to centre himself. All he found inside was a dull familiar burning. The voices said nothing.

"My Lord, we can close the door back up again," shouted one burly guard pushing back slightly on the door.

"...so humiliating and unfair- to me!" he wept.

"Be justice - considering he put you in the fire, My Lord," yelled the other and began pushing also so that the door moved.

"No!- Stop that!!" the angry treasurer ordered imperiously and then fawned, "No... no please - please, mercy... have mercy- Pity me. Please. O great noble compassionate magistrate, please please... I, I'll give you anything you want."

"This is what we came for, I supposed," called Dashi covering his mouth and nose, "Tie him up, and drag him."

They removed the treasurer from the hole he was blocking with his legless mass. Once gone, the irregular white-bricked chamber beyond was visible.

Two children stood there.

On one side, the source of the wrenching stench - a large garbage chute that went straight up out of the lantern light and to the kitchen, the other end out to above the door to the river. A small opening had been appended, and a pile of moulding bones and rotting matter lay in an alcove below.

On the other side of the room stood a charred work bench, long metal pans and an iron pot over a low fire. On the bench there were five bars of gold, along side four small hammers and fragments of gold leaf. Beside the bench sat the bags of lead shot. The ones needed for the guard's guns, but hoarded by the treasury. Dashi understood.

"Come away, children," Dashi shouted, beckoning them. And when they came, the flies arose off the garbage in a cloud. The children moved in jerks, and Dashi saw in the light their faces, their half smiling mouths hung open, and beneath their tiny teeth ran a dark blue line like soot. Their hair matted and lost in patches. They said nothing. If the kitchen staff had heard them, they'd ignored them.

Dashi looked up at a noise from above of buckling hot

metal that said the kitchen was now ablaze. The children pointed to him, and he saw the palms of their hands were spotted with blackened lesions, no doubt from burning themselves he thought. Whatever they had been doing here, the investigation would wait. He lifted up one and the burly guard took the other.

He noticed the children were still silent. But the treasurer trussed in the rear was not. He blubbered like a wet cat on the sorriness of his fate.

Downstream, Dashi knew, ended in the falls coming out from beneath the palace wall. Upstream was uphill. Even if the ledge continued all the way, every six paces they'd have to lean backwards going around the arches, and even then, where this river met the lake - it was sure to have an iron gate carefully hidden against the outer wall with, Dashi suspected, another hidden lock. But that must be how they brought the children in - how they brought the bars, bones and whatever else they were doing, out.

The water was becoming easier to see. From a few openings in the cavern's ceiling on their side cast the orange glow of the fire above. Bits of flaming debris peppered the water. Dashi saw a substantial piece of flaming material fall through one of the holes and land hissing half out of the river. Meaning while the water was swift, it was also shallow.

He put the child he carried in another's arms and had the guard tie the coat rope around Dashi's middle. He pointed to the other side. He then lowered himself down the rocks to the river. The water, although fast moving, only came up to his knees. So Dashi aimed himself a bit up stream and walked. He could hear the sound of the men jumping in behind him. The rocks underneath the water were jagged and shifted under his feet. Slowly he waded across until he reached the rock face of the other side.

"Hold on!" he shouted to the guard behind him, and he let him self slide downriver to get to the platform. Finding the ladder going up onto the rocks Dashi pulled the rope off and secured it onto the ladder. He tugged the rope.

Soon the guard were coming across The treasurer they brought by lift and drop.

"I'm drowning!" he cried.

Dashi spied the palace's kitchen disposal chute further downstream. Then he climbed up and opened the trap door above. He climbed back down and as the guard came across he pointed up. After the first few had gone up Dashi did likewise, coming up into the palace meat locker, which was thankfully empty.

"This way," said the magistrate and led them upstairs. When Dashi opened the door he smelled smoke. Considering there was a fire raging next door, this in itself was not unusual. But this was no burning building smell. All the kitchen staff turned to see as Dashi, Lord magistrate, half clothed and sodden wet, reentered his palace.

"Hello Dashi," said the master who sat at the table, chair tilted back, pipe in hand.

"Yeah..." said Dashi flopping into the chair beside his master, "Hello Master."

The guard came through. Taking some porridge, they wandered away, outside, to watch the treasury burn with everyone else.

Hearing the wailing from down in the cellar. "We have the treasurer," said Dashi, as if talking about the weather.

"Isn't that what you wanted?" asked the master.

"Have you met him?" asked Dashi back.

The master said, "Oh, yes. He's quite a specimen."

Dashi changed the subject. "Master I really felt... with the mirror... even when the captain got shot-"

"I heard," said the master.

"I almost lost it - but I held on to it. I could hear the minds. Instead of changing into them- or resisting," he said. "But then, I saw that," said Dashi pointing, as it was only now that they'd managed to haul the bawling treasurer up the stairs. "Dungeon. Take food for yourselves. Don't let anyone near him," he said to the guards. "It's slipped away again. I was so close."

"Why do you think that is?" asked the master.

Dashi knew. "Because he makes me feel defeated. He's so *loathsome* - and I *want* to help the people. Well... he's one of them."

"One of us," suggested the master.

"But I need to forgive him, right?" said Dashi.

"No," said the master, "Listen," he said tapping his ear, "The only person you ever need to forgive is yourself. If you don't like the way you feel about this rapist cannibal slaver, and I don't know why you would - if you want to be more understanding, because you know his minds, no matter how stuck, are the same as yours - if you want no mind left behind - then embrace his minds as the mirror of what stuckness could be in your own. You can't make the treasurer change. But you can make everyone who angers you your teacher."

"I don't know whether I can - I despise him," said Dashi, "and pity him... and I'm disgusted-"

"Embrace this," said the master, "If you want to get away, finally, from pretending, then you have to embrace *what is*. You forgive yourself to not be stuck gnawing on old bones. What you feel after you free yourself - is what is. It is your faith in yourself. And, by oneself, that is the best that one can do.

"Everything I have told you, is to stop you focusing on the immature, which only maddens your minds. It isn't that you won't see – but having seen, you don't allow yourself to become ensnared by the resentments of one mind. Instead you focus on their whole."

"How do I focus on the whole of them, when they're so selfish?" asked Dashi with bitterness.

"Not them – the whole of you," said his exasperated master, "If one is caught up in the idea that people are stealing from you – this is a stuck mind. Even if they are.

"Those who steal are stuck there too – concerned they aren't getting their fair share, or not as much as they want, afraid others will get more – they take all they can grab. Better you free yourself, and give them everything, than to become one of them."

"Oh..." said Dashi, and somehow that made sense. "Why didn't you just say that in the first place?" he joked.

The master laughed, "You think they're bad because you keep trying to be their teacher. Embrace this pretending, this romantic delusion. Do not sacrifice your joy to them. Who do you think you are?"

Dashi imagined the dragon in the mirror. Dashi said, "Apparently, I'm a dragon."

"So I heard. What would this dragon do?" asked the master.

Li's face came to him. "He'd go find Li," Dashi said – and his stomach growled – "...and get something to eat."

The master nodded, "A very practical dragon."

Then Dashi began to tear up, "Master, I was the dragon," explained Dashi, "And then I lost it– It vanished. One second I was in it, I was of it," Dashi said with frustration, his hand gripping the empty air. "But I couldn't hold on to it." He breathed in deeply, and then let it out. "I feel somehow I failed."

forsaken...

"That's all right," said the master, comforting his student, "That's how it comes. You've had your taste of it. Now the real adventure begins."

"Oh master – I don't know if I can take any more adventure," Dashi said.

"Oh Dashi," the master said, and he chuckled, "On and on, the world goes on, and has its way. Everything continues. The path you are on, the destiny you have chosen by your actions, and all the connected interactions of infinite being – when you realise this, and accept that it is so, then you are the paragon of humanity – a monkey king, and that is all. Because there is something more. A silence beneath everything. The centre of being," said the master.

"IT? said Dashi.

"IT," said the master, smiling, "And releasing is the action of faith, to wait upon the creative to awaken in your intuition. And what does following give you that you couldn't take using your own minds to control your life? Why give your life over to something inside you cannot see? How can you know it has your best interest?

"Well, you're here aren't you? All is in its keeping and *all* is what you want. This is the call to adventure you need to answer."

When the magistrate went to bed he was no longer alone. And that should have been a greater comfort than it was. In the dawn twilight of early hours he lay awake.

In the dark, Li's sleepy voice said, "Dashi..."

"Yes, Li?"

"Why are you awake?" she asked.

Dashi wanted to say, "I don't know," which felt more and more like the only truth he had. Or more prosaically, "My hands still hurt," which they did, even with his having removed the tight gauze bandages. What he chose to say was, "I think... my minds are discussing my future."

"Oh," she said, and turned over to face him. "Do you want to talk about it?"

Dashi looked inside his head. It was hollow and empty. "I don't think I have anything to say yet," he replied.

"Mmm," she purred, putting her hand out to find his. Her hand was warm and soft and small and delicate, and invisible, save only to his touch. She yawned, "What are they talking about?"

Dashi listened. He felt his breath flow in and out, just naturally. He flexed his hands. He heard the ringing in his ears. The song of the dark, his brother used to say.

It was the bright song of the dragon that rang in his ears, awakening echoes of loss in his every breath. While underneath, in the black silence, the ancient king of the frozen forest incanted low - conjuring fires of rage and appetite - howling sorcery, the flames crept up his aching belly and loins in hunger.

"Where is the song of the man?" Dashi opened himself to the place his heart might be.

"Mmm?" she said.

"I think-," he said, "I feel... that I'm going the wrong way."

Li said, "Which way is the right way?"

Said Dashi, "I think that's what they're discussing."

"Oh," she said. "Don't worry. When they're ready, they'll tell you."

That little bit of wisdom – and Dashi felt an ease of comfort. He nodded slowly, "When it's the right time," he said. And he looked down at her, prone beneath the blankets, thinking she deserved to be loved more than he, at the moment, was able.

Though the outer wall bordering the treasury compound had a hole blown through, its gate to the outer courtyard was closed, as was the palace gate. In the inner courtyard the braziers burned and the twisting wind made them rush, tossing up crackling sparks.

"Faithless," thought the black draped magistrate as he looked down from his ornately-carved, heavy chair, set upon the raised platform. A throne set upon a stage. Dashi looked into the fire, his burned hands bandaged. To either side of the courtyard, a long line of tables had been prepared with many drinking cups.

And then the gate opened. Up the centre of the courtyard they marched, the crows, four wide and many deep. Guards, of both uniform, along either side, their swords at the ready. When they were all in at the gate, they were closed behind. The courtyard fluttered with the garb of officialdom.

The magistrate stood. Dashi looked within for a beginning. "I have never been one of you, it is true. And I've also never been more aware of, nor happier for it than I am now," he said, "Even though I've been brought into your midst – I ally myself to those who labour in the earth for life, rather than you who've, for gold, dug your grave." He paused.

"A desire for vengeance has given me some grief over

the past few days. I sought out my advisors, and I have since calmed my heart's distress. I realise now that you are like mad dogs, and therefore, I seek two ends: to protect the people, and to release you from your misery.

"Because I continue to desire compassion, I recognise the impairment you have cultivated as an illness. Albeit a self-inflicted one. That being so, there's no cure that can be attempted without your consent. A consent, that your victims, the murdered children, and undoubtably many others, never gave. Another division between us for which I am glad.

"Therefore I take this action." Dashi indicted to their right. "On the tables to either side of you are potions. In the cups to your right, there is a poison. It is quick acting and painless," the magistrate said pausing, "The potion to your left, will determine by the colour of your subsequent urine whether you have consumed human flesh. Should you choose this route you will be individually tried – fairly – and if found guilty, sentenced to be held for life in prison. It is my hope that over the years at least some amelioration will be found for your suffering."

Other than the rustling of their feathers, the crows remained silent, they gave no indication they were listening, or alive. Their faces grey under the grey sky.

"I recognise that voice!" said one of the black crows, and stood out to the right of his fellows. The mouth that'd spoken only from shadow now brought into daylight – his mottled cadaverous skin revealing blood red gums and long yellow teeth. "You fooled me, My Lord," said the librarian.

"It is my prerogative," said Dashi.

"Then you deceive as we do," countered the librarian, "no better."

427

"When I wandered into your library I had no premeditation to deceive you," said Dashi.

"And yet you did," he countered.

"Perhaps poisoners had made me cautious," said the magistrate.

"And this is what you offer us? Again, you admit circumstance moved your choices," argued the librarian.

"I do not control the river," said Dashi. "I only swim where I may. Nor do I completely deny our kinship – these black robes. I put it on of my own free will, and of my own free will I wore it. I know your minds in mine, I know the lure, but I seek more than mere conformity. Let me be clear then that I am like you, and we are brothers. And also that I am more. By embracing unity I transcend uniformity's burden."

"Baaah," said the librarian, "Bring me my cup of poison. I'd rather be dead than listen to this drivel." One of the guard poured the librarian a cup and handed it him. "My only regret is the flesh *not* consumed," he proclaimed, "The sight not seen, and the palpation untouched." He held up the cup to his peers. "I have eaten the forbidden and drunk the unspeakable! For this in right thinking society, they called me *master*.

"The emperor will fall! The Hand will rise!" he trumpeted, his right hand out and fingers splayed in salute, and then enunciating in a rasping sneer, "When we're in control, we'll be free. And no one – will ever tell us again – what we are allowed, or not allowed – to do," he spat, and drank back the liquid, smashing the cup to the ground, laughing. In a few moments he collapsed, and was taken away.

Dashi looked to the mistress. She nodded.

"Any others?" asked Dashi. But none moved. "There is

428

still the potion to prove your innocence," he waved towards their left, "We will do what we can to aid forgiveness." Again they merely stood silent, defying his authority to the last.

"Then there is one more choice. I proffer these for you to decide your path. The choice is the one I gave many months ago when first I became magistrate. That is - for you to leave." At this there was a great murmur. They were alive after all. "However," said the magistrate holding out his bandaged hands, "Should you leave, you will be outside the law. None of my men will harm you, on my command. Beyond these walls, you will be free, at least in this. But you will be beyond civilization, both outside my protection - and my mercy."

Suddenly there was derisive laughter. And the crows they began to openly mock him. And what's more - they mocked the position of magistrate, and the law, and the emperor.

How could it be, Dashi wondered, that those who carried out the work of the empire were so contrary. But he understood. As far as they were concerned - they were the law - and the empire. It was they who wrote the law, oversaw the rules, their hands that controlled the strings of empire.

What was the emperor to them, but a figurehead, empty of true legitimacy? What was a magistrate to them, but a mouthpiece for a puppet? What was the military to them, but dogs? And the people? - less than dogs.

"Open the gates!" called out Dashi. And the gate opened to the outer square. The crows turned, and almost to a one with rude gestures, marched outside the magistrate's walls.

Watching them leave, the magistrate said to himself, "I

embrace the joy in this. I release it from everywhere it is stored within." He breathed. "Now I am free," he said quietly. Then when the last had gone he called out, "Close the gates!"

And when they had fully closed, there began the most terrible sound. The sound of fear. Cries spilled over the high walls, cries for mercy, and for pity, and calls for the humanity they'd themselves abandoned in their brokenness. They beat the doors to be let back in. And every blow Dashi felt, and was sorry.

But the magistrate accepted. What they had done, now returned to them. Balance returned, as is the law. Not of the emperor, nor his magistrate, but of heaven and earth.

Dashi gazed now at three petrified remaining bureaucrats, standing at the table with the potion to prove their innocence, their eyes darting to each other. They were frozen, in the din. And when the beating stopped, and the last voice had died away, they abided still, quaking.

"Drink," said the magistrate, and this they did. "Take them to their cells to await trial," he said to a guard.

Dashi came down from the platform to the mistress, "We will question them first before the librarian wakes up, and compare that with what the treasurer said," said Dashi, "You were right. They chose to not choose. Only escape moved them."

"To escape themselves," she offered. "Their whole lives they've run from the minds they rejected. The great pretence. Escaping is how they became what they became."

Dashi nodded.

"At least they've helped with the grain shortage," she offered.

Dashi laughed. He said, "I can't believe you said that," then he embraced the joy and released it. But it was still funny.

"I know, in such bad taste"-she smirked-"that mind."

He beckoned servants who carried steaming basins of water, "Excuse me," he said to the mistress, and went to the gates, which were opened for him.

Out in the square the mud had been swept away, but now there were blood and bodies to clear. Dashi nodded to the captain, as the guard came out from the palace yard and began to drag them off to one side. But it was not the guard who'd slayed them. Dashi had given his word.

Dashi simply stepped around the fallen robes. He strode towards a group of people he knew: farmers, shopkeepers, mothers and fathers, servants, rounders. Blacksmith, chef, musician and thief, their hands were red. They shivered and shook, some gazing blankly at their hands, some looking anywhere but.

As he came to each, no one said a thing to him except the old man who'd stolen his hat, his voice atremble, "Some things you have to do."

Dashi removed the bandages from his burned hands, and one by one, Dashi took their hands in his - flowing the spilled blood with his own. He held their gaze as he washed their hands, intoning, "We embrace this. We release it from everywhere it is stored within. Now we are free." And to a one, they let their held breath go.

When the magistrate went back in, there was a small group of disheveled people, feet bound in bandages, many whose heads had been shaven, or half shaven. The mistress looked deeply upset.

When she relayed their request, Dashi merely nodded at

her that she supply them with what they wanted and she
led them away.

In the dungeon. The treasurer, gagged, bound to a
chair, his eyes wide, looked from side to side. A bottle of
his own reserve wine and a goblet sat nearby.

"It was your brother," began the mistress, as she filled
a small pot that sat over a low alcohol flame with water,
broken roots and fungus.

Dashi shrunk, "Please don't say he was part of this."

"Well, in a way, yes," the captain said hoarsely, his un-
buttoned collar revealing the thick bandages, "It was his
attacking the supply trains that meant they had to be
armed. Which meant they needed guns and with them,
ammunition."

"Lead shot, which was used as ballast under carriages
carrying food," said the mistress.

"Uninteresting to rifle-less bandits focused on food,
even if they found it," said the captain.

"But when the grain taxes were paid at harvest time,
there was plenty. So your band of thieves didn't attack,"
said the mistress, "You had no way to store the grain. The
grain therefore went south. Perhaps your brother thought
better of attacking what was now the emperor's.

"The lead was taken to the treasury, melted down into
bars by the children, who later papered them with gold
foil. That was why there was so much lead shot sent, but
none to be found for the rifles. Which had they kept some
for the treasury guard..." - she shrugged - "In any event,
the false gold bars were sent to the imperial treasury."

"And no one there noticed? said Dashi incredulous.

"The treasury is also run by bureaucrats. They who wrote the book," - and she pulled it from her sleeve. She picked up Dashi's pen that Li had found again. "The book, made by whose hand?" she asked, and Dashi noted the similar sounds, and she then wrote: "To have them in your hand - to make them into sheep." Dashi noted the similar characters.

"It is a code?" he asked.

"They're puns," said the mistress, "The kind of thing you do when you are clever and have a too long a time to think out your plans. Continuing with: when the wagons returned with the grain tax, the ballast was changed to mud bricks."

"Ah," said Dashi, "But really it was the gold covered in mud."

"No, just mud bricks," croaked the captain, "The gold was in the sacks of grain. Received by their accomplices."

"This is why we sent so much grain away only to buy it back later," said the mistress.

"Paid with gold-covered lead bars," said Dashi.

"Exactly," said the mistress. "I suspect similar trans-formations of gold into lead have been taking place every-where. Stockpiling the real gold in some hidden vault while filing the treasury with counterfeit. It is also why the bureaucrats purposefully orchestrated poor growing practices so there would always be a shortage that kept the supply trains coming and going, so the gold could be shipped out in the bags of grains."

"You mean the starvation was on purpose?" asked Dashi.

"And it brought out desperate thieves that required the requisitioning of bullets," said the captain, and coughed.

"We unwittingly helped," said Dashi.

The captain merely nodded.

"What about the children? Why-" began the magistrate.

The mistress said, "I believe that was incidental to the plans to steal the gold. A side benefit from starving an impoverished population," said the mistress "and then a means by which to ensured loyalty. A kind of addiction.

"It was the payment for babies that made me suspicious. Why not just wait? Poor women would bring them to you for nothing. Especially since they'd orchestrated a star-vation - families couldn't keep their children. But if you have someone else's wealth to spend, and a need..." she left off.

"It makes one glad one was merely abandoned," said Dashi.

"We've learned from our prisoner," - she glanced at the treasurer - "that the orphanage woman was expressly told not to handle them. Thus they became sickly even though fed," she said, "They could then be drowned, collected and-"

"They farmed despair," said Dashi.

"As I said, an addiction," said the mistress.

"The original chef was obviously one of them," said Dashi, and winced, "The ovens in the kitchen... were they used for this?"

"Fortunately the treasury had its own kitchen and ovens, said the mistress, "The babies' bones were taken back to the fields-"

"We assume taken up the river under the palaces to the lake," said the captain, his voice a croaky hiss, "And from there to some hiding place."

"Along the ditches," said Dashi.

"It's also how they took the children in," said the mistress, "We now know they were also blackmailing the couple, threatening to expose all the deaths. That was how they kept the price down."

"Babies for cheap? With all that gold?" said Dashi disgusted all over again.

"It wasn't their gold – it was the Hand's," the mistress said taking the pot from the flame.

The captain cleared his throat, and said, "They'd take back the bones with some ashes from the kitchen fire – they told the woman and man they'd been cremated. Then the man went out through the hole in the wall and buried them where he was told – in the mass grave, by the ditch."

"And the bureaucrats told the farmers not to dig in those fields – they didn't want the alarm to go up," reasoned Dashi.

"Which is in a way fortunate because your master got to looking at the soil," said the mistress, "Far better than in the fields they were constantly churning with plows. Well away from the grave, the plants growing healthier and stronger where the natural process of decay was allowed to continue in place. With the discovery of the skulls it was easy to get the farmers to switch for fear of what remains might be unearthed. Also it kept him rather busy."

"That's why the harvest was so good?" asked Dashi.

"It appears that way," the mistress said.

"And because of that, people were keeping their children," said Dashi.

"Also you tried their orphanage suppliers, the man and woman," said the captain, and cleared his throat again.

"Who they killed to keep–" said Dashi.

The mistress interjected, "As I was saying – it was buying the babies for cheap that revealed their otherwise hidden hoarded wealth. The gold meant for buying persuasion."

Dashi nodded, "Persuading who?" he asked.

"I am coming to that," said the mistress, "I realised it when they wrote your name in red. The calligraphy was pretending to be rough but they could not hide the refinement. Further you, My Lord, made the comment about how the brush must have been been a broom. By the thickness of the lines a very wide broom. The kind used for sweeping grains. It was you that led me to the granary," said the mistress. "Which you'd already had partially emptied. Stealthily," she added, "A few bags at a time."

"I had?" Dashi said.

"You had the grain distributed so it wouldn't be vulnerable to, for example, fire," she said.

"Oh yeah," he said, "Good for me."

"Indeed," she said, "Upon discovery, the empty granary must have presented a problem for the bureaucrats supposed to be managing it – one for which they found a creative solution. And because the sacks were also how they moved the gold, it was no doubt interpreted as a signal we were on to them.

"That is where I found the broom. And because I had all court documents sent to me, and I made all queries, I could quickly assemble samples of writing. There were only a couple dozen who would have had the training and position to call me by my title."

"Ah," said Dashi, "Clever."

"Thank you," she replied.

Dashi thought about this. "I should've just had them all rounded up. They weren't armed and the treasurer's guard was no match for mine," said Dashi. The captain stood slightly taller inside.

"Round up who exactly" she asked. "It is only in hindsight that we may conclude it was most of them. If we'd attacked the treasury directly it could only have been interpreted as a direct attack upon the emperor. To be tried by bureaucratic official review, and judgement, and it would be you who'd be facing torture."

The treasurer reacted to this, squirming.

She glanced at him and continued, "If we'd taken those we suspected most, we'd tip off the rest and they'd have escaped. Even then, they wouldn't have willingly told us anything. Should we have tortured the whole bureaucracy in hopes one would tell us what we wanted to know? And now considering the executioner–"

"What about him?" asked Dashi, looking over his shoulder at the body's now familiar blotchy red skin lying nearby, "Obviously one of them too."

"No, just bribable," she said. *"There's bad folk everywhere, and what's far worse, weak ones,"* said the mistress, "Just as the third chronicler was one of ours."

"Him?"said Dashi.

"He was their go between. We simply offered him greater personal wealth versus his would be meagre take from the collective spoils. Like our poisoner, he'd realised the history of the gold in the vault underground," she said, putting her hands onto her sleeves, "Several hundred years ago there was a previous coup in which the treasury was secretly emptied. By one of the princes I assume. I'm not even sure which, because any witnesses were massacred and they themselves were apparently killed – merely another body added to the heap of bodies.

"No one ever found the gold, and it was assumed stolen away. So the gold lay hidden, forgotten, like the river. A fortune, about which the Hand had no knowledge."

The treasurer's eyes grew wide, and his breathing laboured.

"But, unknown to them, a few bars at a time, the bureaucrats automatically began sending – because that's what bureaucrats do," she said, smiling.

The treasurer wriggled against his restraints, his red face near bursting.

Dashi chuckled.

She said, "We can only guess how recently was the gold rediscovered – the painted bricks that line the chamber. Everyone previous probably figured the chamber was just part of the garbage chute's construction. But we can surmise they found it when they began to traffic children in and out of the treasury."

"Ah..." said Dashi, "But why didn't anyone at the imperial treasury notice all the extra gold?"

"They never received it," said the mistress, "The larcenists just piggybacked their larceny on the Hand's thieving scheme, with a thieving scheme of their own."

"Right..." said Dashi, "It's a lot of betrayal to keep track of."

"That's why they made mistakes," said the captain.

"I see," said Dashi, "So if it wasn't the chronicler who was it?"

"The court clerk. It was his handwriting," said the mistress triumphant. "It was also probably he who shot you with an arrow."

"Twice," said Dashi.

"Very likely," she replied, "I assumed if they wanted a new magistrate they should have just kept trying to kill you – eventually you'd have exposed yourself – gone looking for soup–"

"Nothing wrong with that," Dashi grumbled.

"–and that'd be the end of it," she said.

"The end of me, you mean," Dashi corrected.

Continuing she mused, "But instead they spent time writing slogans and spreading gossip. For what purpose? And why at the festival was it so important to get so close to taunt you? – to put their plan into such danger of being exposed should they be captured? And then I knew... not everything but enough.

"This was political theatre. This was for the crowd. Immediately I sent a letter to my friend in the provincial capitol. I think it may have been just in time. This was never about you personally, Dashi– My Lord. That was my mistake. This was always about the empire. The book of remembering, is a coded book for how to overthrow the emperor.

"At first they may have wished you dead. The loss of my sister as an allied magistrate must have been a blow to their plans. To have a..." she paused, "a countryman take the position, a man of the common people? How could they hope to compete?"

"Compete in what?" said Dashi.

"In popularity," she replied.

"Why?" he wondered aloud.

"The bureaucrats certainly weren't going to fight the emperor's army," she said, "Or any ones that can't be bought. They needed the peasan... the people to rise up."

"Cannon fodder," Dashi said.

"Sacrificial idiots," offered the captain.

"But then when they saw you were... imaginative with your judgments... they felt you could be manipulated–" she continued.

"Stupid you mean. They thought I was stupid," said Dashi.

"And so they wanted you to stay," she said excited like it was a compliment. "What they had in mind is to goad you until you reacted in a ridiculous draconian way. They thought they could make you come down hard on the people. Which they felt, from such a one as you-"

"An idiot," said Dashi.

"-would be seen by the people as insult to injury. Then they could overthrow you and promote their agenda."

"Which is?" Dashi asked.

"A government run entirely by them. Hidden of course. On a need-to-know basis. No one would ever know who ran things, not even the other bureaucrats. A figurehead of some sort would be found. Just as my sister was never truly magistrate, there would be a kind of emperor in name only. It would be sold as the people's government.

"But... you didn't become cruel," she said with animation, and Dashi glanced down remembering his night in the forest, "In fact you opened a space for the people to speak. They thought they understood how you'd react, but you started to make reforms that would made their revolution redundant.

"They couldn't see what you saw in the people. And too late they realised they didn't understand you. Because the minds you saw with they'd long ago abandoned. Thus they revealed to me their blind spot. They thought you were like your brother.

"By the time they'd decided again to be rid of you, my spies had already infiltrated their ranks and we knew they were planning a coup where you would be killed!" she said victorious.

"You knew?" asked an incredulous magistrate.

"Well, I knew they'd attack," she explained, "but I didn't know when – nor could I stop it." Dashi just shook his head, as she went on. "No, they had to make the first offensive. We could make contingency plans but ultimately we'd be forced to improvise.

"That's why I made up a story to get you to dress out of your usual robes so that you wouldn't be recognised. That day seemed a very likely day for the attack. Auspicious even. I admit it went a bit sideways getting you to safety. Fortunately Li had the good sense to shout for you to be thrown out at the gate-"

"That's why I was-" began Dashi.

"Hoping to spare your life," she explained.

Dashi grunted.

"Fortunately, your luck carried you to your master," she continued.

"I was shot with a poison arrow," said Dashi, "I almost died."

"And that's why I'd been making you drink antidote every morning," she said.

"It tasted like it," said Dashi.

"I like to be prepared," she replied.

"Prepared?" said Dashi, "You've been running things from the beginning. Deceiving and leading them where you wanted. Concealing, covering, masking, screening. Keeping me in the dark."

"And me," said the captain, "I did some too."

Dashi looked at him, irked.

"And the other women," she added.

"I guessed," said Dashi.

"If I had told you everything, you would've changed the way you acted," said the mistress. "It would have signalled that we knew - and we couldn't have that, and win."

Dashi acknowledged the rationale, "But it makes me suspicious," he said.

"You asked me to teach you about politics," she said, "Now you know."

Dashi kicked the straw at his feet.

"I apologise again for not foreseeing every possibility and have offered you my life for these oversights and any appearance of betrayal."

"Which I have declined," said Dashi, "But I think it is you who are the greatest spinner of webs – and even now, should I try to untangle a single thread I would be caught." Dashi looked the mistress straight in the face, "As my instructor in politics I suppose this is a compliment."

"Then I will take that as a compliment," she said bowing. Then she poured some wine into the goblet.

Dashi embraced his feelings and breathed out, releasing. "So... after they have all the gold, what then?"

"War," said the captain. "That was their plan. It's all in the book. A popular uprising. To ferment dissent and then – attack everywhere – all at once to stop reinforcements from being sent."

"Is the empire so brutal everywhere that the people would rise up so eagerly?" asked Dashi.

"It is never so much what you, Dashi, mean by the people – the poor," said the mistress, "It is the aristocracy, the merchants, the clergy, the scholars, the bureaucrats – they and their children are the ones who reap the benefits of an empire disproportionately, and it is they who, when things are not to their liking, begin the mechanisms of discontent. All the poor will get of it is an early grave"

"Except if they fight for the winning side," said Dashi,

"Especially then," said the captain, "They've already proved their disloyalty."

"And of course they've all the gold to buy whoever they can. The emperor's gold revealed as mere lead," said the mistress.

"So therefore it is the military they are likely *persuading*," said Dashi. "But they must have failed," he said, "If they'd attacked everywhere, the beacon fires would've been lit, and a messenger would've been sent from our tower."

"Ah," said the mistress, "But our tower did begin to signal distress."

"What? Why wasn't I- never mind," said the magistrate stroking his hand over his hair.

"The beacon fire was lit, but then was doused," the captain said.

"Consider the reaction of the, as you call them, crows," said the mistress. "You banished them from the city - in winter - yet they weren't afraid - they were cocky. They'd already been told they'd a warm nest awaiting them."

"An aerie," coughed the captain, to the annoyance of the mistress.

"I think having experienced what we have, we will find the tower is captured," the mistress said.

Dashi nodded. "Then that's why they waited for the snows. To cut everyone off. Each city a war unto itself."

The captain said, expanding, "Which if won, could in the thaw, rejoin as if still on the emperor's side to see who was who."

"Madness. The entire empire could be engulfed in war," said Dashi, "and we don't know. And if they win they will appear as before - but not."

"From atop the tower, on a poor day, you will be able to see five mountain beacons," said the captain, "On a clear winter's day, you'll be able to see the smoke rising out to the horizon. Each fighting just as we have, separated by the snows. And should those cities be captured, it is only the snow that protects us - but spring is coming."

Dashi said, "Then we'd better see for ourselves."

"Indeed," said the mistress, who poured the cooled contents of the pot into the goblet of wine. "But we'd better arm ourselves with as much information as we can get," and she pulled the gag from the treasurer's mouth, "Sing, little birdie, sing."

Later Dashi sat in the sunny cleaned and scrubbed square. And many more sat with him. He didn't quite know who they were, or why they were there. He said nothing, he taught nothing. He didn't feel there was much to say after so much had happened. But also there was a sense of something green sprouting up from the soil of the old, and that happening was what he guessed these people had come to be a part of.

"Indeed," he thought, as to why he was there himself.

So he got up. The reinstated magistrate ambled through the palace gate towards the broken treasury wall and crawled over it. While a sooty crew of men and women carried baskets of black rubble and burned wood into awaiting carts, Dashi found an out of the way place to sit in the ashes. The people from the courtyard soon peeked over the tumbled stone wall. Some climbed over to join their master, and sat in the surprisingly still warm remains.

Though they didn't know why, a painful bittersweet joy streaked their happy contorted faces. After, they agreed why - because of the senseless destruction - and because the heat that rose through their skin was like that of a slain but still warm animal - it moved them.

For Dashi, he felt he was where he was supposed to be - that everything was as it was supposed to be. The smokey warmth was pleasing and he was contented. Time passed him by.

He closed his hand upon some char. He crawled back through the gap and came to stand at the blank wall. Writing with his still bandaged fingers in a claw, he wrote:

forgiveness of ashes
benign freedom
beginning again, again

Master Dashi returned to leading the meditations as before, though now there were so many more students – and each following week came more still. As the master had said the practice was over, Dashi no longer sat, but walked among those sitting. When they were quiet like this, he felt he was within a community of people who liked what he liked.

When they ceased practice, they pestered him. They asked endless questions. They talked about how they were feeling. Mostly they talked about how they were angry.

"No enemy," he said.

"No preference?" they asked.

"Yes preference," he replied, "but not the categorical exclusion of someone as completely unlike yourselves."

"But didn't you say we had a unique nature?" they said.

"All oak trees are unique oak trees," said Dashi.

"Then maybe their nature leads them to that, and ours to this?"

"Certainly," said Dashi.

"So why shouldn't we be angry?" they said.

"No shoulds – even no, 'no shoulds'," said Dashi, "But why fill your minds with the pains of others who you can't help and do not want to? See their plight, but don't allow yourself to be pulled into another's stuckness.

"Be with the kind of people who like what you like. Go looking for the light where you can find it in others, in beauty, in nature, in yourself. Focus on each of your own Joys, even when bitter sweet, to make for yourself your heart of Joy. When whole you can think about saving the world, if you still want to. Otherwise, practice - let go of confusion and ineptitude."

"And what if you can't find the light?" they asked.

"Then your shadow will spread across everything you touch in life like a plague," he said. "The demons of our lesser nature. So practice." Then they were silent once more - and he liked their presence better.

As he walked between them he felt a sense of responsibility to help each and every one of them. He also considered how the master and mistress, with just the one student, had been fatigued. Truth was - Dashi was tired.

He'd given back the land. He'd driven out corruption. He'd led the charge to save the city. Responsible as he felt, he did not savour the idea of sitting in the red chair for three more years of servitude. Because although he'd faced the darkness within, no matter how he tried embracing it, no matter how he attempted releasing, the one inside himself had settled in to become a companion - alive within, it cast its shadow.

The dragon also was within, though hidden like a mystery - someone whistling in the night.

One night Dashi ambled down to the kitchens to get himself a bowl of soup, and there found the master, enjoying dumplings.

"Master," said Dashi, as he sat down.

"Dashi," said the master.

The chef put a pot of water onto boil. One of the kitchen maids brought the magistrate an empty bowl, and he thanked her.

"Have some of mine," said the master and poured soup and a few dumplings out into the empty bowl.

"Thank you, master," said Dashi, and he fumbled with the spoon in his bandaged hands.

"I've been meaning to say," said the master, "You can stop the releasing if you get to feel like you did when you'd finished with the firebreath."

"That I don't know who I am?" said Dashi.

"That's it," said the master, popping a dumpling into his mouth. "Just use the two when you feel you need to."

Dashi tried to scoop out a dumpling. "What's next?" he asked, distracted.

"Nothing's next," said the master, "If you mean a practice."

"From here on it's just me?" asked Dashi, as another fell back into the soup.

"No," said the master, "Up to now it's just been you. Your sticky reactions. Now you step into the world."

Dashi turned the spoon around and stabbed a dumpling, biting it off the handle. He chewed. The warm comfort of the food somehow distant.

"Like that," said the master, nodding.

"I know how to eat," said Dashi.

"Your body knows," said the master. "And you know through the minds of the body."

Dashi answered, "The somatic minds," slurping at the soup.

"Correct," said the master.

"How many?" said Dashi per usual – now holding his face close to the bowl, spearing at the elusive dumplings.

"Forty-two," said the master, "and a half."

Dashi's soup spoon fell to the floor with a clatter. He stared at the master. "You answered."

"You never asked," said the master.

"I asked all the time," replied Dashi.

"Only about the temporal minds," said the master shaking his head, "Or the total. I would have told you," he said shrugging.

"Forty-two," said Dashi.

"And a half," said the master.

"And a half," Dashi repeated, "What half?"

"Time," said the master.

"Is that why you told me now?" Dashi asked, "Because it's time?"

"It's why you asked me the right question," answered the master.

"Is that how you do it? – always showing up at the right time?" Dashi asked. "And catching the snowball?"

"I told you, I don't *do* anything," said the master. "Why do you think you're so lucky?"

"I don't know," said Dashi.

"It will turn out, that that is the right answer," he replied.

"I *know* I don't know," said Dashi.

"You don't know that you *do* know," corrected the master, raising his eyebrows, "At least forty-two of you."

Dashi felt an immediate forty-two years older. "Master why do you always speak in riddles?"

The master smiled, "I thought you'd never ask," he said. "The same reason my wife tells you stories – to distract your very capable thinking minds. Don't let anyone tell you different. The purpose of which is to seek the other way, that of the heart."

"How's it working?" Dashi asked.

The master leaned forward and said, "Who are you?"

Dashi slumped back in his chair. He sighed, "At first I was Dashi, and then the magistrate- and I thought I was a dragon, but now- I don't know."

"It's working," he said. "Let me give you a piece of advice, young Dashi," said the master, "Keep my grand-daughter close."

Of course he knew thought Dashi, a bit embarrassed. "Anything else?"

He said, "Yes, Dashi." The master put his emptied bowl aside. "Forget about being good. Embrace your heart."

Weeks passed and more came to sit at his passing feet. Dashi's responsibility to his students felt like fraud.

"What I'm trying to be good at - is being me," he thought, "How is that even teachable - to be yourself?" A map leading back to your own gate. A crutch to be thrown away.

He understood why the master said there was no more practice. Freedom is the practice. Beyond the walls of the ideas of self. Freedom means you don't have to keep turning the crank. In fact, it means exactly that you stop turning the crank. Yet, here he was teaching.

"When you get rid of everything stuck and distorting, you still have a personality," he heard himself telling them, "You still have a full slate of minds and their desires. You are a something. Just in its unified state. The heart of Joy is you."

"Whatever *I* am," he thought to himself.

Why did his master take interest? Why when they called him demon had he reacted like he'd been bitten? Maybe they knew, dragon and demon aren't so far apart.

Perhaps he didn't need to know. Perhaps it was unknowable, except in its immediate changing reflection in the world. So, not knowing why, Dashi gathered heavenly scented flower petals from the garden in a basket and cast them onto his students' heads. It said something he didn't know how to say.

I thank Li for this pen.

I held out high hope for everyone after the events of the last year. The crews, mostly of volunteers, move through the streets setting things to right. There is cheer in repairing, and mutual commiseration. For this I am pleased.

However I also begin to see the signs in those who's lives were not torn apart, of a return to sleep. After being shocked awake I'd assumed there could be no possibility of this. I was wrong.

The desire to settle back into normal - to the little joys now held onto by pretending, to not having to deal with the desires of the minds that call you, like a music unheard by any but you - is an empty desire wished by everyone.

But no matter how much I wish to return to these enjoyments, the dumplings here have changed their taste. I suspect this is true for those others who, through all that has happened, have trouble going to sleep.

Poetry appears on the wall, about those who died, couched in the language of heroism, not terror. A language and therefore a mind, that does not want to face that you survive because someone else was willing to die. Shielding you to the pain of the people dying. And more importantly to your vested interest in their being willing to die so that you can live. I will remember you in glorious verse – is a bribe we pay to the dead. An easy thank you. And a culture of this stuckness is mutual hypocrisy.

Of course I want to live. That's the point. I think of the young man who died on the bridge – like a porcupine, so stuck with arrows. I recognise his courage in my gratitude, but I do not ascribe to him a desire I do not have in order to minimise my debt. Unless he was a sage, he died with at least one mind wishing it didn't have to be so.

I spend most of my time tending the dancers. I've invited them into the garden, as it is the most healing space.

"There are no dragons, no demons, that is all nonsense. The bitter ones, who could not accept their lot, who tried to break everything, just went crazy," – that is what some have said to me – they call themselves the sane ones, the adults, the mature. They twist my words.

But the dancers know there are monsters. They arose out of them. Lived in them. I try to tell them, as I do myself, that as there is darkness there is light.

I hope some will continue – "Maintain your practice," I say, knowing there is nothing else worth saying. They smile, thinking they understand that as praise.

Others just want to forget. Hiding from the ferocious. Convincing themselves this was a dream. Or it was someone else's doing.

Temporarily present, they will vanish back into incredulity, lessons-learned unlearned. I do not blame them. I walk with them in the garden looking for myself as well. Just in a different layer of illusion.

I know a dozen ways to say fool. I have been every one.

It is only the coming to adulthood's full awakeness – not the fractured inherited drives of the individual minds but their sum, the intelligence that they radiated out from, and to which one can return only as one's whole self, in the form of the drive of the self, the soul, uniquely inflected by the reality of body, origin, and time. My hand like your hand, but unique as yours. So too our minds are each other's, but unique in expression, because of the opening shape through which the consciousness waxes and wanes.

Again, not as an identity for consumption by peers, but a metaphorical identity which is my total course of action. Any deviation into doing what is 'good' is a degrading of the project for which I am I. That sounds as though I am rejecting and drifting back to sleep. In fact I am embracing finding what I am driven towards – that being myself. Thus the totality desire. The desire not of becoming whole, but the why of my being, of my soul. The dragon inside.

All those things that we pretend are sleepwalking dreams that we live, if we dismiss those desires as fantasy, then we do so to not deal with the reality they express – that of being a feeling – desiring conscious manifestation. Consciousness is not a means to see, but a navigation to creation.

From the master's book:

> *Travelling without footprints, reckon-*
> *ing without tally, speaking without error,*
> *securing a door without a lock, binding*
> *without rope.*

> *Constantly saving everyone, and every-*
> *thing – all is accepted, nothing is rejected.*
> *Turning the light around.*

It seems perhaps this means not travelling, speaking
as such, but coming to a way of being that does without
doing. The mastery beyond usage. Then it says:

> *What is the good but the teacher of the*
> *bad? What is the bad but lessons for the*
> *good?*

Seems true, but considering what was just said? – and
then:

> *If you do not understand this you will get*
> *lost. No matter how clever you are.*

A trick question!

Meaning therefore: they SHOULD *honour me for my*
great efforts and attained wisdom. I DESERVE *respect.*
Stuck identity. Servant to it. Addicted.
One's intelligence only serves the division – to rationalise
the delusion. Without calling it good and bad of course,

call it wholeness versus stuckness, or immaturity.

But wholeness is only the wholeness it is, of one's self, because of the path of its beginning. One's adulthood can only come via one's childhood. One's wisdom from suffering. To cherish one over the other is a confusion. There is no opposition. No enemy.

Yet there is something still inside me - a desire to be accepted. To wear a mask. Try as I might to remove it.

Maybe it is me. Maybe it's all of us. Maybe it's necessary.

What if when I was trying to do what was expected, I was just feeling what others wanted? That's all.

The ability to unite with one's minds must also be the ability to unite with another's minds. What if instead one presented not a pleasing mask to their desires, but the language of unity? To make their desires your own, and find not a mask, but the river.

Who was I with my brother, then with the master, then as magistrate, and now - as son of the thunder dragon? Who was I in the winter or now in the spring? Surely what I think of as my motivations have flowed to me and will flow on without me. Borrowed as mine.

If instead of feeling myself apart from the world I was with the world, accepted it, embraced it - what would that be?

- Dashi

IV
The Dragon

With the coming of the spring rain, the snow lay on the valley floor, here and there, in patches. The sun shone, and then hid behind bulbous clouds; a light rain fell and then abated; a blossom-fragrant breeze caressed and was still again. The road to the mountain pass was cold. The stoney peaks – a friendly embrace from the distant city, from the winding, climbing path revealed their defensive strength.

The twenty-odd guards rode forward, their numbers their only assurance against the fortified few they suspected held the tower. The magistrate rode with them, hoping he might stem any more blood letting.

He rode beside the captain. Alongside him on his other side was Li, who'd wished to come – though the captain had made it clear, that with neither armour nor weapon, she was to stay back beyond the range of arrows. She did, however, have the same long rectangular shield tied to her saddle, as did all of those mounted in the column.

The magistrate's mood had shifted since the mass trial. He spent much of his time in the gardens, whether with those he let wander there, or when they were absent, by himself. The budding trees had surrendered in flowering, and he walked under their canopy, shaded. Sometimes Li had also strolled with him, taking his arm – a plucked flower from a tree placed behind her ear. For some reason that made him smile.

She noted that although he smiled when addressed, and was considerate, polite and dutiful in all his dealings – within, some part of Dashi became more distant. Increasingly taciturn, punctuated by rhetorical questions, and silence. On the occasion that the two chanced meeting with her grandmother in the garden, the mistress had bowed her head as if confirming something unsaid and Dashi nodded as though he understood.

Thus Dashi had been silent for the journey. Even Li's promptings had only produced nods and shrugs - so the two had let him be.

"When we reach the approach, My Lord, you and the mistress's granddaughter will remain out of archers' distance. We will dismount and advance with shields together," said the captain, more for something to say than to inform, as he knew they knew. His voice now contained a minor rasp, which if not controlled worsened at higher volumes. He wore it - as his neck bore its scar - with forbearance.

The magistrate spoke, "Should a distant tower be lit - what assistance could we bring?"

His two riding companions wondered if he was merely speaking this question aloud, and not until he turned to gaze at them did they respond.

"None, My Lord," said the captain, "We have no army to send forth. We've barely enough to keep peace with shopkeepers, drunks and erstwhile nobles. If they are under attack then it will be up to the warlords and the emperor to send their armies."

"We ought to send scouts though," said Li, "to know how goes the battle. To know whether we should bolster our defences - to defend the pass."

"We would be overwhelmed," stated the captain, "If they want to gain the valley, most generals would not hesitate to bridge any defences we could raise with the bodies of dead soldiers. Better we should escape into the mountains, if their intent is murderous - or surrender, if they will spare us."

"Scouts could tell us whether we should choose to run or lie down," countered Li. The captain's brow dropped, then he too sunk into a silence.

Dashi nodded, saying, "Poetry is reality – politics is madness."

As this was obviously from out of his inner musings and said to no one in particular there was no more to say and the three proceeded as before, in silence. The guard, did as their captain and leader did. The magistrate, for all his strength, had been made mute by a mood.

Even this day, which was clear, and sweet with the scent of new growth in the valley; even spring's forgiveness, that brought forth excitable birds which flitted about in every treetop; when every farmer's cottage they passed was well kept, and the land all around was beginning to green; when even the sight of young goats frolicking in a field, beside their mother – alive through the famine because of the sustaining milk she gave; although a sense of well-ness, deepening, radiated from the heart of the land – at the same time, the valley's magistrate had seemingly fallen back into his own winter.

The road began to steepen. The trees that dotted the sides of the incline changed from white and pink speckled branches, budding with leaves, to spiny pines, which the higher the horses climbed, became dwarfed and twisted, bent away from the alpine wind, until even these were sparse – as snowy stillness reasserted its dominion. The road wound slowly up the mountain. The sound of wind and falling hooves filled the riders' ears – and increasingly, that of their hearts' beating.

Upon reaching the crest, the simple cut-stone markers, bordering the road at interval, gave way to an ancient carved stone railing that elegantly curved forward through the gap between the high steep slopes on either side. As they rode forward the way opened out and wound around the side of a frozen alpine lake. Beside the lake of ice, the horses' and their riders' breath rose white against the black broken rock which towered above their heads. The way bent ahead. Coming around its corner the riders now could see the tower - and that meant also, the tower could see them.

It stood at the end of the road, a large, squat, square, brick building with sloping sides. In its centre it had a wide, round-topped open gate, through which the road passed, with three narrow windows above. The teeth of the battlement were jagged from neglect. Their missing bricks fallen to the wall's base, or now gone entirely. From out of the middle the tower arose, atop which the smoke beacon could be lit. Dashi's eye went to the small holes under the parapet. Holes from which archers might fire.

The captain held up his arm to halt the column. "My Lord, from here we should go on foot."

Dashi nodded, and dismounting removed his shield from his horse where it hung aside the saddle.

"My Lord, we discussed, you are to remain-"

"I will announce us," Dashi said, holding out his hand, walking through the men who'd taken this as the signal, dismounting and forming a line behind him with shields at the ready. He stood front and centre.

"I am magistrate, Dashi," he called out to the tower. His voice echoed from the stone face of the mountain. He waited for a greeting - should they be friendly - or an arrow if they were not. But the tower stood menacing in silence.

"Your comrades are dead," he shouted, and waited for the echo to die. "The usurpation of me - as the appointed magistrate - and the subjugation of the valley - has failed." Again Dashi waited as his word's reverberation dissipated. "I have no wish to spill blood - without necessity. If you will surrender peacefully - you will be treated fairly - and with honour - as befitting an imperial guard." Again there came no sound.

"It's catching on," said Li aside to the captain who shushed her.

"You have my word," Dashi shouted. And after some moments he turned to look to the captain.

A jerk of the captain's head at a swift movement made Dashi spin back around. He spied the cause of the captain's reaction - a crow.

Dashi walked back to the captain. "A crow," he said.

"Several," said Li, and they watched them appear upon the battlements curious at the cavalry's arrival.

The captain nodded, and with his hand bade the magistrate and Li to remain, "My Lord," he said, and joined his men.

Dashi watched as the line advanced, shields held together angled to the loopholes to deflect incoming missiles. They marched slowly forward. They moved in locked step. Each one resting his life upon the other. Their fellowship - to let no gap come between them - lest they divide and perish one by one.

Watching them inch forward Dashi thought, "More crows," knowing it to be a bad sign.

Together the guard advanced. Slowly, the protective wall of shields gained ground. But a rain of arrows did not fall. There was, no response at all.

"That's puzzling," said Li, pulling her coat closer from the blustering winds.

"Indeed," said Dashi.

Soon the captain and his men were at the great gate. This was the most perilous, entering they would expose their flank. They formed a circle and moved through cautiously, expecting attack any moment, and when none came, they advanced into the guard tower, disappearing from view.

They were gone a long while.

"No sounds of fighting," said Li hopefully.

Dashi was now guessing what the captain and his men were seeing. Soon enough a guard came running and waved for the magistrate to come. Li waved back and pointed to herself. The guard disappeared for a second and then returned nodding.

When Dashi and Li entered the gate they entered a tunnel-like side passageway, upward slanting with a rounded roof, which twisted at angles for close-quarter fighting. The clucking of a hen was the first thing Dashi heard as they rounded the corner into an open inner courtyard above the tunnels. As with the rock which surrounded the keep, the mountain winds had blasted it bare of ice and snow.

Around the courtyard, a few ladders leaned against a raised walkway, from which yet more ladders led to the top of battlement wall, and from off the battlement a great ladder rose to the top of the tower. Off the courtyard was an empty stable, its barely-hung door wide open, from which several curious chickens emerged. Here and there, frozen to the ground, clumps of feathers and bones could be seen. The work of crows.

A guard ushered Dashi through a door into the tower guards' kitchen with its iron pots and crumbling rudimentary clay and brick stove - and past, through to the soldiers' cramped white washed quarters - where six of them lay dead. Frozen upon the floor. Their hard cold skin looked pecked. There were also a couple dead chickens.

Dashi put his hand to the small heating stove in the corner. It had long burned cold. About the soldiers, on the beds and on the floor, were wine bottles – their spilled contents frozen. This perhaps explained, thought Dashi, why the court clerk had left the treasury by way of the kitchen and its cellar.

"Tell the men not to eat the chickens," said the magistrate.

"My Lord?" – came the captain's voice from outside, and Dashi and Li exited the icy room and returned to the courtyard. From above them on the tower the captain looked down. Dashi gestured for Li to climb up the ladder to the walkway before him, and followed. They walked the way around to the next ladder, up to the battlement, climbing up likewise. In circling around the battlement to the base of the tower's ladder they found there a crumpled frozen soldier, his skin already drying-out in the harsh winds. Apparently fallen from its heights.

But instead of being laid to rest, he had been posed as though meditating. His legs broken into odd angles. His fingers removed. A black mandala of his own blood encircling him.

The captain looked down from above. To the top of the tower the two climbed the rickety ladder. The captain offered his hand, which Li took as did Dashi behind her. Dashi looked down at the fallen guard, the captain leaned over beside him.

"It wasn't the fall that killed him," said the captain, "It was a blade."

"Before he fell or after?" asked Li looking over as well.

The captain looked about him on the tower's edge.

"After."

"I'd think I'd better have a word with my court clerk," said the magistrate.

"I think you'd better," said Li.

"My Lord, this is what you needed to see," said the captain and the three of them walked around the charred signal pile raised in the centre, to the southernmost side of the platform. From there they looked out over the distance. The black smoke of war rose in great columns into the spring air as far south and west and east as they could see.

"I would say that half the fires are lit," said the captain, "The others either have not been attacked yet - or are already taken."

Dashi nodded. "Why kill them?" he said.

"My Lord?" queried the captain, brows furrowed.

"The tower guard," he clarified to the captain, though his eyes scanned the horizon of smoke. "It was they who put out the beacon, and they who didn't report the others burning," he said, "They were part of it."

"The court clerk - he leaves no one," said Li.

"I agree," said the captain. One of Li's eyebrows nudged upward. "If they were alive we'd be questioning them right now. We'd know from whom they got their orders - in short order."

Dashi shook his head. "If the trail led to anyone it would lead to a scapegoat. A dead end, or a false name. Me probably," he said, "they were told they'd be rich if they played along - but they were always to be expendable. They knew nothing and the Hand couldn't care less if we boiled them alive." Dashi looked at the two. "Why go to the risk of murdering soldiers? Surely he could have just slipped through," asked Dashi.

"Because they knew," said Li.

"Because they knew something," repeated Dashi.

"The gold," surmised the captain. "They must have known where it was bound for. Therefore they had to die."

"If they knew, why wouldn't the clerk just stay here until the snow melted? They were already in on it," said Li. "Then they could go together – using them as bodyguards."

"Well, we're here now," said the captain, "The clerk realised we'd be coming, and although the path down is treacherous it's still better chances than what I'd do to him."

Dashi brooded. "But he killed them," he said. "Why should he? Even using poison? One unforeseen complication can ruin everything. Like the one at the bottom of the tower," – he indicated with his chin – "Like the prince who tried to steal the gold before him..." said Dashi. "It only takes one sword thrust to end years of meticulous planning."

His eyes wandered back to the pillars of soot. And then to where the tower-guard must have fallen. "I think he was the one that tried to light the fire," said Dashi.

"The clerk only escaped recently, that would have been many months ago," said the captain.

"Look at his skin," said Dashi. "He's been sitting there some time."

"Then it was the other guard who did this," said Li.

The captain nodded, "Did you notice, My Lord, the broken guard below is muscular but the ones within the quarters are not."

"Not fighters," said Dashi.

"Not real imperial guards" said the captain.

"Loyal replacements," said Li.

Dashi shook his head. "Even if the guard at the bottom

of the ladder wasn't in on the theft, and he did try to light the fire, and the other guards who were in on it murdered him, it only deepens the question. Explain why the clerk poisoned them in the first place, when he could have slipped away?"

"You heard the mistress," said the captain, "He was double-dealing the Hand. These guards were loyal to the Hand. Loose ends."

Li said, "Dashi, he's killed a lot of people. He's a babyeater."

"But he's a logical babyeater," said Dashi. "If that makes sense."

"I'm afraid I agree with her," said the captain. Li wrinkled her brow. "He's escaping. He's lost his composure. He's just killing everyone in his path to get away without any witnesses."

Dashi weighed this. "You're not thinking like a thief. He brought bottles of wine," he said, "This was premeditated. Probably planned. The gold's already been taken wherever it's being stashed. Just because the tower guards knew about the swap – didn't mean they knew where..." Dashi said.

Then Dashi smiled, and he laughed. A big bold laugh came tumbling out. The captain and Li looked sidelong at each other as the magistrate chuckled to himself – amused by something hidden.

Dashi looked down from the tower to the empty stable. "Isn't there supposed to be a horse so a rider can bring a message to the city?"

The captain looked down. "The court clerk must have taken it," said the captain.

"Why?" said Dashi, smiling.

Li nodded. "You mean he already had a horse," she said,

"We know he stole the one from the inn keeper."

Dashi said, "He should be in a hurry, but instead he stops here to steal a horse and kill everyone?"

The captain said, "You take another horse only when you have something to carry."

"The gold," she said.

"Too heavy," said the captain.

"Just a bar of it," she said, "He went right past the vault."

"The vault he had just stuffed the treasurer down," replied the captain.

"He had one stashed away, a whole saddle bag full," she said.

"Too heavy to escape with," said the captain.

"He stashed it outside the walls in case he needed to get away," she replied, annoyed.

The captain had to think for a moment and said, "Enough for one horse. Why take the other one?"

"To spread the load, so they didn't get tired," she rebutted, hands instinctively on her hips.

The captain looked up, "A saddle bag full of gold, or wine, or old broken sticks can only be as heavy as the clerk can carry and lift to put on the horse. The clerk himself was much slighter than the third chronicler who normally rode the horse, and less again than that of the inn keeper.

"Then he got someone else to put the saddle on," she argued, "the inn keeper."

"The clerk was seen riding off with the horse, that's all," said the captain. "Any amount he could lift would be insignificant to the load on the horse. There's no need to take the other. And as was already said – he was in a hurry."

Dashi interjected between the two, "The motive. Why he did – what he did – here?"

"Which is?" asked Li.

"The gold," said Dashi.

"That's what I said," said Li.

"And right you were," he said. The captain's eyebrow twitched. "The second horse is needed only if he's going where the gold is," said Dashi. "And so the only reason to kill the guard is if they knew where that was, which no one would possibly tell them unless..."

The captain smiled too, "The gold is here."

"Here?" said Li.

"Here," said Dashi. "What better place?" he asked, "The court clerk realised what the mistress realised. That his superiors in the conspiracy didn't know about the gold in the hidden vault - left over from the previous massacre. The treasurer was too drunk to notice anything. And the crows, wrapped up in revolutionary fever, just processed it unquestioningly like they were trained to do. All he had to do was keep the lead coming to make the fake bars going back to the imperial treasury; place the real ones from our treasury vault to return hidden in the sacks of grain, to be recovered by the Hand; and divert those from the hidden vault, unloaded by accomplices here. All without lifting a single one."

"Here?" Li repeated. "Not somewhere he could secure it - farther away?"

The captain nodded. "Here, exactly because you need a vault, a stronghouse, a fortress," said the captain. "And how do you inconspicuously acquire that as a mere exiled bureaucrat?"

"And you need guards," said Dashi.

"Ones paid enough, or afraid enough, to not steal the gold when you're away," said the captain.

"And especially for no one else to know," said Dashi.

"This is a small fortress. At the top of a treacherous mountain pass. Manned with the emperor's own trained guards. Well, maybe just one of them."

"For free," said Li.

"Paid for by the Hand, to steal the emperor's gold – on pain of punishment for theft. Whatever gold you leave here is as safe as gold can be." Dashi wagged his head at the audacity. "The clerk would have told them this was the Hand's secret stockpile – and they, held secret positions as its keepers. And as caravans frequent through, he could arrange for whatever movement of gold he required," said Dashi, shrugging in admiration of the clerk – a strange kinship – robbers of the same caravan.

"The tower is a bank," Li said, hands wide, "and all the guards were in for a cut."

"Some got more of a cut than they were looking for," the captain said deadpan, glancing towards the edge.

Dashi breathed in, "Gold," he exhaled. "I'm afraid he was sent because of the mistress's letter," Dashi sighed. "Captain, tell the men to scrape the walls of the quarters with their swords. If it's here there must be a lot of it, and no reason not to use the same white paint trick from the vaults."

"Yes, My Lord," said the captain who called down the instructions to his men.

"If they find it," said Dashi, "send for wagons. Take it back to the city."

"Yes, My Lord," said the captain glancing at a drifting snowflake.

The magistrate looked out over the distance. Tiny flecks filled the space between the burning towers. The towers of smoke that marked war – over there, properly understood, foretold of war here. Only the mountains defended them. Only nature.

"If we wait here," he said, "the beacon fires will, one by one, day after day, go out. Meaning that the rebellion is quelled – or, that it was successful. Until the snow melts enough for a caravan or a military force to come through, there is no knowing if–"

"We are surrounded," finished the captain.

"Not to the north," said Li.

"There are tribes there. We are surrounded," he repeated, glancing up at the white-grey sky, now shedding its skin.

Dashi turned north to gaze at the icy silence. "A war no walls can withstand, because it's already inside. Walls surround a city. Crops surround a settlement. Decisions surround our lives." His gaze turned upwards. Dashi was silent in that moment.

"Ah..." he said in the next, staring at the opening in the wall, the only direction in which peace existed. "It's only a habit," Dashi said, "I embrace it, and I release it."

As before, but not.

The magistrate looked at the captain. "I'm done."

Dashi turned, walked around the dead fire, and stepping upon the ladder began descending from the tower. "My heart of Joy calls me!"

"My Lord?" called the captain in concern from the top, with Li looking over as well, "What do you mean?"

Dashi looked up on the ladder, "What do I mean?" he said thinking, "I mean, I was never inside. Would I have been the son of a farmer, a landowner, I still would never have been allowed in. But even that was taken from us. They couldn't bear the possibility we might rise within the city ranks, so they took our gardens and our families, and stole our children and left us to fend for ourselves, outside. Envious, that we knew to embrace life, and all they had were more walls. Walls I have no reason to honour."

"That is the past, My Lord – you have given the land back to the farmers," said the captain.

"And the next magistrate may tell you to take it back from them again," said Dashi continuing his climb down. "Already the people choose to forget. I hoped to change them, but I failed."

"Not totally," said Li.

Dashi laughed. He stood now beside the fallen soldier – the frozen, fingerless guard, head down in a death medi-tation of the circle of his life-blood. Dashi looked up at the two looking down from the heavens, over the para-pet. "Thank goodness I failed," he said. "I remember tell-ing the master I thought his philosophy sounded selfish. It still does – but I didn't understand what he was telling me."

Dashi smiled. "I thought I was going towards others but I was going away. A fugitive from myself. I've spent my entire life doing the right thing – always choosing what was best for others – for us. Even when I was a thief. And it was the right thing – then. I see that. How else could I have come to now, to forgiveness, to what time it is?" The magistrate started around the battlement.

"Time?" said the captain.

Dashi halted his forward march, turning again to them. "What is it I wanted for everyone? – that they become fully themselves. To stop pretending, and take off their mask.

"What is it I'd have done if I succeeded? Just given them a different mask. Because I was denying myself. Not being Dashi – but like Dashi. Not my self, but self-ish. A child trying to please a parent – pretending I understood what they felt, what they needed. It's time I grew up," he said, and continued along the top of the wall.

Li called out, "What about the followers you've gathered? What about your responsibility?"

"I want them to flower!" Dashi laughed. "Full responsibility for yourself is the greatest freedom," he said, and leaned on the ladder down. "Ten thousand decisions a day - this or that. The road always forking before us. Our minds reaching out into time to see - and squabbling." He laughed at the ridiculousness of it, swinging onto the ladder. "Oarsman all paddling in different directions.

"So, we strongarm some out of the boat and call it culture - a strategy for survival - for cake. Do it for us. Dance the dance. Stay in the middle, where it's safest.

"At least until the group goes mad. Which is inevitable. In it's very conception lies discordant potential," he said climbing down.

"And it doesn't matter, someone else made the mask. You can trap yourself in a drama of your own devising. The only way out is nature. Our nature. The hole in the wall. The unified centre from which I can make ten thousand decisions.

"Because I'm not in here - and everything else is outside. I'm just a point of view." Dashi reached the bottom of the ladder and began walking around the perimeter of the walkway.

"The I is everywhere. I am addressing from it and to it. The centre of everything is my centre too. There's no one to judge but ourselves - and I've had quite enough of that."

"Where are you going?" Li asked Dashi.

Dashi tilted his face skyward, blinking at the falling flakes "Go?" said Dashi, "I have thrown out those who could not abide by the agreement of civilisation," he said,

"And I find I can't agree either – so I too must go. I'm throwing myself out," he said, continuing around, "A rebel, an outlaw, an outsider – outside this game for gold and power – I'm sick of it. I need to go find my own way. Tell the mistress she's magistrate until I should return or until they send someone else. That's her punishment for being so clever," he said, "But I'm taking the hat."

Dashi took hold of the last ladder that led to the courtyard. On top of the tower Li was now crying. He was leaving – just as she'd feared.

Halfway down the ladder – "My Lord, what of the gold?" shouted down the captain.

Dashi called back, descending, "Ask the mistress what to do with it. She can distribute it to the people, throw it in the lake – put it back in the mountain where it came from – it doesn't matter." And finally down on the ground, he shouted up, "You've been a good friend, captain – I thank you," – as chickens idled over to peck at his boots. "There are a number of well-furnished houses now empty. Make sure all my loyal guard get well paid."

"I'm going with you," said the captain, his voice breaking.

"No, you deal with this gold problem. If I return I'll bring real gold," said Dashi.

The captain not knowing what Dashi meant didn't argue and bowed to the magistrate.

Weeping – Li held out her hand outstretched.

Dashi looked up. "My flower," Dashi called to Li. "You coming?"

Stay tuned
for the final book in the trilogy

THE EMPEROR

INTERVIEW – FEB. 29, 2020

The two philosophical pillar characters of the Dashi series, the mistress and her newly wed, though long term partner, the master presents something of a mystery for readers. Actually they're all mystery. Although they seem so calm and simple on the surface they obviously have much going on beneath.

The metaphysics of the Dashi books, which are mostly given in dialogue to the titular character, arrive in the story through these two portals into the deeper wisdoms of life. But is this just story magic? – or does any of this hold up under inquiry?

I sat down today with the master and mistress to discuss the deeper meaning of their life view and find out about what's going on backstage.

MEJP
Thank you for coming to discuss the... I suppose, philosophy behind the Dashi books.

MISTRESS
Our pleasure.

MASTER
Indeed.

Master pours some green tea for the mistress, the host and himself.

MEJP
The first question I want to ask is the one that everyone will be wanting to know because in the books Dashi is always asking–

MASTER
IT?

MEJP
Well... that can be a follow up question. No, I was going to ask how many minds are there? And why is it such a big secret? Why keep it from Dashi? Is there some reason?

MASTER
Alright. So there are sixty-four minds–

MISTRESS
For humans.

MASTER
Yes. But forty-two and a half of those are the senses, and the drives, and some of the deeper emotional equipment of consciousness–

MISTRESS
Sex, motherhood, aggressive predatory impulses, defensive protective reactions–

MEJP
A half?

MISTRESS
The forty-third acts as both somatic and temporal.

MEJP
Ah...

MASTER
The basic interior psychology for any mammal. That's why we get along so well with some animals – dogs for example – because we have similar minds to them.

MISTRESS
So we understand each other.

MASTER
At a higher level.

MISTRESS
A deeper level. You can understand part of what a crocodile is thinking because we have some of that. It's just not very... friendly.

MASTER
Low level.

MEJP
So to get back the sixty-four – you break them into two categories.

MISTRESS
Somatic and temporal. The forty-two and the twenty-two.

MEJP
Interesting numbers.

MASTER
Frankly annoying numbers. You think you're exploring some new territory but you realise someone else has
been there before you. It's how it is. However, working
from scratch you do get a feel for the whole of the subject
personally, not just the six-thousand years of meandering
commentary.

MEJP
So the twenty-two then...

MISTRESS
The twenty-two are the temporal minds, or voluntary
minds. Not that you get to opt out, but you have some
small measure of... I'd rather not say control...

MASTER
Interaction.

MISTRESS
'Interaction.' The twenty-two we hypothesize began as
a result of the forty-third mind being able to experience
time. To be able to experience the multiple pathways that
are implicate in any situation to the individual. That's why
the time mind is also the observer mind. Something that
people get confused with.
    Then specialization occurred. The other twenty-one
minds were then temporal languages for the prediction
of different... ah, aspects of life. Like social life versus
valuation–

MASTER
Via–

MISTRESS
'Via,' or humour via might.

I think we're a little deep here. Let me back up. Right from the very beginning of minds, they are desires. In the case of the first mind it is clearly procreational. Though for some time we thought it was the desire to eat didn't we?

MEJP
Wait, 'via?'

MISTRESS
Non-dual.

MASTER
In meditation, when you're looking at these presences, they feel like something. And there is sometimes a visual element, in this case just an oval with a horizon line, white above and black below, with this bump in the middle.

MISTRESS
A drowned man in a bowler hat.

MASTER
But when you're looking at it – feeling it – it's not an easily comprehensible thing, this part of your own interior workings.

MEJP
Like looking inside a computer.

MASTER
Sure. So the first desire is procreative. Then you can step through them one by one. Most of them are boring. Not much going on from a top down point of view.

MISTRESS
Like visual consciousness.

MASTER
Right. There's sixteen different consciousnesses in you that just handle different aspects of your being able to see: edges and contrast and colour context, and so on.

MEJP
But no one to talk to.

MASTER
Exactly. Once you get into the twenty-two, this is where the real fun and also the true predicament of consciousness begins.

MISTRESS
Though that's a projection.

MASTER
Where will comes to joy.

MISTRESS
Maybe.

MASTER
Maybe.

MEJP
I'd just like to clarify before we go much further. Why it is that you feel the need, I assume, to keep this material from Dashi?

MISTRESS
Because he'd think about it too much.

MASTER
He'd dither. It's easy to see. Not telling him is so he can get on with being himself, without all this noise.

It's part of what we're saying to him. That if you want to do something or you want to understand something that those aren't always the same thing. There is the condition of knowing too much, and having to, as they say, unlearn it.

MISTRESS
Also this ties in with the idea of, when you go to do a thing, that often to do it, to be able to do it well, you have to actually focus yourself on something else.

MASTER
It's the same thing.

MISTRESS
It is, but I think it's worth pointing out that particular aspect of it. Anyway... so that's why we don't tell him. At least not yet.

MASTER
He'll find out for himself.

MISTRESS
You keep saying that.

MASTER
Because it's true. That's why I keep saying it.

MEJP
All right, let's move on.
Now, in the second book you bring in the idea of levels or as Dashi likes to say layers of a cake. And these represent the stages of maturation.
What can you tell me about that? Was there anything you felt wasn't presented sufficiently or highlighted in the book as much as you'd like?

MISTRESS
Well, we don't want to pick holes in the book. It's very good, isn't it?

MASTER
I like it.

MISTRESS
But the 'six layer cake,' from survival to wholeness of the minds – and the will, which we can get to later – is predicated on this idea of the evolutionary aspects of this being both an internal representation of the group – humans being group animals – and at the same time because it is the foundation of our communication with each other and our understanding, and therefore languaged representations of the world – that the group, and indeed, the reality around us is a projection of that cognitive structure.

The master sipped his tea.

MASTER
Indeed.

MISTRESS
So both coming in and going out. We achieve a kind of congruency with the world.
Watch a child looking at a tree flowering and they aren't flabbergasted at the complexity of a universe that can bring this into being. It's just there. They are in the world and the world is in them.

MASTER
That's why we always start on the inside.

MEJP
Because?

MASTER
Because you can influence your own consciousness more easily than trying to get everyone else to do what you want them to. You may have noticed this in your own life.

MEJP
I have.
So you're saying, if I may paraphrase, that there was an evolutionary pressure on humans to form certain kinds of temporal predictive minds, which themselves sit atop the more autonomic ones, and that these minds, the twenty-two, form a kind of internal community, which in coming

to terms with – coming to wholeness – that we then have a model for our interactions with others – who also have these same... drives–

MISTRESS
Languages.

MEJP
And that's why we understand each other!

MASTER
That is why we even *can* understand each other.

MEJP
Right.

MASTER
One of those funny ideas that people have, that everyone can be totally different with no points of reference – if people were that different, if there weren't underlying structures, we'd have no basis to even begin to have any kind of dialogue. The minds, in many ways similar, but being different from each other, are amply capable of disastrous misunderstanding. It's the underlying structure that one matures into.

MEJP
In wholeness they come together?

MASTER
In wholeness they come to trust one another, to have faith in the tribe instead of rationalizing intellectually.

MEJP
I don't understand.

MASTER
Exactly.

MISTRESS
What he means, is the minds continue to be different even when it is felt they all come from the same origin–

MASTER
The entelechy–

MISTRESS
Or beyond that–

MASTER
IT – or any... you know – Tao... God... Love...

MISTRESS
Though again those are just projections.

MEJP
Master, hold that thought. Mistress, the minds don't come back together?

MISTRESS
They do and they don't. As I was saying, you realise they come from the same origin and also in wholeness you come to recognise the seed, regenerated from out of the remerging energy of it's essence. But the branches of the tree stay where they are. The minds do not come to full comprehension of each other. That would defeat the

purposes of them.

MASTER
And also make you go crazy.

MEJP
Why crazy?

MASTER
Part of the brilliance of minds is that they're repre-
sented inside of each other. So in mind A, is a small copy
of minds B, C, D, and so on, and this is repeated in each
mind. They're not really individual qualities so much as
the absence-

MISTRESS
Invisibility.

MASTER
-of that quality making a difference to the whole.

MEJP
Embedded.

MASTER
Yes, so that when you are not at the wholeness level and
you think you can boss yourself around, or you're scared
or there's some trauma, and so on, you simply ignore that
internal copy of the other mind.

MEJP
Like booting out the ambassador from another country.

MASTER

Except that they're still there and they want your attention.

MEJP

Ok, more like having a bank of hotlines, a whole bunch of colour-coded old phones, but you just shove the ones you don't want to hear ringing in the desk drawer.

MASTER

Nice.

MISTRESS

So what is happening internally is, like I said, what will happen externally.

The minds, at wholeness, come to trust each other even if they don't totally understand each other. And of course because A may trust B more than C, but B says C is ok, then there is this vetting process that tries to smooth out relations.

MASTER

I want to say, and this is a good juncture, that instead of an evolutionary model there are some people who think–

MISTRESS

You.

MASTER

Me... that the forty-third mind blossomed into the other twenty-two. They were already tucked inside that mind waiting to come out. Which means there won't be a sixty-fifth.

It explains why they – because my wife was explaining *how* they can vet for each other – they also are sources to heal each other out of stuckness. Each language, having one other, that it is most able to translate.

If you match them all up with their best friend, so to speak, not only do you not get any overlaps or most popular mind, they arrange themselves into a circle which joins up at the ends. Which would be very odd if the twenty-two weren't just explications of the forty-third.

MEJP
Interesting.

MASTER
Further, because having two things in a dynamic is the best, or simplest level of comprehension, 'but not more so' you see? – because they are in a circle you get these axises... is that right?

MISTRESS
Axes.

MASTER
They form stable pairs. And that around the circle's circumference you can see things like politics playing themselves out in predictable ways as the pressure behind any particular stuckness blows it into the next category of mind, with its desire, language, and so on.

MISTRESS
Survival on the outside – wholeness in the centre.

MEJP
Sacred geometry.

MASTER
Wait, isn't that a projection?

MISTRESS
A very tidy one, too.

MASTER
Hmm... Well, the difference is, that I didn't make the circle, and then shove the minds inside. They themselves describe a circle.

MEJP
I see.

MISTRESS
I'd like to add that - back to the relations of the minds to each other - in this trusting community that is built up, that although any one mind is in seeming competition with the others, that in coming to wholeness they can mix with all the other minds and as my husband was talking about, pair up with the compatible mind across the way.

MEJP
A kind of interior dating service.

MISTRESS
It's the logical conclusion of your growing up. Find the love within yourself first. Then go find someone to love.

MASTER
Someone like you.

The mistress batted her eyes.

MEJP
Someone who likes what you like.

MISTRESS
Indeed.
Then you do evolution - and make copies of yourselves.
That's why it's the first mind.

MEJP
Huh... It's a tight little package isn't it? I mean it seems
to have an angle on whatever you point it at.

MASTER
Almost.

MEJP
Alright... Would you expand on that?

MASTER
Well, you asked about IT. And you were just talking
about how minds... were you taking about how they're
chosen?

MISTRESS
Chosen? No.

MASTER
How any mind gets to be in the spotlight?... Ah - you

were talking about competition, and then how the actors become more cordial, hopefully. Unless you get stuck, and then you have a real battle on your stage. Or a staged battle in your reality. The-

The master paused and drank some tea. She picked up her cup as well.

MASTER CONT'D
-The way in which the minds work is they just run on stage and start giving their opinion.

MEJP
Their soliloquy.

MASTER
Or there can be conversations, absolutely. But how is that not just chaos?
And the answer is, that there is an agreement. In fact a series of them.
What's the agreement? One mind will have the best idea of how they can achieve their mutual goals.

MISTRESS
Mutual agreement. A mutually advantaging language. You can't force them to agree, to coordinate. At lower levels this is where your phones start to get shoved into desks.

MASTER
So then the first language being survival, the second being power. Having a fish lets you eat for a day, knowing how to fish lets you eat for life. Then comes your-place-

in-the-tribe language – which for most of history just focused back towards the power to try to secure more food.

MEJP
Ah, so the layers, they're self-generated out of the minds
themselves.

MASTER
Right, only the minds exist.

MEJP
What do you mean by that?

MASTER
Ok, exist... perhaps a strong word. The minds are au-
tonomous structures, ideals actually. Prototypical kinds of
memory. As opposed to say a point in between the minds,
our everyday objects, which are... even more illusory.

MEJP
An illusion created by an illusion. Ok.

MISTRESS
Any name we use for the minds, although we try to get
the flavour right, is just describing the petals of an entire conscious being – from which they flower. And there's
more to us than that.

MASTER
So now that when we arrive finally at wholeness we arrive back at the place we started. The mind that saw time.
The observer. That's the language of wholeness. The
mind connected to the body. That's why I say it's half in

and half out of both categories.

Also why I think the twenty-two are explications of the forty-third mind. It's the mind that holds the image of the entelechy, the desire towards your maturation, your coming to be, the fulfillment of your particular consciousness.

And that entelechy is itself undergirded by any entelechial impulses of IT. Towards complexity and consciousness, perhaps.

MISTRESS
The oak matures and bears acorns, like that from which it came. In maturation the knowledge of what you are, the acorn/oak, reifies, is projected before you. And you realise this body is the first metaphysical proof – your connection to the earth and the sun and the rain. To the reality outside your subjective, in which the minds are embedded.

MEJP
(gestures head exploding)
Pshhh... mind blown.
Ok... And you sit around and think about this stuff all day?

MASTER
Not any more. We have better things to do.

MISTRESS
This is just the ladder.

MEJP
Ok. As you describe it, it only has six rungs. So why, why – can't we humans seem to get up it? Why does everyone stay stuck? If inside of us there's this urge towards

wholeness?

MISTRESS
Firstly it's not a very strong voice. The mind of the observer isn't about to rush the front of the stage. If you've been in an accident you've experienced it. The observer is calm. And some therefore mistakenly believe without desire.

It's revealed when the... the pain of adolescence, or self-aggrandizing makes the other minds recede. Self-righteous behaviour, that ends badly.

Or when your friends try to help you to self-reflect. That's your external tribe taking the place of one of your minds if that mind is being sticky. They observe you.

MEJP
(laughs)
You mean they're externalized minds on loan which can... pick up the slack... yeah.

MISTRESS
So it is with silence. Which is the why of meditation. That you can hear those quiet voices. The ones that aren't your dominant voice.

Which let's give them their due, those loud ones, when they mature will go on to become the Joy of your being, but merged together with the more subtle consciousnesses.

MEJP
I'm thinking of a new kind of educational model then–

MASTER
Good luck.

MEJP
But wouldn't that be the logical conclusion?

MASTER
Sure - but you have to be at that level to teach at that level. You can't fake it. You can't make it into a program. Religion tries to do this all the time.

You have to have someone who's been there. Not only that, but who has understood they do not understand.

But those kinds of people won't follow many institutional rules. Not that they're against structure. All the levels are what they need to be. There's no rejection. But that isn't the structure that starts getting imposed.

MEJP
Stuck structure. From bureaucrats.

MASTER
Exactly.

They just don't make any sense to people who can see holistically. So the brass get rid of them.

The self-acclaimed administration make up some rules that kind of sound like what the visionaries would have said. All subtleties are missed and then they lord it over everyone, and steal their dreams. For a profit.

MEJP
Some would say that's just cynical.

MASTER
'Some would say.'
If you think of it from their point of view, the observer

is just a sidekick to the central mind of the fifth layer – the map maker, the analyser. They think if they just make their simulation better it will become the real thing.

Which is perhaps why it seems so hard to make the jump from five to six. Because when you make the jump you don't actually leave, you just float half way between.

MISTRESS
You go from being me to us. From an individual mind to an individual collective, and so on. Which you still call, "me."

MASTER
And this is why so many civilizations just fall apart here when the pressures have built up.

MEJP
So if the map maker can't make the jump across...

MASTER
It just starts around the outside of the circle again with a new vision, an inspiration, usually in the form of some religion.

MEJP
Ah...

MASTER
Now here is my point about the system not being able to explain everything. It isn't about explaining, it's about just looking at things. That's what consciousness does. Explaining is a map. A useful thing, but you can't really draw a map of wholeness.

MEJP
One to one correspondence.

MASTER
Right.
The trick is that the seed from which you came, not just the zygote or the informational matrix or whatever, but right down at the very bottom, is the will, the consciousness itself, which appears to be... I say appears to be because you can't put it in your pocket – IT. That by going all the way within, you find yourself at the external.

And if you don't. If you can't find the consciousness of the universe around you, if it's just a figment of your interior existence and nothing else – then that isn't just nihilism – it's solipsism. And what that is – that's hell.

MEJP
Hell isn't other people?

MASTER
Hell is slowly drifting without a compass into the vortexes of madness which surround the minds. People visit them recreationally with drugs, but if you can't come down, if you're trapped there, it's a hell. I assume the minds divided into separated languages to escape these border dysfunctions.

MEJP
Checks and balances.

MASTER
One mind, no matter how profound, won't do it. You

need somewhere else to go, so you won't go nuts! Just as the denial of an underlying reality undermines any kind of knowledge about the world – and I mean science. Otherwise we're just chasing figments of our imaginations.

MISTRESS
Madness is a very good survival-fitness filter.

MEJP
And yet our seers and creative geniuses are all mad.

MISTRESS
Are they?
Or are they not able to be understood by a world obsessed with gadgets? Isolation is a terrible force on the consciousness.

MEJP
You're saying they are driven mad by trying to tell everyone something they can't hear. The Cassandra principle.

MISTRESS
More like Van Gogh. Often high function is just the one mind, a small constellation, while the others stay stuck.

MEJP
Like a savant.

MISTRESS
That's why we talk about getting unstuck so much.

MEJP
Do you think that your theories, your philosophy could

be taken up by someone who doesn't have the maturity of awareness, and thereby turn it into some sort of oppressive–

MISTRESS
Nonsense.

MASTER
Yes, they certainly could. It's pretty much assured they will. Par for the course.

MISTRESS
We were just speaking about how a single mind has no bearing and can veer off into places where it can't get itself out of, and goes mad. The same is true for ideologies via their mad proponents.
No – whatever they make of what we are saying – it would not be the way. Even what we say is not truly the way. Anything they might make would just be..."

MEJP
Stuck!

MASTER
Exactly.

MISTRESS
Indeed.

MASTER
Exactly, indeed.

MISTRESS
Well someone might decide the best way to avoid the feelings of madness is to, I don't know, let's say they are stuck somewhere in reciprocity, to guilt people for being different, or if stuck in the power level, beat them for being *crazy*.

MASTER
For their own good, of course.

MISTRESS
To make them whole.
What I mean is there is always a mismatch for those who can hear. Words can be stolen but not the language. Any statement can be taken away by a sneaky consciousness bent on interpreting things their way. But to do so they have to change the language.

MASTER
Like the inside / outside, ground and figure problem where you try to say it's one or the other. This vs that, instead of this via that.
Human consciousness has a lot on its plate. Some oddness is to be expected.

MISTRESS
This is why when we speak about the inside and outside, which seems so academic, it really isn't. Trying to solve problems on the outside is part of the problem on the inside. Not that outside problems shouldn't be dealt with.
But being able to hand people the tools to detach themselves from their own rejection of themselves. It's about

their own self-unacceptance, not any external oppression to whatever lifestyle they want.

An even easier version of the same thing is there is no out there and in here. If it isn't all in, then it must be all out. And the states of our minds are just the flux of what is washing over us.

MASTER
That's an old idea and very pretty. But I don't think it addresses the issue of the comprehension of minds. The primary thing they do is not just slosh around in some state of mauve jello. The thing they do is to comprehend.

There's a there in here, and here is also in there. That's the self-supporting duality, it's the clearest a primate brain is going to get without getting muddled up in reductionist paradox. It's a feedback loop into the centre.

MISTRESS
It's a donut.

MASTER
Not a cake.

MISTRESS
In time.

MEJP
Ok – that's too much for me.

MASTER
That's what I mean.

MEJP
Mistress, Master, thank you for speaking with us today.

MISTRESS
My pleasure.

MASTER
Thanks for having us.